HIS STEADFAST

ALSO BY
GOLDEN KEYES PARSONS

The Darkness to Light series
In the Shadow of the Sun King
A Prisoner of Versailles
Where Hearts Are Free

HIS STEADFAST

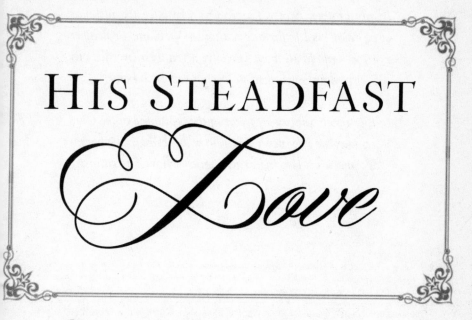

Love

GOLDEN KEYES PARSONS

THOMAS NELSON
Since 1798

NASHVILLE   DALLAS   MEXICO CITY   RIO DE JANEIRO

To my brother, Scotty Lee Keyes, who gave the ultimate sacrifice of his life for our nation in Vietnam, September 1, 1967. And to all those who have given their lives for our freedom—whether on foreign soil or at home.

In this 150th anniversary year of the beginning of the Civil War, may we vow never again to walk through the horror of Americans bearing arms against fellow Americans.

© 2011 by Golden Keyes Parsons

Published in Nashville, Tennessee, by Thomas Nelson. Thomas Nelson is a registered trademark of Thomas Nelson, Inc.

Thomas Nelson, Inc., titles may be purchased in bulk for educational, business, fund-raising, or sales promotional use. For information, please e-mail SpecialMarkets@ThomasNelson.com.

Scripture quotations are taken from the King James Version of the Bible.

Publisher's Note: This novel is a work of fiction. Names, characters, places, and incidents are either products of the author's imagination or used fictitiously. All characters are fictional, and any similarity to people living or dead is purely coincidental.

Page design by Mark L. Mabry

Library of Congress Cataloging-in-Publication Data

Parsons, Golden Keyes, 1941–
  His steadfast love / Golden Keyes Parsons.
    p. cm. -- (Darkness to light series ; bk. 4)
  ISBN 978-1-59554-629-6 (soft cover)
  1. Texas--History--Civil War, 1861-1865--Fiction. I. Title.
  PS3616.A7826H57 2011
  813'.6–dc23

2011029950

Printed in the United States of America

11 12 13 14 15 16 QG 6 5 4 3 2 1

CHAPTER ONE

SEPTEMBER 1860

My concern is not whether God is on our side; my greatest concern is to be on God's side.

ABRAHAM LINCOLN

The sweet, gooey peach pie filling had overflowed its crust and dribbled down the side of the plate. Amanda Belle made a quick swipe on the side of the tin, then turned her back on the table laden with pies and licked her index finger. A husky voice interrupted her surreptitious snack.

"Which pie do you recommend? They all look tasty."

Startled, she looked into a pair of blue eyes as clear as a cloudless Texas sky.

She cleared her throat and bobbed a curtsy. "I'm afraid you have observed me being rather impolite. Please excuse my bad manners."

Ignoring the heat rising in her cheeks, she waved her hand over the desserts lined up on long tables covered in calico tablecloths. The special offerings of the ladies of the Methodist church dotted the tables—and each woman watched eagerly to see which platters and baskets emptied first. A young slave stood at each end of the table steadily waving a palm fan to keep the flies away.

"Our Elsie baked the chess pie, and it is a favorite. So you are fortunate that there is still a piece left—if you like chess pie, that is, Lieutenant."

The stranger grinned. "I don't blame you for sampling the goods. I don't know that I could have resisted either. And it's Captain."

Flustered, Amanda flicked open her fan. "Oh, my soul. I'm sorry. I'm not very conversant with military ranks."

"Give it no mind." Pointing to the chess pie, he said, "That must be a Southern dish. I've never tried it, but upon your recommendation, I'm happy to indulge." He held his plate toward her, and she lifted a sugary, buttery slice of the chess pie onto his already full plate. "This is such a treat for my men—to sit down to home cooking. Thank you for your hospitality."

"You are very welcome, sir."

"I am Captain Kent Littlefield." He tipped his hat with his free hand.

Again she dipped a slight curtsy. "Amanda Irene Belle, sir. My father is filling in as pastor until we can call a permanent one." She nodded toward her father, who lingered at the front door of the church, visiting with members of the congregation. The shoulders of his lean, lanky form slumped forward, as they usually did—a habit formed because of his height. "That 'temporary' position has lasted for two years already." She smiled. "I am pleased to meet you."

"The pleasure is mutual." Captain Littlefield nodded his head and grinned as he walked to join his men at a nearby table, balancing his overloaded plate. He glanced in her direction several times, but she averted her eyes and looked away.

After dinner, as they were clearing the tables, the captain walked toward Amanda carrying several plates. "Here, let me help you."

"Thank you, Captain Littlefield. We're almost finished."

He handed her the plates and then pulled the cloth from the serving table. He shook it out, folded it, and handed it to her. "Well, thank you again, Miss Belle." Their hands brushed, and he took hers and raised it to his lips. "I like it."

"Pardon me?"

"The chess pie—I like it."

"Oh . . . yes . . . the pie." She fumbled with her basket.

Before she could pick it up, Captain Littlefield had it over one arm and offered her his other. "May I escort you to your buggy?" He cupped her elbow in his hand and assisted her. "I shall look forward to seeing you again . . . at church?"

She laughed. "Yes, I'm here every Sunday. You know, when you're the pastor's daughter, it's expected." She cleared her throat. "So to speak."

He fixed his gaze on her and lifted his eyebrows, then stepped back as her father approached. The two men shook hands and introduced themselves. Amanda touched her cheek, which had started to blotch, displaying her disquietude to those around her. She twisted the cameo ring on her finger and turned to watch as the captain mounted his horse and waved good-bye.

❦

Father's bass voice boomed out the familiar line of the closing hymn. "Rock of Ages, cleft for me, let me hide myself in Thee."

Amanda, her brother, Daniel, and the three little Belle sisters turned to leave when they spotted Captain Littlefield across the aisle toward the back.

Daniel bounded toward him and shook his hand. "Welcome again, Captain Littlefield. I'm Daniel Belle, Amanda's brother."

The captain glanced over Daniel's shoulder at Amanda. "Yes, I remember from last week. Good to see you again."

The two young men turned and walked out the back door where Father stood at his usual place bidding members of the congregation good-bye. Captain Littlefield shook his hand and lingered a moment, chatting. Her father smiled and clapped the officer on his shoulder.

What were they talking about? Grabbing Mary and Catherine's hands, Amanda skirted around the bevy of women moving slowly down the steps and waited for Daniel and Captain Littlefield.

Ten-year-old Emmaline had broken away from her sisters and run to her brother. Suddenly shy, she ducked behind Daniel's long legs, and he laughed and pulled her in front of him as they approached the hitching rail. Captain Littlefield gathered the reins of his horse.

"Good morning. Is that a new bonnet?" Claire, Amanda's best friend and Daniel's sweetheart, stopped them. She patted Catherine, who was six, on the head and knelt down to hug little Mary. "How are you girls today?"

"Hold you." Mary held her arms up.

Claire laughed. "You're almost too big for me to hold anymore, but I'll try." She swung the four-year-old into her arms and settled her on her hip, and kissed her on the cheek. "You're growing up too fast."

"Not fast enough." Amanda smiled. "Sometimes I think they will never grow up."

"I'm sure it does seem like that to you sometimes. But look at Emmie. She's getting so tall." She waved in the direction of Daniel and Emmaline, who were chatting with Captain Littlefield.

Daniel motioned for the girls to join them. Amanda felt her face flush as they drew near to the men. Daniel reached for Claire's arm, still holding on to Emmaline with the other hand.

"Captain Littlefield, may I introduce my fiancée, Claire Beecham. I believe you've met my sister Amanda. And these are my two youngest sisters, Mary and Catherine."

"You are surrounded by beautiful women, it seems."

Daniel chuckled. "Yes, so it seems." He took Mary from Claire.

"I noticed you visiting with my father at the door," Amanda said.

Captain Littlefield grinned. "Yes, I asked him if it was permissible for a Presbyterian to attend your Methodist services when my duties at Fort Washington allow me to do so."

"And . . . ?"

"He assured me that it was." The captain mounted his large gray. "I must return to my duty station."

"How long have you been stationed at the fort?"

"Just a couple of months."

Amanda opened her parasol against the vivid noonday sun as she looked up at him. "I hope you and your men know how much we appreciate the protection of the federal troops. We feel most vulnerable here on the frontier, with the wetlands and swamp on one side and the ocean on the other. Thank you for your service."

He smiled and tipped his hat. "You are most welcome. Ladies, Daniel. I trust we will have the opportunity to meet again soon."

⚜

Amanda saw Captain Littlefield in church every Sunday after that for a month, although he did nothing more than tip his kepi and say, "Good morning, Miss Belle." She wondered if he was more interested in chess pie than he was in her, yet there was something in his expression when he looked her way. His eyes seemed to smile at her.

One Sunday morning in October the captain entered the pew behind the Belle family. He held his cap in his hand. "Good morning, all you beautiful Belle women. You too, Daniel."

Amanda ducked her head and blushed.

Daniel turned around to shake the captain's hand. "For a Presbyterian you are becoming quite faithful to this Methodist church."

Kent laughed, and even his laughter sounded husky, like his voice. "I guess I am. I enjoy your father's sermons."

"Would you do us the honor of coming to our home for dinner? Then you and Father could have more than simply a few moments to talk."

Amanda turned around in her seat. "Please do, Captain Littlefield. We have great plenty at our house."

"You are certain that it is acceptable with your father?"

Amanda nodded. "Guests are always welcome in our home."

"Will you be serving chess pie?"

Her lips lifted in a demure smile. "I can't guarantee chess pie, but I can guarantee that the meal will be delicious."

"How could I resist such a tempting invitation? I heartily accept."

⁂

The three young people passed the time on the veranda before dinner. The day was cloudy and threatening rain, and Amanda could smell the moisture in the air. She and Daniel sat in the swing as they chatted, and Captain Littlefield leaned against the railing. The family's big yellow dog lay sprawled at Daniel's feet.

The captain let the dog sniff his hand. "Pretty dog. What's his name?"

"Sam Houston—after our governor—we just call him Sam. He's a mutt, but he's a good dog."

Sam wagged his tail and nuzzled the captain's hand.

He chuckled. "Looks like I've made a friend."

Amanda leaned forward, stopping the gliding of the swing. "Daniel tells me you are a graduate of West Point."

"Yes. It's a family tradition that all of our men go to West Point. And since I'm the only son . . ." He grinned. "I have four sisters."

Daniel slapped his knee. "Very good! That's something we have in common."

"And where is your home, Captain Littlefield?" Amanda asked.

"Pennsylvania."

Daniel leaned back in the swing and put his arm around his sister. "How do you like Texas?"

"I love Texas, especially here on the coast where you can see the ocean from every part of town. And since horses are my passion, well . . . there's no better horse country than Texas."

"Texas is indeed horse country, even though some have attempted to make it camel country as well."

They all laughed at the mention of the less than successful experiment of bringing camels to south Texas.

"Camels will never replace horses in Texas," Daniel said.

"I agree. However, the army does use camels to carry large loads of equipment across the desert."

Daniel nodded toward the captain's gray. "That's a fine horse you have. What's his name?"

"Sterling Prancer, but I just call him Sterling. He's a bit of a show-off—likes to prance around in front of people. My father gave him to me when I turned eighteen."

"Before you went to West Point?"

"Yes, and then my orders brought me to Texas. I truly love this area. In fact, I'd like to buy a ranch and settle here someday—after I retire from the military. There is a charm about the West that tugs at me."

"How would your family feel about that?"

"I'm sure they would rather I settle in Pennsylvania." He looked at Amanda. "But I have nothing to tie me down there—no sweetheart, I mean, or anything like that."

Amanda avoided his eyes and put her hand to her neck. As usual, she could feel the embarrassing mottling of her skin that she inherited from her mother spread to her cheeks.

⁂

"Is that Captain Littlefield?" Amanda asked as an officer on horseback approached their fence.

"I invited him to come by this evening after he got off duty." Daniel rose from his seat on the porch swing and strode out to meet the officer.

Captain Littlefield walked through the gate and stopped to greet Emmaline, Catherine, and Mary, who were playing in the yard. The girls giggled as he handed each of them a wildflower he had plucked somewhere along the way.

"Welcome, Captain Littlefield. I'm glad you could get away from your post and drop by for a visit," Ezekiel said.

The captain shook his hand. "Good evening, sir."

"Please, have a seat." Her father moved to the swing beside Amanda, and indicated a chair next to a table.

The captain turned and handed one remaining flower to Amanda. "There are still wildflowers in the fields. I thought you might enjoy . . ."

Amanda rose and took the flower. She opened the front door. "Elsie, would you bring the lemonade and cookies, please?"

Captain Littlefield cleared his throat and took a deep breath. Leaning over the railing of the veranda, he looked out over the ocean. "I love the fragrance of the ocean. Did you know that it smells different on the East Coast?"

Amanda turned her attention to the young man. "Well, Papa's family is from Alabama—on the coast, but that's still the Gulf. Why would there be any difference?"

"I suppose it has to do with the different vegetation and sea animals, but the odor is definitely different." The glow from the setting sun sent brilliant shades of pink and orange across the waves. "You have a beautiful view." He turned to Amanda's father. "May I have permission to escort your daughter on a stroll along the beach, sir?"

Her father sputtered and stood, sending the swing twisting from side to side. "It's getting late, and we need to get the girls to bed."

"Kitty can do that," Amanda said. "Daniel will come with us—won't you, Daniel?"

Daniel laughed and leapt over the railing. "Of course. A walk on the beach is always in order."

"Very well," their father grumbled. "Don't be gone long."

The young people, accompanied by Sam, were down the steps before he could voice any other arguments.

They walked toward the shoreline, the rhythmic swooshing of the waves punctuating their conversation. Daniel plied the captain with a plethora of questions about military life. "Do you get homesick? What is the most difficult part of being an officer? Is the food horrible? Aren't those uniforms hot? What has been your most difficult order to carry out?"

"Little brother! Give the poor captain a rest. I'm sure he's growing weary of your questions."

"Little brother?"

Amanda laughed. "Yes, but barely. It gives him pause for me to call him that. There's only eleven months between us."

"Oh, I see."

An awkward silence followed before Daniel interjected, "I'm nineteen."

"Yes, well, I don't mind the questions about being in the military. They are all questions I had prior to going to West Point."

Daniel held up his hand. "Very well, then, one more question: what do you find is the main difference between living in the North and living in the South?"

Captain Littlefield hesitated before he answered. "Isn't that rather obvious? It would be the issue of slavery."

Amanda and Daniel both stared at the captain, and Amanda felt her pulse escalate. "You have servants in your home, do you not?"

"We do. We have servants. Not slaves. They are free to come and go."

"Is it . . . is our way of life offensive to you?"

"I would say different. I see that your slaves are well cared for and seem to be content, but—" He stuck his hands in his pockets.

"Go on, please. But what?"

"But . . . they are not free. I must admit that I am offended by the fact that human beings are owned by other human beings."

Amanda snapped her fan. "My father says he will free our slaves soon, especially with President Lincoln backing the abolition of slavery. But how will we run our farm then? Bellevue is not a true plantation, but we are a very large farm."

Daniel stepped in. "This is nothing we can solve today. It's a difficult question."

"Yes, and I must admit that I don't have all the answers. Nobody does."

The three fell silent. Daniel ran to the shore and began skipping rocks on the water. Amanda and the captain fell behind.

"Miss Belle . . ."

"Please call me Amanda."

"Yes, well, Amanda. I hope this discussion about slavery won't discourage you from . . ."

"Discourage me?"

"Discourage you from looking upon me with favor. I would like to ask permission to call on you."

Amanda pulled her shawl around her shoulders as the sun sank lower on the horizon. She looked up at him, and her emotions quickened. Daniel, the ocean, the sunset—all were a blur of faded colors, but the captain's face. His face smiled down at her in perfect focus. "Captain Littlefield—"

"May I request you return the favor and call me Kent?"

She smiled. "Kent, I do believe my father has concerns."

Daniel whooped just then and pointed at a dolphin frolicking in the bay, then another one, and another appeared. All three watched, transfixed by the beauty of the creatures' graceful gyrations.

Amanda exhaled slowly. "Aren't they beautiful? I never tire of watching them."

The captain nodded and turned his attention back to her. "I hope I can prove to your father that he needn't be concerned. Haven't I already said that I love Texas and want to settle here?" He reached for her hand and kissed it, then covered it with his other hand. "From the first moment I saw you at the church dinner, I was struck by your beauty. I would consider it a privilege to get to know you." He kept hold of her hand and drew her closer to him. "I would like to ask your father permission to court you."

Her breath quickened. "You flatter me, Captain . . . Kent. I would like that very much." She lowered her eyes and felt her cheeks begin to blotch. "But I must ask you to delay. My father is a reasonable man, and given some time, I think he might come around. But there are things that you don't know about my family. Before my mother died she gave me this cameo ring as a symbol of my promise to her that I would take care of Emmaline, Catherine, and Mary—and of course, Daniel." She twirled the ring on her finger and laughed. "He's all grown up now, but the girls are still young."

"Surely your father doesn't expect you to wait until they are grown to give permission to an interested party to court you, does he?"

She touched her cheek. "No, I don't think so, but . . . please honor my wishes and wait . . . just a bit."

CHAPTER TWO

MARCH 1864

Let me tell you what is coming. After the sacrifice of countless millions of treasure and hundreds of thousands of lives you may win Southern independence, but I doubt it. The North is determined to preserve this Union. They are not a fiery, impulsive people as you are, for they live in colder climates. But when they begin to move in a given direction, they move with the steady momentum and perseverance of a mighty avalanche.

GOVERNOR SAM HOUSTON

The strains of "Yankee Doodle" and the rumble of supply wagons filtered through an open window on the warm Texas morning. Amanda looked up from her sewing and cocked her head. Rising from the wingback chair, she peered through the parlor window, and watched the U.S. federal troops trudge along the road in front of their house. She stepped onto the veranda and shaded her eyes. Vines of purple wisteria trailed along the fence that separated the road from the large two-story house and coated the spring air with a heavy fragrance. Fronds of palmetto palms waved in the breeze. She moved down the steps to the end of the walkway and stopped at the gate.

Captain Littlefield rode atop his dappled gray beside a column of soldiers and stopped in front of the fence. He dismounted and strode toward Amanda. "I wish to speak with you, Miss Belle."

"Has something happened?" She looked down the column, unable to see the end of it.

"Yes, I—"

"Captain Littlefield?" Father rounded the corner of the house and stepped through the open gate toward the officer. "I noticed you were in church last Sunday."

The captain shook his hand. "Good afternoon, sir. Yes, I enjoyed the sermon, sir."

Her father waved off the captain's comment. "When we get a permanent pastor, then we'll hear some good sermons."

"Yes, sir." Black curly hair tumbled out as Kent removed his hat and smiled at Amanda, revealing his deep dimples.

Her cheeks flushed as she remembered their last conversation.

Daniel rode up from the stable and dismounted alongside his father, who motioned toward the soldiers. "Can you tell us what is going on?"

Kent fingered the reins in his hands. "Federal troops on the frontier have been recalled. We are being shipped north." He hesitated. "Texas has seceded from the Union. Some of the men have chosen to stay and join the Confederate forces. I'm afraid, sir, that we are at war."

Stunned, Amanda caught hold of the fence. Her father shook his head as he stared at the column of men continuing to march past.

"I came to inquire if you would allow me to correspond with your daughter. I initially had intended to ask permission to court her, but it appears the politics of the times have interfered."

"You will fight on the side of the Union?"

"Why, yes. I—"

"Then I am sorry, young man." Her father folded his arms

across his chest. "Our country is going to war over a state's right to determine how its people will live their lives. I cannot agree to a relationship between my daughter and a Northern abolitionist. My desire is for her to marry a Southern gentleman one day."

"I see." Kent replaced his hat. "Please excuse me. I must attend to my men. I am truly sorry, sir, to have been the bearer of bad news." He looked at Amanda with intense, clear blue eyes, and nodded. "Ma'am."

She whirled around to her father. "Papa!" She hesitated at the gate. "I'm sorry, Captain Littlefield."

His expression warmed. "Please know that I will not forget you." He reached for her hand and kissed it. His tanned complexion presented a stark contrast to hers as his moustache brushed the back of her hand. He held it a moment longer before releasing her. "I pray God will allow us to meet again when this is over." He swung onto his horse and, casting a glance over his shoulder, rode toward the bay to catch up with his men.

No one spoke as they watched the young man ride toward his troops. Only a mockingbird squawking in a nearby tree broke the silence. Amanda felt nauseated. Her legs seemed unattached to her body. The trio walked back to the house, where her sisters had huddled on the veranda. Amanda gathered them around her. She turned toward her brother. "Daniel, what will you do?"

"Why, I'll enlist, of course. Those Yanks won't dare come close to Texas."

"No, no! You cannot. You're not even twenty. We need you here."

The young girls, sensing the tension of the moment, began to sniffle and cry.

Amanda looked at her father. "Papa?"

Her father sat on the veranda steps. "We have the disadvantage of being on the coast. I'm certain the Union will try to blockade the bay." He stared at the road. "There have been rumors of secession for years, but this is not what Governor Houston wanted. Mark my words, children, our home will never be the same. We will never be the same. The world will never be the same. Our lives will forever be defined by this act."

⊷❧⊷

MAY 1864

Kent shaded his eyes as he looked up at the bright green leaves of the oak trees that arched over the driveway leading to his home on the outskirts of Bethlehem, Pennsylvania. The shimmering shades of spring announced to him that God had sent abundant rain. The cornfields he had passed by were bristling with flat green leaves that waved in the wind like verdant hands welcoming him home. The landscape offered a vivid contrast from the tropics of the coastline of Texas. Although the trip had been long, he enjoyed seeing the different parts of the country. But most of all he looked forward to his leave and being with his family.

Each city, town, and small village hummed with talk of war. The defeat of the Union soldiers at Fort Sumter had spurred the military into full-fledged war. Now there would be no turning back, no more negotiations among the politicians.

Reining in Sterling Prancer, he tied the horse to the hitching post in front of the large Georgian-style house and looked around. No one in sight. He had sent a letter informing his parents of his arrival. Surely they were expecting him. He walked up the brick steps to the large, heavy wooden double doors and stepped inside the cool foyer.

"Hello?" He set his kepi on a long credenza and walked toward the parlor. "Hello-o. Anybody home?"

A squeal penetrated the quiet afternoon air from upstairs, and he heard someone running toward the spiral staircase.

Their head house servant, Felix, poked his head around the door from the kitchen and hurried toward him. "Mister Kent. Please forgive me. I dint hear you come in."

Felix's wife, Mathilda, bustled behind him fussing. "Oh, my! This is no welcome for you. We thought you wouldn't be here for a few more days. We've been cookin' and cleanin' and—"

Kent laughed and held up his hand. "No worries. I was eager to arrive home and ran a bit ahead of schedule." He looked up and saw his mother and sister, Fannie, just older than he, coming down the stairs, their laughter and greetings tumbling over each other. Fannie held on to the chubby hand of a curly-headed toddler, who slowed her progress with his need for two steps on every stair. She finally picked him up and carried him the rest of the way.

His mother ran into his arms and embraced him, then stepped back to look at him with her intense blue eyes, so much like his. The rest of the family had dark eyes, but he had inherited his mother's distinctive color. She patted the stubble on his cheek. "How handsome you are, son. You look fine. Just fine."

"I haven't been away *that* long, but I wouldn't mind cleaning up a bit. It's been a long trip."

"Your room is ready. Mathilda?"

The portly maid was already headed for the kitchen. "Yes, ma'am, Miss Luvenia. I'll get some water heatin' right away."

"Just enough to freshen up. I'll bathe later."

"Yes, sir. I'll get that done in no time."

"Do you have a hug for your sister?" Fannie set her little boy down, and he ducked behind her skirt.

"Of course, always." Kent kissed her hand, then pulled her into a tight hug. He knelt down and tweaked the boy's nose. "Don't you know your Uncle Kent, Jacob?"

Jacob stuck his thumb in his mouth and stared. He moved farther behind his mother and shook his head.

Kent pulled a piece of penny candy from his pocket. "How about this? Can I coax you out with a sweet?"

Slowly the boy smiled and nodded, then held out his arms to his uncle. Kent knelt beside the child and took him in his arms, unwrapping the candy for him. "You've grown into such a big boy since I've been gone." He picked the boy up. "My goodness! I believe Mathilda has been feeding you well." He looked toward the back of the house. "Father? Is he here?"

His mother answered. "He's been commissioned into the army, as a general. He's gone to Washington."

"Oh, I see. And Samuel?"

"He's stationed in Maryland right now. We're staying here until this unpleasantness is over." Fannie took Jacob from Kent and set him on his feet, and the child scampered out the front door.

"I don't think this will last long. What about the rest of the family? And other men from Bethlehem?"

"All of our boys are gone, except Elizabeth's Robert. He's waiting on his orders. She will be coming home with the twins as well after that. Olivia's staying at Kathleen's in Philadelphia." Luvenia motioned them toward the parlor to sit. "James Peifer came by to inquire after you last week. He's waiting for orders. Even the Moravians are justifying the need to take up arms in this situation."

Kent smiled. He had hoped he would get to see his best friend from childhood. "I must go into town tomorrow to see him."

Mathilda appeared at the door, her forehead covered in sweat. "You have hot water in your room, Mister Kent . . . uh, Captain

Kent . . . uh, I don't know what to call you now." Her belly shook with laughter as she wiped her face with her apron. "I'm just so glad you're back home for a bit."

"Mister Kent is fine, Mathilda. Thank you."

Luvinia stood. "Go on, son, and freshen up. Supper will be ready in a couple of hours. Try to rest some if you can."

He bent over the small frame of his mother and kissed her forehead. Her hair had become much grayer in his absence. "I'm not that tired, but I will freshen up and perhaps read the paper. Do you have the latest newspaper?"

"Of course. I'll have Felix take it up to your room."

"Thank you. And Fannie, do you have time to visit with your little brother before supper?"

"Time seems to be all I have these days. The hours creep by since Samuel left. I have to concentrate on staying busy."

Kent took his sister's hand and kissed it. "Dear one, hopefully our lives will resume normality before too long."

"I pray so." She shooed him toward the stairs. "Go clean up, and we'll talk later."

"I'll be back down after I change."

He took the stairs two at a time and walked down the landing into his room. The smell of the citrus oil and beeswax that Mathilda used to polish the wood enveloped him, stirring unbeckoned memories of childhood. A smile teased his lips when he noticed that the old servant had laid out clothes on the four-poster bed for him. He supposed she would never cease being his nanny.

The similarity between the Belles' household and their slaves and the Littlefield house and their servants struck him. Of course, their servants were free. They could go to another employer if they chose, but they remained with the Littlefields. In theory the difference was a giant chasm, but in practice . . . he didn't know if there was much difference.

He removed his uniform, grimy with road dust, and washed up. Donning the clean pants and shirt Mathilda had laid out for him, he reclined on the settee to read the newspaper his mother had saved for him.

FORT SUMTER FALLEN

"Our Southern brethren have done a grievous wrong," says Major Robert Anderson. They have rebelled and have attacked their father's house and their loyal brothers. They must be punished and brought back but this necessity breaks my heart."

Kent read on. Major Anderson had been his gunner instructor at West Point; the commanding Southern officer, General P.G.T. Beauregard, had served as the major's gunnery assistant. Now they were commanding opposing troops and shooting at each other. He laid the paper in his lap and looked out the window at the rolling hills of the countryside he could see beyond the rooftops of the town.

This was what this war was going to look like—friend firing upon friend, brother firing upon brother, father firing upon son. The fields of battle would be in their familiar woods and pastures. Kent shook his head. *God have mercy on our nation.*

⤜✥⤛

Kent rode into town to the bookbinder's shop where his friend James worked. The bell jangled overhead as he entered the shop.

James looked up from behind the counter, and a wide grin spread across his face. "Kent. Your mother told me you were coming home on leave." He darted around the end of the counter and vigorously shook his friend's hand. "I was afraid we were going to miss each other. The Grays are being mustered into the 1st Pennsylvania Volunteer Infantry Regiment for ninety days."

"When is your departure date?"

"Day after tomorrow."

"Well, I'm glad I arrived early." He looked around the shop. "Do you have to work today? Do you think your sister would allow you to come to the house for supper?"

"I'm just finishing up some manuscripts, so I can leave things in order here. I'll have another evening with Mary. I would like to come to supper. It's good to see you, friend."

"You, as well."

"What do you think? Can this war be settled quickly? Surely . . . surely . . ." James's eyes pooled with dark concern.

An older man with a cane approached the entrance of the shop, and Kent held the door for him. "We'll talk tonight, James. See you around seven o'clock?"

"I'll be there."

Kent went outside the shop onto the brick walk into the increasing warmth of the spring day. His horse nickered a greeting. Patting Sterling's neck, Kent surveyed the familiar serene village street scene. He mounted and rode down the street where he had raced along as a boy playing tag with his sisters; the street where he and James had sold newspapers, then invaded the general store to buy penny candy with their earnings; the street where he had stolen a kiss from Penelope Abshire after the church service one October Sunday morning.

At the end of the street he turned his horse around. "Let's go home, Sterling. Things look pretty much the same, but I fear the change will prove to be vast in the coming days."

Kent and James retired to the parlor after supper, much as their fathers had done in former years. Kent expected to look up at any time and see his father walk through the door with his political colleagues.

James spoke up. "This feels strange, doesn't it—just you and me sitting in the parlor drinking a brandy?"

"Yes, it does. Would you like to go out on the porch?"

"I would."

The young men settled in wicker chairs on either side of a table. Mathilda followed them onto the porch with a plate of rhubarb cake, covered with a napkin.

James grinned and rubbed his hands together. "Ah, Mathilda. You know how to make a young man happy." He pulled a slice from under the cloth and downed it in just a few bites. "I'd rather have a piece of Mathilda's rhubarb cake than brandy any day."

Kent laughed. "I agree. Remember how we used to hide in the kitchen while she was baking and snitch cookies right from under her nose?"

"And she never caught us."

Mathilda threw back her head and laughed. "You two. I knew full well where you were and what you were up to. I was just playin' along with your flummery."

The two chuckled as the old woman waddled back into the house.

Kent cocked his head and looked at his friend. "Tell me about the Moravian men deciding to enlist. Your people have traditionally been pacifists."

"True." James leaned back in his chair. "But my heritage was not always Moravian, you know. It was French Huguenot. My ancestors, the Clavells, fled to this country from France and converted to the Moravian church after homesteading up in the Schuylkill Valley in the 1700s."

"I think I remember that. But I thought your mother's name was Clewell."

"The Clavells changed their name soon after arriving in this country. And I guess they were not staunchly pacifist, because one of my ancestors, Jacob Clewell, fought in the Revolutionary War." He paused. "And the attitude among the Moravians has changed greatly. They view this as a just war—to support the Constitution."

James reached for a second piece of dessert and looked at Kent, quirking his eyebrows.

"No, thanks. Go ahead."

"My family loves this country, and we are willing—yes, eager even—to lay down our lives for the government that has protected our sacred rights of person and property. We cannot allow the country to be trampled under by men who have built their success on the backs of Negro slaves."

"You are an abolitionist?"

"Are you not?"

"I . . . well, you know I've just come back from duty in the South, on the frontier in Texas."

James brushed crumbs from his lap. "I know."

"It's hard to explain if you haven't seen the slavery system in operation with a good and kind master."

"You don't mean you agree with the concept of men owning slaves, making greedy profit off the misery of their condition?"

"The slaves I saw were not miserable."

"But they were not free either."

"No, they're not, and no, I don't agree. I'm just saying that I can perhaps understand their position a bit better than I did before."

James stood. "Well, I don't understand it at all, and I say that any man or family who owns slaves is evil and should be dealt with."

Kent rose also and shook his head. "You cannot put people all in one heap, James. The pastor of the church I attended in Indianola owned slaves, and their family is good and kind."

"Evil lurks beneath the surface then." James's lips grew taut.

"I'm telling you, they are not evil people. Trapped in a flawed system perhaps, but not evil."

James stepped close to Kent and poked him in the chest with his finger. "If that's the way you feel, perhaps you should change that Union blue to Confederate gray and fight for the South."

Kent's heart thudded against his temples, and he took a step back. "I don't think you mean that."

"Oh, I mean it. Looks like my friend is a turncoat, if not on the outside, certainly on the inside."

"James, I'm an officer in the Union army, but I have a degree of understanding for the South that I would not have had if I hadn't been stationed there."

"And I'm saying that you've been swayed by evil."

Kent stared at his friend and took a deep breath. "I think you'd better go now, before both of us say things we may regret."

"Yes, I think so." James walked down the steps to his horse. He mounted, his jaw set and his mouth tight. "My heart is heavy for you."

"And mine for you."

James whirled his horse around and rode away without any further word.

Fannie stepped out on the porch. "Is James leaving already?"

Kent turned to his sister and sighed. "Yes. We had words. He thinks I'm empathizing with the South because I said I could understand somewhat how they feel. And in truth, Fannie, their slaves are not treated much differently than our Mathilda and Felix, from what I observed."

She sat in the chair James had just vacated. "Well, are you?"

"Am I what? Empathizing with the South? Maybe somewhat. But agreeing with them? No, I don't agree with the secessionist movement. I think it will tear our country apart." Kent sat back down, facing his sister. "Fannie, I've met someone."

Her eyes lit up. "You have? Tell me about her."

"Her name is Amanda—Amanda Irene Belle—and she's the pastor's daughter of the church I attended in Texas."

"That is quite a Southern name, isn't it?"

Kent chuckled. "I guess it is."

"Were you courting her—officially, I mean?"

"No, I wanted to, but I was recalled before I could ask her father's permission, although—"

"Although what?"

"Her father wouldn't even give me permission to write her, because they are from the South and I'm from the North."

"Well, that seems pretty final to me. How can you pursue her if her father forbids it?"

"I don't know. I definitely feel God brought us together. Won't he make a way for us somehow?"

"Those are daydreams. You have your military duties and will be fighting against her very way of life. Better try to find someone with whom you have a common background. Hanging on to something that can never be will only lead to heartache."

CHAPTER THREE

JULY 1864

*Do your duty in all things. You cannot do more, you should
never wish to do less.*

ROBERT E. LEE

D aniel bounded down the stairs with his carpetbag. He
started out the door, then grabbed Amanda by the shoulders as she waited by the ornate banister. He pulled her
into a smothering embrace. "I'll be back before you know it, sis."

She clung to him, silently begging him not to go. Amanda had
promised to take care of the children. Now Daniel, barely a man,
was walking headlong onto bloody battlefields of death.

Emmaline, Catherine, and Mary jumped up and down with
excitement as he hugged them. He swung Mary in circles as she
wrapped her legs around his waist.

"Now you girls take care of Amanda and Papa until I get back,
you hear?" He let Mary down and kissed her cheek.

Giggling, the girls bobbed their heads up and down.

The Belles' house servants gathered on the veranda to send
off the young Mister Belle—Elsie; her daughter, Kitty; and her
older son, Washington. Elsie's younger son, Hiram, was Daniel's

personal servant and stood ready, holding the reins of Daniel's treasured horse, Cannonade. Several other youths, also with their Negroes, waited for him on the road, their mounts pawing at the dirt.

"Hurry up, Daniel. We're gonna miss the barge to Houston."

The enthusiasm of the new recruits collided with the somber fears of those left behind.

Daniel kissed Amanda on the forehead and loped down the steps. She chewed on her lower lip to prevent it from trembling as her brother met their father at the gate and stuck out his hand.

Father brushed it away and enveloped his son in his long arms. "Lord, I implore thy protection on this, one of thy children . . ." He looked at the others, who had removed their hats and bowed their heads, shifting their eyes toward one another.

"For all of these thy children. Be merciful and spare their lives in this awful time of brothers fighting brothers, fathers fighting sons. Thou hast told us in thy Word that the Angel of the Lord encamps around his people. I ask thee to do that for these boys . . . these men. I commend my son to thee." He broke away and motioned for them to go.

Daniel and Hiram mounted their horses and joined the eager new soldiers as they rode toward the bay, waving their hats in the air. "8th Cavalry, here we come!"

Father turned toward the house. "And God have mercy on us all." He walked up the steps to the veranda and leaned against one of the white columns, his shoulders heaving with silent emotion.

A tear tracked down Amanda's face as she and her sisters watched their father grieve.

Amanda put her signature on the letter to Daniel, sealed the envelope, stood up, and stretched. She walked to the wardrobe and slowly pulled out a dress as she cut her eyes toward her sleeping sisters. Mary's dark hair, like Father's, created a startling contrast to Emmaline's and Catherine's blond curls. She tried to dress before they awoke, and before Kitty came upstairs to help, but Emmaline sat up, rubbing her eyes. "Where are you going, Mandy?"

"Shhh. I'm—"

But the little girl threw aside the bedcovers and, scrambling after her big sister, stepped on Catherine in the trundle bed below.

"Stop it." Catherine swatted at her. "You stepped on my hair."

"Please, both of you. You'll wake Mary. I'm going to the Flag Society today."

"Can I go with you?" Emmaline felt she was much more mature than her little sisters.

"No, sweetie. This is for grown-up ladies today."

"I'll be good. I promise." She began to remove her nightgown.

"No, not today."

Her mouth turned down. "But . . ."

"No tears. Papa needs you to be a big girl. Maybe we'll hear from Daniel today. It's been over a month since he left."

The door opened, and Kitty tiptoed in. "I'm sorry, Miss Mandy. I didn't know you was already awake."

Amanda smiled at the young servant who was still a head shorter than she, but surprisingly strong in spite of being thin and wiry.

"It's fine, Kitty. Get Emmaline's robe for her. We're going down for breakfast."

The little girl plopped onto the bed. "But I wanna go with you."

Amanda finished lacing her boot and stood. "Put on your robe and come downstairs with me." They left Kitty to tend to Catherine and Mary.

Ezekiel had already finished eating his breakfast of ham and biscuits, sorghum molasses, and coffee, and was still sitting at the dining room table reading the newspaper.

Elsie bustled around the table, her apron dwarfing her thin frame. "Yes'm. Y'all sit down. I'll get your breakfast right away. Miss Emmaline, you up mighty early this mornin.' "

"I want to go with Mandy to the Flag Society, but she won't let me. She says I need to stay here in case we get a letter from Daniel." Her lip poked out in a pout.

Their father looked up from his paper at Amanda, and her pulse quickened. "Anything in the paper, Papa? Anything about . . . ?" She couldn't bring herself to say the unthinkable: *Is there anybody we know on the list of the dead or missing in action?*

He shook his head and turned to Emmaline. "Your sister is right, sweet pea. I need you to stay here with me. We'll go into town later, and you can get some taffy." He folded his paper. "How about that?"

Emmaline nodded and grinned. "Yes, Papa. I'd like that." She sat down in her place at the large dining room table.

Elsie returned and set more biscuits in front of the girls. "We's getting low on flour, Master Zekiel, and there's very little wheat left to grind. Last time I tried to buy flour, they tell me at the mill they don't have none. We gonna be eating cornbread for every meal 'less we be able to buy some flour somewhere."

"I don't think the war will last long, but if it does, we might run low on provisions. It probably would be wise to start rationing the corn as well. Elsie, tell Washington to spread the word that no one is to take corn without permission from now on. Give only half the usual amount to the hogs. We have plenty of lobsters out of the bay to feed them."

"Yessuh." She nodded her head with the colorful scarf wrapped around her graying hair. "Coffee gettin' low too."

Father stood. "Don't fret, Elsie. The Lord will provide."

"Why are those in here?" Amanda nodded to a case sitting on the buffet. She knew it held the dueling pistols that had belonged to her grandfather.

"I brought them down from the attic," her father said. "Times being what they are, well, one never knows . . ." He rested a hand on Amanda's shoulder. "Daniel has not even gone into battle, Mandy. The paper said that the 8th Cavalry is mustering in Houston and hasn't been sent out yet. Pray diligently for his protection. He'll be home before we know it." He tousled his younger daughter's hair. "Get dressed, Emmaline. We're going to town."

Amanda smiled. Her father was a stern man, but he also possessed a gentle side. She ate her breakfast and glanced at the newspaper with the battle reports on one page and the society column on the very next page. Strange, how their everyday lives continued more or less in a normal fashion in Indianola while young men were being killed on their country's battlefields in places with names like Fort Sumter and Bull Run.

She left half her breakfast and went into the hallway. Stopping at the hall tree in the foyer, she pulled her long hair back in a ribbon and twisted it into a knot. She wished it were still as blond as Catherine's, but the older she got, the darker it became. She supposed it would end up the caramel color that her mother's was when she died.

Amanda put on her hat, tied the bow beneath her chin, picked up her parasol and sewing kit, and went down the steps to the buggy. Washington stood ready to drive her into town to Hettie Moore's house, where the women were meeting to make flags for the Confederate troops.

Washington, Kitty, and Hiram were about the same ages as Amanda and Daniel, and had been their constant childhood playmates. Amanda had not realized the vast chasm between their races until she announced one day, in her six-year-old innocence, that she was going to marry Wash when she grew up. That resulted in a spanking from her mother and her mouth being washed out with soap. She was not allowed to play with Elsie's children for a few days after that, but eventually things settled back to normal.

As they grew into adolescence, Wash's father died, and the young Negro gradually took on the duties of head servant of the household and stable. He had matured into an imposing handsome man with a natural ability for sizing up situations quickly and astutely. Despite being a slave, his demeanor bespoke authority. Washington and another slave, Harriet, had jumped the broom last year, and he had a family of his own now, with a newborn son. With Daniel gone, the Belles depended on him more and more.

Wash drove Amanda to the Moore home and assisted her out of the buggy.

"I'll be here until after lunch, Wash. Come back for me around three o'clock, please."

"Yes'm. I'll be here. Don't you go wand'rin' off if I'm not here right when you're ready to leave. It's dangerous these days on the streets. Soldiers are everywhere—up to no good."

"Oh, Wash. This is Indianola. Nothing's going to happen here."

"Being a major port, second only to Galveston up the coast? The North is gonna be plenty interested in Indianola. You stay put. I have errands to run, and I needs to go down to the saddle shop. I'll be back by half past two o'clock jes to make sure."

"Suit yourself."

Amanda walked to the Moores' front door and knocked. The maid ushered her in. As the door closed behind her, she saw that Wash held the buggy whip in his hand until she was safely inside.

❦

Hettie's home was the gathering place for the women of society in Indianola. The older woman still wore mourning black, although she had been a widow for over twenty years. She stood, sending her hoop skirt swinging, to greet Amanda. Women of various ages sat in a circle around a large Confederate flag.

"Come in, dear. We're just getting started." She indicated a chair for Amanda next to her friend, Rebecca Davis. "We're sewing on stars today."

Amanda nodded and joined the ladies. They chattered as they worked, filling each other in on the latest gossip.

"A Confederate officer and his family have set up headquarters in our home," Rebecca told her, "and we are having a party for them and some of the soldiers Friday evening. Would you and your family like to come?" Her needle darted up and down, expertly tacking the stars on the blue field with hardly a stitch showing.

"A party?" Amanda threaded a needle.

"Yes, it will be a good diversion from the news of war. We shall play charades and perhaps even put on a play. Wouldn't your little sisters enjoy that? We might even dance a bit. It will be most gay."

"I shall ask my father. Perhaps we could come." She tried to be polite, but the situation just didn't feel right to her. How could they go to parties and dances when Daniel was putting himself in harm's way, fighting for their way of life in the South?

She glanced around the circle and smiled at Claire, who lifted her eyebrows.

"Any word yet?"

Amanda shook her head. "No, we haven't heard a thing. I suppose you haven't either?"

Claire sighed. "No. I know they are keeping the recruits busy with training and all." Her dark hair, almost the same color as

Daniel's, fell in soft ringlets around her face as she went back to her stitchery. Amanda thought the two of them looked more like brother and sister than did she and Daniel.

Hettie served a light fare of oyster pie, soda bread, butter, cucumbers and onions, and wine made from Mustang grapes. Access to the waters of Matagorda Bay afforded plenty of seafood at least. Pastries made with strawberry jam rounded out the meal. After working another hour or so after dinner, the women put on their bonnets and took their leave.

Amanda put her supplies away and peered out the window. She didn't see Wash. She looked at the grandfather clock beside the front door. The black minute hand crept a couple of marks past two o'clock. She put on her hat. "Hettie, I think I shall go outside and wait. It's a beautiful day. I'll sit in the swing in the shade. Washington will be here in a few minutes."

"Oh, dear." Hettie fanned herself vigorously. "It's pretty warm this afternoon. Are you certain you want to wait outside?"

"I'm certain. Wash is surely on his way."

Hettie fidgeted with her hands. "I don't know, Amanda. I think you should stay in here until he comes. The streets are not safe anymore, what with the soldiers on every corner and runaway slaves wandering into town."

Amanda waved her hand. "I'll be fine. I'm not going to be on the street. Thank you for a wonderful morning. We'll meet again next week?"

"Yes, of course." Hettie stood at the door and watched as Amanda seated herself in the swing under the shade of the big live oak near the gate. Amanda waved at her and began to glide the swing back and forth. She opened her parasol and pulled the brim of her hat down to shield her face from the sun filtering through the lacy leaves. Bees hummed around the honeysuckle vine winding around the fence pickets.

Fifteen or twenty minutes passed. Amanda left the swing and stepped to the gate. She creaked it open and stepped out on the wooden walkway, then into the road. Wash was nowhere in sight. As she turned to go back to the swing, three young Confederate soldiers appeared and leaned against the gate. They were not in uniform, but they wore Confederate kepis.

One skinny soldier, hardly more than a boy, grinned at her, showing tobacco-stained teeth. "Look-ee here. What's a beautiful young lady like you doin' out here on the street unescorted?"

"I . . . I'm not . . . alone, that is. That is my friend's house. I'm waiting for my driver."

The second soldier, shorter but more muscular, backed her up against the fence. "Well, it looks to me like you're alone. I don't see no 'driver.' Do you, Zeb?"

The third soldier hung back toward the street. "Come on, y'all. It's broad daylight. This is a refined lady. Leave her be. We don't need no trouble." He tugged on the arm of the skinny soldier. "C'mon, y'all are drunk."

Zeb jerked his arm free. "This is no trouble. No trouble at all." He leaned toward Amanda. "I've always wanted to kiss a refined lady. How about a little kiss, missy? No harm in that, is there?"

She cringed and shrank from him.

The stocky soldier laughed and slapped his knee. "Naw, no harm in that. Go ahead, Zeb, show that refined lady what a real kiss is."

He caught hold of Amanda's arm and pulled her toward him. The whiskey on his breath sickened her, and she wrenched herself away from him. "How dare you!"

"How dare . . . ? Why, you little spitfire! Think you're too good for a common soldier of the South?" He reached for her again, but was stopped by a dark hand on his arm.

CHAPTER FOUR

We soon began to feel the privations which war entailed upon us, but we met them with brave hearts for we were full of patriotism in those days.

EUDORA INEZ MOORE

You'll be leavin' Miss Belle alone now." Wash towered over the soldiers. His big shoulders blotted out the sun overhead as he offered her his hand. He still had on the black top hat that he always wore when he drove Amanda to town.

Zeb whirled around to face him. "Look here. No darkie orders us around!"

"Nobody doin' no orderin'. I jes come to take Miss Belle home." His velvety deep voice commanded the moment.

The soldiers stepped back, and Zeb shook his head, snickering. "Aw, didn't mean no harm, ma'am. No need to get excited. Just having a little fun."

"Don't look to me like the lady havin' much fun." Wash looked at them as he assisted Amanda into the buggy. Then he turned again toward the soldiers with the buggy whip in his hand. The men backed up into the street, holding up their hands.

Wash got the reins and swung onto the driver's seat. As he pulled the buggy away, Amanda looked back at the soldiers, who were laughing and slapping each other on the back as they headed toward the saloon.

She took a deep breath. "I'm sorry, Wash. You were right. I should have stayed inside until you got there."

"Yes'm."

Amanda gripped her hands in her lap to keep them from shaking. "I've never been treated with such disrespect—and by Southern men."

"Not all Southern men are like your daddy and your brother."

"Evidently not. Once again you come to my rescue."

He looked over his shoulder at her. "This is a mite different than when we were growing up—pushin' you away from a snake or catching a runaway horse. Things is more serious now, 'specially with the war and all." He chucked the reins to hasten the pace of the team. "We'll be home shortly."

"I don't approve of the way those soldiers talked to you." She was speaking to the back of the young Negro's head. She hated that they had treated him so rudely—and on her account.

He kept his gaze on the road ahead. "I know. You and your family been nothin' but good and kind to us."

"We couldn't run Bellevue without you. You're like . . . well, like family to us."

Wash stopped the buggy, turned, and looked directly at Amanda. "Miss Amanda, I'd give my life for you, you know that. But you also know that we're not really like your family. If we were . . ." He turned back to face the front.

She leaned forward. "What, Wash? If you were . . . what?"

"Giddyup." The buggy lurched forward. "Nothing. Things would be different, that's all."

Amanda sat back and twirled her parasol. She could not imagine what life would be like without Elsie and her family at Bellevue. She knew that in her heart she loved Wash and Kitty nearly as much as Daniel and her sisters, but to say that aloud to anyone would be scandalous. The spanking and mouth washing her mother gave her years ago flashed through her mind. What was going to happen if the Union won the war, and the slaves were freed? Her father always said he would give his slaves their papers voluntarily if it came to that, but slavery was just taking hold in Texas. How would they harvest the crops without slaves? She felt torn and confused.

They rode the rest of the way in silence.

On Friday evening, the Belles' carriage once again rode into town. Wash jumped down and held the team of horses as the family gathered their things. Father assisted Amanda and the younger girls as they chattered excitedly.

The Davis house was similar to Bellevue, but slightly smaller. However, this evening the guests were gathered outside in the gardens to the side and back of the house. The Davises had decorated with red, white, and blue bunting and two of the flags that the women had sewn, hanging them from the second-story railings.

Servants lined up along the walkways and paths in their crisp white aprons like white irises along a fence. The female servants served drinks and refreshments as the guests arrived, and the men cooked a hog and steamed clams over the pit down by the pond, smoke billowing into their eyes. They wiped the perspiration from their foreheads with white handkerchiefs and laughed and cajoled with each other.

Rebecca rushed toward them. Her cheeks were flushed with

excitement, fairly matching her auburn hair. "Oh, I'm so delighted that you decided to come. You look ravishing, Amanda. And I love your hat. The color of that bow makes those hazel eyes of yours fairly glisten."

Amanda smiled and touched the wide brim of her straw summer hat with the teal-colored ribbon that tied underneath her chin. Her teal-and-white-print cotton dress had a large flounce around the neckline and a voluminous ruffled skirt with a large matching sash and bow down the back; it was one of Amanda's favorites. She always received compliments when she wore it.

"Thank you. You look beautiful as well." She bussed Rebecca's cheek.

"Oh, you are so sweet." Rebecca motioned to the Belles. "Come and meet our honored guests."

She led them to the shaded arbor where her parents, Theodore and Sylvia Davis, conversed with three Confederate soldiers and two women. The Davises arose and greeted the Belles, and Theodore introduced his guests. All of the men wore dark blue frock coats with white trousers. Naval officers.

Her three sisters hid behind Amanda's skirt as they were introduced. She laughed and pulled them in front of her as she acknowledged the introductions. "Mind your manners, girls."

"Ahem."

The girls stood upright when their father cleared his throat.

"These are my younger sisters, Emmaline, Catherine, and Mary." Each of the girls curtsied and giggled. "Go on now and play. We'll organize for charades later on. Don't go far."

"Yes'm." They bounded out of the arbor to join the other children.

Rebecca introduced a young lieutenant who stepped forward, took Amanda's hand, and clicked his heels.

"Horace Miller at your service, ma'am. I'm very pleased to make your acquaintance." His voice was soft. He wore his blond hair cut short, as well as his moustache. His eyebrows and brown eyes seemed too dark for his blond hair.

Amanda nodded and removed her hand. "Yes, nice to meet you as well."

Rebecca ducked her head and giggled. Her eyes sparkled.

This lieutenant must be more than simply an acquaintance.

"I understand that your family supports the war effort."

"We do what we can. Sewing flags and knitting socks seems a paltry contribution."

"Not at all. And you have a family member in the Confederate army?"

"Yes, my brother, Daniel. He is in Houston with the 8th Cavalry."

"Ah, Terry's Rangers. I just came from Houston. The word is that they are mustering and will be shipped out soon." He smiled. "Of course, 'soon' in the army could mean weeks."

"Oh." Amanda stepped toward the young officer and Rebecca. "Do you know where they might be sent? We've not heard from him since he left."

Horace shook his head. "Don't worry yourself about that. They don't give them much time to write, and you know how the mail delivery is these days. I don't know where they are going—east of the Mississippi, I would guess. They need cavalry over there."

"I see." Screeches from the children playing, little boys antagonizing little girls, pulled Amanda's attention away. "They seem to be having fun."

Rebecca laughed. "Yes, they do. Lieutenant Miller is a graduate of the Naval Academy."

"Yes. Just a year ago."

Amanda sat on a garden bench next to Rebecca. "Did most of the men from the academy go with the South or with the Union?"

"Sympathies for the South run high in Maryland. About a hundred and fifty of us went with the Confederate states' navy, and I'd say around twenty-five percent of the officers, including General Lee's brother, Commandant Sydney Smith Lee. The fighting in Texas thus far has been in the west, even into New Mexico Territory. But we are here to take care of the coastline. It's no secret that the Union forces will soon try to capture the coastal cities to prevent supplies being shipped to Confederate troops. We expect a major thrust this fall. I'm afraid it may get bad in these parts before this thing is resolved."

"Oh-h-h." Amanda exhaled. "I didn't think that . . . or perhaps I wouldn't allow myself to think about the fighting touching our little town."

"The Union forces are going to try to capture every port they can, whether large or small. You'd best be prepared."

"What would you suggest we do?" Rebecca asked. "How do we prepare?"

"Stock up on what you can—flour, coffee, medicine, bandages, candles. Those of you on farms are fortunate and will fare better than those in town. Unless, of course, your darkies flee."

Amanda shook her head. "Ours won't. They are loyal to our family."

Horace stroked his moustache. "You may be surprised. When freedom is offered, they will scatter like fireflies on a warm summer's night—unless, of course, they have been trained to stay put."

"What do you mean?"

"You know as well as I do that there are ways to—shall we say—encourage our coloreds not to run."

"We do not whip our slaves at Bellevue, if that's what you mean. I tell you, ours will not run. I know our Negroes. They will stay with us."

"Forgive me." He bowed slightly at the waist. "I did not mean to pontificate. I hope you are right. But with word of freeing the slaves spreading like wildfire, we are seeing runaways headed north all over the country." He offered his arm to Rebecca. "Would you ladies care for a cup of punch?"

Amanda snapped her fan and followed Horace and Rebecca, who rested her hand lightly on his arm. He threaded his way through the guests to the refreshment table.

The evening passed with gales of laughter at the children's antics playing charades. The Davises had hired a fiddler who entertained and provided music for dancing. Amanda laughed along with the others, and danced, but her mind was on Daniel and the young Captain Littlefield, not on her immediate surroundings.

❧

Amanda looked down at her sleeping sisters as moonbeams danced on their faces through the window of the buggy. She held Mary in her lap.

"Papa, did God plan this war? Did God plan for our lives to be in upheaval because some people hundreds of miles from us think we should not have slaves?" She brushed a lock of hair out of her little sister's face. "We treat our slaves fairly. Can we not decide for ourselves what is best for our families? I don't understand. I don't understand why my brother may lose his life in a war that we don't want." Tears threatened.

"That is what the war is all about—giving the states the right to decide what is best for its populace, not the federal government. There's much that we don't understand, my dear."

Amanda brushed away a tear that escaped down her cheek.

Her father reached across and patted her hand. "We simply have to follow what we know is God's will at the time. What I know is God's will for me right now is to provide for you girls and pray for Daniel. That's all I know to do. If it comes to a point where I have to protect our home, I will do that to the best of my ability. We have to trust God for the rest."

CHAPTER FIVE

> *Beautiful dreamer, wake unto me,*
> *Starlight and dewdrops are waiting for thee;*
> *Sounds of the rude world, heard in the day,*
> *Lull'd by the moonlight have all pass'd away!*
>
> STEPHEN FOSTER,
> "BEAUTIFUL DREAMER"

Rebecca looked more beautiful than Amanda ever remembered. Of course it was merely a fitting for her wedding dress, but Amanda couldn't imagine how her friend could look any more stunning on her wedding day than now.

"Oh, Rebecca. You look . . . you look absolutely radiant."

Rebecca picked up the heavy lace skirt of the dress and twirled around. "I can hardly believe it. I'm getting married—and next week."

"Quit being such a fussbudget, or we won't have this dress finished by next week." Her mother took her by the shoulders and stationed her in front of the full-length mirror. "Fortunately we have little left to do. How I wish this didn't have to be such a hurried affair."

"But the war, Mama. Horace is being shipped out in just three weeks. Who knows when he will be back?"

Claire spoke up, her voice barely rising above the bustle of the women in the room. "I wish Daniel and I had taken time to get married before he left."

Amanda reached for her friend's hand. "I know you must miss him."

"As do you." Claire smiled and turned her head away, but not before Amanda detected her friend's eyes reddening.

"Oh, Claire. I hope I've not been insensitive." Rebecca turned from the mirror. "This ole war has interfered with every phase of our lives. I just hate it." She walked to Claire and put her arms around her. "But our boys say they'll make short order of the Yankees, and they'll all be back before the turn of the new year. Daniel will be home before you know it."

"I hope you're right." Claire wiped her eyes with a handkerchief that Amanda handed to her. "Thank you. And you have your Captain Littlefield that you're waiting for, Amanda."

The underlying drone of female chatter ground to a halt, and heads turned toward Amanda.

"Why, I . . . Captain Littlefield and I never . . . We made no commitment to one another. Besides, my father refused to allow him to communicate any further with me."

"And do you agree with that?" Rebecca's brown eyes flashed as she challenged her friend.

"I . . . I don't know. My father feels that because he is a Yankee officer and we are Southerners that there could never be anything—"

"Your father feels? What do you feel? I saw the two of you together after church several times. It was obvious he cared for you and you for him. And he's quite handsome."

The girls in the room tittered.

Rebecca's mother turned her around to face the mirror once again. "Please, Rebecca. And mind your tongue, young lady."

"Times are different from when you grew up, Mother. A girl ought to be able to follow her heart."

Mrs. Davis shook her head and began to pull the loops from the buttons down the back of the dress.

"Captain Littlefield is quite handsome. I do agree with that." Amanda sat in the window seat and looked down at the street brimming with supply wagons and Confederate soldiers and sailors. "But . . ." She picked up a fan. "It was simply not to be. I have the girls to raise, and that's going to be a few more years."

Claire remained in a chair beside the window. "Do you plan never to marry, or to wait until your sisters are all grown and married? Daniel and I can help care for them after he comes home."

"I promised my mother before she died that I would take care of them."

Rebecca caught Amanda's eye in the mirror as her mother placed the lace veil on top of her hair. "And you think she meant for you to sacrifice your desires for a husband and family to raise them? Do you think she didn't mean for you to find love and happiness?"

Amanda fanned herself. Someone had finally dared to speak aloud the fears that had whispered in her ear for so many years—fears she had kept shut in the deep recesses of her heart. Only when Captain Littlefield wooed her for a brief few weeks did she allow herself to imagine that maybe, just maybe, she could fall in love and have a family. Then the war slammed that door shut, and her father's disapproval locked her heart's desire in a prison of doubt and self-denial. She dared not even test the lock.

"I'm sure my mother wished me to find contentment. I can be content caring for my family."

Rebecca stepped out of the dress and drew a robe around her shoulders. "But what about love, Amanda? Do you love Captain Littlefield?"

Amanda looked around the room and felt herself blush. "I . . . I think perhaps I was beginning to have feelings for him. He was attentive and kind. We had different views on some things. This slavery/abolitionist matter has thrust our entire nation into war. Could we expect any less between individuals?"

"I know how happy I am to be marrying the man I love. I cannot imagine what it would be like to refuse to acknowledge the fact that I care so much for him. By this time next week we will be Lieutenant and Mrs. Horace Miller." She spun around the room, laughing and humming "Beautiful Dreamer."

Amanda was glad when Rebecca turned her attention elsewhere. Mrs. Davis had handed the wedding dress to Callie, their slave girl who attended Rebecca. Amanda watched the girl smooth the dress out on the bed with care, then hang it on the door of the armoire. She moved to the corner of the room and folded her hands at her waist.

For the first time Amanda observed a slave other than Wash and his family as a person. She stared at the young girl. She was pretty.

Callie kept her eyes down.

Maybe we are wrong about the slaves.

Callie looked at Amanda, and then looked away quickly.

Amanda shook her head. *I'm staring.* She turned to Rebecca. "I must go." She hugged her friend. "I'm delighted for you, and cannot wait for the happy day—I'm truly happy that someone has found love in the midst of all this turmoil."

⚬⚬⚬

Wash chucked the reins and headed for Claire's house. Amanda shifted back and forth in her seat.

Claire opened her parasol. "What is it, Amanda? Are you uncomfortable?"

"Only with the conversation at Rebecca's."

"About Captain Littlefield?"

Amanda nodded. She looked down at the lacy gloves that protected her hands from the brilliant afternoon sun. "I know my father wants to try to prevent any heartache that he feels might come my way. At the time I felt he had done the right thing by insisting that we not pursue our feelings for each other. But now . . ."

"But now, what? Are you having second thoughts?"

"I don't know, Claire. You and Daniel have loved each other since you were children. You all always knew that one day you would marry. And your parents don't object. How am I supposed to know whether Captain Littlefield and I are to be together? Shouldn't I submit to my father's wishes?" She shook her head. "My heart tells me one thing, and my head tells me another."

"And what is your heart telling you?"

Tears sprang to Amanda's eyes.

Claire reached across and took her future sister-in-law's hand. "I didn't mean to make you cry."

Amanda pulled a handkerchief from her bag. "I know. My life seemed so simple before Captain Littlefield came along, and then the war. I didn't think I wanted or needed anything else other than Bellevue and Papa and the girls—and, of course, you and Daniel. But every time Kent, er, Captain Littlefield . . . came to call, it was as if seeds of desire began to sprout in my heart. When he had to leave, I plowed everything under. However, today, when you and Rebecca probed . . ." She looked at Claire. "It made my heart hurt."

"Oh-h-h, honey, I didn't mean to hurt you." Claire gathered Amanda in her arms.

"You didn't hurt me. Having to look at my hidden longings hurt me. You were just the messenger of truth."

"What are you going to do?"

"What can I do? The war has split not only the country, but our family. I'll most likely never see Captain Littlefield again." She sat up and put her handkerchief away. "I need to do what my hands find to do and stay busy."

They pulled in front of Claire's house at the end of town. Oleander bushes were bursting with vibrant pink blossoms around the porch. Wash helped Claire out of the buggy.

Claire closed her parasol and leaned toward Amanda. "Have you prayed about this?"

"What's there to pray about? I live in a home that follows the Book. We do what it instructs and obey the head of the household. I think God does whatever he chooses with people. Prayer doesn't seem to make much of a difference."

Claire put her hand over Amanda's. "Don't become cynical. It's true that being on opposite sides of the war complicates your association with Captain Littlefield. And I'm certain your father is looking out for your best interests. He loves you very much. But you never know how God is going to work things out for his children."

"I think 'things' have already been worked out for my life." Amanda watched Wash climb back onto the driver's bench. "See you at church tomorrow?"

"Of course." Claire turned to go inside her house. She called over her shoulder. "Think about what I said."

Amanda nodded. "I will. Let's go home, Wash."

Amanda watched the Confederate soldiers in town, leaning against the hitching rails along the wooden sidewalks. She could hear their laughter and joking, and she shuddered thinking of the unpleasantness she had experienced. Surely all the soldiers were not like those ruffians. One of them could be a young man like Daniel—courteous, chivalrous, kind. Daniel was probably in a town somewhere with his colleagues, purchasing coffee or sugar or tobacco. Or perhaps he was camped in a woods somewhere waiting to go into battle. Maybe he was hungry or short of supplies. Or maybe he was wounded, and there was no one to care for him. And Kent. Where was he, and was he well?

Her mind flitted from one extreme to the other as she watched the landscape pass. She wished there were something else she could do besides knit socks and blankets to send to the troops.

She closed her eyes as the buggy jostled along. She thought of Captain Littlefield—Kent—his incredibly blue eyes, his smile that coaxed a dimple to appear in his right cheek, his black curly hair. She thought of his husky voice as he asked for the chess pie that first Sunday she met him, and then how serious it turned during their discussions about slavery. She opened her fan.

Wash turned around. "Are you too warm, ma'am? We'll be home shortly."

"I'm fine. Thank you."

Wash pulled in front of Bellevue and assisted Amanda from the buggy.

"Wash, did you overhear my conversation with Claire?"

Wash shifted his weight. "It was hard not to hear, Miss Amanda."

"Would you please cease being my servant for a moment and be my friend—someone who has been my friend longer than anyone else?"

"Yes'm. I'll try."

Wash looked at her with his dark eyes that looked like melted chocolate. They seemed sad, as if he knew a secret that would be harmful, but he couldn't tell . . . wouldn't tell. A bead of perspiration rolled down his forehead. He flicked it away with his hand and took off his top hat. "It's mighty hot out here today."

"Yes, isn't it?"

Amanda hesitated at the gate. "Did you love Harriet from the first moment you saw her? Or did you learn to love her because my father bought her for you and arranged your marriage? Would you have been happy simply living here taking care of us, with no wife and family?"

"Those are powerful questions, Miss Amanda. Questions that hardly seem fittin' for a slave to be talking to his mistress about."

"I need my friend Wash—not my slave, Washington."

"Yes'm." His whole demeanor changed, and he straightened his posture. He lowered his voice, but the deep tones were weighty. "It would have been hard not to fall in love right away with a woman as beautiful as Harriet. She's a powerful-looking woman."

Amanda smiled. "That's so true."

"But deep, true love is different. That comes from walkin' alongside of each other when one of you's sick or discouraged or happy or fearful. It builds one step at a time until you's one, like the Good Book says." He took a deep breath. "Would I have been happy not bein' married and havin' our little Zachary? No'm. I might have been content, but not happy without a wife and family."

The word *content* echoed in her ears. "My father has forbidden me to communicate with Captain Littlefield again, but my heart longs to be with him. I find I cannot stop thinking about him."

"Don't look to me like there's much you can do at the moment, with the war an' all. Mistah Zekiel, he mean good for you, Miss Amanda, but if'n your heart is pullin' you the other way . . . seems like you could appeal to him. He's a reasonable man."

"I don't know. He can be pretty stubborn."

"Pray."

"Pardon me?"

"Like Miss Claire tell you. Pray for God to do something to bring you together, if that be his will. God jes loves to surprise his children, if'n you let him. Pray for him to change yo' daddy's heart. Pray for a chance to see the man again. Jes pray." Wash returned his hat to his head.

Amanda smoothed her skirt. "Thank you, Wash. You've given me wise words to contemplate. Seems like everyone is doing a heap of praying these days. Put the team away, please, and I'll see you in the house."

Amanda opened the gate and walked to the steps leading to the front door. She startled to the sound of her father's voice coming from the swing on the other end of the long porch, where he was partially hidden by the tall vases of palms.

"Evening, Amanda. You and Washington seemed to be having an awfully serious conversation."

CHAPTER SIX

SEPTEMBER 1864

*Lord, I'm going to hold steady on to You, and You've got to see
me through.*

HARRIET TUBMAN

manda sat on the veranda in the descending twilight and
rocked back and forth in rhythm with her fan and the hum
of the cicadas. The leaves of the trees hung motionless in
the calm of the gathering dusk. Emmaline, Catherine, and Mary
played at her feet with their dolls, making a tent with a quilt. A flock
of ibises rose gracefully and flew over the rising moon.

Father sat across from her, his sleeves rolled up, whittling on a
trap to put out tomorrow for small game—rabbits, possum, and, if
they were fortunate, bobwhite quail. Elsie and Kitty were putting
the finishing touches on the evening meal in the outdoor kitchen—
it was too hot to cook inside.

"Ach!" Father slapped at his neck and rolled down his sleeves as
the mosquitoes made their nightly appearance. The high whine of
the pesky insects zinged by Amanda's ear now and then, but they
didn't bother her as much as they pestered her father and Emmaline.
Both of them went to bed every night in the summertime with

several new bites. Emmaline would awaken Amanda scratching at her legs.

Harriet walked around the side of the house with her apron full of tomatoes, okra, and onions from the garden and dumped them on the table, where Amanda was dusting off the seats of the chairs. Zachary's head poked over his mother's shoulder from a sling she had fashioned out of a scarf and wrapped around her body to carry the baby on her back. She dumped the produce in a large wooden bowl on the veranda. "This'll be enough for a good gumbo tomorrow. I'll get some shrimp out of the bay in the mornin'."

She untied the scarf and brought the baby around in her arms. His big black eyes blinked at his surroundings as she sat him down on a quilt. "You play there while I help Grammy finish supper."

Wash brought more wood for the outdoor oven. He tossed the logs into the glowing pit, stood up, and wiped his forehead with a rag. Kneeling on one knee in front of his son, he planted a kiss on the baby's cheek. The boy squealed and kicked his legs as his father tickled his feet. Wash laughed and returned to the woodpile for another armload.

Harriet's skin glinted bronze like polished copper in the setting sun. High cheekbones set off her angular face and deep-set green eyes gave her a hauntingly different look from most of the other slave women.

Father had purchased her several years ago from a neighbor at the insistence of the owner's wife. He never told Amanda why, but it wasn't difficult to figure out. The arrangement had been satisfactory for both families. Not only was she a handsome woman, she was a good worker and devoted to Wash and their son.

Kitty and Elsie brought sliced smoked ham, tomatoes, onions, and cornbread, and a pitcher of buttermilk to the table.

Amanda called her sisters. "Come, girls, suppertime." The white wicker chair scraped across the planks of the kitchen as she pulled it out from the table. The sound of dogs baying in the trees beyond distracted her, and she walked to the front of the house, peering into the dusky twilight.

A riderless horse raced toward them, with someone riding behind it, headed for the house at full gallop.

"That's Daniel's horse. It's Cannonade!" Amanda cried. As the horseman came closer, she could see the frantic expression on his face. "And Hiram! Oh no. No! Wash. It's Hiram!"

Wash ran around the side of the house and caught Cannonade's bridle. Hiram leapt from his horse and dodged behind Wash. "The d . . . dogs are after me, Wash—the Home Guard!" He bent over with his hands on his legs, gasping for air. "I got almost all the way home. They . . . they think I'm a runaway. Daniel give me my papers, but they don't pay no mind. They just out to get a colored."

The baying grew louder as the dogs came into view in front of eight horsemen riding with torches in their hands.

"Get on the porch, Hiram." Ezekiel grabbed his rifle. Sam leapt off the porch, his hackles raised. Ezekiel took the reins of the horses from Wash as the horsemen reined in their mounts. The dogs howled and began circling.

"What can I do for you gentlemen?"

"We're chasing down a runaway slave, and the dogs brought us here."

Ezekiel looked around. "I don't see any runaway slaves here. These are all my Negroes. You men have been on a wild goose chase."

The lean wiry spokesman for the vigilantes scrutinized the servants and Hiram on the veranda. "You say this slave belongs to you?"

"That's what I'm saying. He went with my son, Daniel, to Houston to enlist in the 8th Cavalry, and Daniel sent him home with the horses. The boy has papers, if you'd bothered to look at them."

The man whirled his horse around, then faced Ezekiel once more. His low voice rumbled. "Very well. I'll accept your word as a Southern gentleman. There are runaway slaves all over the country. We're simply trying to keep the peace."

"For a price, I assume."

The bounty hunter's jaw worked back and forth as the flickering torches cast eerie shadows on the faces of the posse. "Landowners sometimes offer a reward to have their property returned."

"Yes, well, I don't seem to have lost any of my . . . property. Seems the boy came back voluntarily, doesn't it?"

"Humph. Wonder if he'd have returned if he hadn't been chased back."

"I think you need to get off of my property, and I am using the term properly this time. You'll ride a couple of miles before you get to the end of my land. The most direct route is straight down that road along the coastline." Ezekiel shifted his rifle to his other hand. "Farewell."

The men swore, but turned to lead the yelping dogs down the road in the direction from which they had come.

Amanda ran toward Hiram. "Hiram, where's Daniel? What's happened to Daniel?" Her voice, tightened with panic, was almost a shriek. "Where is Daniel?"

Hiram wiped the perspiration from his brow with his sleeve. "Miss Amanda, Daniel's fine. They sent the 8th Cavalry to Kentucky without they horses or boys. Say they get them the best horses in the country once they gets to Kentucky." He chuckled. "Our Texas boys don't believe that for one minute. Mistah Daniel send me home with my papers and his horse. He know'd I may run into trouble, but he didn't have no choice."

Elsie stood by her son, wringing her hands in her white apron.

"I almost made it without no trouble." Hiram grinned and put his arm around his mother. "I sho was glad to see the turnoff to Bellevue."

He dug in the bag that was slung over his shoulder. "Mister Daniel sent this for you." Hiram thrust the treasured correspondence in his still-trembling brown fingers toward Father, who took it and ripped open the envelope.

He skimmed through it quickly, then smiled at Amanda. "He's fine. Says he's proud of his unit—that people have dubbed them Terry's Texas Rangers—appears the name is going to stick." He read down further in the letter. "He says for us not to worry."

Amanda shook her head and blinked away tears as her father read the last paragraph aloud.

Don't worry about me, but do pray. I am certain that the Confederate army will win this conflict, and we will be home in no time. Please tell Claire that I will write soon.

Love and regards,
Daniel

Amanda's legs felt like jelly, and she feared they would not hold her up. She collapsed onto a chair and held her head in her hands, fighting rising emotions, and reached for a fan on the table.

Her father leaned his rifle against the railing, pulled up another chair, and sat in front of her. He poured a glass of water and held it out to her. "Here, drink this."

She wrapped her quivering fingers around the glass and took a token sip, then gave it back.

Father set the glass on the table and took both of her hands in his. "You have your mother's beautiful slender hands." He patted them affectionately. "Mandy, we cannot live our lives in constant fear that Daniel is going to be wounded or killed."

"But, what if . . ."

"We cannot live day to day saying *what if.* That's not living a life of faith. We must live our days saying *Yes, Lord,* and trust him with our lives—and Daniel's."

Amanda chewed on her quivering lip. "I know you're right, Father. But I can't seem to gain control over my fears and my emotions. Every time I think about Daniel fighting for his life . . . I . . . I can't gain control of myself."

"He's a fine young man, and I'm sure he's a fine soldier as well, skilled and brave. All the worry in the world is not going to do him any good. Only prayer for God's protection will have any effect. Spend your time praying for Daniel instead of worrying about him."

❧

NOVEMBER 1864

The days turned cooler, and Amanda watched wagons carrying half a dozen of their slaves toward the coast. Her eyes filled with tears as she stood on the porch with Elsie and watched men who had worked the fields of Bellevue all of their lives leave. The Confederate army was conscripting slaves as labor. The Belles were fortunate that they were allowed to keep their house slaves, but half of their field hands were taken. Elsie turned and looked at Amanda without speaking and dabbed at her eyes with the corner of her apron.

Maintaining Bellevue became more difficult week by week. Heavy cannons rode by the house nearly every day as the military began to place them along the coastline for defense.

The slaves kept busy killing hogs and putting up the meat for smoking now that cooler weather had finally reached the coast. Remembering Lieutenant Miller's admonition to stock up on

57

supplies, Amanda and Harriet had assumed the task of making tallow candles like the old-timers. The oil supply for their lamps was almost gone. A foul odor from the animal lard lingered around the house, and try as she might, Amanda couldn't wash the smell from her clothing after making candles all day. It even lingered in her nostrils.

For the first time that month, they heard cannons booming in the distance. Amanda ran to the front of the house as the reports punctuated the air and rattled the windows. Ships appeared on the horizon in the bay. She could see smoke billowing from the cannons on the ships, then a report from Confederate cannons on land. The ground vibrated beneath them.

The servants stopped their chores, tools in their hands, and went to the front of the house as well. Confusion rippled through the group.

Father ran from the stable holding his rifle. "Wait! Don't panic." He motioned to the slaves to gather around him. "Listen to me. None of those rounds are hitting close. It sounds like they're aiming for Lavaca and Aransas Pass. They most certainly are trying to blockade the bay. Quickly, hide the meat in your cabins as we planned and put supplies in the smokehouse. Go to your cabins and don't come out until someone comes for you. Make haste." Dark heads nodded, and the servants scattered.

Wash ran toward the smokehouse. "Harriet! Harriet! Where are you?"

Kitty called to her brother over her shoulder as she gathered up the candle-making supplies and started for the house. "She was going down to the shore to gather crabs for supper."

Wash sprinted toward the shoreline, his feet scarcely touching the ground. Amanda watched as he disappeared from sight, but she could still hear him calling for Harriet. She gathered up a box of wicks and ran to the back of the house. She dashed through the back door as Wash and Harriet hurried toward the house from the beach.

Harriet's breath came out in gulps. "I . . . I was already heading back when I saw the ships."

"You take the baby and get inside. I'll finish up here."

All night long the cannons boomed, but Union troops never came ashore at Indianola.

⚜

Cannonading persisted off and on as November passed into December. Amanda almost became accustomed to hearing the explosions. There continued to be a shortage of supplies. However, occasionally a shipment would get through the blockades, and they would be able to purchase coffee or sugar or even fabric. Christmas came and went with simple celebrations.

Amanda searched every page for news of Terry's Texas Rangers and read everything she could find about the war. The papers proudly reported that the unit had begun to distinguish themselves by their skills and willingness to fight, acting as shock troops. Daniel's letters attempted to assure them that he was doing well.

> You may hear reports of the Confederate cavalry, but they are little more than mounted infantry. They ride to the battle and then dismount and fight. Not so our Terry's Rangers. We ride into the battle with our double-barreled shotguns, two revolvers, and a Bowie knife and fight from atop our horses—and splendid horses they are. They seem to sense that we are in a fight for our lives and perform nobly.

But that one paragraph served to erase all his avowals of well-being. The newspapers also brought distressing reports of battles with heavy losses on both sides. Daniel's letters became fewer and farther between as the war dragged on.

Father strode into the kitchen where Amanda was sorting out potatoes on the table for Elsie. He pulled on his jacket and got his hat from the peg in the kitchen. "I'm going to the post office."

She grimaced. "Do you want me to go with you?"

"Suit yourself. I need to check on our flock."

Amanda's stomach churned as she took off her apron. She did not want to go with her father to check the list of missing and wounded on the bulletin board at the post office, but something in his voice told her that he wished her to do so. "Give me a minute to freshen up."

She washed her hands in the pail beside the kitchen pump, smoothed back her hair, and went into the hall to get a bonnet. She looked in the mirror and realized how pale she looked. She tweaked her cheeks and tied the ribbons beneath her chin, then hurried out the front door where Father waited with the carriage.

"Thank you for coming with me, Amanda." He clicked his tongue, and the horses lurched forward. "The longer this war goes on, the harder these trips will be."

Amanda nodded. "I know."

The trip to town passed with little conversation. As they drew up in front of the post office, the wind whipped around the corner and caught Amanda's cloak in a small whirlwind. She pulled the string around the top of the cloak tighter, grabbed hold of her hat, and ran into the small building with her father behind her.

A small cluster of people huddled around the bulletin board, turning away one by one, the men's faces grim, the women wiping at their eyes with their handkerchiefs, clutching a muffler or a crocheted purse as they exited. One by one the eager-but-hesitant purveyors of the posted list turned away—some crying, some stoic and dismal of face.

Father walked into the middle of the group, giving words of comfort where he could, offering a compassionate embrace. Amanda stood on the edge of the little knot of Indianola citizens, reluctant to intrude on the intimate grieving of families. Father moved to the bulletin board and ran his finger down the list. Amanda held her breath as he stopped about three-quarters of the way down. He hung his head and turned to leave.

She rushed to his side. "What is it, Papa? Who . . . ? It's not Daniel, is it?"

"No, no, dear. It's . . . it's Claire's father. He's listed among the dead—not from a wound, but from pneumonia."

Amanda gasped. "Oh no. We must go to them."

"Just a moment." Father went to the postmaster's desk, and Amanda saw the man nod his head in response. Her father made his way back to Amanda. "They already know. They were in earlier. Come, let's go offer what comfort we can."

Amanda's heart banged against her chest as they pulled in front of the Beecham residence. Three other buggies were already stationed at the hitching rail. Father pulled theirs to the side of the house and tied the team to the fence. As they walked around to the front door, she could hear wails from within.

She hung back, but her father pulled gently on her arm. "Come, my dear. They need us."

"I don't know what to say." A lump knotted itself in her throat.

He shook his head and patted her hand. "You don't have to say anything. All we have to do is weep with them."

The good pastor raised the door knocker, but the door opened before he could bring it down. Claire flew into Amanda's arms— and the two wept together.

CHAPTER SEVEN

Skimming lightly, wheeling still,
The swallows fly low
Over the field in clouded days,
The forest-field of Shiloh—
Over the field where April rain
Solaced the parched ones stretched in pain
Through the pause of night
That followed the Sunday fight
Around the church of Shiloh—
The church so lone, the log-built one,
That echoed so many a parting groan
And natural prayer
Of dying foemen mingled there—
Foemen at morn, but friends at eve—
Fame or country least their care:
(What like a bullet can undeceive!)
But now they lie low,
While over them the swallows skim
And all is hushed at Shiloh.

HERMAN MELVILLE,
"SHILOH: A REQUIEM"

Daniel rubbed down his Morgan mare as the thin sunlight of early morning splayed through the dense thicket on the outskirts of Corinth, Mississippi. He coughed and grabbed his ribs, sore from his insistent cough, and tied the mare to a tree. The miserable march through snow and freezing rain as the Confederate forces fell back from Nashville to Mississippi had taken its toll on the men—pneumonia, colds, dysentery. At least the weather was beginning to warm up, and they were able to relax and try to recover from the brutal winter.

"That cough is sure hanging on." Johnny Jennison held a coffee-pot in midair and looked up at Daniel. Johnny's freckled face made him look much younger than his twenty-two years. He could have passed for fifteen or sixteen, like many of the boys who lied about their age to join the troops. And the drummers—some of them were no older than twelve or thirteen.

"It's much better. Luckily I haven't contracted the 'evacuation of Corinth'—yet."

Johnny smirked. "Nearly everybody else has. Don't know how you escaped it. I'd be willing to wager that we've had more men die from the dysentery than wounds from battle."

Daniel sat down on a tree stump and held out his cup. "What do you think we are waiting for, Johnny? I hear Yank reinforcements are on their way. Why don't we attack before they come?"

Johnny shook his head. "I don't know, but the scuttlebutt is that General Johnston is ready to move, despite Beauregard's objections."

"I hope you're right. This waiting around could addle a man's brain." He set his cup beside the woolen blanket that Amanda had sent for Christmas. Not all of the men were so fortunate. He settled down, using his saddle as a pillow, and pulled the blanket around his chin. He closed his eyes—and dreamed of the ocean.

It seemed he had just fallen asleep when someone shook his shoulder roughly. "Get up, Daniel. We're heading out."

Daniel scrambled to his feet. He reported to his company along with the others and stood at attention beside his horse. His knees knocked. They always did that before he went into battle, but once the shooting started, he knew his fear would flee.

General A. S. Johnston sat tall and straight in the saddle. Mud slugged under his horse's hooves as he rode in front of the men. His large dark handlebar moustache hid his mouth until he spoke. "We are only a mile from the unsuspecting enemy, where they are encamped on the west side of the Tennessee River. Their object is to push farther south into Mississippi. We must not allow that. If we attack now, before their reinforcements arrive, they will be taken by surprise. Tonight, gentlemen, we will water our horses in the Tennessee. God be with you—and give you good aim."

Daniel swung into the saddle and fell into line. Both sides claimed God's favor and protection in battle. How could God be with both the North and the South? He shrugged his shoulders to no one. *I don't have to philosophize about the politics of the war. All I have to do is follow orders.* He spurred his horse, and caught up with Johnny. "Let's go get us some Yanks!"

❦

Major Kent Littlefield walked among the tents in the early morning fog that hovered over the hill, not far from a little Methodist church built of logs. The locals called the place Shiloh. The Stars and Stripes hung limp from the staff, fluttering occasionally with a passing breeze.

He stopped and chatted with his men, hovering around the embers of their fires, encouraging them.

"Mornin,' Major." A sergeant with a barrel chest and bushy moustache saluted Kent, then offered him a seat on a campstool outside his tent. "How long are we going to wait for reinforcements, sir? The Rebs are coming closer and closer. I can smell 'em."

Kent looked around the pastoral landscape. "Surely General Buell will be here any day now." He pointed toward the church. "Reminds me of my church in Pennsylvania. I'd be on my way to services if I were at home on this beautiful Sunday morning."

Suddenly the ground shook with the blast of cannons, and the air was filled with deadly missiles and the Rebel yell. Streaks of fire creased the sky and expired in flashes of light and billows of smoke. Kent and the sergeant jumped to their feet.

"No church today. Sounds like Armageddon is coming to us."

Kent ran to his aide and ordered his horse to be saddled while he got his rifle and sword. He looked down the hill. Those crazy Rebs were storming up the hill, three out of four falling from the fire that had already opened up from the Union troops. He mounted his horse and rode through the camp, ordering the men into battle alignment, but confusion and chaos spread like a wave on the sea. Most of his men had never seen combat. It seemed they had forgotten all their preparatory drills.

One soldier, running toward the river, dropped his gun and shouted over his shoulder, "Somebody told me it would be like shootin' squirrels. Squirrels ain't my fellow countrymen."

The smell of gunpowder hung in the air all day long. The metallic ring of bursting shells and the spinning fragments sent dirt flying all around them. By evening the wounded and dead from both sides dotted the pasture, sprawled over the fences and lying where they fell at the bottom of the hill. Their moans and cries for water haunted the encroaching darkness.

The officers gathered to the rear of the line. General Ulysses S. Grant rode his large and spirited roan into their midst and dismounted. "The Confederates have pushed us back two miles and surrounded us on three sides. Unless our reinforcements come soon, I fear we are defeated."

Flashes of lightning and claps of thunder provided an ominous backdrop as the rain began to fall. The general swung back on his horse. "I suggest you take shelter and pray for reinforcements before daylight."

Federal gunboats sitting like turtles on the Tennessee River began to lob shells into the Confederate camp during the night, joining the lightning in a deadly dance as flashes of the cannon's reports answered nature's light display.

Spotting the overhang of a cliff, Kent and his sergeant huddled beneath the protective rock. The groans of first one wounded soldier, then another, from the field in front of them rose in a macabre rhythm. With each flash of lightning Kent could see the fallen, some as still as stone, others trying to crawl to safety.

One man, close to his shelter, reached for his canteen. "Water. Would . . . somebody . . . please give me some water?"

"C'mon, Sarge. Help me." Kent and Sergeant Kelly dragged the young soldier to their makeshift shelter and gave him a drink.

The boy couldn't have been more than nineteen or twenty. A bloody chest wound gaped through what remained of his ragged jacket. He enclosed Kent's collar in his fist and pulled him close. "Am I . . . am I going to die?"

The boy's breath brushed warm and damp on his cheek, but Kent could barely make out what he was saying. He swallowed. "I don't know, Private. I'm not a doctor. Just try to rest." He pried the soldier's fingers from his jacket and rested the young man's head in his lap.

"I've m . . . made my peace with God. Jesus and the angels will come and get me. I'm not scared. But I sure wanted to have . . ." He drew a ragged breath. "I sure wanted to have a son."

"I understand."

A crooked grin spread across the young soldier's face. "I have a wife . . ." Another belabored breath. "W . . . waiting back home for me. We married the day before I left."

"That's good." Kent covered the boy with his blanket. "Don't try to talk anymore. Just rest."

"If I don't . . . don't make it, would you look up my family and tell them that I was a good soldier? And that I was thinking . . . of . . . "

"What's your name, son, and where are you from?"

"N . . . name's Henry Yost. I'm from Pennsylvania."

"Are you in the 77th Pennsylvania?"

"Yes."

One of his own men. "I'm Major Littlefield. I'll see that your family gets your message."

"Would you take this to my wife? Her . . . her name's Amy." He closed his eyes and smiled, then opened his hand in which he held a locket. His eyelids fluttered open. "She gave this to me when I left. I want her to know . . ." His voice faded away as he struggled to breathe. "I want her to know I was thinking of her to the . . . the end."

Kent took the locket covered in the young soldier's blood. "I will see that she gets it."

"Th . . . thank you, sir. My folks live east of Emmaus, on a f . . . farm." He closed his eyes, and Kent thought he was gone, but the boy still breathed. Kent didn't know how. The wound was massive.

Kent looked toward the dark night sky. "God in heaven, you are a compassionate Father. Have mercy. Have mercy on this young man." He could think of nothing else to pray.

The moans from the men on the bloody field continued throughout the night as if an evil maestro walked among the bodies conducting a symphony of agony. Sounds of suffering came from first one section of the field and then another. Kent covered his ears until the moans were no more. The whistles of shelling from the gunboats persisted throughout the night.

Shortly before dawn he heard the sound of soldiers marching. He touched the soldier's face. Cold. Kent covered his face with his bloody cap. "Rest in peace, my young friend."

He picked up his blanket, folded it, and tied it onto the back of his saddle. He felt a twinge of guilt at leaving the soldier as they prepared to ride to the general's quarters. He surveyed the battlefield. The bodies lay so thick that it was going to be difficult to find footing to ride out. All of those men had families who loved them . . . sweethearts waiting for them . . . children who would grow up without their fathers.

He looked down at his bloody pants and hands, and his stomach churned in revulsion. *This has only just begun. Our brothers' blood will cry out from every river, every pasture, every hill and mountain of this country for years to come. What have we done?*

Kent and Sergeant Kelly's horses picked their way through the bodies. Suddenly Sergeant Kelly's voice boomed. "Whoa! Wha . . . ? Shoo! Get out of there!"

"What is it, Sergeant? Oh, God, send your angels!"

To their horror, wild hogs snorted and rooted around the bodies, feeding on them. Kent whooped and hollered as loud as he could. "Yee-haw! Get out of here. Shoo!"

They shot at the hogs and scattered the scavengers for the moment, but had to abandon the morbid scene and report to the general's quarters.

Kent approached the general. "Sir, we must do something about the bodies. I sought shelter under the cliff next to the field last night, and I saw . . . sir, hogs were feeding on . . ."

The general's grim expression never changed. "Take care of it, Major Littlefield. Put someone in charge of a burial detail and get as many of them buried as you can, but I want you at your regular post. The army of the Ohio is arriving with 25,000 fresh Union troops."

Kent saluted. "Yes, sir." He rode to his company and appointed a corporal to head up the grisly detail. "Bury them in mass graves. That's all we can do for now, but get the dead in the ground and the wounded back to camp."

Kent quickly organized the men he had left—appeared to be less than half. "Advance—in battle formation! March!"

Twigs snapped and birds flew into the air as the men marched through the underbrush. The Stars and Stripes streamed at the front of the column, but beyond and approaching, a mass of gray uniforms.

"Woo-ooo-woo!" The shrill, earsplitting cry of the Rebel yell pierced the early morning air, sounding like a cross between the war cry of Comanche warriors and howling coyotes.

Shivers crawled down Kent's spine as the yell increased in intensity. He raised his sword. "Form your battle line! Ready! Fire!"

Explosions pummeled the ground until he grew deaf. Kent shouted above the noise of battle—the repetitive popping of the rifles, the shouts of the soldiers, the drum roll, the exclamation of pain from those hit by a volley—as he rode up and down the line encouraging his men. He was aware only of the faces of his men and their bravery as one after another fell in front of him. The flag went down, and a young private picked it up with one hand and held a pistol in the other. Young drummer boys *rat-a-tat-tatted* orders to move forward.

The Rebel line fell back, firing as they went. Fresh troops and increased numbers were proving to be too much for the weary Confederate army. A cavalry unit covered the Rebs' retreat.

"Fire at will! Don't let them escape!" His voice rose above the clamor as he led them in a charge.

The Confederate riders brandished not only rifles, but six-shooters, firing relentlessly and fearlessly. A soldier next to him shouted. "It's the 8th Cav. Let's show 'em what us Yanks are made of."

Kent spurred Sterling through the lines and rode hard after them. Hoofbeats resounded in his ears. He was gaining on them when his horse stumbled, sending him plunging to the ground. Leaping to his feet, he scrambled for the shelter of the woods and turned to fire at the cavalry rider who pressed down upon him. He got off a shot as he made it to a stand of trees and ran headlong down the embankment to a creek, rolling down the steep incline until a log stopped him. He slithered over and ducked behind it.

The Johnny Reb pursuing him jumped his horse over the log, then whirled around to aim his six-shooter at Kent.

Kent stared at the cavalryman. "Daniel!"

The soldier lowered his gun. His eyebrows arched underneath his hat. "Captain . . . uh, Major Littlefield?"

Kent raised his hands and nodded. The two stared at each other, not speaking.

Finally Daniel dismounted, still holding his gun on Kent. "What do we do now?"

"I suppose I'm your prisoner."

Daniel shook his head and holstered his gun. "Not by my doing, you're not."

Kent lowered his hands and put his gun away as well. "How are you, my friend?"

"As well as can be expected." Daniel gave a wry smile. "You Yanks have us running this time, but watch out for the next battle."

"You're in a pretty fierce unit, it appears. Your reputation is spreading."

Daniel stuck out his chest. "Humph. We're one of the few true cavalry units that fight on horseback."

"That's a nice Morgan you have there."

"She's not Cannonade, but she's a good horse." Daniel patted the mare's neck as the horse pawed at the leaves on the forest floor.

"You'd best rejoin your unit before one of my men decides to shoot you."

Daniel swung into the saddle. "I suppose I should. Do you hear from Amanda?"

"You know your father forbade it."

"My father is a wise man, but I didn't know if my sister would heed his wisdom." He calmed his anxious horse and his expression turned sober. "This war is changing our land, our lives. It probably is best that you forget her."

Shots whizzed by, ricocheting off the tree trunks.

"I shall never forget her." Kent reached up and grasped Daniel's hand. "Get out of here and stay safe, my friend."

"You as well." Daniel turned his horse to go. "Perhaps we shall meet again one of these days . . . hopefully not on a battlefield."

"Yes, in better times."

Daniel spurred his horse and disappeared quickly into the trees to catch up with his regiment.

Kent whistled for Sterling, who stood at the edge of the stand of trees. He ran his hands over the gelding's ankles. "Looks like you escaped injury this time. I'm grateful." He mounted and looked through the trees at the rear of the retreating 8th Cavalry. "Very grateful."

Amanda picked up the *Indianola Bulletin* and read about a battle at a place named Shiloh. "Papa, doesn't *Shiloh* mean 'peace'?"

Her father looked up from his desk. "Yes, it does."

"Ironic. The paper has reports of a battle in Shiloh, Tennessee, with heavy losses on both sides." She read on, then gasped. "Terry's Rangers were there."

Father stood and reached out his hand. "Let me see." His dark eyes flitted back and forth as he read down through the column. "And valiantly they fought, from what the newspaper says, although the Confederate army lost the battle." He looked at Amanda over his spectacles. "They've listed the dead and wounded."

Amanda's pulse quickened as she waited for him to read the list. He shook his head. "He's not on the list. That means he must be well, or at least alive."

She took a deep breath and clasped her hands together in her lap to calm the trembling. "This is torture, being afraid to read the newspaper for fear of what it may hold, or fearful of going to the post office to look at the lists of dead and wounded and missing."

Her father gathered her in his arms and kissed the top of her head. "I just pray that this madness will come to a swift conclusion. God, let it be so."

CHAPTER EIGHT

OCTOBER 1862

FEDERAL FORCES CAPTURE GALVESTON!

Amanda crumpled the newspaper in her lap as a sick feeling washed over her. The dreaded morning ritual of reading the newspaper enticed her and her father like a magnet, drawing and repelling at the same time. Supplies were becoming critically scarce. Confederate troops in Sabine City had been forced to withdraw after heavy bombardments; headlines splashed reports of Confederate soldiers killing fellow Texans in Nueces County who sympathized with the North; then came word of the unspeakable hanging of forty suspected traitors just a few weeks ago in Gainesville.

"What are we doing—killing everyone who doesn't agree with us? Texans killing Texans? This is madness." She folded the paper and handed it to her father. "I wish we could go get Daniel and bring him home."

"All the wishing in the world won't bring him home safely—but praying might."

"I know that, Papa. I'm simply making conversation." She picked up her cup and swirled the muddy brown liquid with a spoon. "I wish we had some real coffee."

"Still wishing, eh?"

She smiled. "As I said, making conversation. A brew from peanuts is a poor substitute for the real thing." She took another sip of the concoction. "Christmas is already around the corner again, and now with . . . with the blockade, it's going to be difficult to buy gifts. . . ." Swallowing a sob, she pressed her napkin to her mouth. "I don't mind for myself, but for the girls. They will be so disappointed if . . . if we can't do something for them for Christmas."

She pushed the heavy, polished dining room chair back and turned her back on her father, hiding her tears as she busied herself at the buffet. She did not want to burden him anymore than he was already. How could he keep on running Bellevue and pastoring a congregation in the midst of war without collapsing? Weariness deepened the wrinkles around his eyes.

He rose and walked to her, putting his arm around her shoulders. "Don't cry, sugar. We'll do something for them. We always manage. We'll cut down a salt cedar–got plenty of those around. And we'll put pine cones on it and string popcorn." He held up the newspaper. "We'll make chains out of the newspapers we're saving. No matter what's going on around us, we will celebrate our Savior's birth, one way or another."

Amanda smiled. "I know. We are blessed. When I think of poor Daniel out there in a tent, cold and possibly hungry . . . ach! I can hardly stand that. I have a package of cakes and blankets and socks to send to him. Emmie has knitted him a scarf from the last of the wool yarn. We'll send it off this week." She snuggled against her father's chest like she used to when she was a little girl. "I'm just feeling a little blue today, that's all."

Father kissed the top of her head and smoothed her hair. "I need to go check the traps." He gave her another quick hug, then walked into the foyer and plopped his hat on his head. "I shan't be gone long." He went out the door, bending his shoulders against a stiff breeze blowing in from the bay.

⁂

Later that evening the cannonading increased in the bay. Her father motioned the family to ignore it and sit down to dinner as usual. Elsie came through the swinging door from the kitchen and jumped, nearly dropping the tureen of stew, as a different-sounding, larger explosion shook the windows and rattled dishes in the china cabinet. She gulped and set the bowl on the table in front of Father.

"W-we has rabbit stew made with the game Mistah Zekiel brought in from the traps today. And it sho tastes good too." She managed a smile. "Kitty's jes pulling the cornbread out of the oven." She shook her head as she went back through the door. "Listen at that wind blow. Mercy!"

Catherine turned up her nose. "I don't like rabbit stew."

Amanda spooned the brew into the girls' bowls as their father passed them around. His tone grew firm. "We should be grateful that we have food on the table. You'll eat it or go hungry."

Catherine ducked her head and sniffled.

A loud clang from the kitchen startled Amanda, causing her to hit the side of the tureen with the spoon. "What was that?"

Catherine laughed. "Just Elsie knocking a plate off the table. She's getting clumsy in her old age."

"Catherine! That's rude." Her father glared at the girl.

Sam, who had been asleep in front of the fireplace, raised his head and began to growl.

They heard voices and scuffling, then the door from the kitchen banged open. Three Yankee soldiers burst into the dining room, shoving a frightened Kitty and Elsie in front of them. Two of them pointed pistols at the family, and one held a rifle.

"Sorry to disturb you folks, but it's frightful cold out there, and we need shelter."

Sam snarled and began to bark wildly.

Emmaline screamed and jumped from her chair. It clattered to the floor as she started to run toward the front door.

"Stay right where you are, missy." A tall, lanky red-headed corporal pointed his pistol at the girl. "And you'd best shut your dog up, or I'll do it for you."

Father stood and held his hands in front of him. "There's no need to point your guns at us, especially the children. We are people of peace. Sit, Sam."

The dog sat, but stayed beside Father. He motioned to the younger girls, and all three of them ran to the shelter of his arms. Amanda scooted her chair from the table and stood, her heart thudding. She glanced at the dueling pistols, too far out of reach on the sideboard.

The soldier who seemed to be the spokesman, a burly sergeant with a large handlebar moustache, nodded his head toward the kitchen. "We have a wounded officer who needs help—bad."

Father shuttled Emmaline, Catherine, and Mary toward Kitty. "Take the girls upstairs, Kitty. And take Sam with you. Amanda, come with me."

"No, Papa, no!" Catherine wailed, and Mary started crying.

Emmaline jutted out her chin and assumed the role of older sister. "Shush, girls. Come, let's go with Kitty."

The young servant swooped Mary up in her arms and shooed the sisters to the winding staircase.

Father and Amanda went through the swinging door, followed by the Yankee with the rifle. A young officer sat propped up against the table leg on the floor in front of the fireplace. His shattered left leg lay at an awkward angle, and he appeared to have a head wound as well. Her father knelt beside him and removed the officer's cap that stuck to his bloody wound, revealing curly black hair.

"I told my men I thought you would help us." The wounded officer's raspy voice was barely above a whisper. He turned his head, and Amanda looked into the startling blue eyes of Kent Littlefield.

"Oh-h, Papa, it's Captain Littlefield." All of the emotions she had buried because of her father's disapproval came rushing to the surface with that one look from the officer. She glanced at her father out of the corner of her eye.

"Looks like you've gotten a promotion, Major Littlefield."

He tried to prop himself up on his elbow. "Yes, it is major now. I apologize, sir. I . . . I know this is awkward, but we . . . needed . . ." He labored to pull in a deep breath.

Father hoisted the young officer to a standing position and drew his arm around his shoulders. "Amanda, help me take Major Littlefield to the guest bedroom behind the parlor. Elsie, get hot water and all the bandages you can gather and send Hiram for Dr. Greer."

Sergeant Kelly pointed his pistol at them. "Stay right where you are. Nobody's going anywhere."

Amanda and her father moved past the sergeant with their grisly cargo, ignoring the weapon.

"Unless we get a doctor for him quickly," Father said, "I'm afraid your major here is done for. He's lost a lot of blood, and I have very limited medical experience. Does your unit not have an assigned physician?"

The sergeant stepped back and shook his head. "We are an advance party. The full company doesn't attack . . . er . . . arrive until tomorrow."

They assisted Major Littlefield to the bed in the guest room. Amanda was surprised at how heavy his body seemed as they half carried, half dragged him down the hallway. The metallic smell of blood invaded her nostrils, and she watched her skirt grow red as the fluid oozed from his battered leg. She peered at his face, twisted in pain. She wanted to ease his suffering, but didn't know how.

"Amanda, we need a knife and a lantern. Elsie, hurry on now. Get that water and bandages ready for Dr. Greer when he arrives."

Major Littlefield reached up and pulled Amanda's father down to his face. He rasped into his ear. "No doctor. No doctor. At least until tomorrow. Just get me through the night."

The windowpanes shook and the crystals on the overhead chandelier rattled. The boom of the cannons sounded closer and louder as they set to work.

Amanda held the lantern as Father cut the captain's pant leg with the knife. He pulled the blood-soaked garment from the leg. Exposed bone poked through the skin. "This leg is full of dirt and shrapnel. Looks like you got in the way of an explosion."

Amanda turned her head and swallowed the wave of nausea that rose in her throat. The lantern rattled as her hands began to shake.

The redheaded soldier chuckled. "He got in the way of an explosion, all right—like the explosion of the bridge over the bayou, so the rest of our troops can take over your little ole port here in Indianola."

"That's enough, Corporal Robertson." Major Littlefield leaned on a shaky elbow.

"Keep that light steady, Mandy." Her father looked intently at her. "Can you do this? If not, go get Wash."

She nodded. "I can do it."

"If we don't clean all of this trash from the wound you're going to lose the leg for sure, or die of infection. I'll do my best, but we need a physician to set the leg. And we need medicine."

"In the morning we'll send for the doctor, but not until then."

Father brandished the knife in his hand. "Giving your troops time to invade in the morning without prior warning?"

Robertson pointed his pistol at the older man, and the room grew silent as the two stood their ground. The light from the lantern flickered on their faces and glinted off the knife and pistol.

Major Littlefield groaned, breaking the tension. Father stepped back and looked at the wounded officer. "I suppose they sent you back down here because you are familiar with the area."

Kent drew in an uneven breath. "'Fraid so."

"Amanda, you and Elsie wash out the wound. Give him enough whiskey to knock him out. We'll disinfect to the best of our ability and pick out as much of the shrapnel as we can. The leg is obviously broken, probably in more than one place, by the looks of it." He looked at Amanda. "Hold the lantern high, so I can see."

She lifted the light for her father to look at the head wound. He brushed the officer's hair away. "There's much blood, but it appears this wound is superficial. However, it still needs to be washed out." He glowered at the soldier brandishing the rifle as Elsie returned with bandages. "Elsie, we need some whiskey. Fetch it quickly, and let's get to work."

⁂

Amanda opened the door to the guest bedroom for Dr. Greer. The doctor handed his hat to her and set his bag down on the table beside the bed. Elsie shuffled in behind them and opened the draperies, allowing the morning sun to filter into the dark room. The

Union officer lying on the bed moaned and shielded his eyes from the light.

"Let's see what we have here." The doctor felt Kent's forehead and pulled his hair back from the abrasion on his head. "Feels a little feverish, but this wound will heal just fine." He pulled the blanket aside and looked at his leg. "Now this . . ." He gently lifted Kent's leg as the young man grimaced. "This is another matter."

"Thank you, Doctor, for being willing to treat an enemy officer."

"Young man, I have taken an oath to do what I can to administer healing when people need me. Don't I recognize you, Major? You were stationed here before the war, if my memory is correct."

Kent answered through teeth clenched in pain. "Yes, sir."

The doctor looked at Elsie. "I need hot water and towels, please." He adjusted his eyeglasses and peered at the leg. "We'll need to set it. Amanda, you and your father actually did a pretty good job removing most of the shrapnel, but I see a few more pieces that need to come out." He took a scalpel out of his bag, muttering as he worked. "Where is Ezekiel this morning?"

"He went out to ride the property to check on . . . on things."

The doctor nodded and adjusted his spectacles. "You are fortunate, young man, that the leg is only broken and dotted with shrapnel instead of being blown off by one of those blasted Minié bullets. You take one of those and the bone is shattered, giving us no recourse but to amputate. As it is, the setting of this will probably be complicated and painful. It should have been attended to last night. If we can keep the infection at bay, however, we might have a chance to save . . ." The doctor's voice trailed off as he bent over the captain and continued to examine him. "Well, let's get to work."

The cannonading increased throughout the morning as the makeshift medical team worked on Kent's wounds. The pop of

gunfire joined the booms of the artillery. Ignoring the bombard-
ment outside their window, Amanda focused on the daunting task
immediately before them. All too aware of her inexperience, she
fluctuated between fear of harming Kent and the composure that
comes from knowing that one must do what is necessary.

Dr. Greer nodded toward his bag. "Get the bottle of chloroform
and pour some onto a rag. Hold it over his nose until he passes out.
We need to set his leg."

Amanda removed the bottle from the doctor's bag and got a
towel from the washstand. "How much?"

"Just a few drops. When I nod my head, then cover his nose
with the rag, and when he passes out, we'll set the leg. Send for that
sergeant. We're going to need him."

Amanda quirked her eyebrows at the doctor.

"It's going to take some manpower to pull his leg back into place."

Amanda grabbed her stomach. "Elsie, fetch the big man with
the long moustache."

"Yes'm."

"Take these soiled towels and bring more clean towels when you
return."

Sergeant Kelly cracked the door open and stuck his head in.

"Come in, Sergeant. We're going to need you." Dr. Greer looked
at Amanda and gave her a reassuring smile. "You can do this, my
dear. Focus on the task at hand, not on your emotions."

Amanda nodded and followed the doctor's instructions. She put
one hand underneath Kent's head, and when the doctor gave the sig-
nal, she held the chloroform-laden cloth over his nose. She felt his
head grow heavy.

"Now, pull, sergeant, and pray that the bone snaps back into place."

Sergeant Kelly took hold of his superior officer's foot and pulled as Dr. Greer manipulated the leg. A loud snap echoed through the room as Kent flailed in his delirium and tried to free himself from their grasp.

"More chloroform."

With trembling fingers, Amanda placed the rag over his nose again, and he returned to the blessed sleep of the anesthesia. She bit her lip and blinked her tears away.

Kent drifted in and out of consciousness. Amanda wiped his brow with a cool cloth. She brushed his hair back from his face. He reached for her, and she held his hand—and her emotions for him escalated, in cadence with the reports from the cannons from the bay.

The morning passed. Dinnertime passed. Elsie brought broth in a cup for Dr. Greer and Amanda. Early in the afternoon, the doctor straightened his shoulders and took a deep breath. "We've done all we can for this young man. The rest is up to God. Pray against infection." He rolled down his sleeves. "I need to get back to my patients in town."

Father pushed the door open and stepped into the room. Stomping of boots and commotion in the foyer swept in with him.

Amanda looked up from her station at the head of the wounded officer. "What on earth is going on out there?"

Her father's jaw worked back and forth. "I rode into town to check on things. While we have been nursing an enemy officer back to health, our home has been taken over as headquarters for the Union troops that have just invaded Indianola. The soldiers are helping themselves to whatever they desire, and what little provisions we had left are being 'appropriated' by the Union army." His eyes flashed his exasperation. "And we are harboring the enemy."

Dr. Greer took off his bloody apron and shrugged on his jacket. He put his hand on her father's shoulder. "Pastor Belle, you know as well as I that our professional positions place us in no-man's-land. We may have our personal opinions, but our service to our fellow man must know no limits." He closed his bag and put on his hat. "Besides, it's not as if you invited the enemy. Your home was invaded."

"Yes, led by a man that we once entertained in our home. He took advantage of our goodwill."

The doctor turned to Amanda. "Feed him some of Elsie's broth as soon as he comes to. He's going to need all the strength he can muster. And get Wash to make a pair of crutches for him. I have none left. When he feels like it, he can start trying to walk. Pneumonia will set in if he lies there too long."

Amanda nodded.

"Elsie can take care of him." Father stepped aside to allow Dr. Greer to leave. "It would not be seemly for a single young woman to take care of him."

"Hmm. It's wartime, Ezekiel. Our stuffy decorum needs to go by the wayside. Elsie's going to be needed to keep the kitchen going with all these Yanks around."

Amanda collected the bloody towels and followed the two men out. They shouldered their way through the soldiers, who held rifles and pistols at varying positions, looking as if they didn't know how to treat them.

Dr. Greer ignored the soldiers. "I'll check on him in a few days."

A young private took up his rifle and pointed it toward Father.

Sergeant Kelly stepped between them and the eager soldier. "At ease, Private. That's the doctor who treated Major Littlefield, and the other is a pastor. They are no threat to us."

The solider lowered his rifle slowly and rested it by his side. "Whatever you say, Sarge."

"Besides that, the pastor and his family are our hosts. We don't want to do anything to be ungrateful guests now, do we?" Coarse laughter rang out as Dr. Greer walked out the door toward his buggy.

Amanda shuddered and headed to the kitchen with her gruesome bundle.

She watched him sleep—watched the even rise and fall of his chest, and gently touched his shoulder when he moaned in pain. She took note of every detail in his face—a chicken pox scar on his forehead, a wrinkle beginning to form where a deep dimple appeared every time he even tendered the thought of a smile, his dark eyebrows, the beard that hid his angular jaw, a few prematurely gray hairs. She memorized every one of them, fearful that she would never see him again after he recovered. While he was unconscious and no one else was around, she gave herself the license to touch his forehead, to caress his beard and his hair, to hold his hand. Her love for him expanded until at times she thought her heart would burst.

A thunderstorm grumbled in the distance, and the wind whipped the waves in the bay onto the shore. Moving shadows of late afternoon darkened the room. Soldiers tromped through their house, but Amanda never left Kent's bedside.

Finally his eyes flickered open, and he stared at her. "Is . . . is that you, Amanda?"

She smiled. "It is I."

He struggled to sit up. He felt the bandage on his head, then he yanked back the quilt covering his leg. He touched the limb, and his eyes widened. "I still have my leg?"

She nodded. "So far. The doctor says if we can keep the infection down, there's a chance we can save it." She covered her mouth with her hand as she felt her chin quiver.

He collapsed on his pillow with his arm over his eyes. "I . . . I thought for sure I was going to lose it." He leaned up on his elbow. "My men. I need to see to my men."

"You don't need to do anything for a few days. Your sergeant is taking good care of your men."

"I need to confer with him."

"You need to rest. Dr. Greer said—"

His voice, firm and authoritative, took her by surprise. "I'll thank you to summon Sergeant Kelly for me."

Amanda inhaled. "Very well, if you insist. I'll send for him shortly."

Kent looked directly into her eyes, sending her heart aflutter. "Thank you, Amanda. How can I ever thank you?"

"No thanks needed. Lie down. You've lost much blood and are weak. Could you manage to eat—maybe some broth?"

He nodded, lay back, and closed his eyes. "In a minute. Sit here with me, please." His voice sounded weak.

She chuckled. "That's what I've been doing all day." She thought he had dozed off again, but when she shifted her weight in her chair, he opened his eyes. "Please don't leave just yet."

"Let me get you something to eat."

"Could I have a drink of water?"

Elsie had placed a tray with a pitcher of water and goblets on the washstand across the room. Amanda rang for the maid before pouring a drink for Kent.

Kitty poked her head into the room. "Yes'm?"

"Kitty, bring some broth for Major Littlefield, please. And would you find Sergeant Kelly and tell him the major wishes to see him."

The slave wrung her hands in her apron. "Yes'm. Mama made soup."

"That'll be fine." Something about Kitty's behavior bothered her. "What's wrong? Are the soldiers . . . is everything in order in the house?"

Kitty looked over her shoulder, and Amanda could see the cloud of blue uniforms in the hallway. "I'm frightful scared, Miss Amanda. They looks at me with no good in they eyes. Wash done got crossways with one o' dem over Harriet."

Kent rose again on his elbow. "I'll take care of that, Kitty. Fetch Sergeant Kelly right away, please." He pulled himself up, and tried to prop the pillow against the headboard.

Kitty left, closing the door behind her.

"You need nourishment before you start giving orders again. Here, let me get that for you." Amanda leaned over and plumped three pillows behind his head for support. She could feel his breath on her cheek. A warm surge of emotion flooded through her. She pulled back, certain he could hear her heart thudding.

"Thank you, once again." He tried to straighten his shirt. "I apologize. I'm sure I don't smell very good."

"Dr. Greer and Elsie and I—we—well, we washed you off before the doctor worked on you."

Kent cleared his throat. "Oh. Well, I am . . . uh . . . rather discomfited."

Amanda smiled as her cheeks blotched. "I'll have Hiram come and bathe you later."

He ran his fingers through his hair. "Ow." He touched the bandage. "That's a bit tender."

"Dr. Greer said a bullet must have grazed your head." She pulled his kepi from the chair where they had placed his clothing and held it up, poking her finger through a jagged hole. "Not much left of your cap."

"Guess I'm lucky to be alive." His splinted leg stuck over the side of the bed at an awkward angle.

Amanda pulled a chair alongside the bed and propped the limb on it. "You have orders not to move that leg much this first day, because of the bleeding."

Nodding, Kent grimaced as he tried to get in a comfortable position.

Kitty entered with a tray holding a bowl of soup and set it on the bedside table. "You needs to eat too, Miss Amanda. Mistah Zekiel say for you to come to supper. I'll take care of the major."

Amanda tucked in the blanket at the end of the bed and hesitated.

Cocking his head toward the door, Kent encouraged her. "Go ahead. Eat and get some rest. I need to talk to Sergeant Kelly. Did you send for him, Kitty?"

"Yessuh, I did. He say he be here directly."

"I . . . aghh." The pillows shifted, and Kent grabbed his leg.

Kitty and Amanda both rushed to his side.

"Now see there. What did I tell you? You don't need to be trying to take care of your duties today. You are too weak." Amanda readjusted the chair and stood back with her hands on her hips.

Kent grinned and his dimple appeared, even through the beard. "Ah, the lady has a strong side." He laid his head back and closed his eyes. "I submit to the lady. Let me speak to Sergeant Kelly and that will be the extent of my 'duties' today."

Amanda picked up the soup bowl and spoon. "Kitty, please fetch his sergeant right now. Explain to him how weak the major is, but that he insists on speaking with him."

"Yes'm." Kitty left the two in the room alone once more.

Amanda fed him spoonfuls of the nourishing liquid. She'd best get him to eat before he got distracted with his duties. She offered him one spoonful after another—not speaking, so that he would down the soup without talking.

"I must admit, that tastes good." Kent took hold of Amanda's hand as she held up the spoon for another gulp. "After Sergeant Kelly leaves, I must speak to you and your father as well."

Amanda shook her head. "I . . . I don't think this is a good time for that, Kent."

"No, you don't understand. This isn't about us, although I must admit that is very much in my thoughts. Especially now that I am here . . . in your presence. . . ." His voice trailed off and his eyes met hers, unguarded and vulnerable.

An urge to reach out and touch his face, caress his beard, rose within her. She clasped her hands in front of her, willing them to maintain a proper decorum. "What then? What is it?"

"It has to do with your brother. I have news for you."

CHAPTER NINE

OCTOBER 1862

We have shared the incommunicable experience of war . . . In our youths, our hearts were touched by fire.

OLIVER WENDELL HOLMES JR.

itty fussed over Major Littlefield, smoothing the quilt on the four-poster bed.

Kent heard someone knock softly on the door. He pushed himself up. "That'll be Sergeant Kelly. Thank you, Kitty. That's all I need for now."

The sergeant came in as the young servant scuttled out. He closed the door and saluted.

"At ease, Sergeant. Pull up a chair."

The chair scraped as Sergeant Kelly pulled it across the floor and creaked as he sat in it. "These fancy chairs are not made for bulk like mine." He removed his cap and sat on the edge of the chair. "How are you feeling, sir? How's the leg?"

"If we can stay free of infection . . . maybe I'll get lucky."

"Beggin' your pardon, sir, but I think we're all gonna need more than luck in this war. I don't mean to preach, but we're gonna need the protection and blessing of God himself. None of us imagined how tough this would prove to be."

"You're correct, of course. I hear you had a hand in getting my leg straightened out."

"Yes, sir. I hope you're not too mad at me. That was . . . mmm . . . a bit unpleasant."

"Not to worry, Sergeant. I don't even remember." Kent paused. "Give me a report on the operation, the men."

"We have occupied the town. It was fairly simple, after all the bombarding from the ships."

"Any fatalities? How many wounded?"

"No fatalities." He shook his head. "You are the most seriously wounded."

"That's good. Lieutenant Warren? Where is he?"

"He's in town with the men."

"Instruct him to report to me first thing tomorrow morning."

"Yes, sir. Anything else, sir?"

"Yes, there is." Kent leaned on his elbow toward the sergeant, facing him with an uncompromising stare. "I will tolerate no foolishness here in this house—no looting, no terrorizing, no stealing, and certainly no harassment of the women—and that includes the slaves. Do I make myself perfectly clear?" Kent's voice rose with every phrase.

Sergeant Kelly blinked at each point his superior made and nodded.

"This is a pastor's family. They are friends of mine and no threat to our cause." He sank into the pillows. "What about in town?"

"Men are men, sir."

"Give my instructions to the men here, then go into town and try to keep things in order. Make sure every man understands my mandate."

The sergeant stood. "I'll do my best, sir. But—"

"But what, Sergeant?"

"I fear accusations of favoritism, just because you know these folks. We need provisions for the troops."

"We are going to be here for a few weeks. There's no need to strip the land. We will take what we need, but we will not leave the local residents destitute. That is to no one's advantage."

"Yes, sir." Sergeant Kelly put on his cap and saluted once more.

"One more thing. You and Corporal Robertson may bed down in the house. The other men are to sleep in the barn."

The sergeant shuffled his feet.

"Sergeant, this home is mostly girls and women, except for Pastor Belle. I want no complications."

"Yes, sir. I'll see to it." The sergeant turned and left the room.

Kent closed his eyes and dozed. The roar of cannons filled his head and a boom roused him from his fitful slumber, causing his head wound to throb. But the boom was nothing but the click of the doorknob. Kent opened his eyes and watched as Amanda lit a lantern in the waning light of the evening.

Ezekiel walked in behind his daughter and stood at the end of the bed. "Are you comfortable, Major Littlefield? Is there anything else we can do for you?"

His words were cordial, but to Kent's ears his voice did not carry the warmth of the genuine hospitality that he had experienced in the Belle home before the war.

He stared at the head of the house, which at his orders had been invaded and violated. *I can't say that I blame the man. We've confiscated his home, and he knows of my interest in Amanda.*

"No, you've been most kind." He tried to pull himself up straighter. "I asked to see you, sir, because I wanted to tell you that I saw Daniel . . . at Shiloh."

Amanda's hand flew to her mouth as her eyes grew wide—those

eyes that drew him in every time he dared to gaze into them. Her head snapped toward her father.

Ezekiel unfolded his arms and grabbed hold of one of the posts at the foot of the bed. "Is he well? Is my son . . . did you simply see him or did you speak with him? I suspected he was there, but Daniel mentioned nothing in his letters—how—"

Kent smiled and held up his hand. "I know you have many questions. Let me assure you that at the time I saw him he was very well. And understandably he would not mention battles he has been involved in for fear of concerning you.

"The 8th Cavalry is an outfit Texas can be proud of. They were covering the rear of a Confederate division that was in retreat. I was leading a charge on them in front of my men when one of the Johnny Rebs got the drop on me when my horse stumbled. It was Daniel. We recognized each other about the same time."

"What did he say? How did he look?"

"He looked like a soldier. He was riding a magnificent Morgan. We found ourselves in a standoff—there in that woods." Kent hesitated. "Then we both dropped our weapons and exchanged greetings. This is a strange war indeed. Who is the enemy?" Kent looked into the father's eyes of his former pastor. "He's a fine soldier, Reverend Belle. You should be very proud of him."

"I am. I am very proud of my son." Ezekiel turned toward Amanda as she moved into his arms. Kent could hear her sniffling, and turned his head, not wishing to be an intruder upon the intimate familial scene.

⚜

A week later Kent hobbled into the parlor on the crutches Wash had fashioned for him. He dropped into a chair in front of the desk, which he had set up as a makeshift office. Propping his splinted leg on a small upholstered stool that Amanda insisted he use, he flexed his foot. The leg seemed to be healing—slowly. He stared out the window at the bay sparkling in the late afternoon sun. Winter in this part of the country was entirely different from the snowy days in Pennsylvania. Although the temperatures would drop during the night and there was always a breeze, the weather was pleasant most of the time—hardly any need for a jacket.

Kent's musings were interrupted as Hiram pulled in front of the house with the buggy.

Reverend Belle walked into the hallway and paused as he pulled on his gloves. He turned toward Kent through the open doorway to the parlor. "We've lost another one of our boys." His anguish was reflected in his grim facial expression. "I must go into town. Amanda has not returned from her ladies' society meeting, but I need to go lend whatever comfort I can to the family."

"I am truly sorry, Reverend Belle."

"Humph." Ezekiel stalked away without further comment.

The house grew quiet. All Kent could hear were the muted voices of the little sisters upstairs. Occasionally a giggle would filter down the stairwell into the parlor. His men had gone into town.

He sorted through backed-up paperwork for an hour, then realized his leg was growing numb. He stood to change position and lit the lantern on his desk.

Wash pulled in front of the house then, and Amanda hurried through the front door. She stopped in the archway to the parlor and glanced down at Kent's leg.

"Good evening, Major Littlefield. Is your leg some better?"

Kent nodded. "Somewhat." He motioned with his hand. "Won't you sit with me awhile?"

Amanda looked down the hall. "I really shouldn't . . . Father . . ."

"Your father has gone into town. Another family has lost a loved one."

"Oh-h." She removed her cloak and hat, draping them over a chair. "Did he say who it was?"

"No, he didn't."

Amanda sat on the settee and removed her gloves. "The wind is chilly today."

Kent clomped to the settee on his crutches and sat beside Amanda. She stood and moved to the piano and sat on the stool.

"Do you play?"

Amanda nodded and fingered the keys, wiping dust from them. "All of us took lessons, even the boys. My mother insisted. She believed music was an essential ingredient of a good education. But since she's been gone . . . I . . . don't play that much anymore."

Kent noted that she said *boys* plural, but let it pass. "Would you play something for me?"

"Oh, my soul, I'm so out of practice. And the piano needs tuning." She hit a key that klunked out a discordant note. She laughed. "I'm afraid a tune would be rather sour."

"Please. I'd love to hear you play something."

Amanda slowly ran some *arpeggios*, then began to play Beethoven's "Moonlight Sonata." The notes fell beneath her fingers as she played through the movements, the volume rising and falling.

Kent burst into applause as she finished. "Bravo! That's wonderful. You are really very accomplished."

"Oh, it's nothing." She closed the lid over the keys and turned toward Kent. The stool squealed as she turned around.

"Amanda, don't go. I must speak to you." He patted the cushion on the settee beside him. "Please sit here with me for a moment." He reached for her hand. "Please . . ."

She moved to the couch and sat on the edge, fingering the cording on her sleeve.

"You must be aware of my feelings for you."

"Kent, please don't. I cannot—"

"No, please give me this opportunity. It is torture watching you walk by me every day, exchanging pleasantries, making small talk, but never speaking out the deepest yearning of my heart." Amanda started to rise, but Kent held on to her hand. "Please don't go. Hear what I have to say."

"But my father—"

"Just listen to me . . . for the few moments we may have." He released her hand.

She looked down as he continued.

"Surely I have not misread the messages of unspoken love I have seen in your eyes." He touched her cheek with the back of his fingers. "Those beautiful eyes that reflect the color of the ocean outside your window."

Amanda raised her head and looked directly at him. She spoke barely above a whisper, "No, you have not misread anything." Tears swam on the edge of her eyelids. "I find myself utterly awash with tenderness and—"

"Tenderness? Only tenderness? Amanda, I am overwhelmed with love for you. I want to take you away from all the ugliness of this war to someplace safe, where no harm can come to you. I want to hold you in my arms and comfort you. I want to watch you sleeping. I want to wake every morning to your beautiful face. I want to have a house brimming with the laughter of our children. I want to build a life with you. I want to grow old with you. Amanda, I want to marry you."

Shaking her head, she stood and fumbled for her handkerchief.

He took her hand and kissed her fingers, pressing his cheek against them.

Slowly she withdrew her hand. "I . . . I . . . if we were not in these perilous times, and if we were not on opposite sides of this horrible war, I would—"

"You would what, Amanda? Please be honest with me."

She turned away from him as he struggled to his feet on the crutches. "What good will baring the depths of my heart do when nothing can come of it?" She slowly faced him. "It's better if we never speak of these things again, and when you are healed and your troops leave, you will no longer have any ties with the Belle family."

Kent stepped toward her and gently took hold of her arm. "We can try to deny how we feel, but that will not negate that those feelings exist. What if we are truly meant for each other? Of all people, you surely believe in God's providence. Your father is a pastor who teaches that from his pulpit. What if God intends for us to be together?"

"What God intends for me is to take care of my family as I promised my mother on her deathbed. I aim to keep that promise." She stifled a sob with the back of her hand. "I already feel I have failed in watching after Daniel. He's liable to be killed at any moment."

"Those are unrealistic expectations—a burden your mother would not have wished you to bear. We are at war. She never could have foreseen that. There was nothing you could have done."

"I could have prevented him from enlisting."

"And how were you going to accomplish that?" Kent smiled at her. "Seems to me Daniel has a mind of his own."

She lifted a face twisted in anguish toward him. "I cannot fail again. I cannot lose another . . ."

"Another?" His voice was soft and compassionate.

Gradually, between broken gasps and swallowed sobs, she

related the tragic story as if it were being squeezed out—painfully and haltingly.

"Brilliant sunlight. When I think of that day I remember the blinding sunlight. We were at a church picnic on the beach, and I was supposed to be watching the children. I got distracted by a silly . . . a silly hermit crab and . . ." She took a breath. "There was another brother, David, between Daniel and Emmaline. The children were playing in the sand, and nobody saw him wander out onto the wharf." She walked to the window and looked out. "His b . . . body washed up on shore a few days later." She lowered her head as her shoulders began to heave. "It was my fault. I was supposed to be . . . to be wa . . . watching them."

Kent hobbled to Amanda and propped his crutches against the desk. "Come here. Let me hold you." She kept her head lowered, but allowed him to gather her into his arms. He leaned against the desk and embraced her. He didn't speak; he simply held her. Her weeping subsided after a few moments.

"Surely you realize that it wasn't your fault. How old were you?"

She drew back and looked at him, her tearstained cheeks reddened and blotched. "I was sixteen; Daniel was fifteen; David was t-ten. Mother was pregnant with Mary. And it *was* my fault. Father put me in charge of them. I neglected my duty."

"That was too much responsibility for someone as young as you—to watch all those children. Your father should never have put that burden on you."

"And who are you to judge what a father does with his children?" The deep bass voice of Ezekiel Belle resounded from where he stood in the archway, his hat in his hands. "Amanda? Come." He held out his hand, and Amanda scurried to gather her cloak and hat and followed her father upstairs.

CHAPTER TEN

OCTOBER 1862

There's a yellow rose in Texas
That I am going to see.
No other soldier knows her—
No soldier, only me.

"THE YELLOW ROSE OF TEXAS"

aniel walked toward her through a foggy swamp, smiling. A shot rang out. He fell into her arms, blood oozing from the wound. Placing her ear to his chest, she frantically listened for a heartbeat. Was he dead or alive? A Yankee officer stood in the distance, watching the scene, but somehow she knew that he wasn't the one who fired the shot. Her mother ran out of the fog, crying, "I told you to take care of him. Why didn't you take care of him?"

Amanda opened her eyes. The eerie silver-light of a full moon illuminated her room. Her heart banged against her chest, and her hair stuck to her neck in sweaty clumps despite the chill in the air. She reached for Emmaline curled next to her and gently moved her over. She sat up and looked into the trundle. Catherine and Mary were sound asleep, Mary snoring lightly. Amanda pulled the kicked-off quilt around their shoulders.

She sat on the edge of the bed and blinked in the darkness. The same dream every time. Would she continue to have this dreadful nightmare until Daniel got home from the war?

❧

Amanda stood in front of the mirror the next morning in her pantaloons and camisole as Kitty helped her dress for church. She touched her face. The tingling warmth of Kent's fingers lingered on her cheek. She swallowed hard, forcing the lump in her throat to go away. She would put Major Kent Littlefield out of her mind and heart. Her father simply wanted what was best for her, didn't he?

Kitty yanked on the corset ties, cinching them in a suffocating closure. Amanda gasped for air as she stepped into her dress and slipped her arms into the sleeves. Kitty began to push the buttons through the button loops down the back of Amanda's dress.

Being in love was new territory. How was she supposed to deal with her emotions? Now she understood why Rebecca and Claire were all atwitter over their Lieutenant Miller and Daniel. She'd thought them foolish. Now she repented of her intolerance. If she should obey the dictates her heart shouted to her at this very moment, she would run downstairs into Kent's arms and declare that she would marry him immediately.

"There. I'm glad you don't wear that dress every Sunday, Miss Amanda, what with all them buttons . . . my, my!"

"It's too heavy to wear most of the year, but I'm chilled today. Thank you, Kitty."

"That thick fabric is why it's so hard to button." Kitty removed the matching blue velvet carriage cloak from the wardrobe. "All those flounces—I don't know how you walk in that skirt."

Amanda smiled and put on her bonnet, and Kitty placed the cloak over her shoulders. They walked into the hallway and started down the stairs where her father waited. Emmaline, Catherine, and Mary were already running out the door to the carriage.

"You look lovely, my dear, as always."

"Thank you, Papa."

Either he didn't notice her cool tone or he chose to ignore it.

She risked a sidelong glimpse as she passed the parlor, hoping to see Kent flash his quick smile her way. But the room was dark and empty, and his Bible was missing from its usual place on the corner of the desk. Her heart plunged.

Father's sermon bored Amanda today. Beyond the church windows, a ship lay at anchor in the bay, and her thoughts carried her away on that ship. Kent was the dashing captain, and she would sail to any port with him. She couldn't stop thinking about what he had said to her. *I want to grow old with you . . . I want to marry you . . . Too big of a burden—*

"Amanda?" Emmaline tugged on her sleeve. Their father had just closed the service. "Amanda, let's go."

"Oh, my soul." Amanda jumped. "I'm sorry. I guess I was daydreaming." She gathered her things. She couldn't wait to get back to Bellevue. She may have only been daydreaming, but in those fantasies she had made a decision. She must talk to Kent.

❧

The parlor was still empty, and no light came from beneath Kent's room down the hallway. Where was he? Strains of a hymn played by the regiment's band filtered from the barn. Amanda removed her outer garments, stalling as her father trudged up the stairs. She waited for him to close the door to his room before tiptoeing to Kent's room. She knocked softly. No answer. Holding her breath, her heart thudded as she pushed open his door. Empty. Did she dare check the barn?

"Looking for me?"

Amanda whirled around to encounter the man who had captured that fluttering heart. "Why . . . uh, yes . . . The parlor was empty, and I . . . I thought you'd probably be in your room."

He balanced himself on his good leg and removed his cap and woolen cape. "I woke up late and decided to try to walk outside a bit. My men are either lazing around the barn or have gone into town. Although we must stand ready at all times, I try to allow them to observe the Sabbath."

Amanda lifted her eyebrows.

He nodded his head. "We have a chaplain. The band plays a few hymns, we pray, and have our own services."

"What do you pray for?"

A slight smile tugged at the corner of his mouth. "Probably the same things that your Southern troops pray for: protection, victory, an end to the war."

"Both sides cannot be victorious."

"I know." He paused. "But surely you realize the Union must win. The slaves must be freed. And if we don't win, that means the end to our great country, this great democracy."

"I did not intend to discuss politics or the war with you. I came to . . . I've been thinking about what you said last night." She twisted the cameo ring on her finger.

A door closed upstairs, and her father's boots clicked first on the wooden floor of the landing, then on the stairs.

Amanda clutched Kent's arm as she whispered, "Meet me in the library tonight—late." She scurried across the hall and disappeared into the kitchen.

Kent started toward the parlor as Ezekiel came down the stairs. "Good afternoon, Pastor Belle."

"Good afternoon, Major Littlefield." Eyeing the officer's cloak, he asked, "Ventured outside on that leg, did you?"

"Yes, I decided to start exercising it."

Ezekiel eyed the empty hallway. "Have you seen Amanda?"

"I believe she's in the kitchen."

"May I speak with you?" He motioned toward the parlor.

"Of course." Kent took a deep breath and led the way into the room. He set his cloak and cap on his chair and turned to face the older man.

Ezekiel's dark eyes glinted with determination. "I want to make myself very clear, Major. It is obvious that you are a fine young man of character and integrity, from a good family, educated. It is equally obvious to me that you have feelings for my daughter. Under different circumstances I might be persuaded to allow you to court her, even though our ways of life are very different. However, at this time in our country, we are technically enemies. Therefore, I am going to ask you to refrain from pursuing Amanda or from expressing your feelings toward her. I do not want her loyalties to be torn. She is a Southern woman."

Kent cleared his throat as he balanced on the crutches, doing his best to stare eye-to-eye with the formidable figure of the man before him. "May I speak frankly?"

"Please do."

"It is true. I find myself very much in love with Amanda." He reached for the chair.

Ezekiel motioned toward him. "How thoughtless of me. Please, be seated." The pastor sat across from Kent in a wingback chair as the major lowered himself into the chair beside his desk.

Kent propped his leg on the stool. "I love your daughter and want to marry her when this madness is all over. And . . . you are too late."

"Too late?"

Kent nodded. "She already knows how I feel."

"I see. Does she return your affections?"

"I think so, although she has not said so in words. Sir, I want to honor your position as her father, but feelings in this matter will not change. I beg you to reconsider."

Ezekiel shook his head. "This situation is utterly impossible. I will not sanction it in any way." He rose from his chair. "I want your word as a gentleman and an officer that you will honor my request."

Kent pulled up and steadied himself on the edge of the desk. "Based on my love for your daughter, I cannot agree to that. However, I will agree to wait until after the war to pursue her further."

Ezekiel's eyes bored through him. Uncomfortable under the man's scrutiny, Kent wished for the first time since donning the Union blue that he were wearing civilian clothing.

Ezekiel spoke, his tone low and compelling. "I suppose, based on the strength of your love for Amanda, that is the only answer you could honestly give. In spite of your feelings for my daughter, may I have your word then—that you will not pursue my daughter until after the war?"

"You have my word—my very reluctant word—but you have it."

Ezekiel strode toward Kent and offered his hand. It was warm, human. When he left, Kent sank once again into the chair. He pulled out his watch—not even one o'clock yet. It would seem forever until he could meet Amanda later that evening.

Amanda sat in the rocking chair in her room reading by the light of a lantern as she waited for her sisters to fall asleep.

Emmaline was restless. She rolled over and leaned up on her elbow. "Are you coming to bed?"

"Go to sleep, Emmie. I'm going to read for a bit."

Emmaline turned her back on the light and curled into a tight ball. At last the heavy, steady breathing signaled Amanda that all three were asleep.

A soft knock startled her, pulling her out of her chair. She went to the door with the book in her hand. Turning the knob, she peeked through the crack.

Her father cocked his head. "Still up, my dear?"

"Y . . . yes, sir. I couldn't sleep, so I thought I'd read for a while." She opened the door wider and motioned toward her sisters. "Shh. The girls are asleep."

He nodded. "Don't stay up too late."

"No, I won't. Good night, Papa."

"Good night."

She closed the door and leaned against it, her heart racing. She listened as her father moved down the hall to his room and his door snapped shut.

She returned to the rocking chair and opened the book, but found herself reading the same passage over and over. She put the book aside and simply rocked—and waited. Finally the household settled into the solitude of the night. Picking up the lantern, she tiptoed to the door and slowly pulled it open. She held her breath as the hinges squeaked. Catherine stirred and mumbled incoherently.

Amanda hesitated until the child became still once again, then eased out the door and down the hall. Her slippered feet made no noise as she sped noiselessly down the stairs. She stopped in front of the pocket doors of the library and glanced toward the parlor across the foyer. Dark. She pulled on one side of the door. It ground in its track. She paused, then slithered through the small opening, returning the door to its closed position. She lifted the lantern in the musty, dark room.

"I'm over here, Amanda."

She whirled around to the voice behind her. Kent was struggling to his feet from a leather chair beside a tall wooden bookshelf. "I thought you'd never come."

She set the lantern down on a round table next to his chair. "I had to wait for the girls to fall sound asleep." She suddenly found herself very nervous. "And my father saw the light in my room and came to check."

"Do you think he suspected anything?"

"I don't think so."

"Come here. Let me hold you." Kent leaned on his crutches and held out his arms toward her. "This may be the only opportunity we have to be together."

She put her hand on his arm and felt the muscles ripple beneath his shirt. "I . . . I don't want to throw you off balance."

He pulled her into his arms. "I'm fine. I need to feel you close to me."

She moved into his embrace as if she had been there hundreds of times and laid her head on his chest, comforted by the thud of his heart.

He buried his head in her hair and breathed deeply. "Mmm— lavender. Even when I was unconscious those days following my injury, I could smell lavender every time you came into the room. How do you manage to always smell so good?"

"Lavender powder and perfume—and shampoo when I can get it. It's pretty scarce these days." She pulled back from him and searched his eyes, the prominent blue of his irises darkened in the dim light. "We need to talk. There are things I must to say to you. I've made some decisions."

Kent steadied himself on the bookcase.

Amanda pulled back and motioned across the room to an uphol-stered couch in front of a shuttered bay window. "Shall we sit over there?"

"We'd better extinguish the lantern, don't you think?"

Amanda nodded and blew out the flame. Then she led the way across the dark room to the couch, aware of the soft *clomp-clomp* of Kent's crutches behind her. Slivers of moonlight poked through the slats of the shutters, creating a soft silver glow. Kent took both of her hands in his and lifted them to his lips. How could she think with him kissing her hands like that?

He reached toward her and cupped her chin in his hand. "You are so beautiful."

Amanda shook her head and removed his hand from her face, holding on to it. His hand felt cool, his skin rough.

"Has no one ever told you that before? Surely you have had many suitors."

"No, not one."

"I find that difficult to fathom. Perhaps your father has shooed them all away without your knowledge." He chuckled, but his little joke died in midair. "No one has ever told you before how beautiful you are?"

"Only Daniel and my father."

"And you didn't believe them?"

"They are my family. They are supposed to think I am beautiful."

"Well, the fact is, my dear—you are the most beautiful woman I have ever known."

"Stop—you are embarrassing me . . . and my heart is pounding so that I cannot think what I need to tell you."

Notes of soft laughter escaped from his throat and seemed to caress her. "I'm sorry. What is it you need to say to me?"

"I made some decisions in church this morning."

"That's a good place to make decisions."

"But they had nothing to do with church, or God, or the sermon. All I could think about during the service was you, and what you said to me yesterday in the parlor." Amanda stood and walked to the window. She opened the shutters and let the moonlight flood the room. "When you marched off to war over two years ago, I thought I would never see you again, so I determined to forget you and any feelings I had for you. I thought I succeeded in doing that. Then you returned, wounded and vulnerable, and . . ." She sat back down and searched his eyes. "Kent, I have completely lost my heart to you. Every time I went into your room during your recovery I wanted to gather you in my arms and comfort you. I wanted to tell you how I felt, but my father . . . I convinced myself that he knew what was best for me, and that the only thing for me to do was to deny my feelings." She paused. "But I cannot do that anymore. I've decided that even though he adamantly opposes us, in spite of that . . ." She leaned in toward Kent and touched his cheek. "Kent, I would be honored to be your wife. If you're certain—"

"I've never been more certain of anything in my life." Kent covered her hand with his own, then pulled her toward him and brushed her lips with a gentle whisper of a kiss. "And, my dearest, the honor would be all mine." He embraced her, and she felt his breath quicken. "However . . ."

Amanda stiffened, afraid to move. "Yes?" Her voice clouded with doubt.

"Amanda, look at me."

She straightened and allowed herself to gaze into his eyes.

He gathered her hair in one of his hands. "I've wanted to touch your hair from the first day I saw you cutting pies at the church picnic. I thought then that it looked like spun honey."

She waited.

He cleared his throat. "I love you, and the strongest desire of my heart is to marry you. But your father asked to speak to me after you came in from church."

"And?" She was almost afraid to breathe.

"He requested, rather firmly, that I give him my word that I would not pursue you any further. He said that if I truly loved you, I would wait until after the war. He asked for my word as a gentleman and an officer."

"Did you give it to him?"

"I did. It was not what I wanted to do, but I did give him my word."

"You intend to honor that?"

Kent stared at her as clouds moved across the moon, plunging his face into shadows. "I must honor my word. If a man cannot be honorable in his word, what does he have left?"

She didn't answer him for several minutes. At last she found her voice. "Of course, you are right. We must honor your word." She reached out and touched his beard. "That's one of the things that I love the most about you—your integrity."

He took her hands again. "Amanda, it doesn't change how I feel, or the fact that I want you to be my wife. It simply changes the time frame. When this war is over, I will come for you." He shifted his leg. "I don't think we will be here much longer. As soon as I can travel, I expect orders. Will you wait for me? Promise me you will wait for me, no matter how long it may take me to return."

She nodded slowly. "I will wait for you. How much longer do you think this horrible war is going to last?"

"Who can know the future? But I fear the longer it goes, America's fellow countrymen killing each other, the more difficult will be the healing. Not only are the men wounded, but the land is fractured and wounded. And the schism between North and South grows wider with each day."

"Can we write to each other?"

Kent grinned. "I did not promise that we wouldn't correspond. I will write every opportunity I have."

"I suppose you should send your letters for me in care of Claire or Rebecca."

"I suppose." He gathered her in his arms with her back against his chest as they gazed at the night sky. "The moon is beautiful tonight."

"I don't know if I can stand to watch you leave again, not knowing if you will come back to me."

"I will come back."

"You cannot know that."

He nuzzled his cheek against her hair. "Surely God would not be so cruel as to bring us this far, only to part us forever. He brought me back once. I believe he will do it again."

"You believe it was God who brought you back and caused your leg injury?"

"I don't believe he caused my leg to be wounded, but obviously he did allow it. I believe in the providence of almighty God, and that he is in complete control of all things." He held her tightly. "We have to trust God with our lives, our future, Amanda. There is no other stability in this whirlwind in which we find ourselves."

She turned around to face him. "Are you speaking of God who is on the side of the North or the side of the South?"

He leaned his head back, closed his eyes and sighed. "I am speaking of the God of the Bible, who is just—and full of mercy."

"You sound like my father."

"Your father is a good man, Amanda. Let's not waste this little time that we have discussing troublesome subjects. Let us simply enjoy each other's company."

She stood. "I must say good night. I cannot stay any longer."

"Why must you go? Sit back down with me. Can we not wait for the dawn together? Please don't say good night."

"Oh." Amanda felt her face begin to flush. She hoped Kent couldn't detect it in the dim light. "But my father . . . he . . . he wouldn't . . ."

"No, he probably wouldn't approve. But I haven't broken my word to him, because, after all, you pursued me this time."

He grinned at her in the moonlight, and she wanted to plunge through a crack in the floor. "But . . ."

"Put everything aside except being here with me." He took her hand and kissed it. "My dear, I simply want to be with you this night before I'm ordered to another post. You are safe with me."

As the sky lightened from inky navy blue to velvet gray, Amanda slid the door of the library open, leaving behind in the shadows a love she never imagined possible for herself. She tiptoed up the stairs and, halting at her bedroom door, heard Kent shuffling to his room downstairs. She entered her bedroom noiselessly and sat once again in the rocking chair. She should be sleepy, but she wasn't. The sun began to finger the horizon with delicate shades of pink.

Part of her heart loved her Southern way of life and would always be with her brother fighting in the Confederate army . . . but the other part of her heart had changed. She was in love with the enemy. Did that make her a traitor?

She pulled her knees to her chest and hugged her arms around them. She didn't have answers. There was so much that she didn't understand. All she knew now was that she wanted to marry Kent Littlefield and would never be happy until she could rest in his arms at the close of every day. It didn't matter to her whether he wore Confederate gray or Union blue.

CHAPTER ELEVEN

NOVEMBER 1862

Whatever may be the result of the contest, I foresee that the
country will have to pass through a terrible ordeal.

ROBERT E. LEE

The faintly sweet fragrance of the breakfast cornbread tickled Amanda's nose as she carried the breakfast tray toward the parlor. Kent had been busy at work when the family gathered in the kitchen to eat. It was midmorning. She'd missed him, but dared not show it. A lingering glance, the brush of hands were the only indications of their night together in the library. She hungered for his touch, but would not risk another clandestine meeting. Her father had been especially attentive to her whereabouts, and she did not wish to jeopardize his goodwill toward Kent.

The parlor door stood slightly ajar. She halted at the door, detecting an unfamiliar voice, and took a step backward.

"I am sure you realize, Major Littlefield, that this information is top secret."

"Of course. When do I need to report?"

"After the first of the year."

"The operation isn't immediate, is it?"

The stranger lowered his voice, and Amanda leaned in to hear.

"Because of the threat of Maximilian in Mexico, President Lincoln wishes to put a federal flag over Texas as soon as possible. Generals Grant and Sherman are not fully convinced that it is necessary. Since you know the lay of the land and have experience here, your counsel would be helpful. It may take as much as a year to set this in place."

"So the president wishes to advance troops to Shreveport via the Red River, then on into Texas?"

"Roughly. We'll bring troops down from Arkansas to augment. The details haven't been worked out." The man chuckled. "That's why we want you. And, if this goes well, it will most certainly mean another promotion for you."

Amanda heard the rustle of paper at the same moment that footsteps sounded on the stairs. She turned to see her father. A cup rattled on the tray, and the men in the parlor ceased their conversation.

"You look as if you've seen a ghost, my dear."

"I was just bringing Major Littlefield's breakfast to him, but his door is closed. I heard voices. Should I knock?"

"A Union colonel came to pay our Major Littlefield a visit early this morning. Knock and see if he wants breakfast. He may have already eaten with his men."

"Elsie said he had not."

Father went toward the kitchen. "Very well. I'm going to the barn."

The dishes on the tray rattled again.

He turned as he pulled his cloak around his shoulders. "Are you certain you are well?"

"Yes, yes, I'm fine."

The parlor door opened as her father went into the kitchen, and

Kent greeted her. "Good morning, Miss Belle. I was hoping that was you. Come in."

"Have you had breakfast?"

Kent's smile washed over her and landed in the pit of her stomach, sending it aquiver as she entered, and his touch on her elbow caused her to flush.

"No. You may leave the tray. And would you bring a cup for my colleague?"

Amanda set the tray on the corner of the desk.

"May I present Colonel William Townsend?"

She nodded and curtsied to the distinguished man with a bushy gray beard and moustache. "Pleased to meet you, sir."

He bowed slightly. "The honor is mine, Miss Belle."

"To what do we owe the pleasure of your visit, Colonel Townsend? I hope you have brought good news to Major Littlefield. Although good news for the major might perhaps be bad news for the South, mightn't it?"

"Purely military business, young lady. Nothing to worry your pretty head about."

Facing the colonel, Amanda struggled to keep her tone civil. "You'll forgive me, Colonel, if I am offended by your remark. Military business seems to be of concern to all of us these days. I am always worried about our family, and the fact that our home has been invaded—"

Kent cleared his throat. "Amanda, you brought coffee?"

The colonel turned his back to her and addressed Kent. "Actually I fear I do not have time for coffee, Major Littlefield. I must be on my way." He fetched his hat from the hat tree. "You will excuse me, Miss Belle?"

"Yes, of course, Colonel. I'll get my . . ." The word *boy* stuck in her throat. Terminology that she had grown up with now sounded abrasive and offensive. She rang the servant's bell. "Wash."

The young man appeared at the door. "Yes'm, Miss Amanda?"

"Would you show Colonel Townsend out, please, and help him with his horse."

"No need, Miss Belle, I can show myself out. And my horse is tied up right in front."

"Please, I insist, Colonel."

The colonel bowed again and handed Kent an envelope as he settled his hat on his head. "Your orders, Major Littlefield."

Kent pulled himself to attention as much as his broken leg would allow and saluted the colonel. Amanda's heart wrenched as her beloved grimaced.

The colonel returned the salute and nodded. "Major Littlefield. Miss Belle." Then he followed Wash to the door.

As the front door clicked shut, Kent wrinkled up his forehead and looked at Amanda. "Well, we knew I would be receiving orders soon. This is not entirely unexpected." He opened the envelope and read down through the orders quickly, returning the paper to the envelope.

"Where are they sending you?"

"To join General Grant in . . ." His voice trailed off as he folded the letter and replaced it in the envelope.

Waves of affection for this man in the uniform of the enemy consumed her—the man who had vowed his undying love for her and for whom she had declared that she would wait. But what she had heard this morning . . . and seeing him in an official capacity . . .

"Kent, I don't know what to say. Seeing you in your role as a Yankee officer frightens me." She brushed past him to leave.

He caught her by the arm. "Amanda, it's me. I haven't changed. My feelings are stronger than ever."

She stood with her back to him. "If I'm honest, mine are as well. They grow every day. The highlight of my day is when I see you. B-but I don't know if I can go through with this. Perhaps our worlds *are* too far apart, as Papa says."

"Don't make any rash decisions, my love." He took her shoulders and gently turned her toward him. "Wait until this is over. All you need to do is wait for me." He glanced toward the door. "How long . . . did you hear something that has upset you?"

She shook her head, the guilt of her denial causing her cheeks to flush. "No, I just . . . please let me go." She twisted away from him and ran from the room.

⸙

Amanda descended from the buggy in front of the mercantile and shooed the girls inside. "I'll not be long, Wash."

Inside, the jars of penny candy enticed her little sisters like corn kernels would a flock of chicks. Their squawks in favor of the various taffies—licorice, maple, molasses, and peppermint—made Amanda laugh. "I'm surprised they have such a variety, with the shortage of sugar. Why don't you get a bag of assorted flavors? Then you can each have some of what you like."

She wandered back to the dry goods section and fingered the bolts of fabric. It would be nice to have a new dress, but she really didn't need one. She looked at the sparse shelves—about half what they carried before the war. She moved to the notions counter and found what she was looking for in a large glass jar—the perfume buttons. She selected a delicate filigreed brass one.

"Anything else, Miss Belle?" The proprietor peered over his spectacles at her as she placed the button on the worn wooden counter.

"Have you gotten any lavender shampoo in yet?"

He shook his head. "Not a drop since the blockade. You'd be the first to know if I did." He bent over and placed a box on the counter-top. "But I do have some lavender perfume for that button."

"No, thank you. I still have perfume."

"Anyone special you'll be giving the button to?" The man smiled and stroked his beard.

She ignored his question. "How much will that be? Please add a bag of taffy."

"That'll be eighty cents. Five cents for the candy and seventy-five for the button."

Amanda paid the owner and left, gathering the girls into the buggy as they fussed over the candy.

❧

November 1862

The company of soldiers stood at attention in front of Bellevue. Amanda and her father waited in the foyer as Sergeant Kelly and Major Littlefield strode toward the front door. Kent, now using only one crutch, paused in front of them, his mended kepi in his hand.

"Pastor Belle, Miss Amanda, I don't know how to thank you enough for your kindness and compassion under this difficult set of circumstances." The major donned his cap and turned to Amanda. He searched her eyes. "Miss Belle, I shall never forget the time you spent caring for me."

"Nor shall I." Amanda clasped her hands in front of her with the perfume button hidden in her palm.

"Perhaps . . . no, certainly we will see one another after the war."

"Yes, just as we spoke." She felt a smile warm her face, and she ducked her head.

The officer reached for her hand and kissed it. As he did, she took his hand with both of hers and slipped the perfume button to him. Her eyes flashed a warning as she looked up at him, entranced once again by the startling blue eyes. He palmed the button.

Kent turned. "Sir, you have my utmost respect. You have exhibited true Christian charity."

Amanda's father narrowed his eyes. "We didn't really have much of a choice, did we, Major Littlefield?" He took the young man's hand, then in a surprise move, pulled Kent into an embrace. "But I would hope someone in Yankee country would do the same for our Daniel." He cleared his throat and straightened his jacket as he released him. "I pray the protection of the Almighty on you, Major Littlefield."

Candles on the scrawny cedar Christmas tree winked as the Belle family gathered around the piano. The evening was cool enough for a flickering fire in the parlor fireplace. With Father's bass voice, Emmaline's sweet soprano, and Amanda's warm alto, they sang a hearty "Deck the Halls," with Catherine and Mary joining in on the *fa-la-las.*

Amanda leaned back from the piano as the song ended and laughed. "We offer a pretty fair choral rendition." She caressed Emmaline's head. "Your soprano sounds more and more like Mama's."

Emmaline smiled. "Play 'Silent Night,' and let Catherine and Mary sing it."

"Very well." Amanda swept the keyboard, setting the new key for them. "Stand up straight, girls, and quit giggling."

The two younger girls stood beside their father at the piano and began to sing in their thin, innocent voices, Catherine taking the lead and Mary following a beat or two behind her sister.

"That's wonderful, girls." Father patted the two younger sisters on their heads. "Now, it's time for bed."

"I don't want to go to bed. I want to stay up with you," Catherine whined.

"We are going to bed shortly as well. Besides, Santa Claus won't come until we go to sleep."

"I want to stay up and see Santa Claus!" Catherine stomped her foot.

Amanda pushed the piano stool back. "You know that Santa cannot come until the whole house is asleep."

Mary tugged on Amanda's skirt. "Will Santa be able to get through the blockade?"

Amanda shot a look at her father, and they both began to laugh. Amanda hugged Mary and spun around with her. "Of course he will. Santa knows all the secret ways to get to little girls' houses for Christmas." She paused. "He just might not be able to bring as much as he usually does."

"Will he fill our stockings?" Catherine pointed to the three stockings hanging on the mantle.

"I think he will be able to bring something for them. Now come, girls. Off to bed with you." She pulled the bell cord for Kitty and kissed each of the girls, sending them scurrying up the staircase, which was gaily decorated with cedar boughs and pine cones.

❧

Amanda walked to the parlor door and listened to see if the girls were quiet upstairs. "I think they are asleep now."

Father went to the library to uncover the hidden homemade gifts he had worked on for months. He placed them under the tree for the three younger girls . . . cradles for Catherine and Mary's dolls and a small wooden chest for Emmaline. He passed his hand once again over the lid, checking the finish. "I suppose I could work on this forever and never be fully satisfied with it."

Amanda smiled. "You did a wonderful job, Papa. The inlay is beautiful. Emmie will love it." She opened a drawstring bag and removed four packages wrapped in brown paper, three of them tied with colorful ribbon.

"What have you there?"

Amanda smiled. "I did some work of my own. It's just hairclips made from old buttons and some of mother's earrings." She placed the packages bedecked with ribbon under the tree. "I wanted them to have something of hers even as young as they are. They can use the ribbons in their hair."

Father chuckled as he rubbed his beard. "You are maturing into a mighty enterprising young woman."

"I have something for you as well."

"My dear, no need for that." He reached for the small parcel, and she giggled and pulled back. "No, no, no! Not until morning like everyone else."

Wash entered the parlor quietly and waited.

Amanda glanced over her shoulder at him from where she knelt, placing the packages under the tree, and smiled. "Yes, Wash?"

"Will you be needin' anything else this evening?"

"Would you please bring me the box in the pantry with the oranges and nuts for the girls' stockings?"

"Yes'm. Anything else?"

"Yes, Elsie hid a bottle of peach brandy behind the fireplace when the soldiers were here. Would you ask her to bring that to us, please?"

Wash grinned. "Yes'm. I'll be right back."

Amanda walked to the desk and picked up another package. "Wait a moment, Wash. One more thing—this is for Zachary . . . and you and Harriet. And there's something in there for Elsie, Kitty, and Hiram as well."

"Oh, Miss Amanda. Times is hard. You shouldn't have—"

Amanda flicked her wrist. "It's very little, Wash. But I . . . we wanted to express how much we appreciate you and your family, especially in these days. I don't know what is going to happen in the future when this war is over, but . . ."

"Don't none of us know what's gonna happen, Miss Belle. But I thank you." The young man bowed and took the package.

"Go on now, and have a Merry Christmas."

"You, too, Miss Amanda, Mistah Zekiel." The young servant turned and left.

"Ahem." Father cleared his throat and smiled at his daughter.

"It's Christmas Eve, Father. We have reason to celebrate, though in the midst of a war. Even the Lord partook at a wedding celebration."

"Yes, well, just a small glass."

Elsie brought a tray with a decanter of brandy and two goblets and set them on a small round table. Wash followed with the box of fruit and nuts.

"Thank you, Wash and Elsie. Merry Christmas."

"Yes'm. Merry Christmas to you."

The two, father and daughter, stayed up late into the night chatting and reminiscing. Amanda finally spoke out loud the thought that tugged at her at every corner she turned in the house, at every meal they ate, every holiday that passed.

"I wonder where Daniel is tonight. I wonder if he's warm; if he's had a decent meal; if he's well."

"I cannot stop thinking about him either—my son." Father rose and returned his glass to the tray. "I believe, I pray that this awful conflict will end soon, and God will bring him home."

Amanda ran her fingers over the etching on her half-full glass. Another issue besides Daniel's situation tormented her. She must tell her father. She didn't want to, but her conscience could bear the burden of keeping it from Father no longer. She inhaled, then let her breath out slowly. "Sit down, Papa. There's something I must tell you."

"This sounds serious." He declined to sit, but stood in front of his daughter and waited.

She rose from the couch, walked to the table, and set her glass on the tray. "Yes, it is serious, but it is of such magnitude that I don't know if we should attempt to deal with it." She wrung her hands and turned away from her father. "Rightfully, I shouldn't have this information."

Father took her arm and turned her around to face him. "What is it, my child? Whatever could it be?"

Motioning for him to join her, she returned to the couch. She fidgeted with the lace on a handkerchief she held in her hands. "I know that you talked to Major Littlefield—Kent—before he left regarding our affections for one another."

Her father's mouth creased into a terse slit.

"He told me about your conversation."

"The man gave me his word he would not pursue you further."

"And he kept his word, Father. I instigated that rendezvous."

He folded his arms across his chest. "Rendezvous?"

Amanda put her hand on his leg. "Please listen to me, Father."

His dark eyes glinted at her as he nodded.

"We simply met one night and talked—talked about the war, our families, and how we feel about each other. Kent told me that he had given his word to you not to pursue me any further, and that he intended to keep his word. But he did ask me to wait for him until after the war."

"And?"

Amanda nodded her head ever so slightly. "I agreed."

Her father rose to his feet and began to pace in front of her. "You don't have the maturity to understand, Mandy. There are some decisions that a father must make for his children; some issues that a child cannot foresee, but a parent can. Too many differences divide you. Our heritage is thoroughly Southern, and your young officer's men are the ones trying to kill your brother." He stopped and looked at her. "You know all this. I see no need to go over it again."

She peered directly into her father's eyes and held his gaze steady. "I'm not a child any longer, Papa. I'm a grown woman." She looked down at her hands. "You keep talking about the division in our country and the differences in our ways of life, but isn't that what the war is all about? To unite the country?"

"To unite us how? By force? By killing all of our men? By destroying our work force? By denying the people of the South the right to make decisions for our states?"

Amanda covered her ears and shook her head. "I don't know. And I don't know what I'm going to do about Major Littlefield, even though he has won my heart. I am so torn." She rose and walked to the Christmas tree, and began to blow out the candles. She sniffled. "This man is what I've dreamed of and prayed for. But that's not what I wanted to talk to you about." She swiveled to face her father once more, her skirt brushing against the sparse branches of the cedar tree. A small glass ornament, a delicate, spun-glass angel, fell to the floor and broke. "Oh, no." She stooped to pick up the shards.

"Leave that for now. Tell me what is troubling you."

Amanda rose with pieces of glass in her hands and looked at them. "We cannot fix this; we cannot put it back together. It's too shattered. . . ." She placed the broken pieces on the desk. "Do you remember the colonel who brought Kent his new orders?"

Her father nodded. "Yes."

"Did you not think it strange that a colonel was sent to deliver orders to a major? Why not simply send his orders with a courier?"

"That thought did cross my mind at the time."

"I overheard the colonel and Major Littlefield talking in the parlor as I delivered his breakfast tray that morning. What I heard was so unbelievable that the colonel's words were meaningless. I didn't know how to make sense of them. But as I've contemplated their conversation, the seriousness of what is to occur began to dawn on me. What I heard them say was that the Union is planning a major offensive to move up the Red River in Louisiana into Texas next year."

"This next year? In a few months?"

"No, no. A year from now. The colonel said that because of Maximilian's presence in Mexico, President Lincoln wants to establish a federal base in Texas." She paused.

"What else?"

"I didn't hear much more—except that it will take a year to set this into place, and Generals Grant and Sherman are not in favor of it, and something about troops from Arkansas joining them." She left out the part concerning Kent and his involvement.

"You're certain, Amanda? What you've told me is accurate?"

She nodded. "I am certain, regrettably certain."

"This information is too dangerous to the state of Texas and the war in the South to remain silent. We must do something." Her father stood and stoked the embers in the fireplace back to life, and put a large log on to last through the night. "I need to think about this and pray."

CHAPTER TWELVE

MARCH 1863

> *We have sent the bravest of our land*
> *To battle with the foe,*
> *And we will lend a helping hand.*
> *We love the South, you know.*
>
> CARRIE BELLE SINCLAIR
> FROM "THE HOMESPUN DRESS"

The long winter months evolved into the warm, blustery days of spring. Amanda spent her days writing to Daniel and Kent, walking the beach and wondering how they were faring.

She stepped through the back door and tightened the strings of her bonnet. Although Kent had ordered his men to leave the Belles' provisions intact, the Yankee soldiers had eaten or taken most of their meat. She opened the door to the dark smokehouse and waited until her eyes adjusted. She took down a side of ham that the slaves had managed to hide and started back to the house. Glancing about for Wash and not seeing him, she dashed for the house. If Wash knew she was taking care of duties that ordinarily belonged to slaves, he would not allow it. She walked into the kitchen and tossed the slab onto the table.

Elsie turned from the stove. "Miss Amanda! I'd have sent Hiram out fo dat meat."

"It's something I can do, Elsie. I feel I'm contributing somehow when I pitch in with the chores."

Elsie shook her head and began to slice the meat and throw it into the frying pan. "I jes don' know what this world comin' to. Breakfast will be ready shortly."

The smoky fragrance of the ham followed Amanda as she walked into the foyer and removed her bonnet. She proceeded through the large archway into the dining room where her father sat at the table drinking a cup of roasted chicory coffee and reading the paper.

"Ah, Amanda. I'm glad you're here. I've made a decision."

"A decision about what?"

"The information you overheard. We cannot sit on it any longer. We must take action." He motioned to her. "Please, sit down."

Amanda pulled out her chair and sat down. "I agree that it is pertinent information, but what in the world can we do?"

"I have decided to send you, accompanied by Wash and Harriet, to Austin to take this information to your Uncle John."

Elsie bustled into the room with a pot of steaming liquid. She poured a cup and set it in front of Amanda, who sniffed it and wrinkled up her nose. Waiting for Elsie to disappear through the swinging door into the kitchen, she set her cup back on the saucer. "I don't know how you drink this stuff."

"It's better than nothing."

"I suppose." She dipped her spoon in the cup, took a taste, screwed up her face, then pushed the cup and saucer to the side.

"Your Uncle John has been assigned as Commandant of Conscriptions in Texas. Although he does not have a battlefield command at the moment, he will know what to do."

"Why not send Wash or post a letter? Or why don't you go?"

Father drummed his fingers on the table. "I have thought this through, Mandy. I cannot leave my congregation during these calamitous times. A letter might be intercepted, and coloreds are not safe traveling alone. We saw what nearly happened to Hiram. No, I think that a Southern lady traveling with her servants would be the least suspected. You have the information in your head, so there's no letter to intercept. If someone detains you, your explanation is that you are simply going to visit our family in Austin. This is the best solution." He paused. "And there's another reason I need you to go to Austin. Although our Southern boys have regained Galveston, Dr. Greer told me his medical supplies are practically down to nothing. He needs morphine and opium, and with warm weather coming, quinine. We need you to bring those supplies from Austin."

"Won't it be dangerous?"

Father steepled his fingers and pushed back in his chair. "Yes, my dear, there will be danger involved. You'll take weapons with you, of course, and Wash is very capable of defending you. And I will pray for God to protect you."

"Little good prayer will do. I've done plenty of praying these past two years, and God seems to be deaf."

Father narrowed his eyes. "Amanda, that's blasphemy."

"It may be, but at least it's honest. How do you know you're not just praying to somebody's idea of what God should be? Have you seen any answers to prayer? Has this war ended? Is Daniel home? No, no, no." She stood and leaned forward with her hands on the table. "I, for one, am not going to waste any more time praying into the air for some nebulous god to hear. Either God is not real or he refuses to answer when people pray, and neither premise is acceptable to me."

The color drained from her father's face. "You don't mean what you are saying."

"Oh, yes, I do. I'll go to Austin and deliver the information to Uncle John because it is something real I can do for the war effort, but I'm through praying for safety and protection and for the war to end. The only help we are going to receive is what we gain by our own wits."

"Sit down, Amanda, and eat your breakfast. I'll entertain no more outbursts."

"I'm not very hungry." She replaced her napkin on the table. "If you'll excuse me, I believe I'll go check on the girls and send them down for their breakfast." She walked to the door, then turned toward her father, her jaw set. "When do you want us to leave for Austin?"

"The sooner, the better. Can you be ready by the day after tomorrow?"

"Yes, of course."

❧

Amanda held a green carriage cloak in her arms and her carpetbag at her side. The day was mild, with a balmy breeze blowing in from the water, the humidity thick with the fragrance of the ocean. But the weather would turn cooler the farther north they traveled. The wind ruffled the feathers on her matching bonnet.

Wash pulled the carriage in front of the house. A rifle lay beside him. Father assisted Amanda into the carriage.

Harriet waited with Zachary in tow on the veranda, a cloth bag with their belongings slung over her shoulder. Harriet and the toddler climbed in behind Amanda and sat across from her. A wooden box containing pistols and another rifle sat on the floor between the two women.

Father stuck his head through the window as he closed the carriage door. "You should be able to get to Austin before Sunday, weather permitting. I sent a post to John yesterday. He'll be expecting you."

Amanda nodded and settled a pillow under her arm. "Good-bye, Papa. We'll be fine. Wash and Harriet will take good care of me." She smiled at her traveling companions.

Harriet nodded. "Yessuh, Mister Zekiel. We'll be just fine."

Father stepped back. "Go on now, Wash. Take care of the women folk."

"Yessuh. You can count on me to do that."

"Godspeed."

Amanda ignored her father's parting blessing and waved to him as they pulled away. Questions of whether they were doing the right thing tugged at her, but she also looked forward to the adventure of traveling to Austin for a change of scenery. She was weary of haunting the newspaper and post office for news of the battlefront, stitching quilts and knitting socks with the women folk—some of them newly widowed, some of them having no idea where their loved ones were, dreading the worst when no correspondence arrived. The citizens of Indianola, with mouths set in tight lines, cast their long shadows on the streets of the town as they greeted one another in passing, reluctant to look directly at one another, fearful of the grim message that could be lurking behind the eyes.

Miles of South Texas farmlands, interspersed with palm trees and salt cedar, slipped by the window of the carriage. More trees appeared on the horizon the farther from the coast they rode.

Was she doing the right thing? She thought so, but guilt had tormented her ever since she agreed to make the trip. If she informed the

Confederate army of the Union campaign of which she had knowledge, she was arming the enemy of her beloved. Would he be leading a company of soldiers in this particular siege? What if he were killed because of the information she was about to turn over to her uncle? But what if she didn't inform the Confederacy, and then Texas was overrun and defeated by the Union forces? And what if Daniel were killed? To her knowledge he wasn't in Texas, but wouldn't any advancement of the Union forces be to the detriment of the Confederacy?

Zachary played on the seat across from her next to his mother. The life of a slave was simple. They made no life-changing decisions. They didn't have to provide for their families—it was all done for them. She watched the little boy play with the blocks that she had given him for Christmas. As he separated them according to color, Harriet asked him, "What color is this? And this?" and he answered correctly every time.

The child was only about two years old. Thoughts began to swim in Amanda's head, nipping at the surface, not allowing her to dismiss them, like an insistent wave on the shore. Surely Wash and Harriet wanted more for their child than for his life to be "simple." The boy was intelligent. Like all parents, wouldn't Wash and Harriet want their child to advance and learn? But most folks she knew did not even believe that a Negro was capable of learning. What kind of future did Zachary have as a slave? He didn't have a future. At this point he could look forward to only an existence—a simple, static, drudgery of an existence.

As a boy, did Wash have dreams of more than being a slave? She herself had taught him to read when they were children—covertly. Her mother knew about it and gave her consent. Her father turned his head and chose to ignore it. Wash learned quickly. There was no reason why . . .

Amanda shook her head. She was thinking like an abolitionist—and it frightened her.

"My dear Amanda." Colonel John Ford rose to greet his niece. "How wonderful to see you. I received Ezekiel's post a few days ago informing me that you were coming. Here, have a seat, please." The colonel pulled a chair over for her and waited until she was seated, then lowered himself into the office chair behind a huge desk. He leaned back and smiled at her, running his hand over his bushy beard. Although only in his midforties, his hair was almost completely gray, and his beard was becoming so.

Amanda still thought him handsome. She remembered him as a dashing officer in his younger days, with a commanding voice and light blue eyes that took in every detail around him. The fragrance of cigar tobacco permeated the room, evoking childhood memories.

"How are the rest of the family—Ezekiel and the girls? Was your trip reasonably pleasant?"

"Everyone is well. The girls are growing. How are Addie and the baby?"

Colonel Ford broke into a wide smile. "Wonderful. They both are well, and Lula is the delight of my life. I consider myself blessed indeed."

"Yes, you are. The trip was fine, aside from the constant wind."

"It has been bad this year." His eyebrows knitted together. "Did you see anything of concern along the way?"

Amanda swallowed a quick intake of air. "No. Are there problems in the area with Indians?"

"We've been dealing with deserters and scallywags of all sorts. Since all of the federal troops left the frontier to fight in the war, we're shorthanded. We have only skeleton forces to protect the homeland." Colonel Ford dismissed the subject with a wave of his hand. "But I think you should be fine." He picked up his cigar and stuck it, unlit, into his mouth.

She chuckled at the sign on his desk: *Colonel John S. "Rip" Ford.* "Very well, Uncle John—or should I call you Uncle Rip now?"

He shook his head. "Looks like that's going to stick with me long after the war with Mexico."

"Why are you called that?"

"I had the grim duty of writing families of the deceased soldiers, and always signed them 'Rest In Peace.'"

"What an awful reminder. I hate going to the post office these days and reading the wounded and fatality list."

Colonel Ford swiveled in his chair and looked out his window at the bustle of wagons and soldiers on horses in the street below. "We are living in a time that will always be remembered with great sadness. I fear the schism will not be easily mended."

The chair squeaked as he turned back toward her. "Now, to what do I owe the honor of your visit to Austin? It's delightful to see you, but I think that the whole family would have come had this been simply a social visit."

Amanda's gaze flitted around the room, then settled on her uncle's Confederate gray uniform—and she thought of Kent. North—South. What was she doing? She didn't know if she was being loyal or traitorous. Colonel Ford waited with his hands resting on the arms of his chair. She took a deep breath and heard herself begin, almost as if her voice belonged to another.

Colonel Ford watched her face intently, unblinking, as she revealed what she had heard through the crack in the parlor door that day. He placed his cigar in an ashtray and came around to the front of the desk, leaning against the edge and folding his arms.

She wrung her hands as she finished. "That's all I heard. Father and I didn't know what to do at first with the information, but felt somebody in authority needed to know. So of course you were the first one we thought of. Father couldn't leave the congregation, and we feared a letter might be intercepted, so here I am." She stood. "Did we do the right thing, Uncle John? Is this helpful?"

The colonel embraced her around her shoulders. "Yes, my dear, very helpful. There have been rumors of such contemplated action, but nothing we could nail down. After the first of next year, eh?"

"That's what they said."

"That gives us time to plan our counterattack." Colonel Ford straightened a few papers and slid them across the polished wood of his desk. "Thank you, Amanda. This is significant. The Confederate army is indebted to you."

She rose as he indicated the door. "There's something else. Father asked me to purchase medical supplies. We were cut off during the blockade and still don't have what we need. Can you help us?"

"Yes, I'll inform my aide. You'll need to be doubly cautious on the trip home carrying that kind of booty. But first, you, of course, will stay a few days with us?"

"Of course."

"Just be alert on your return trip." He scribbled a note on a piece of paper. "I will send my personal escort with you when you are ready to go home."

"That's not necessary. I have Wash with me."

Colonel Ford smiled. "I didn't ask your permission. It will be my pleasure to offer this extra protection for my brave and loyal niece." He walked with her out the door into the wide, dark hallway where Wash waited.

The servant assisted her down dozens of steps into the bright sunlight, the crowd blurring before her. She looked at Wash and shook her head.

"Miss Amanda?" Questions hung in his eyes.

"I don't know, Wash. The whole world has gone mad, and I can't tell right from wrong anymore." She stepped into the carriage and stared out the window at the wagons and soldiers milling around in the street. She felt dirty, but it wasn't from the dust being stirred up on that busy Austin road.

Chapter Thirteen

The deep waters are closing over us.
MARY BOYKIN CHESTNUT

The wind increased as the sun slipped toward the horizon. The carriage lumbered and creaked under the extra weight of the medical supplies that Colonel Ford had ordered for Amanda to take back to Indianola. She straightened the boxes piled in a teetering stack beside her.

Harriet caught a small chest that threatened to fall from the top. "Washington needs to re-tie these or we're going to have boxes on top of our heads." She chuckled, and the two women rearranged the cargo.

Amanda lifted the edge of her hoop skirt and reached down to feel the packages of quinine that they had sewn into the hoops. They made her skirt heavy and cumbersome, but Uncle John had insisted.

"If you get stopped by enemy soldiers or marauders and they steal the supplies, at least you have a chance of getting through with the quinine. And be wary of anything that looks out of the ordinary on the road. Don't trust anyone."

Amanda shifted her weight. Their trip had been boring and uneventful. They were close to home.

Zack lay asleep under a quilt beside his mother, undisturbed by the jostling.

"Does he always sleep this soundly?"

Harriet nodded. "Yes. Just like his daddy. Washington can sleep through a hurricane."

"Would you mind if I asked you a question?"

"No, ma'am. I wouldn't mind." Harriet sat erect, as she always did, lending an air of elegance to her demeanor. Her green eyes locked on Amanda's and did not waver. She reached up and tightened the knot on her head scarf.

"Are you happy at Bellevue, Harriet?"

"Yes, Miss Amanda."

Amanda had never thought about Harriet's proper speech before. In fact, she had never talked to her much, as Harriet didn't work in the house. She didn't sound like the other slaves when she spoke. If Amanda's eyes had been closed, she would not have identified her as a Negro. "You have good command of English. How did that come about?"

Harriet looked down at her sleeping child and pulled the quilt up around his shoulders. She turned back to Amanda, and gave her head a slight shake.

"Please, I'm truly interested."

Harriet hesitated. "Very well. Before I came to my previous owner—the one Mister Ezekiel bought me from—I was born and lived on a plantation in Missouri. The master's wife believed in educating the slaves."

Amanda knew that in some states to educate slaves would have been to risk one's life. "So you read, then?"

"Yes, ma'am. Learning to read and write changed who I was."

Neither woman spoke for several moments in an atmosphere

pregnant with questions. Finally Amanda broke the awkward silence. "How did you get from Missouri to Texas?"

"My owner's Texan cousin visited for Christmas one year when I was a young girl. He saw me and offered to buy me." Harriet's mouth tightened. "Then my new owner, your neighbor, well, he just wanted to bed me. That's when Mister Ezekiel bought me." Her eyes fluttered as she turned her gaze back on Amanda. "Am I happy at Bellevue? I was grateful that Mister Ezekiel bought me and got me out of that situation. I love Washington and adore our little boy." A smile creased her face. "You and Mister Ezekiel have been good to us."

"If President Lincoln frees . . . if he issues freedom to the . . ." Why was she having such a difficult time verbalizing her thoughts? ". . . the slaves, what will you and Wash do? Where will you go?"

Amanda would never forget the expression on Harriet's face as she answered.

"Wherever we need to go to educate our son and allow him to succeed in life."

"You would leave Bellevue?"

"Perhaps you should talk to Washington about this."

Amanda stared at the woman, then looked out the window as the landscape grew flatter the farther south they rode. Tears that surprised her swam in her eyes. She ducked her head and flicked them away with her finger. She couldn't bear to think about Wash leaving them. He had always been with them. Would Elsie and Kitty leave as well? Surely not. What would they do without them?

The military escort pulled up beside the carriage and called to Wash to halt. The young lieutenant tipped his hat and dismounted. The two enlisted men waited on their horses. Opening the carriage door, he leaned in.

"This is where we leave you, Miss Belle. Colonel Ford said for us to return once we got you into Calhoun County. We passed that line back a piece." He removed his hat and hit it against his leg, sending dust puffing around him. "I believe you'll be safe from here on out. I've not seen much of anything on our trip, save a coyote or two."

Amanda smiled. "Of course, Lieutenant Clifton. We will be home in a couple of hours. We'll be just fine. Thank you for your service." She offered her hand, which the lieutenant took as he bowed and then stepped back.

"It's been our pleasure, Miss Belle."

❧

The carriage slowed. Amanda stuck her head out of the window to see a wagon halfway across the road and half in the ditch ahead. Four bedraggled children sat in their path so that it was impossible to ride past them without going into the ditch on one side or the field on the other. A fifth child, an older boy, stood in front of the team of horses. She saw a man standing by the wagon, but no woman. She tapped on the window. "Wash, stop. It looks like they could use some help."

Wash turned around on the seat and shook his head. "I don' like the looks of this, Miss Amanda. They done cut off any way for us to go around very easy."

"It's children, Wash. Stop and see if we can help."

"Yes'm. Whoa, whoa." Wash halted the carriage and climbed down from his driver's perch.

Amanda opened the carriage door and paused on the foot iron. Dust from the hasty stop billowed up in her face, and she waved it away with her fan, coughing. "Do you need some help?"

Wash helped her down and motioned for Harriet to stay in the carriage.

The man appeared to be in his late thirties, but it was hard to tell. A shaggy beard hid most of his face and flowed down onto his shirt. He removed a floppy hat and grinned. Most of his teeth were missing. "We'd be most obliged, ma'am. The missus died just a couple of months ago, and me and the young'uns—well, we're trying to get to Mexico to make a new start. We don't want nothin' to do with this war." He put his hat back on his head. "Horses spooked awhile back and ran us into this ditch. Prob'ly a snake. I think the axle may be broken."

"Wash, take a look. Do you need food?"

"We could use some."

Wash walked to the wagon and knelt down in the dirt to check the axle on the wagon. "This axle looks fine to me—"

The man pulled a pistol and held it on Wash as one of the "children," who actually turned out to be a woman, jumped up and walked toward them.

"We could use about anything you got there, missy." She looked in the carriage. "I don't know what they are carrying, but they have a load here." She got in the carriage and began to pull boxes out.

Amanda ran toward the woman as the boy aimed a rifle at her. "I don't think you want to do that."

"These are medical supplies for our town. Leave them alone! You couldn't possibly use all of this."

"No, but we could sell it. Looks like we've struck a gold mine here, Pa." The woman's teeth matched her husband's. She continued to unload the boxes, aided by the older boy.

Harriet sat in the corner of the carriage holding Zachary, who had awakened, in her arms. He stared with wide eyes and his thumb in his mouth at the intruders.

Clem motioned to the boy holding the rifle. "C'mere, son, and keep this young buck steady." He stuck his pistol in his belt and walked to the carriage in four long strides. Sticking his head inside, he gave a low whistle. "Woo-eee! Lookee here! This is one purty colored." He climbed into the carriage and pulled Harriet's skirt up as Zachary began to wail.

A roar rose from Wash as he knocked the rifle from the boy's hands, hit him over the head with it, and dashed toward his wife like a wild man. Pulling Clem from the carriage, he began to swing the rifle like a scythe. A deafening thud, and the crack of Clem's skull stopped the scuffle.

The woman ran to her husband. "What have you done? You've killed him. You've killed him!" The children by this time were screaming and gathering around their father.

Wash spoke quietly as he held open the door to the carriage. "Miss Amanda, get in. Quickly now!"

Amanda scrambled in, and Harriet picked up a whimpering Zachary and sheltered him in her arms.

"Hyah! Hyah!" Wash whipped the horses into action, leaving most of the medical supplies in the dust at the side of the road. The carriage banged over the ruts as they sped away.

An explosion ripped the air, and the back of the carriage shredded open. Amanda dived onto the floor and waited for them to gain some distance from their attackers.

Harriet lay over Zachary, her arms encasing him.

Amanda raised her head slowly and looked around. "Is everybody well?" She touched Harriet's arm. It felt warm and slick. Amanda pulled herself from the floor and found blood pouring from the back of Harriet's head. "Oh, no! Harriet! No!" She raised the young woman up off the child, and gathered Zachary, who was now screaming, in her arms. "Wash! Stop!"

Wash shouted. "I can't stop now. We gotta put some distance between us and those thieves."

Amanda set Zachary down on the seat opposite his mother beside the boxes and lifted Harriet's head. She was gone. "Wash, it's Harriet. You must stop!" Her screams escalated.

Wash careened the carriage into a small grove of trees and leapt off the driver's seat, rifle in hand.

Amanda threw open the door and stumbled out with Zachary as Wash reached inside and pulled Harriet's lifeless body out. Blood poured over both of them from the head wound. Wash stumbled in circles like a crazed man. His black silk top hat fell into the underbrush. He put his wife's body down on the ground under a cedar tree and attempted to wipe the blood from her face.

"No, Harriet. Don't leave me. I need you. Our son needs you. Don't go. God, don't take her now." He lifted his head toward heaven and bellowed. "No-o-o-o. Not like this. Not Harriet." His cry echoed through the woods to a silent heaven.

Amanda, sobbing, cradled Zachary in her arms, trying to soothe him. She paced back and forth, not knowing what to do. "Oh, God, oh, God, oh, God. Help us, Father. God in heaven, help us."

Wash crumpled in a heap beside his wife and stared, dry-eyed, into the woods. He turned an unseeing eye toward Amanda, and it seemed he looked through her as if she were not there, until his eyes settled on his son. He pushed himself up and held out bloody arms for his child. Amanda handed Zachary to his father and turned away as Wash buried his head in the child's shoulder and wept. Finally he handed the baby back to Amanda and turned to the dead body of his wife and mother of his son. He picked her up in his strong arms and carried her to the carriage and settled her gently on the floor, covering her with a quilt.

"Miss Amanda, if you wouldn't mind, would you ride up here on the driver's seat with me and my son? We be home before too long. Harriet be . . . be fine in the c . . . carriage." A sob caught in his voice as he helped Amanda, with Zachary in her arms, climb onto the driver's perch. He walked back to the edge of the trees and picked up his top hat. He put on the hat and pulled himself up to his perch. "Giddyup." The slap of the reins signaled the horses, and they lurched forward.

❧

Amanda could not stop her tears. Father drove a small buggy with the girls inside, following a small cart lumbering toward the back of Bellevue property. Lines of singing, chanting slaves, some carrying torches, some carrying cloth bags filled with seashells shuffled behind the cart. Elsie held Zachary and rode in the cart with Wash and Kitty. A simple wooden coffin lay in the back.

Wash backed the cart up to the hole in the ground and stopped. He descended and helped his mother and son. The Belle family got out of their buggy and stood quietly as Wash waited for the slaves to gather round the yawning hole. The setting sun sank behind the trees and haunted the mourners with elongating shadows.

Wash took off his hat and began to speak, softly at first, then gaining in strength. "Tonight I commit to the ground the person I most loves in the whole world. There never was a better woman than my Harriet. She was everything that was good in my life. She believed in me. Harriet had plans for us, for our son. She planned that he would be educated. He was gonna have more than we ever would be able to give him here in the South." Wash flickered a look toward Amanda and Father. "I don't know how I'm gonna to raise him by myself." He paused. "She loved livin' here on the ocean—the smell of the sea, the beautiful sunrises, the bounty of the waters. Her favorite was my mama's shrimp gumbo."

A chuckle rippled through the crowd. Everybody knew how much Harriet loved gumbo. Elsie held a handkerchief to her eyes where the tears would not cease. Kitty sobbed and held her handkerchief over her mouth.

Amanda's shoulders heaved with her weeping. Emmaline, Catherine, and Mary huddled around her skirt, sniffling and blinking at their sister in innocent bewilderment.

Father stared, dry-eyed, at the ground.

Wash continued. "With the war surrounding us on all sides, it seems almost unbearable that my wife was taken by thieving vagabonds. It weren't for no noble cause, but for simple thievery." He paused and looked up into the sky. "Lawd, I jes don't understand, but I trust You." He turned to Ezekiel. "Mistah Zekiel, would you say a few words?"

Father stepped forward and opened his Bible and read: "The Lord is my Shepherd; I shall not want. . . ." He looked up and continued the psalm from memory. ". . . Surely goodness and mercy shall follow me all the days of my life; and I will dwell in the house of the Lord forever."

If those words are meant to comfort, I hope they are more comforting to Wash than they are to me. Amanda looked around, afraid someone heard her thoughts, but the slaves swayed and offered "Yes, Lawds" and "Amens" to the reading of the passage.

Wash beckoned to several men who came forward to help lower the coffin into the ground. Father joined them. Mourners stepped forward one by one to throw clods of dirt on top of the wooden box. *Thud! Thud!* It was as if a shot hit Amanda's chest with each clump of dirt. She gathered her sisters tighter and cried uncontrollably.

The men finished filling up the hole. Then Wash stepped forward.

"The sea brought us. The sea shall take us back. So the shells upon our graves stand for water, the means of glory and the land of demise."

All the women carrying the seashells came forward and placed them on the grave. The slaves continued to sway and sing.

Amanda started toward Wash, but her father took hold of her arm and motioned to his daughters to get into the buggy. "But, Father, Wash—"

"What Wash needs now is to mourn with his people and his Savior. He will be fine. Leave him be."

Amanda glanced over her shoulder at her childhood friend. His dark eyes swam with tears as he acknowledged her gaze.

The Belle family rode by the glistening torches that caught an occasional glimmer of the swaying figures, but all else was plunged into darkness. The singing followed them home, and even into the night, as Amanda lay awake on her bed, the humming and singing continued.

If only the military escort had still been with us. If only I hadn't told Wash to stop. He sensed the danger. She tossed from side to side, carried on the waves of the mournful songs. *Why didn't I listen to Wash? If only . . . if only . . .* Guilt ground into her soul.

Finally, close to dawn, the incantations ceased and she drifted into a fitful slumber.

Chapter Fourteen

There's not a stately ball,
There's not a cottage fair,
That proudly stands on Southern soil,
Or softly nestles there,
But in its peaceful walls
With wealth or comfort blessed,
A stormy battle fierce hath raged
In gentle woman's breast.

A Soldier's Wife,
"Victories of the Heart"

Father brought the buggy to a halt in front of Claire's house. Amanda waved him off as she stepped out of the carriage. "I'm fine, Father. I can manage." She stepped onto the wooden sidewalk and shaded herself with her parasol. Irises unfolded in blossoms around the trees, and the pink and white oleander blossoms cascaded alongside the house. She opened her fan. "Oh, my soul, it is unseasonably warm for this time of year. What is summer going to be like?"

Father held the team steady. "After I go to the post office and take care of a matter at the church, I'll come back and pay my respects to Mrs. Beecham. I shan't be long." He removed his hat and wiped his brow. "I'm not feeling too well. I'd like to get back to Bellevue by midafternoon."

Amanda stopped at the gate. "Are you ill, Father?"

"A headache I can't seem to shake. I'll be back shortly."

"Very well. Claire and I have some catching up to do." She hurried up the steps and clanked the brass knocker, remembering the day a year and a half ago when they stood outside that same door to offer comfort upon the occasion of Colonel Beecham's death.

"Good afternoon, Miss Belle. Miss Claire is in the back parlor."

Amanda handed the maid her hat and parasol. "Thank you, Lucy. I can find my way."

"Yes'm."

Amanda wanted privacy with her friend today, so was glad that she was in the back of the house where little activity took place.

Claire looked up from her embroidery hoop and smiled as Amanda walked through the door. "Come in. I thought you might drop by today." She rose and embraced Amanda in a soft hug. The delicate fragrance of rosewater hovered around Claire. "I have something for you."

She went to the desk in the corner of the room, opened a drawer, and removed a small key. Standing on tiptoe, she reached to a shelf above her head in a wall-length bookcase and pulled down a small chest, which she unlocked. She grinned at her friend. "You cannot be too careful." Claire sorted through a sheaf of letters, then pulled out three unopened envelopes. "These are for you."

Amanda's eyes grew wide as she reached for the letters. "At last. I had grown discouraged that he would write to me." She looked at the date and opened the one written earliest.

April 26, 1863

My dearest Amanda,

Am I too presumptuous to call you "my dearest?" For that is how I think of you. You are my dearest treasure, and I intend to spend the rest of my life cherishing that precious treasure. It is sundown—the time of day when I think of you the most. But how that could be, I know not, for my thoughts are of you all day long. When I look out over the ocean, I think of beautiful Bellevue and our walks along the shore.

The weather has been wet and cold, but is warming up more every day. The fields are turning green and the trees are budding as if the Almighty is sending us the message that new life will triumph even amidst the death and carnage.

How long I will be in New Orleans I cannot say, but keep sending your letters to the headquarters here and perhaps they will catch up with me. Of course, I'm sure you understand that for military security I cannot divulge any more than that.

She sat down in a large wingback chair by the window. Claire returned the chest to the bookcase, then resumed her embroidery. A surge of guilt spread through Amanda as she remembered her mission to Austin last month. Everything within her now regretted that they had taken that journey. If Kent were stationed in New Orleans, would the information she gave her uncle put him in danger? With the exception of bringing Dr. Greer quinine and a few medical supplies, the trip had proved to be a disaster. She closed her eyes and took a deep breath.

"Amanda? Is all well?"

"Oh, yes, just fine. I was resting my eyes—and thinking." She continued with Kent's letter.

Please be careful. Perhaps it would be wise not to venture far from
Bellevue until the war is over. The roads and woods are full of
thieves, deserters, and vagabonds these days—not safe for anyone, let alone women and children. I cannot bear to think of
anything happening to you.

She smiled, touched by his concern for her. Would he not
inform her of his condition? Her eyes raced down the page.

My health is good. The officers at headquarters fare better than
the soldiers in the field, and that fact affords a point of guilt that
I wrestle with continually. I long to be with my men on the battle-
ground, but my leg has not healed to the point where I can ride.

Thank goodness for that fact. Perchance the war would end
before his leg heals, and he wouldn't have to ride into battle ever
again. And they could be married. She resumed her reading.

I am walking with only a cane now. The flexibility in the leg is not
good yet, but I exercise it vigorously and expect to recover fully
in due time.

    I must close for now, my love. Would that I could gather you
in my arms and drown myself in the heady fragrance of the lavender
that surrounds you. I have sewn the perfume button you so gra-
ciously handed me upon my departure into the inside of my jacket.
Each time I catch a whiff of the sweet scent my thoughts are immediately filled with you and your beautiful face. I cannot wait until the
day that we can be together as one. I am praying for God to change
your father's mind concerning us. In the meantime, I remain . . .

                    Devotedly yours,
                    Major Kent Littlefield

Amanda folded the letter and replaced it in the envelope. She tore open the next letter and read quickly through the short paragraphs. Not much news, but she clung to the words of endearment.

To think of you lightens the day and my burden as an officer; to write to you eases it even more; but to receive a letter from you is the most encouraging of all. Thank you for the package of a blanket, socks, and shirt, though how you managed to get them to me without your father's knowledge is beyond me. Surely the postmaster in Indianola suspects something. Can he be trusted not to reveal our secret correspondence? Give my undying gratitude to Claire for being willing to act as a go-between.

Our time together was all too brief. I long for the day when I can hold you without fear of discovery and kiss your sweet lips for as long as we desire. I do not like the fact that we have to keep our correspondence a secret. It does not feel honorable to me. And the last thing in the world I want to do is dishonor you.

I must close. Forgive the brevity of this correspondence. Duty calls, but I remain . . .

Devotedly yours,
Major Kent Littlefield

A knock interrupted her as she was opening the last letter. She leapt to her feet and stuffed the letters into the crocheted purse tied to her belt. She heard her father's voice as Lucy answered the door. Claire motioned for Amanda to pull a chair alongside hers and handed her a hoop with a needle stuck in the fabric. Amanda pulled it through just as her father walked into the parlor.

"Ah, looks like you girls are hard at work."

Claire laughed. "I wouldn't say that. We've done more catching up on . . . mmm . . . news from the war than anything."

"Oh? What do you hear from Daniel?"

"He is well, and, I must say, seems rather proud of his unit. They are in Tennessee."

"Yes, that's what his last letter told us. In fact, when the post-master learned I was coming over here, he asked me to deliver these letters for you." He held up a bundle of letters tied with twine and handed them to Claire. He waved a second stack in Amanda's direction, addressed to the Belle Family.

Amanda uttered a small cry. "That's Daniel's handwriting."

Father glanced around the room, then spoke to Claire. "Is your mother available?"

"Yes, she's probably upstairs. I'll call for Lucy to inform her that you are here."

"Thank you." He went into the front parlor and sat down reading through his own mail while he waited for Mrs. Beecham to come downstairs.

Claire untied the string holding her letters together and looked through them. She caught her breath and looked at Amanda with her eyes widening.

Amanda took the envelope Claire offered, glancing first at the familiar script, then toward the front parlor. She spoke softly. "Do you think my father saw it?"

"N-no, I don't think so. Wouldn't he have said something if he had? And he wouldn't have gone through my letters, especially being all tied up together, would he? No, I'm sure he didn't notice anything amiss."

Amanda folded the letter quickly and ferreted it away with the others. She sat down to read the letters from Daniel, as did Claire.

They chuckled and wiped tears from their eyes as together they shared the precious letters from brother and fiancé.

⁂

"Would you mind taking the reins, Amanda? I'm—I'm not feeling so well." Father handed Amanda the reins and slumped against the side of the buggy.

"Papa!" She took the reins and felt his face with the back of her hand. "You have a fever. We'll be home shortly, and we'll get you to bed."

"Hurry, Mandy. I feel nauseated."

"Hyah." Amanda slapped the reins, and the horse broke into a gallop. Dust flew from the wheels of the small buggy as they pulled in front of the house. Amanda looked over at her father, who was slumped against the seat, eyes closed. She gathered her skirt, jumped down from the buggy, and ran into the house, calling, "Wash, Hiram! Somebody help me. Father's ill. Come help me."

Wash and Kitty came out of the kitchen and ran down the hallway outside to the buggy. "Mistah Zekiel." Wash shook him.

Father looked around, dazed.

"Can you walk, Mistah Zekiel?"

"Yes, yes, of course." He pressed his palm against his forehead. "It's just a headache, but I feel nauseated. Help me to my room."

Wash assisted him out of the cab and half walked, half carried him upstairs to his room, with Amanda close behind. He hefted his master into the bed, and Amanda tugged his boots from his feet.

"Get the chamber pot, Wash. I need to . . ."

He got the chamber pot just in time as Father began to retch into it. Amanda pulled a towel from the washstand and sprinkled water on it.

After the episode, Father lay back on the pillows of his bed, breathing heavily. Amanda folded the towel and placed it on his forehead.

"I'll let you rest, Mistah Zekiel, but I reckon we better try to get that fever down. I'll send Mama up with a cool water bath." Wash closed the shutters, and the two eased out of the darkened room.

"What is it, Wash? What's wrong with him?"

Wash shook his head. "I don't know for sure, Miss Amanda, but it sure is lookin' like yellow fever—the vomiting, high fever, headache."

Amanda took a step backward. "Oh-h-h, no." She leaned against a wicker chair on the landing in front of the open window. "Send Hiram for Dr. Greer."

"Yes'm, right away."

"Thank you, Wash."

Wash hurried down the stairs as Amanda tiptoed to her father's door and peeked in. He lay motionless in the darkened room. Ezekiel Belle was never sick. He always took care of everybody else. What would they do if . . . No, she would not let her thoughts dwell on speculation and what-ifs. She would pray. That's what she would do. She would pray for this not to be yellow fever and for her father to be well quickly. Surely God would answer this prayer. After all, Father was the pastor in town. Not only did the family need him, the whole community needed him. God knew that. He knew that they needed . . . him. . . .

Amanda leaned against the doorjamb with her head buried in the crook of her arm. "O Father in heaven, please, please . . . we . . . need . . . him."

Within the hour Dr. Greer walked in the front door without knocking. Kitty took his hat as Amanda ran down the stairs, meeting him halfway. "Thank you, Dr. Greer, for coming so quickly. Father is suffering from a severe headache and vomiting—"

"Hiram filled me in." He pointed to his bag as they climbed the stairs. "Thanks to you, I have quinine. How long has he been feeling ill?"

She shook her head. "I don't know. He didn't say anything until today."

"If he's vomiting, he's been sick for more than just today."

Amanda wrung her hands. "He never complains. I was not aware that he was feeling ill." She creaked open the door and ushered the doctor in. Elsie sat beside her master's bed, bathing his forehead. A quilt lay over his legs.

"Open the shutters so I can see. Get that quilt off him."

Elsie removed the quilt and moved to the windows. Bright afternoon sunlight flooded into the room, revealing dancing dust sprites in the air.

Father moaned and opened his eyes, squinting against the bright light. He pushed with his hands to a sitting position. "Dr. Greer. They needn't have bothered you. I just have a terrific headache and—"

"And have been vomiting?"

"Well, yes, when we first returned home from town."

"Lie back and allow me to examine you."

Father took a deep breath. Dr. Greer looked at the pastor's eyes and felt his forehead and cheeks, then probed his abdomen. "Elsie, continue the cool water. If we can get the fever down, he'll rest more comfortably." He crooked his finger at Amanda and went out in the hall. "His eyes are jaundiced, as is his skin. Had you not noticed?"

"N . . . no. He is so dark naturally, and with his beard, I didn't."

"I'm afraid it is yellow fever, and I equally fear it is too late to save him."

The room began to spin, and Amanda grasped the doctor's arm. "No, surely you cannot mean that. Start the quinine. You must save him, Doctor. We'll pray. God won't take him—not now."

Dr. Greer patted her hand and steered her to the wicker settee on the landing. The parlor palms swayed in the afternoon breeze that blew through the open window as if it were only a warm spring day of no consequence. The sun glinted off the polished dark wood floors.

Dr. Greer's voice continued. "I'm sorry, my dear. Aside from divine intervention from the Almighty . . ." He paused and latched his bag. "We just don't know what causes this. Keep everything disinfected and clean. Here's what you can expect: in just a few days—four or five at the most—the vomiting will increase, and he'll become delirious. Then a blessed coma will overtake him, and he will slip away. I will leave as much quinine with you as I can, but I honestly don't think it will help."

Amanda's mind was swirling. She heard what the doctor said, but the preposterous words wouldn't settle into a rational, reasonable context. They floated in the air with no place to land. She took a deep breath. Finally the words hit her with the force of one of the cannonballs that had boomed around them during the occupation of Indianola last fall. She folded her hands in her lap to stop them from shaking. "What can I do to make him comfortable?"

"Not much. Try to keep him hydrated. With the constant vomiting it's almost impossible."

Emmaline appeared at the top of the stairs. "Mandy?" She walked to Amanda's side and cuddled up to her. "Hello, Dr. Greer. Is someone sick?"

"Papa's not feeling well. He has a headache."

"Oh." She put her hand up to her temple. "That's strange. So do I."

CHAPTER FIFTEEN

MAY 1863

Year that trembled and reel'd beneath me!
Your summer wind was warm enough, yet the air I breathed
*   froze me,*
A thick gloom fell through the sunshine and darken'd me,
Must I change my triumphant songs? Said I to myself,
Must I indeed learn to chant the cold dirges of the baffled?
And sullen hymns of defeat?

WALT WHITMAN,
"YEAR THAT TREMBLED AND REEL'D BENEATH ME"

Amanda closed the door to her father's bedroom and leaned against it. She'd never felt so weary in her entire life. Rolling down her sleeves, she wiped away the tears that left watery trails on her cheeks. She walked down the hall, rang for Elsie, and collapsed into a chair. She couldn't recall when she'd last cleaned up and put on fresh clothing.

The longtime servant plodded up the stairs, her head swathed in a black scarf. "Yes'm?"

"He's gone, Elsie. Begin preparations on the body."

"Oh, Miss Amanda. This is jes awful. We done lost enough of

our people. We's in hard times, we is. We's in hard times." The older woman began to cry and wiped her nose with a rag that she carried in the pocket of her apron.

"Go on, Elsie. I need to check on Emmie."

She pushed herself up from the chair and let herself into Daniel's darkened upstairs bedroom where they had put Emmaline. Kitty hovered over the girl, rising from her chair as Amanda approached the bed. "How is she?"

"Still running fever, but, praise Jesus, she ain't commenced to vomiting."

"I pray we caught it soon enough." Amanda swallowed the lump in her throat. She leaned over the bed and kissed the feverish face of her little sister.

Emmaline's eyes fluttered open. "Mandy? How is Papa?"

Amanda lowered her voice as she brushed the damp tendrils of her sister's hair from her cheek. "Don't worry about Papa, sweet pea. Let's get you well." She unscrewed the top from the tin bottle on the nightstand and removed a tablet. A glass half full of water sat next to the medicine bottle. "Here, time for your pill."

Emmaline turned her head away from Amanda. "No, Mandy, it's too bitter." She covered her mouth.

"I know, but it will make you feel better." She raised the girl's head with one hand, and gave her the tablet with the other. "Here, wash it down, quickly."

Emmaline's chin quivered as she took the water, then crumpled back down on her pillow.

Her eyelids closed halfway, and she returned to a dreamlike slumber, mumbling incoherently.

Amanda motioned for Kitty to come out into the hall with her. Elsie bustled past them with a bundle of soiled towels. Amanda sighed and re-anchored her bun in place with a comb. "Father's gone, Kitty. Would you assist your mother, please, in preparing the body?"

Kitty's hand flew to her mouth, and her face twisted as she fought to control her emotions. "Miss Amanda. Oh, no. How we gonna get along without Mistah Zekiel to take care of us?" She wiped her eyes with the corner of her apron. "Now, Miss Emmaline done got the fever. What we gonna do? Jes die off, all of us, one by one?"

Amanda glared at Kitty and took hold of her shoulders. "No, do not say that. We are not going to die one by one. The dying stops, and it stops now."

Kitty's eyes grew large, and she ducked her head. "Yes'm."

"Now be done with your tears and go. I'll sit with Emmie while you help your mother." She motioned toward the sisters' bedroom. "Are Mary and Catherine asleep?"

"Yes'm. They been asleep a long time."

"Very well, then. Fetch Wash and Hiram and ask them to carry the b-body—Father—downstairs to the parlor. I'll be with Emmaline if you need me." Her eyes filled with tears again as she walked into Emmaline's room and closed the door. She curled up in a rocking chair beside the bed and rested her head against the back. Her eyes closed, and then she started awake, her heart pounding as her sister whimpered and turned on her side. Amanda stood and straightened the child's bedding around her moist body. She returned to her chair and watched her sister in the glimmer of the bedside lantern.

Her spirit began to pray in spite of herself. *Please, God, please, God, please. Not Emmie.* She didn't even have words to pray, didn't want to pray, didn't trust God anymore. If this was the way God treated his people, she could do fine on her own. But still her spirit groaned and yearned for God to intervene. *Please, God, please, please, please.* She fell asleep with the unbidden prayers on her lips.

Kitty opened the shutters the next morning. The sunlight leapt into the room as if it had no better manners than to disturb one as ill as Emmie.

Amanda jumped to her feet. "Is it morning already? Close those shutters. It's too bright."

The young girl sat up and blinked her eyes. "No, leave them. I like the sunlight." She smiled. "I feel better."

Amanda felt Emmaline's forehead. It was cool and dry. "No more headache?"

Her sister shook her head.

Amanda fell to her knees and let the tears come. "Thank you, Jesus. Oh, my soul, thank you, thank you." She took Emmaline's hands and covered them with kisses. She sat on the edge of the bed, gathered her sister in her arms, and rocked back and forth.

"Kitty, fetch clean water, please, and have Elsie come bathe her. Bring hot water to my room and help me dress. You'll need to assist Mary and Catherine." Catherine and Mary—she was going to have to tell them Father had passed—something she dreaded having to do.

"Members of our congregation and friends will start arriving as soon as they hear the news. Did Wash and Hiram finish preparing Father's body?" When before nothing could be done, now there was much to do.

"Yes'm, and Hiram sat up with him last night. Wash done gone into town early to get a casket."

"Oh, my. I don't know if we can afford one. Well, it's done now. We'll manage. Somehow we'll manage." She breathed in deeply, and her breath caught. "Go on now, and get that hot water up here, so I can ready myself."

"Miss Amanda?"

"What is it?"

"Hiram wants to know which door to use to put Mista Zekiel's body on."

"Oh." Her thoughts flew to when her mother died and David drowned. But she didn't have to make all the decisions then. Papa, her strong papa, had handled them all. Now the burden fell on her shoulders. "Use the pocket door from the library again. It's the easiest to remove."

"Front parlor or back?"

"Front."

"Yes'm." Kitty hurried out of the room.

Amanda remained on the edge of Emmaline's bed, still holding her hand, not wanting to release it. Her sister lay on her back, looking at the ceiling with tears coursing down the sides of her face. Her chin quivered. "Papa's gone?"

Amanda nodded, finding it difficult to speak. "We were afraid we were going to lose you too." She motioned to the quinine bottle. "He was just too sick by the time he started taking medicine."

"What did we have?"

"Yellow fever."

The young girl stared at Amanda. "Am I going to die too?"

Amanda touched her cheek. "No, no, my little sweet pea. Dr. Greer said if the fever broke that you would recover. And we are to keep giving you the quinine."

"The quinine that you smuggled back from Austin."

"Yes."

"Oh." Emmaline looked down at her hands. "I suppose it's up to you and me now to run Bellevue until Daniel gets home, isn't it?" She turned questioning eyes on her sister.

Emmaline grew up in that instant in front of Amanda's eyes. "I suppose so, but we have Wash and Elsie, Kitty and Hiram to help. What you need to do right now is fully recover. You're going to be weak for a while."

Elsie came in with a pitcher of water and clean towels. She set them down on the washstand and raised her hands and face toward the ceiling. "Praise you, Jesus! Missy Emmaline gonna make it." The maid moistened a rag and began to wipe the girl's face. "Kitty's right behind me with your water, Miss Amanda."

"Thank you, Elsie." Amanda kissed the child on the cheek and stood. "I'll check on you later. Try to rest as much as you can. You're going to hear lots of comings and goings downstairs."

Emmaline sat on the edge of the bed and allowed Elsie to start pulling off her soiled bedclothes as Amanda let herself out into the hallway. She grimaced as the hinges creaked on the door to her bedroom. Catherine turned over, still asleep, but Mary sat up and yawned.

"Is it morning?"

"Yes, it's morning." Amanda picked up the six-year-old, although she was almost too big for Amanda to lift. She sat with her in a rocking chair and held on to her for a few minutes. She nuzzled her nose into the child's hair. "Did Kitty wash your hair yesterday? It smells fresh."

Mary nodded and stretched, almost wriggling out of Amanda's lap. "Is Emmie better this morning?"

"Yes, she is. I'm very happy to say that she is much better this morning."

The child jumped out of her sister's lap and started for the door. "I want to see her, and I want to see Papa."

"Wait a minute, Mary. There's something I need to tell you. Let's wake Catherine, so I can tell both of you at the same time."

Mary halted at the open door. "But I wanna see Papa."

Amanda walked to the door and closed it, taking Mary's hand. "Come here and sit down."

Catherine awoke and sat up, rubbing her eyes. Amanda set Mary on the edge of the bed and sat there with her. She took Mary's hands in her own. "Girls, sometimes people are so ill, so terribly ill, that they will never get well on this earth. And Jesus decides to take them to heaven to be with him." She paused.

The two little girls stared at her, not speaking.

Tears spilled over Amanda's eyelids and onto her cheeks. "I'm very sad right now." She tried to continue, but choked on her words.

Mary reached up and brushed the tears away with her chubby hand. "Don't cry, Mandy."

Amanda chewed on her lip. "Emmaline is much better, but Papa has gone to heaven to be with Mama." She gathered her two sisters in her arms, and they wept together.

⁂

The metal door knocker clanked, and Hiram let Rebecca and her parents in, with Claire and her mother close behind. As Amanda rushed down the stairs, she adjusted the black snood around her hair that she had worn only a few weeks before at Harriet's funeral. Someone had already draped black fabric over the mirrors and around the pictures. Amanda twirled the cameo ring her mother had given her around on her finger to bring the figure to the top as she waited for Elsie to open the door.

Rebecca rushed in and embraced Amanda. "Oh, dear, Amanda. We are so sorry. What are we going to do without our pastor?" She stepped back. "I'm sorry. That is very selfish, isn't it? You've just lost

your father, and I am worried because we no longer have a pastor."
She wiped her nose with her handkerchief.

"No, not at all. I understand." Amanda smiled at Rebecca's
expanding figure. "Not too much longer, is it?"

Rebecca placed her hand on her belly. "Just about six weeks."
She blushed. "Horace's surprise leave last fall brought more sur-
prises than one."

"The Lord takes one in death, and then brings new life."
Amanda shook her head. "Life is strange, isn't it?" She motioned
toward the parlor where her father's body lay in state, surrounded by
cedar boughs that Wash and Hiram had placed around him.

The Davises moved into the parlor.

Claire stepped toward Amanda and clung to her. "I know exactly
how you feel, my dear friend, after losing my own father."

Amanda looked at Mrs. Beecham standing behind Claire, and
a rush of warm anger flooded over her exhausted soul. Her words
spilled out in a torrent before she realized what she was saying. "I
don't mean to be rude, Claire, but you still have your mother. Both
of my parents are gone, and I have no one to help me now until
Daniel gets home."

Claire caught her breath and stared at Amanda. "Yes, of course,
you are right. I didn't mean to be insensitive. Please forgive me."

Amanda patted her friend's hand. She covered her face with her
other hand and sighed. "I know you didn't. I shouldn't have snapped
at you." Giving Claire a quick hug, she ushered them into the parlor
to pay their respects.

Buggies and townspeople on horseback lined the road in front
of Bellevue as women brought in food and the house filled with
friends and members of the congregation.

Amanda glanced up the stairs to see Catherine and Mary peering wide-eyed through the railing at the crowd of people. She motioned for the two little girls to come to her, and she took them into the parlor to pay their last respects to their father.

That night, after the visitors had gone and the house grew quiet, Amanda sat in the dining room toying with a cup of tea.

Elsie bustled in with a tray of sweet biscuits. "Miss Rebecca brought these today. I thought you might like one with yo' tea."

"Thank you, Elsie. I'm not very hungry."

"You needs to eat somethin'."

"I know. I will." She took a deep breath. "Would you fetch Wash for me, please?"

"Yes'm. He right here in the kitchen."

Wash walked through the swinging door. She looked up at him and noticed his red, swollen eyes. She touched his arm. "Would you please go upstairs and bring Emmie down so she can say good-bye to Papa?"

"Yes'm." He walked through the archway to the stairs.

"Wash?"

"Yes'm?"

"What are we going to do? How are we going to survive? Will we survive?"

"We will survive, Miss Amanda. God will take care of us."

"Yes, I suppose. Go get Miss Emmaline, please."

Wash carried Emmaline easily down the stairs and into the parlor. He let her down gently on her wobbly, weakened legs. She began to cry and reached out hesitatingly to touch his hand. "Oh, Papa! Whatever will we do now?"

Amanda stood by her side and held on to her waist. "Emmie, he's not there. You know that, don't you? This is just the earthly vessel that contained his spirit."

Amanda found herself trying to ease her sister's distress with a comfort that she could not as yet bring herself to believe. She simply parroted what she had been taught.

Emmaline sniffled and sat down in a chair that Wash pulled up for her. "I know, but I don't understand. This . . ." She motioned to the body. "This is my papa. And now he's cold and stiff."

She buried her head in Amanda's shoulder and wept until Amanda didn't think she could possibly have any tears left. "Wash, take her back to bed and be sure she takes her medicine."

"Yes'm. Then I'll be back down here." Wash picked the young girl up as if she were a rag doll and carried her up the stairs.

Amanda sat in a chair beside her father's body in the dim light of the parlor. She reached up and touched his cool hand. How would she ever fill his shoes? It would be hard enough if Daniel were home, but without him here the entire responsibility of Bellevue fell on her shoulders. She didn't know if she could keep it going.

She went to the piano and sat on the stool. She began to play, just picking out the melody at first, then embellishing with chords and runs: *Rock of Ages, cleft for me. Let me hide myself in Thee.* . . .

Papa had loved to hear her play. She covered her face with her hands and let the tears come.

Wash entered and stood to the side of the body.

Amanda swiveled around on the squeaky piano stool. "Thank you, Wash. I'll sit up with the body tonight."

"No, ma'am. I will. You sat up with Missy Emmaline last night, and you needs a good night's rest. I will sit with Mistah Zekiel tonight."

She smiled weakly. "Are you refusing to do what I've asked you to do?"

He smiled back at her. "Yes'm. I am."

Unlike Harriet's funeral, Father's was held during the morning hours with the sun bright in a cloud-spotted sky. Unlike Harriet's funeral, attended by just the family and slaves, buggy after buggy of the citizens of Indianola stood parked all over the property like a flock of perched blackbirds. Unlike Harriet, Father was buried in the family plot, only a few yards from the house, not on the back of the property.

Rebecca's father, Theodore, one of the elders in their church, comforted the mourners with a passage out of I Thessalonians: "For the Lord himself shall descend from heaven with a shout, with the voice of the archangel, and with the trump of God: and the dead shall rise first: Then we which are alive and remain shall be caught up together with them in the clouds, to meet the Lord in the air: and so shall we ever be with the Lord. Wherefore comfort one another with these words."

For the second time in a month Amanda flinched as clods of dirt hit the wood of a coffin lying at the bottom of a freshly dug trench.

They sang "Amazing Grace," father's favorite hymn, and Theodore prayed a dismissal prayer. The lump in Amanda's throat choked out any attempt she might have made to sing. She simply stood by the casket with her head lowered.

The kindly gentleman walked to the Belle girls, huddled together, and took Amanda's hand, patting it as he spoke. "My dear, we stand ready to assist you in any way we can. Please be comforted by the fact that your father is with your mother and your brother now."

Amanda nodded as tears fell from her cheeks.

Then the fellow mourners extended their condolences and left one by one in their blackbird buggies.

Amanda, Catherine, and Mary watched Wash and Hiram, assisted by two of the other slaves, shovel the dirt into the grave. Sam had crept alongside Amanda and nudged his nose into her hand. Tears trickled down Wash's cheeks. Elsie had stayed inside with Emmaline, and Kitty had already returned to the house. Mary tugged on Amanda's sleeve. "Let's go into the house. I don't want to stay out here any longer."

Amanda took hold of her sisters' hands, Catherine on one side with her blond curls peeking out from under a sky-blue bonnet, and Mary on the other with pastel pink bows sprouting from her tight, dark pigtails. As they walked slowly along the path lined with oleander bushes in full bloom, she looked up to the second story of Bellevue. Emmaline stood at an open window, holding a hankie to her eyes.

The house itself seemed to be in mourning—chipped paint, a roof in need of mending, the broken fence where a sow trampled through the garden, a shutter akimbo on a second-story window—mourning the death of life as they had known it. There was simply too much to do for the small amount of help that remained. Now with Father gone, how could they possibly keep it in working order?

Amanda opened the back gate and shooed her sisters up the walk and into the house. She didn't know how, but they would make it. Somehow they would make it.

CHAPTER SIXTEEN

NOVEMBER 1863

> *But should he fall in this our glorious cause,*
> *He still would be my joy,*
> *For many a sweetheart mourns the loss*
> *Of her Southern soldier boy.*
>
> CAPTAIN G.W. ALEXANDER,
> "SOUTHERN SOLDIER BOY"

Amanda sat at the trestle table beside the fireplace in the kitchen. She wrapped a quilt around her shoulders and pulled Emmaline in beside her. Catherine and Mary sat on the opposite side.

Elsie fussed as she set the breakfast gruel down in front of Amanda. "Jes don't seem fittin' fo you to be eatin' your meals out here with us. The dining room's the proper place fo the ladies of the house to take their meals."

"These are not proper times, Elsie. Besides, it's too lonesome in the dining room without Father and Daniel. I'd rather be out here with y'all. And it's chilly today. The kitchen feels cozy."

"Humph! Yo daddy would not approve."

"Father is not here to approve or disapprove."

Elsie stopped stirring the breakfast concoction in the kettle on the stove and stared at Amanda.

"Oh, my soul. That came out harsher than I intended. What I mean is we have to do what is necessary in these unusual circumstances. I'm sure he would understand relaxing our decorum when it is just the family."

Father is not here to approve or disapprove. That glaring fact had been foremost in her mind ever since he passed away. She had loved and respected him, but now that he was gone, what did this mean for her and Kent? Could she in good conscience allow the love between them to blossom and mature? Would Kent still feel bound to keep his word? She had written Kent concerning her father's passing, but she had yet to receive a response.

She needed to go to the post office. As much as she used to dread reading the daily newspaper, she missed it since the shortage of paper had shut down the *Indianola Bulletin*. They had to travel to town to get the latest news.

She pushed back from the table. "Elsie, tell Wash that we are going into town."

Emmaline looked up from her bowl of porridge. "May I go with you?"

"Me too!"

"Me too!"

All three girls turned their eyes eagerly in her direction, waiting for her answer.

"Mmm, yes, very well. We'll all go. Elsie, after you fetch Wash, you and Kitty come help us dress, please." She kissed Emmaline on the cheek and retied the ribbon in her hair. "We'll make a day of it. Perhaps we could visit Rebecca and her new baby."

"Oh, yes, could we?" Catherine and Mary clapped their hands

and jumped up from the table. They ran toward the stairs, chattering as they went. Emmaline followed after them.

❦

Amanda peered out of the buggy at the soldiers in blue uniforms along the street in town. She leaned against the back of the cab and closed her eyes. The occupation of Indianola for the second time had come as a recurrent nightmare, worse than the first because Kent was not there to intervene in their behalf. At least soldiers were not billeting in their home, but they had helped themselves once again to their chickens and meat and whatever else they fancied. She would never get accustomed to the Yanks frequenting their shops and stores, lingering on the street corners, marching through the center of town—while Daniel was risking his life to fight the blue-coated enemy. But as she searched the eyes of the soldiers she simply saw boys away from home, men torn from their families. The faces of the men were worn and weary, their skin leathery and drawn. Nearly all of them sported bushy beards and moustaches, and they needed haircuts. Most of the troops were terribly thin. Their uniforms hung loosely around their shoulders. Their boots had holes in them, and desperately needed to be resoled.

She couldn't help but put the faces of Daniel and Kent on the soldiers that she observed walking around Indianola. Were her loved ones hungry? Were they thin and drawn? Did their boots flap as they marched with pride for their respective causes? Maybe they were cold and didn't have enough clothing to ward away the winter elements. The weather was tolerable in Indianola, but what about up north, where she reckoned the snow was already flying?

Wash directed the buggy to the front of the Davis home and tied the team to the hitching rail. He assisted the younger girls out first, then Amanda emerged. She ignored a company of soldiers and their sidelong glances as they marched by, stirring up mounds of dust.

A young officer rode beside the column, and she thought of Kent. Dark hair, dark beard, blue eyes. A sudden yearning to feel his touch once again flooded over her, surprising her. The officer turned and looked her way, tipping his hat politely. She gathered the girls and herded them to the door.

In the parlor of the Davis home, Rebecca's baby slept in a dark wooden cradle. A pink crocheted cap cuddled the delicate face, and soft eyelashes fluttered on the ivory cheeks.

"O-h-h, my soul, Rebecca. She gets more beautiful every time I see her. You are indeed blessed. Horace is going to be captured for life by this little beauty." Amanda lightly touched the baby's head as the sisters crowded around. "Will she wake up soon? I want to hold her."

Rebecca laughed. "I hope not; I just got her to sleep. But surely you're going to stay for a good visit. She'll probably wake up before you leave."

Mary could not resist touching the infant. Amanda took hold of her hand and motioned for the sisters to sit on a couch across the room from the baby. "Come, girls. You're going to wake her."

Rebecca stood. "Would y'all like some molasses cookies? We got some flour last week."

"Where on earth did you find flour?"

"Father's brother came to visit from Indiana. He hid it in his carriage and managed to get it through. Coffee too."

Amanda laid her hand on her chest and breathed deeply. "How fortunate you are. I thought I smelled coffee when I came through the door."

"I'll have Daisy bring you a cup."

Amanda smiled at her friend as they sat side by side. "You look wonderful, Rebecca. Are you feeling well?"

"Yes, I am. Finally. I thought I'd never regain my strength after having little Esther." Rebecca shook her head. "Amanda, birthing a baby was the hardest thing I've ever had to do. I didn't think I was going to make it."

The baby interrupted them with a soft cry, then settled into her blanket, making sucking sounds with her mouth.

"But you did make it, and look at the treasure you have now."

Rebecca smiled. "You can rest assured that I am very much aware of my blessings. She was so bruised and beat up when she arrived, I was scared to death. But she's fine now. I just wish Horace could see her."

"I know you do. What do you hear from him?"

"He's in Virginia with Lee's army. I know he was at Gettysburg and there was a terrible loss of men there, but he never writes much about the war. I'm sure he doesn't want me to worry about him. But I read the newspapers. I'm aware of what's going on." She reached out and laid her hand atop Amanda's. "What do you hear from Daniel?"

"Nothing in a long while. The last letter I got from him was over six weeks ago. Of course, I am very concerned, but I try not to be consumed with worry."

"And Kent?"

"Nothing. I did write him of my father's death, but I've not heard a word from him. I don't even know if he got my letter. With the troops moving around so much, I don't know how the mail ever catches up to them." She looked down. "Speaking of mail, I need to go to the post office. Would you mind if I left the girls here for a few minutes while I do that?"

"Of course not. Perhaps the baby will be awake by the time you get back. Would you pick up our mail?"

"I would be happy to." Amanda picked up her cape and gloves. "I shall return shortly." She walked down the steps from the porch to the buggy.

Wash sat on the edge of the wooden walkway holding the buggy whip. He jumped up when he saw her. "Ma'am?"

"Would you please take me to the post office? The girls are going to stay here with Rebecca."

Wash nodded his head and looked directly into her eyes. "Yes'm, I'll take you."

Amanda put one foot on the iron plate and turned toward him. "Wash, I don't know what I'd do without you. Please don't let anything happen to you. We need you."

"I don't plan to go anywhere, Miss Amanda."

Amanda sighed and took hold of his arm as he assisted her into the buggy.

Wash guided the horses onto the street toward town. Amanda felt the buggy halt before they arrived at the post office. "What's wrong? Why are you stopping here?"

Wash pointed toward the post office. "There's a crowd. I can't get any closer. We'll need to tie the horses here and walk."

Amanda descended from the buggy and held on to her hat as the ever-present wind from the ocean made an attempt to pluck the chapeau from her head. She gathered her cape around her and started in the direction of the post office. "Follow close, Wash. They must have just posted the latest notices."

The crowd, mostly women, interspersed with slaves and a few Union soldiers, jostled her from side to side as Wash parted the way for her.

"There it is—on the bulletin board."

An elderly man stood in the front reading an article about the latest battles, following the lines with a gnarled finger. Amanda swept her eyes over the other posted articles as she ducked up and down and examined the lists of names. She skimmed the list of those who had been killed, breathing a sigh of relief that neither Daniel nor Horace were listed. Then the wounded list—not there either. Then the MISSING IN ACTION. Near the top of the list, her eyes riveted on the name, not wanting to believe what she saw . . . a name so dear and familiar to her.

B . . .

Belle . . .

Daniel . . .

Belle, Daniel Montgomery, Indianola, TX, 8th Texas Calvary. Reported missing in action October 15, 1863.

That was over a month ago. She turned around to Wash. "It's . . . it's Daniel. He's m-missing in action." She grabbed his arm.

"Let's go, Miss Amanda. I'll take you back to Miss Rebecca's house."

As Wash cleared the way through the crowd for Amanda, she saw Claire headed for the bulletin board. "Claire. Claire, over here."

Claire turned to see who was calling her. She smiled and started to make her way to her friend. "I didn't see you at first. I was going to check . . . What is it, Amanda? What has happened?" She grabbed Amanda's hands, her crocheted bag swinging from her wrist. "Is it . . . is it Daniel? Is he . . ."

Amanda choked an answer. "He's . . . he's missing in action, Claire. We don't know what's happened to him."

Claire collapsed to her knees. "Oh, no. Oh, no. God, please don't take him too. You can't take him too."

"Wash, help her up. Where's your buggy, Claire?"

Claire looked up at Amanda with tears drenching her face and pointed across the street. Wash assisted the young woman through the milling mass of citizenry to her buggy.

Amanda got into the cab with her, where the two embraced and comforted each other.

Claire spoke through her tears, holding her handkerchief to her mouth and catching her breath between words. "We . . . we should have gotten . . . gotten m . . . married before he . . . he left. N . . . now . . ."

"Wait, Claire. We don't know anything for sure. He may be wounded in a hospital somewhere, and they simply haven't gotten word to us. Perhaps he's been captured and is in prison . . ."

Claire shook her head. "Oh, Daniel, Daniel. I . . . I love you so."

Amanda waited for Claire's tears to subside, then she and Wash bade her farewell and retrieved their buggy.

Snorting horses and mules pulling wagons blocked the road. Wash had to go to the end of the street to turn around. Amanda hardly remembered the short return trek to Rebecca's. Her breath came fast and shallow. She wanted to cry, but her tears were dried up in the staggering shock that took over her body. She clasped her hands together to stop them from shaking uncontrollably. Daniel missing in action. Where could he be? Was he injured? Was he even still alive? *What about the socks I knitted for him, ready to be packaged up and sent . . . what do I do with them now?*

She shook her head. She wouldn't think like that. He was alive. He had to be alive. What could she do? Nothing. Absolutely nothing. She twisted the cameo ring round and round.

The words of her father echoed in her mind: *"All the worry in the world is not going to do Daniel any good. Only prayer for God's protection will have any effect. Spend your time praying for him instead of worrying."*

Only prayer . . . Amanda buried her head in her hands. Hot tears flooded her eyes and something between a moan and a sob caught in her throat. Only prayer . . . but did prayer really do any good? She had given up on praying. Why pray if God's sovereign will overrides the free will of man? And besides that, she had put God himself aside, like a crystal pitcher on the shelf. Beautiful, nice to have on display, but not put into use. Would God answer her prayers for Daniel when she had only given him a passing thought now and then? And even doubted his goodness and mercy?

Honestly, she didn't know, but she didn't know where else to turn. Silent cries from the depths of her soul reached out to the Almighty, fighting through the maze of her uncertainty.

Help, Lord Jesus. I need you. I need you desperately. Please forgive my doubting your goodness and mercy and love for us. Help . . . help us. She stifled another sob with her handkerchief. *Would you protect Daniel and bring him home safely? I vow to trust you from now on.* That was all she could think to say. She breathed deeply and leaned against the back of the cab.

Lord, I know I must be the weakest one of your children here on earth, but . . . one more thing . . . could you at least give me some assurance that you've heard my prayer?

Kent. The Davises' house was in sight when she realized she had forgotten to check the mail for a letter from Kent. She tapped the window once again. "Wash, turn around. I forgot to see if we have any mail."

"Yes'm. We'll go check." He turned the buggy around once more. The crowd had dispersed. Wash helped her out and went with her into the post office. She went to their box and opened it, but it was empty. She closed the small metal door, locked it, and turned to leave.

The postmaster came from behind the wall where he was filling the letter boxes, his hands full of mail. "Oh, Miss Belle. I have two posts here for you. Was just putting them up." He held the two precious pieces of correspondence out to her.

Reaching across the worn wooden counter, she grabbed the letters, her hands still trembling. "Anything for Rebecca? She asked me to fetch hers as well. And Claire. Anything for Claire?"

"Nothing for Claire, but Rebecca has several letters. I'll get them for you."

She quickly glanced at the handwriting as the postmaster disappeared behind the wall. "Wash, one is from Daniel and one from Kent."

The postmaster returned and handed her a bundle of correspondence in a small box. "I'll put those in a box for you to carry."

"Thank you." She handed the box to Wash, and then tore open the envelope from Daniel as they walked outside. Stopping beside the buggy in the bright morning sunlight, she read aloud.

September 3, 1863

Dear, dear Sisters,

It is with heavy heart that I write to you, having just learned of Father's untimely death. Months have passed, and you have been in sorrow and mourning without my knowledge of your grieving. Our unit moves from place to place so swiftly that the mail is weeks in catching up to us. I fear that much of it never reaches its destination.

My agony is great in not being there with you . . . first of all to mourn for our dear father along with you and to encircle you in my arms . . . but I also feel such a profound burden now as the head of the household to be in my proper place.

I see what these Yankees do to the plantations and towns of the South, and I tremble for fear of what may come your way. They leave nothing of value in the wake of their armies—no food, no crops. They destroy and burn homes and ravage the women, slave and free, leaving families destitute. I don't know how our land will ever recover.

I'm not ashamed to say that I left camp one night fully intending to return home and return to Bellevue. But the standard of honor and character that Father instilled in me would not allow me to do so. I returned to camp without anyone even knowing I had been gone. I pray this will end soon.

Tell Wash I am depending on him to take care of Bellevue until I can return. And give him my condolences for the terrible manner in which Harriet was taken.

Winter is coming soon. Please send anything you can in the way of warm clothing. If I cannot use it, someone can. The cold weather here in the North is unlike anything we have ever experienced. Men cry for the severe pain of the cold but continue to fight valiantly for our cause. Pray for us.

My tears are for all of us.

Your loving brother,
Daniel M. Belle

The letter ended rather abruptly, and Amanda wondered why—was he called to battle? Did he simply have nothing else to say? Was the post runner waiting to take the mail? And now he was missing in action. Would they ever see him again? *Thank you, God. I'll take this letter from Daniel as a sign that you have heard me. I must let Claire know.*

Wash helped her into the buggy as she opened the letter from Kent.

October 30, 1863

My dearest Amanda,

I was so very saddened to hear of your father's passing. I would be less than honest if I did not confess that my first concerns are for you now that, aside from slaves, there is no man there to look after Bellevue. I know Daniel feels that responsibility more than anyone else. Have you heard from him? I have taken the liberty of sending this letter directly to you now that . . . and forgive me if I appear insensitive to you at this juncture . . . now that our correspondence will no longer be apprehended.

For security reasons, I cannot tell you where I am nor what I am doing in line of duty. I know you understand that. But I grow more weary and sick of this war with each passing day. I see—no, I not only see, but I ride through and smell the carnage—the dead and the wounded and in the fields of our country. Some of the soldiers are only boys, many not even shaving. My rage mounts—and my sorrow.

Although my military duties demand my utmost attention and focus, when I lie down at night my thoughts always turn to you. Your beautiful face fills my dreams, and you are my first thought upon awaking. Despite our being apart at the present, my heart is with you every moment. I am bound to you with bands of love that grow stronger every day.

The mail is going out with a soldier just discharged. He is ready to leave, so I must close. Please continue to write in care of my regiment. They will find their way to me. Your letters are a lifeline to me. I am depending on you to wait for me. I will come for you after this heinous conflagration is over. I will come for you.

My undying love,
Major Kent Littlefield

She finished the letter as they arrived at Rebecca's. She stuffed all of the letters into her haversack and got out of the buggy before Wash had a chance to tie the horses. She picked up her skirt and ran to the front door, letting herself in without waiting for Daisy to answer the door. She burst into the parlor as the tears gushed forth, and she began to weep.

Rebecca rose from her chair and rushed to her friend. "What is it, Amanda? Did you receive bad news? Oh, dear. Tell me, tell me."

Amanda called her sisters to her, then dug in her bag for the letters. "We have letters, but . . ." She raised her tearstained face to Rebecca. "Daniel . . . Daniel is reported as missing."

CHAPTER SEVENTEEN

MAY 1864

Woe to the hunted man if hunger-maddened hounds overtake him, in swamps or timber, while the mounted pursuers are too far behind to call them off or moderate their savage eagerness. Woe be to a fugitive if the sleuth-dogs once taste his blood!

A.J.H. DUGANNE,
"TWENTY MONTHS IN THE DEPARTMENT OF THE GULF,"
WRITTEN FROM CAMP FORD, TYLER, TEXAS

B y 1864, thousands of prisoners had been taken on both sides of the war, and both governments struggled with caring for the men they had captured. From the deplorable conditions at the Union's Rock Island Prison in Iowa to the South's notorious Andersonville Prison in Georgia, being taken prisoner was often just as dangerous as fighting on the front lines.

The captured Union soldiers trudged single file behind a wagon carrying the wounded along a rutted road under the blazing Texas sun. Kent cut his eyes over to one of the guards walking alongside the column—a young man who couldn't have been more than eighteen and who seemed as despondent as the prisoners he held at bay. His rifle hung loosely in his hands.

Kent stared into the back of the wagon where wounded Union troops lay stacked like sides of beef in the sweltering heat and high humidity of East Texas. Although he had not used crutches for the last three months, he still needed a cane. His leg pained him, and he was limping worse and worse with each mile toward Tyler. *If I didn't have this bum leg, I'd make a run for it.*

A Confederate captain approached on a large sorrel. "Major, you're slowing down the line. Pick it up."

Kent ignored him and continued to stare ahead. He attempted to quicken his steps, but in so doing stumbled and dropped his cane.

The captain poked him with his riding whip. "Well, sir, you're just not doing very well here, are ya?" He whirled his horse around and rode to the wagon carrying the wounded and halted it. Returning to Kent, who still struggled to retrieve his cane, the captain snarled, "If you weren't an officer, I'd leave you here by the side of the road to die."

Kent glared at the captain. "If I weren't an officer and you left me by the side of the road to die, I'd . . ." He held his tongue, swallowing the curses that he wanted to fling toward the Rebel captain.

"Get in that wagon, you Blue Belly." The captain threatened him with the riding whip. "I suppose you need help getting in."

"I can manage." Kent hobbled to the back of the wagon, put his cane in first, and pulled himself into the makeshift ambulance. One of his own men in the front of the line of prisoners gave him a boost. He glanced over his shoulder at the boyish face of the young private. "Thanks, Thurman."

"Yes, sir." The soldier gave his commanding officer a slight grin and a salute.

Kent scooted in next to an older man slumped against the side of the wagon. He touched the man's shoulder, which was tied in a bloody bandage. "You doing all right, Sergeant?"

"I'm making it. Bullet went clean through, but I was lucky, sir. Didn't hit the bone. It's my shooting arm though. That's why they got me. Couldn't hold 'em off." He adjusted his wounded arm and cradled his elbow in the palm of his other hand. "We got whipped pretty good, didn't we, sir?"

"I'm afraid so."

"What happened, sir? I thought we had the advantage."

Kent shook his head. "I don't know. I suppose it was simply a combination of bad timing, incomplete communication, and the forces of nature. It certainly was not for lack of courage or fighting ability of our troops." He removed his hat and wiped his forehead. "Well, it doesn't really matter at this point, does it? At least for us anyway. We're on our way to prison."

The man groaned and pulled himself to a sitting position. "Are we almost there?"

"I think so. Where are you from?"

"Illinois." The sergeant stuck out his good hand. "Ben, Ben Foster. And you?"

"Kent Littlefield. I'm from Pennsylvania."

"Are you married?"

"No. You?"

"Yep. Been married almost ten years now. Got two boys and a little girl waiting for me when I get home. You got a sweetheart?"

Kent nodded and showed the sergeant the perfume button pinned to the inside of his jacket.

"You better not let any of those Johnny Rebs see that. They'll confiscate it for sure." He chuckled. "Does it still smell like her after being in that stinky jacket for months?"

Kent smiled and, holding the button to his nose, drew in a long breath. "Faintly."

"Is she waiting in Pennsylvania for you?"

"No. She's actually from Texas."

"Oh." The sergeant scratched his head. "That could prove interesting after the war."

"Yes, couldn't it?"

Ben laid his head against the side of the wagon. "How much longer?"

"I don't know for sure. Maybe a couple of hours."

"No, I mean how much longer is this war gonna go on?"

Kent sighed. "I wish I knew. I thought it would be over by now. I don't think any of us counted on the Rebs putting up this much of a fight."

"Frankly, Major Littlefield, I don't care who wins now. I just want to go home, work my farm, hold my wife in my arms, and play with my children."

"I understand. I feel much the same way. However, it is imperative that the North win this conflict. If we don't, I fear the downfall of our country."

The sergeant drew a deep jagged breath. "I know you're right, but I don't think I have the will nor the strength to continue. And after all . . ." He motioned with his good hand toward the groaning mass of humanity being jostled from side to side. "For most of those in this wagon, the argument is pointless, is it not?"

Kent smoothed his unkempt beard. "I'm afraid you're right."

Ben closed his eyes and drifted off.

Kent rested the back of his head against the side of the wagon. Bringing the inside of the lapel of his jacket to his nose, he inhaled and closed his eyes.

The sun set upon the lush green of the rolling hills of East Texas, bringing with it a welcome drop in temperature. The wagon pulled through the gate of large logs with well-chiseled points poking into the sky through the gathering dusk. The Rebel captain called the wagon to a halt and ordered the men to get out.

Kent lowered himself to the ground as a scruffy corporal held him at gunpoint, his stiff leg resisting as he tried to stretch it.

Ben followed, and then, one by one, those who could walk were herded out into the night air, which bristled with rifles pointed at them. Those who couldn't walk were carried on gurneys.

Kent touched the face of one of his men who lay very still, too still. The soldier's cool flesh made Kent shudder. He closed the staring eyes and pulled the rough blanket over the man's face. Looking up to the captain, he motioned toward the body. "This one's gone."

"One less mouth to feed." The captain's horse pawed the ground.

Kent clenched his jaw and stepped back as the man was carried away.

After being issued bedrolls and knapsacks, the men were marched through the heavy underbrush past several hut-like log structures about ten feet long. Kent thought at first that they were pigpens, but learned that these were the officers' quarters. He poked his head into three or four of the shelters to find them full, the bunks occupied. Entering one of the last huts in the row, he found an empty bed.

Two lieutenants stood to greet him, coming to attention and saluting. A sandy-haired, slight man introduced himself. "Lieutenant Roscoe Warner, Major, with the 23rd Connecticut."

The other officer followed suit. "Lieutenant John Selvidge, sir, New York 75th Volunteers." Motioning toward the empty bunk with his hand, he grinned. "You are more than welcome to share this here little shebang with us."

The bed stood in the corner of the shelter opposite a crude fireplace. "The good news is that a fire in the fireplace feels good when the nights are cool. The bad news is that when we have to cook in here in the summer, it gets purt' near unbearable."

"At ease, men. This will be fine. I'm Kent Littlefield from the 77th Pennsylvania."

"Where'd they get you, Major?"

"Mansfield. We thought we had the advantage, but they overran us. These Johnny Rebs are like a little yipping dog that won't let go of a bear." Kent sat on his hard bunk, took off his cap, and massaged his leg. "But we'll get them in the end. The South is not going to win this war."

Lieutenant Warner sat opposite him on his bunk. "Are you sure about that, Major? I'm beginning to wonder." He crinkled his forehead and leaned forward. "Tell us what's happening out there."

"Things seemed to be going well as General Banks brought his troops into Louisiana. Sherman's detachment had captured Fort de Russy, but the water level in the Red River was low, and our fleet couldn't get past Alexandria. Banks had to retreat, and . . . well . . . the Rebs may win some battles and may have killed thousands and taken a passel of us as prisoners, but they don't have the natural resources and provisions to continue this nightmare forever. Generals Sherman and Grant are planning campaigns to run over the major cities in the South. We are slowly taking over their land. Surely the Rebs cannot continue for much longer . . . surely . . ."

Kent pushed himself up on his cane and started untying his bedroll.

Lieutenant Selvidge jumped to his assistance. "Here, sir, let me help you with that. You seem to be a bit unsteady on your feet." He unrolled the blanket—threadbare and filthy.

"Thank you, Lieutenant. You are very kind." Kent had none of his personal belongings except his cane and the clothing on his back. He wished he had the blanket that Amanda had sent him. He supposed it was still tied onto his saddle, unless some Johnny Reb had ripped it from Sterling's back. The picture of the valiant horse going down beneath him would remain with him forever. He prayed the horse didn't suffer.

Digging a canteen and metal dish out of the knapsack, he sat back down. "What time do we eat? They didn't feed us all day."

"Around six, but don't be expecting a feast or nothing." Lieutenant Selvidge shoved his kepi over his shock of bushy chestnut brown hair that matched an equally bushy beard.

"That's right." Lieutenant Warner gathered his gear. "They feed us stuff here that we feed to the hogs back home—mostly salt horse. We take mess at the 'Fifth Avenue Hotel,' a larger shebang down the way where six officers are tenanted."

At mealtime Kent followed his two colleagues to the mess hall. There seemed to be lots of vacant land for more huts.

Lieutenant Selvidge introduced Kent to men as they went through the food line. As they sat down at a long table, he indicated a captain further down on the bench. "That's Captain Hicks from Kansas. He and his men are the contractors for building the she-bangs. If you can make a deal with him, he will build you a larger place."

Kent bent forward and nodded toward a man with a close-cropped beard and huge hands. "That one?"

"That's him."

"I'm not going to be here long enough to need another place."

"You're sure about that, huh?"

"I'm sure."

Selvidge hesitated as he spooned another mouthful of cornmeal gruel. "What are you planning to do—escape? On that?" He looked down at Kent's swollen leg, splayed out to his side.

"It'll be all right in due time."

"Sixteen officers attempted an escape last winter." The lieutenant cursed and clenched his fist around his spoon. "Those Rebs got the dogs after them and caught all of them not even a mile from here—all except one, and we don't know what happened to him."

"They sent the hounds after white men?"

"Yep. Colonel Allen had declared far and wide that he would never send the dogs after white men, but they sure did. Said the dogs would catch white men just as sure as they would the coloreds." He shoved his plate away. "So if you're thinking of escaping, you might want to think again." Scratching his scruffy beard, he leaned toward Kent. "However . . ."

"However, what?"

"The last man to escape was supposed to replace the post they had pushed aside to wriggle through, and he forgot. That's why the guards discovered so quickly that the men were gone—that leaning post. In my opinion, if only one or two could get away and get a day's head start, they might have a chance."

"I'll keep that in mind." Kent followed the line of men back to the shebang and lay down on his bunk. He removed his jacket and held the perfume button to his nose. The gentle fragrance, out of place in the fetid odors of prison, carried him to the beach of the Matagorda Bay and Bellevue, and Amanda. He closed his eyes and drifted into a fitful sleep.

Thunder rumbled, and the wind howled through the large oak trees that surrounded the camp. Sheets of rain splashed against the shebang, forcing their way inside, splattering walls. The lightning flashed, one streak after another.

Lieutenant Selvidge sat up in his bed. "This here's tornado weather." He peered outside. "Yep, look at that greenish-colored sky."

Kent hobbled to his feet and went to the window. "It looks pretty nasty out there, all right."

Lieutenant Warner snored and turned over.

"Doesn't seem to be bothering him any."

"Nope. He can sleep through anything." Lieutenant Selvidge lay on his bunk with his arms behind his head. "It's a good night for an escape."

"What do you mean?"

"With the rain, the dogs can't follow you. 'Course, if you don't know where you're going, you're gonna get lost out there in those thick woods. And these woods got all kinds of critters—bear and bobcats, snakes. They say even a mountain lion is spotted now and then." He looked at Kent as the lightning illuminated his grin. "But if a man knew where he was a-going, and wasn't afraid of the animals, this'd be a good night to try. If he knew . . ."

Kent stuck his legs under the blanket. "I suppose, but I need this leg to heal some before I try an escape. But then, you can be assured that I'll be seeing what I can do."

"Yes, sir. That's a natural fact. You need to get healed up. Go on back to sleep, sir. I think this storm's about to play out. Sleep well."

"Yes. You too."

❧

The guard towered over Kent, his face darkening red as he blustered and shouted at the major. Kent stood at attention as straight at the morning reveille as he could with his throbbing leg.

The guard yanked him by his shirt and brought his face within inches of his own. The man reeked of dried sweat and coffee on his breath. "Your first night here, and the men in your shebang have run. You must have brought escape plans in with you. What was your plan? How did he get out?"

"Get out? Escape? I don't know what you are talking about, Sergeant."

"Don't act dumb. It'll not go well with you to play dumb."

"I'm not playing dumb. I don't know what you are talking about."

"Lieutenants John Selvidge and Roscoe Warner—that's what I'm talking about. They're gone. Disappeared. How'd they get out?"

"I only met those men last night. Don't you think if I knew they were going to try to escape, that I would've gone with them?"

"Don't know about that." The guard pulled Kent out of the line of soldiers and shoved him toward the guardhouse. "Come with me."

The burly guard threw Kent into a six-foot-by-six-foot dingy, smelly cell. A bucket sat in one corner of the enclosure for waste and a flimsy blanket on the dirt floor. It was already uncomfortably warm. A small window with bars let in some little bit of light and air.

"You'll have plenty of time in here to think about what you don't know." The guard slammed the door, and Kent heard keys jangling as the lock clicked into place. He shouted out the window, "I want to see the commanding officer. I have a right to appeal to the commanding officer."

The guard ignored him and walked away.

This is a fine fix. Not here even one day, and I'm in the stockade. He smiled to himself as he recalled his conversation with Lieutenant Selvidge late last night during the storm. The man was telling him that he was going to run—without telling him. *Run, Lieutenant, run. And godspeed to you, my new friend.*

The hounds began to bay.

CHAPTER EIGHTEEN

> *Women . . . are the same everywhere.*
> MARY BOYKIN CHESTNUT

Amanda dribbled the fragrant lemon oil on a rag and worked it into the wood of the sideboard in a circular motion. Why they bothered to keep the furniture polished, she really didn't know. They might as well simply cover it with sheets and hope the Yankees didn't chop it up for firewood. She'd heard that was exactly what was happening in the colder states. Fortunately for them, firewood was not needed as much. But Elsie insisted that they keep up the façade of their former lives as best they could. So they polished the furniture once a week.

She pulled a handkerchief out of her apron pocket and wiped her forehead. "My soul, it's hot." She replaced the cap on the bottle of lemon oil and started for the kitchen. Hesitating at the bottom of the stairs, she listened for the girls. It was quiet on the second floor. They must have gone outside.

She went through the swinging door into the kitchen and put on her bonnet. Stepping through the back door, she walked the few steps to the outdoor kitchen where Elsie was beginning preparations for dinner.

Kitty stood at the table dipping cornmeal from a large barrel into a mixing bowl, and Zachary played at her feet with spoons and a cup. She looked at Amanda, her eyes clouded with worry. "Dis is almost the last of the cornmeal. The corn crib is half empty, and that won't carry us through the winter."

Amanda peeked into the barrel.

"We needs to harvest the last of the corn, but there ain't enough of us to do it."

"What do you mean?"

"I mean there's hardly any of the field hands left to harvest the crops. We still has stuff in the garden that need to be picked. We jes don't have enough hands to pick it and get it in. If'n half of the field hands hadn't been sent off to the labor camps for the war that would be bad enough. But add to that those scoundrels that have run off. We jes ain't got enough hands to do the work. And if we gets one more storm, we'll lose the okra, beans, and tomatoes. It's gettin' too hot anyway. We needs to get 'em in."

Amanda put her hands on her hips. "I see." She chewed on her lip. "Well, we shall do what we need to do. We'll all go pick—the girls and everybody."

The two Negro women, mother and daughter, who had always been house servants, looked at Amanda, their brown eyes widening.

"All of us?" Kitty put her scoop down.

Amanda nodded. "All of us. If all of us in the house work—you two, Wash and Hiram, and the girls and I—why that's six of us who will be good help. Catherine and Mary can help too."

"But, Miss Amanda . . ."

"No buts. Get your bonnets, and let's get started."

Elsie wiped her hands on her apron. "What about dinner, Miss Amanda? I don't mind hard work. You know I'se worked hard all my life, but somebody's gonna need to be feedin' y'all."

"Can you do it by yourself? Without Kitty?"

The old slave chuckled. "Why, I reckon I can. I be doin' that before she was even born."

"Very well. You stay here and prepare the meals. Kitty, fetch Wash and Hiram from the barn and then go on to the garden, please, and start picking. I'll get the girls."

The young Belle sisters sat beneath the shade of a tall palm tree in the back of the house, talking and giggling. Catherine and Mary played with their dolls, and Emmaline sat nearby reading. Amanda smiled to herself as she walked toward them. They had matured since the war began. Emmaline was a young lady now and seemed older than her thirteen years. She'd be fourteen in the fall. They were fine girls who would become strong women. Tears moistened the corner of her eyes.

"It's cooler out here under the trees, isn't it?"

"Uh-huh." Catherine answered, but didn't look away from her dolls.

Emmaline closed her book and stood, brushing bits of grass and sand from her skirt. "It was so hot in the house that we decided to come out here. Is it time for dinner already?"

"No, it will probably be a bit before we eat." Amanda reached for Emmaline's hand and squeezed it. Releasing it, she knelt down in front of the younger girls. "We need your help."

Emmaline said, "Our help . . . with what?"

"We need everybody's help. We have crops that need to be picked or we're going to lose them. If we don't get the corn in, we won't have enough food for the winter."

The girls stared at Amanda. Emmaline spoke. "You want us to work in the cornfield?"

Amanda stood and nodded. "We need you."

Mary jumped up. "I can help! I know how to pick. Kitty showed me one time."

Emmaline nodded. "Yes, we all can help."

"Mary, what you can do is help Kitty in the garden. Tomatoes are rotting on the vine because we don't have enough help to get them in."

Catherine flung her blond braids behind her shoulders and continued to fidget with her doll. "It's too hot, and besides that's slave work. Let Wash and Hiram do it."

Amanda stared at the young girl. "Put your doll down and look at me, Catherine." She knelt again to look her sister in the eye and took her doll out of her hands. "It's not slave work anymore. It's work that has to be done if we are going to eat. Most of the slaves are gone, and the ones we have left are here simply because they need a place to live or want to stay and help us. If we want to eat, we shall have to work." Amanda placed the doll in the cradle that Father had carved last Christmas and stood. "So I would suggest that you come with us and help, or you're going to get awfully hungry."

Catherine poked out her lip in a pout. "Where do I have to go?"

"Come with me."

The three girls followed Amanda into the garden, Catherine lagging behind, scuffling her feet. Kitty handed them baskets. Amanda bent down and cupped Mary's chin in her hand. "Work hard and do a good job, little one." She kissed her on the cheek and quickly braided the child's dark hair in one braid down the back. "Put your bonnet on."

Mary grinned at her. "I will. This will be fun."

"Hmm. It's hard work, but I know you can do it."

Emmaline and Catherine followed Amanda into the cornfield. They worked all afternoon with a short break.

It seemed a long time before the sun slipped toward the horizon.

Amanda rose up and stretched her back, groaning. Sam bounded toward her. She gave him a pat. "Too bad you can't help us pick." She searched for Emmaline and Catherine several rows over, hidden by the tall cornstalks.

"Girls. Time to quit. It'll be dark soon."

The two sisters stood, shielded their eyes against the sun, and began to walk toward her. They dragged sacks behind them laden with the ears of corn. Emmaline smiled weakly at Amanda as she brought the sack around. "It's about half full."

Catherine's mouth still sported a pout. "The stalks hurt my hands." She stuck her hands out for Amanda to see. Red welts spotted the girl's skin, with intermittent scratches. Her bonnet hung around her shoulders, and her face was sunburned.

"Where are your gloves?"

"I don't want to wear those ugly old things."

"Suit yourself. But if you don't, you're going to have scratches and cuts all over your hands. I'd suggest you wear them tomorrow. And your bonnet as well. You are too fair to be out in this sun without protection. Look how sunburned you are."

"Tomorrow? We have to do this again tomorrow?"

Amanda started walking toward the barn and spoke over her shoulder. "Tomorrow and every day after that until we get the crop in. Come on now. Elsie probably has supper ready. Be grateful we have something to eat."

"I'll never eat another ear of corn in my whole life."

Amanda laughed and patted Catherine on the shoulder. They walked along the furrows, dragging their sacks in the early evening twilight, with Catherine lagging behind. Amanda loosened her bonnet and wiped her face with a rag. Everything felt gritty—her eyes, her skin, even her teeth. She thought she'd never worked so hard in her life as she had that one afternoon. And they had to do it again tomorrow, and the next day, and the next until they finished.

Amanda saw Wash and Hiram starting down another row. She called to them. "Quitting time. Elsie will have supper ready for us."

Wash raised his head and waved. "Be right in, Miss Amanda."

Sam romped back to Catherine and began to dart his nose in and out of a clump of cornstalks, barking incessantly. Catherine froze staring at the ground. "Mandy! Mandy!" Her voice rose in a high-pitched frenzy.

Amanda heard the ominous rattle. She shouted to her sister as she halted in her tracks and held up her hand. "Don't move, Catherine! Be very still. Let Sam keep him occupied."

The slithering, leathery gray mass of coiled rattlesnake lay immobile, except for the warning rattle and the forked tongue flitting in and out. The dog moved from left to right, nipping at the serpent. Suddenly Sam lunged at him, and the snake thrust toward his head. The dog yelped, but remained between Catherine and the snake.

Amanda lowered her voice. "Now, Catherine, back away slowly. Don't come toward me. Just back away." She looked around for Wash amid Sam's yelping and barking. "Wash! Snake! Wash!"

"I'm right here, Miss Amanda." Wash grabbed Catherine from behind and swung her away from the snake, stepping in front of her as he did. He came alongside Sam, who slunk behind the Negro. Wash held a hoe in his hand, and with one huge swing chopped the head of the disgusting reptile from its body. The rattling persisted for a few seconds, then ceased.

Amanda took Catherine by the shoulders and looked into her tearstained face. "Are you harmed? Are you all right?" She pulled the little girl into her arms. Amanda could feel the child's heart racing as she held her tight.

Catherine cried broken sobs as Amanda smoothed her blond curls. "I . . . I st-stepped on it."

"Oh, my soul. It's a wonder you didn't get bitten. You're sure he didn't bite you?" Amanda bent down and examined the girl's legs and ankles. Rising up, she wiped the tears from Catherine's cheeks with her apron. "You are fine. You're fine. Wash killed the snake. It's gone. It's all over with." Her own heart was pounding.

"Not quite, Miss Amanda." Amanda looked at Wash as he strode toward the house with Sam in his arms. "It got Sam on the nose."

"Oh, oh no. What can we do?" They fell in behind Wash as he half trotted, half ran toward the house.

Wash shook his head. "Nothin'. He will get over it, or he won't. He's a strong dog. He probably saved Miss Catherine's life by takin' the bite."

Amanda took Catherine by the hand and gave their sacks to Hiram. Emmaline followed behind as they ran for the house with the injured animal.

Wash slept with the dog in the outdoor kitchen that night. Amanda got up two or three times to look out the window at the back of the landing, where she could see Wash by the light of the lantern moving around.

She hurried downstairs at daybreak to check on them. "You already up, Wash?"

"Yes'm. When the sun rises, I wakes up. You know that."

"I do. How is he?" She knelt beside the dog, whose nose and face were swollen twice normal size, and rubbed his belly. The dog opened his slit of an eye as much as he could and his tail gave a weak wag.

"Is he going to make it?"

"I don't know. We'll have to wait and see. Should know in a

couple of days. The hardest part will be keeping him still and quiet. He feels so bad now that he's not wanting to get up—and that's good."

She sat on the bench next to the table. "Once again you've come to our rescue, Wash."

Wash shook his head and picked up a bucket. "Twasn't nothing, Miss Amanda. I needs to get the milking done."

"Why won't you ever let me thank you?"

The Negro paused at the steps. He shrugged his shoulders. "No thanks necessary. That's jes what fam . . . families do." He turned his chocolate-brown eyes toward Amanda. "I knows now that to me and my family, Mama and Kitty, Hiram and Zachary, you all truly is our family. And we don't plan on going nowhere."

"What about Zachary's education that Harriet desired so much?"

His demeanor grew somber, but he remained dry-eyed. "We'll worry 'bout that in a few years."

Amanda realized she was still in her robe, and she tightened the sash. "Yes, well, the sun's not going to stand still for us today as it did for Joshua, so I suppose we'd best get about our chores."

"Yes'm. I'll get the milking done, and then we needs to get back out in that cornfield after breakfast."

Elsie came out of the kitchen door and bustled toward the outdoor kitchen. "How's Sam?" She stopped in the doorway. "Oh, good mornin', Miss Amanda. I didn't know you's in here."

"I was checking on Sam. He's holding his own, it looks like. I'll go get the girls dressed, and we'll be down for breakfast shortly."

Wash headed for the barn, and Amanda turned toward the house as they descended the steps from the outdoor kitchen. She caught hold of Wash's sleeve and looked directly into his eyes. "Thank you. Plain and simple—thank you."

Wash nodded his head and went on his way.

The next week Amanda dumped her last sack of corn into the bin and stood back to survey the contents. It was about three quarters full. *If we can keep the Yanks out of it, perhaps we'll make it through the winter.*

Wash came around the corner with his sack and grinned. "We did it, Miss Amanda. We got it in."

"We did indeed."

He started to empty his sack into the crib.

"Wait, Wash. Let's put yours with the rest that we've hidden in your cabin under the floor."

He nodded and started out the door. "I'll see if it'll fit. It's gettin' kinda full in that crate. Where are the girls?"

"They've gone inside to get cleaned up for supper." She smiled. "They are most grateful that the corn is in, as am I. I'm tired of having corn silk all over me, and dirt and dust in my hair."

"Twasn't meant for a lady to be in the field."

"I suppose not, but sometimes the ox is in the ditch, and one has to do what is necessary to get it out—lady or no lady."

"Your momma and daddy would be proud of you, Miss Amanda. You've taken good care of your family."

"I've tried, Wash. But I . . . I can't help but think about Daniel."

"Don't torture yourself about him. Pray him home."

"Pardon me?"

"Pray him home. Pray that God make a way through the enemy lines to get home. That's the best thing we can do for him. He may be tryin' to get back here. Only God can do that."

"I know. And I have been praying. Go on now. Hide that corn."

Wash walked out of the barn toward the slave quarters. He

whistled for Sam. The dog bounded across the barn opening and followed at the Negro's side.

Amanda shook her burlap bag and laid it across a wooden railing. She walked past the stalls to Cannonade and called to him. The horse perked his ears and stuck his nose over the gate of his stall. She let herself into the stall and began to brush his neck. He nickered, turned his head, and nuzzled her shoulder. She chuckled. "You like that, don't you?"

Amanda heard a noise and looked down the aisle of the barn toward the door. The figure of a tall thin soldier blocked the entrance. The sun at his back hid his face. Yankee or Confederate? Her heart banged against her chest as she slowly put the brush down. She moved from the stall to the center of the barn. "What do you want?" Her voice sounded loud—and braver than she felt—in the quiet of the barn.

Cannonade whinnied and pawed at the straw on the floor of his stall.

"I said, what do you want? You have taken nearly all our livestock and food. There's nothing left to pilfer." She picked up a pitchfork leaning against the wall. She could now see that the man had only a stump for his left arm. She raised the pitchfork and walked toward him. "Get out of here! Take your filthy Yankee self and leave us alone."

The soldier put up his good hand. "That's a fine way to treat a returning Confederate soldier—especially when he's your brother."

CHAPTER NINETEEN

AUGUST 1864

> When Johnny comes marching home again,
> Hurrah! Hurrah!
> We'll give him a hearty welcome then,
> Hurrah! Hurrah!
> The men will cheer, the boys will shout,
> The ladies they will all turn out,
> And we'll all feel gay
> When Johnny comes marching home.
>
> PATRICK SARSFIELD GILMORE,
> "WHEN JOHNNY COMES MARCHING HOME"

Amanda gasped and dropped the pitchfork. "Daniel! Oh, Daniel!" She ran with open arms toward the gaunt figure. She flung herself into his one-armed embrace, weeping and laughing at the same time. "You're home. Thank God, you're home." Stepping back to look at him, she caressed his scraggly beard. "You're so thin. Oh, my soul, I'm so happy you're home." She looked behind him. "How did you . . . ? Where . . . ?"

"I walked. All the way from Georgia, I walked. Got my horse shot out from under me. Lost my arm." He held up his stub and grinned. "But I lived to tell about it. That's more than most of my buddies. When I got well enough to stand, I walked out of the hospital and headed home. Wasn't any good to the army anymore. Couldn't fight, so I simply came home." He scratched his chin. "I'm sure I don't look fit to be talking to a lady."

"Daniel! Look at me. I've been working in the fields picking corn. I'm the one not fit to be receiving a gentleman." She mocked a curtsy.

His eyes clouded over. "Working in the fields?"

She flicked her wrist. "Never you mind. Come, come. Let's find the rest of the family. Wash! It's Daniel. Daniel's home!"

He caught her by the arm. "Wait a minute. Let me say hello to Cannonade first."

Daniel shoved his cap back on his head, his long dark hair almost touching his shoulders. He walked slowly toward the horse that he had left behind. The horse blinked at his master, and it seemed as if he were waiting for Daniel to explain where he'd been. The brother she thought she'd never see again held out his hand. Cannonade nickered and bobbed his head. Daniel buried his face in Cannonade's mane. "I missed you. I'm sorry I had to send you back, but if I hadn't . . . I mean they gave me a mighty fine horse to ride, but no horse can replace you, boy." The horse nickered again. "However, I'm home, a little the worse for wear, but I'm back, and we're together again." He gave the animal a pat on his neck, then he turned toward Amanda as Wash came running from his cabin with a barking Sam at his heels.

Elsie and Kitty, hearing the commotion from the outdoor kitchen, hurried toward the barn with Zachary in tow.

Wash entered the barn and stopped in his tracks. "Master Daniel! Welcome home, suh. Welcome home. We sho have missed you." Wash removed his hat and crumpled it in his hands in his excitement.

Daniel stretched out his hand toward his old friend.

Hesitating at first, Wash grabbed Daniel's extended hand, and the two shook hands vigorously, grinning at each other. For a brief moment Amanda caught a glimpse of the two boys they once were, playing together in this very barn.

Sam danced around Daniel, jumping on him, his tail wagging his whole body.

"Hey there, boy. I see you haven't forgotten me."

Elsie took her apron and wiped her eyes. "My goodness, son, you a sight for sore eyes. You sho are." She spotted the swinging empty sleeve and held the corner of her apron over her mouth. "Oh, my. Oh, Lawd, have mercy."

Daniel encompassed the round figure of his former nanny in his good arm. "It's fine, Elsie. Pay it no mind. I've learned to compensate pretty well. I'm lucky to be alive."

"Yessuh, you sho are. And we's lucky to have you back." She turned to go back to the kitchen, muttering to herself and wiping her nose. "Yessuh. Mighty blessed. I'll jes get dinner goin'."

"Look at this big boy." Daniel knelt in front of Zachary and chucked him beneath the chin. He nodded to Kitty as he stood to the side. "Wash, my heart was grieved to hear about Harriet. I . . . I've seen so much death, I'm sick at heart with it."

Wash nodded slowly and raised his eyes skyward. "Yessuh. I know. The Lord giveth and the Lord taketh away. Blessed be the name of the Lord." He straightened his hat and set it on his head. "Do you need help with anything, Masta Daniel?" He looked at the knapsack Daniel had dropped on the sawdust floor of the barn. He reached for it, but Daniel stopped him.

"This is all I have, and I can manage it, thank you." His voice assumed a curt, firm tone. He looked at Amanda and Wash and

Kitty, his jaw set. "We might as well get used to the fact that I only have one arm now. I don't need to be coddled, nor do I need help with most things. I've learned tricks to get done what I need to do. So we'll move on with our lives." He lifted the knapsack with his good arm and slung it over his shoulder.

Wash shifted his weight. "Yessuh. I didn't mean no harm."

"No harm done, Wash. We simply need to understand each other." He adjusted his hat. "Things are not as they used to be."

"Yessuh. I needs to get back to work." Wash took Zachary from Kitty, and they started toward the house, leaving Daniel and Amanda in front of the barn.

Daniel pointed to the shutters that were listing to one side on the second story. "Looks like you could use some help around here. How many of our slaves are still around?"

Amanda took his arm—his good right arm—as they walked to the house. "A handful. About half of them were conscripted into the labor force for the Confederacy, and half of those remaining deserted us. It was hard enough to keep Bellevue running before Father died, but after that . . ." She shrugged her shoulders. "After that we've barely been able to hold on and keep food on the table." Smiling up at him, she opened the kitchen door. "But now that you're home, we'll be doing much better—back to the way it used to be, before the war."

Daniel shook his head. "It will never be the way it was before the war, Mandy. Our way of life is over. There has been too much bloodshed and death. The earth itself grieves for its fathers and sons. If this war doesn't end soon, none of the plantations will survive. The country may not survive. Why couldn't President Lincoln have simply let us choose how we wanted to live here in the South?"

His voice took on a tone that Amanda had never heard before. Gone was the boyish exuberance of his youth. He had become a man—not a normal maturation, but by the unspeakable horrors of war he had seen and participated in prematurely. She turned as he spoke and observed lines of disillusionment etched into his face.

They walked through the kitchen and dining room and started up the stairs as Amanda called out to the girls. Emmaline came out of her room onto the landing, with Catherine and Mary close behind. They still had on their plain dresses, dirty from the dust in the field. Emmaline let out a squeal and ran down the stairs into Daniel's embrace.

"My stars, who is this young woman? It cannot be Emmaline. Emmaline was a little girl when I left."

"It's me, Daniel. Don't you recognize me?"

"Why, sure enough. I can tell by the eyes." He laughed and tousled her hair as they reached the landing. "And, Catherine, you're all grown up as well." He pulled her to him, hugging her around the shoulders.

"We're dirty. We've been picking corn all day."

Daniel shot Amanda a sharp look, but didn't comment. He set his knapsack against the banister. "You look beautiful to me." He playfully tugged on one of her braids.

Mary stood back chewing the nail on one of her fingers, staring at his arm. Amanda swatted at the child. "Stop that, Mary. Your hands are filthy."

Daniel bent down. "You're wondering what happened?"

Mary nodded.

"It's simple. I got in the way of a bullet, and they had to amputate . . . take my arm off or I would have died from the infection. You were so little when I left—do you even remember me at all?"

Mary spoke softly. "I remember you." She stared for a moment longer then leapt into his arms, wrapping her legs around his waist. "I remember I used to do this all the time."

"And then I would swing you around like this . . ." Daniel

swung her in circles holding her tightly with his good arm. He set her down and gave her a peck on the cheek like he had always done.

Amanda took a deep breath. "Well, this calls for a celebration. Let's all of us get cleaned up. I'll have Elsie fix the ham we've kept hidden away from those blasted Yankees. We've just picked beans and tomatoes out of the garden. Daniel, your room is as you left it, except for some blankets that the Blue Bellies helped themselves to. But we certainly don't need them in this heat."

Daniel looked at his family. "You cannot imagine how good it is to be home."

Amanda shooed the girls into their room. "I'll have Hiram bring up hot water so you can take a bath and shave. Your clothes are in the wardrobe. I'll get your boots. I hid them." She grinned at him as he turned to go to his room. "Wasn't about to let the Yankees take everything. I prayed you'd be home."

The corners of Daniel's mouth turned down as they always did when he tried not to cry as a little boy. "There were times when I didn't think I would be." His chin stiffened. "But . . . well, I'm home now." He started down the hall to his room then turned back to Amanda. "Do you hear anything from that Yankee captain who used to come around before the war? What was his name? Littlefield?"

Amanda cleared her throat. "There's much I need to tell you in this regard . . . and it's Major Littlefield now."

Daniel raised his eyebrows. "So you have heard from him?"

"Yes, but not for a long time. His letters came sporadically, then stopped. After the Red River campaign when the Yanks tried to move into Texas through Shreveport . . . well, I've not heard anything." She sniffled. "I don't know that I would be notified if . . . if . . ."

"Notified? Why should the officials notify you concerning Littlefield?"

Amanda bit her lip to keep her chin from quivering. "As I said, I have much to tell you. Kent told me he would come for me after the war, and I told him I would wait for him. But now it's been so long that I fear the worst."

"This is no good. Believe me, Mandy, it's just as well. Those Yankee dogs have no compassion. They're cruel and heartless and are destroying the South. It never would have worked out for you two."

"Kent's not like that."

"They're all like that in war. Trust me. Forget him."

"What about Claire? Does she know you're back? Have you seen her?"

"You let me worry about Claire." He turned his back on her and closed the door to his room.

⚜

Amanda awoke the next morning to the pounding of hammers. "What in the world?" She tied her robe around her and opened the door from Father's old room, which she had taken after his death. She made a mental note to ask Daniel if he would like to have it now.

The hammering came from the window at the end of the landing. She walked toward the sitting area, pushed aside the parlor palms, and looked out. Wash teetered on the top rung of a ladder, hammering the shutter in place. He tipped his hat to her and grinned, then pointed down at Daniel at the bottom of the ladder holding it steady.

She opened the window and stuck her head out. "What are you two doing this hour of the morning? It's barely daylight."

Daniel looked up at his sister. "It appears there's much to do around here. Better get busy."

"I suppose I should be grateful that it's not you, Daniel, on the top of this ladder."

Wash finished his hammering and started down the ladder. "Yes'm. He tried, but I thought it'd best be me to risk my neck up here. Masta Daniel done enough riskin' of his neck."

"Thank you, Wash. Go ahead and get the milking done now." She leaned over the windowsill. "I'll see you inside for breakfast, young man."

"Young man! Uh-oh, I'm in trouble now."

Wash pulled the ladder away from the side of the house. "Yessuh! You in trouble now. Been home less than a day, and you already in trouble." He shook his head, laughing to himself as he walked to the barn.

Amanda swiftly dressed herself in a clean day dress and checked on her sisters before going downstairs. *I'll let them sleep. They've worked so hard the past few days.* She tied her hair back with a ribbon. Even though it would only be for a few hours, she wanted to feel like a lady today instead of a field hand. What was left of their family was all together, and she wanted to snuggle in and revel in that fact.

Daniel sat in Father's chair at the end of the dining room table sorting papers. His hair had grown darker, and since he shaved his beard last night, leaving only a moustache and goatee, he looked so much like his father.

She sat in her regular place. "You remind me of Father sitting there."

Daniel looked up and leaned back. "I guess I hadn't really grieved his passing. The death that surrounded me in the field demanded my focus." He took a deep breath and shook his head. "I expect him to walk around the corner any minute with that ridiculous top hat on and tell me to sit up straight."

Amanda smiled. "I know. I do too. Sometimes I cannot believe he's gone, and then the terrible vacuum left by his passing overwhelms me almost to the point of panic." Tears brimmed on the edge of her eyelids. "I feared for our lives and that we wouldn't have enough to eat." The emotions that she had buried for months began to surface in spite of herself. She rose and pushed her chair back. "I . . . I'm sorry . . ."

She started to leave, but Daniel caught hold of her arm and stood. He gathered her to his chest. "Go ahead and cry, Amanda. You've held it in too long."

"B . . . but what you've gone through is much worse. I should be bra . . . a . . . a . . . ver . . ." Her words were cut off in a choking sob, and she clung to her brother, dissolving in tears.

Daniel let himself cry with her as the two siblings released their grief and sorrow.

Amanda cried until she had no more tears, then she looked at Daniel. She reached up and blotted his tears away with her napkin. "What do we do now? How do we go on?"

Daniel released her, and they sat down at the table. "We do the best we can with what we have. We resist any enemy troops that come our way by outsmarting them."

Elsie stood at the door with their breakfast, her head lowered, waiting.

Amanda motioned to her. "Come on in, Elsie. We're ready to eat."

"I don't have no coffee, Miss Amanda, but we has some chicory. It's not too bad. The Yankees took most of our chickens, Masta Daniel, but some have wandered back from the woods. Kitty found eggs in the barn."

"Anything you fix will taste wonderful to me, Elsie." Daniel put his napkin in his lap.

"Wash fetched some shrimp and crawfish from the bay. I'll be fixin' gumbo for dinner."

Daniel leaned his head back. "Ahhh, how I've hungered for some of your good seafood gumbo. Thank you, Elsie."

The old servant doted on her returned master, shoving breakfast cornbread, leftover ham from last night's dinner, and eggs in front of him until he pushed back from the table. "Stop, Elsie. I'm stuffed. You're going to spoil me."

She laughed and fanned herself with her apron. "Dat's my job, Masta Daniel."

"Not anymore, Elsie." His mouth flattened into a thin line. "Not if President Lincoln has his way and frees your people."

"Miss Amanda and us done had this conversation. Me and my family . . . Kitty, Wash, and Hiram . . . we ain't going nowhere. This has been our home—the only home we ever knowd. Y'all treated us well. We gots work; we gots a roof over our heads; we gots food in our stomachs. Why would we run North? I guess jes knowin' that we could leave if we wanted to . . . but we don't wants to. We wants to stay here with you."

Daniel nodded. "I wish some of those Billy Yanks would talk to folks like you. Not all of us in the South abused our slaves."

"Yessuh." Elsie picked up the dirty plates and went into the kitchen.

Amanda fidgeted with her fork. "But they are owned by another human being, Daniel. Nobody should be owned by another human being."

Daniel narrowed his eyes. "Are you an abolitionist now? Have your feelings for Littlefield caused you to become a traitor to your own people?"

Amanda looked down at her hands, her trip to Austin invading her thoughts. "If you only knew . . . I don't know which side is right anymore. I just want the war to be over. I don't want any further division in our families or our country. I want our family to resume our lives. It doesn't have to be just like it was before the war, but I want us together—you and Claire, and me and the girls. Maybe we can't have a farm any longer, but we have the house and our garden. We can manage, can't we? Can't we, Daniel?" She reached up for his good hand.

He grabbed hold of it. "What about Littlefield? Are you truly in love with . . . that Yankee officer?"

"So much has happened, Daniel. I don't know if he still cares for me. Yes, I am in love with Kent Littlefield, but I've not heard from him for months."

Daniel let go. "Forgive me, Amanda, but you'll be fortunate if you never hear from him again. It will be better for everyone concerned." He stood and walked toward the kitchen door. "I have work to do. Could you help me whitewash the fence?"

Amanda stood. "Of course, but we'll need more lime to mix up a batch. I need to go to the post office anyway, so I'll go to the store as well. Do you have any money?"

Daniel shook his head. "I ran out of what little I had by the time I reached Louisiana."

"Maybe we can gather eggs to barter with Mister Randle at the store. We have not been able to gather in enough of a crop to sell. What we've harvested we've kept as food, but we've been getting more eggs the last couple of weeks. We are going to need money eventually. What are we going to do about that?"

"I don't know, but we'll figure something out."

"Daniel?"

Her brother stopped with his hand on the swinging door and faced her.

"Don't you want to go and see Claire? She is frantic with worry about you."

"Not yet." His eyes darkened. "I can't. Maybe in a few days, but not yet." He touched his stump. "I don't want . . . I don't know . . . whether she'll . . ."

"What do you mean? The fact that you lost an arm will make no difference to her. She loves you. She's waited all this time, and . . . you cannot do this."

"Give me a few days. I'll go see her in . . . in due time." He started through the door, then stopped and turned back around. "Promise me that you won't tell her before I'm ready."

Amanda didn't answer.

"Mandy? Promise me?"

Amanda nodded. "I don't agree with you, but I'll wait until you're ready."

Wash drove her to the store first. Mister Randle agreed to give her lime in exchange for what eggs she had. Wash carried it to the buggy. "Wait here, Wash. I'll just run across the street to the post office."

Before he could object, she dodged a wagon driven by a Union soldier, picked up her skirts, and ran across the street to the post office. The door creaked as she pushed it open. The interior of the office still retained the coolness of early morning. She walked to the wall of mailboxes and stood in front of it motionless. She raised her hand and opened the family's box. A letter rested inside, which she removed with a hand that seemed detached from her body. It shook as she recognized the familiar handwriting.

After all these months, a letter from Kent.

CHAPTER TWENTY

> *Yes, they starved in pens, and prisons,*
> *Helpless, friendless and alone!*
> *And their woe can ne'er be spoken,*
> *Nor their agony be known.*
>
> GEORGE F. ROOT,
> "STARVED IN PRISON"

Amanda caught hold of the side of the door as she stepped onto the wooden sidewalk, blinking in the bright sunlight. She tore the letter open and began to read, oblivious to the men and women maneuvering around her: *May 1864* . . . Over three months ago.

My dearest Amanda,

I have no perception as to whether the Confederates will allow this letter to reach you or dispose of it. And I am equally wondering if you still care for me as before. I've not received letters from you for so very long, but that's to be expected in my present circumstances. Unfortunately I have been taken prisoner and am incarcerated at Camp Ford near Tyler, Texas.

She gasped and stared at the script. That's why she hadn't heard from him. Her beloved had been imprisoned in a Confederate prison—and not just any prison. He was being held in the one named after her uncle. Oh, what a mocking twist of events. She read on, dreading what she might find.

I am faring as well as can be expected, I suppose. My leg continues to pain me, but I've no doubt that as soon as this war ends, and I can rest well and receive adequate medical treatment, I'll be as good as new. The stockade is surrounded by pine and oak trees, which offer relief from the hot summer sun, and on the south side of the camp a hill rises abruptly with a small stream at its base. That spring flows through the stockade—a true blessing.

The commandant of the prison, Colonel R.P.T. Allen, is a West Point graduate and seems to be a man of character and integrity. I did not know him at the academy—he is a few years older than I. His wife is very compassionate toward the prisoners and can be seen bringing sundry niceties, wrapped in napkins, for the injured and infirm.

An interesting side note—on Sabbath days we are allowed to gather to hear our chaplain preach and pray. Mrs. Allen always comes and sits among us, listening to the Word and singing hymns with the prisoners. She seems to see no difference in the Lord between a Johnny Reb and a Blue-Bellied Yankee.

I got off to a rough start just the second day here when I was accused of aiding a couple of officers, my bunkmates, in their escape attempt. The Rebs thought I'd brought in escape plans and set up the whole affair. I had no knowledge whatsoever of their intentions. I was thrown in a cell for a few days as punishment, but they eventually decided that I had not contributed to

the escape and released me. One of the lieutenants got away, and one was captured and returned. He———————————————
——————————————————————————————.

Several lines were marked through. The letter had been censored. She continued.

I know that although I am back in Texas, I am a long way from the coast, but my heart yearns to see you. We are allowed visitors. Do you think you could possibly come? A visit from you would allow me to continue with heartened courage. And if you could bring some blankets and socks, they would be much appreciated. I'm aware that asking you to come this distance is monumental. The facilities have become incredibly crowded since the Red River Campaign, where the Confederate army effectively turned back our advance.

She scoffed to herself. The censors let news of the defeat of the Yankees get through.

Some of the men do not even have shelter and are sleeping out in the open on the ground. Disease and vermin are the bane of our existence. The lice and mosquitoes drive us to distraction. Many are sick with dysentery and typhoid. I am fortunate that, as an officer, I occupy, along with four other men, a small log structure called a shebang. When I first arrived there were only three of us in the shebang, but with the crowded conditions they put two more in with us. Three of us have beds and two sleep on the ground. We take turns sharing the beds. Those sleeping on the ground fight rats and mud when it rains.

She stuffed the letter into her bag and ran across the street to her buggy. She clambered in as Wash assisted her.

"You ready to go home, Miss Amanda?"

"Yes, Wash. Let's go home."

The realization that the information she had taken to her uncle had not only resulted in turning the Union back from Texas, but also in Kent's imprisonment, took her breath away. What had she done? Her stomach churned, and she swallowed hard to keep the bile down that threatened to erupt from her throat. She was responsible for her beloved's being held as prisoner of war. She held her handkerchief to her eyes as the tears started. Her hands shook as she let the tears flow. She could feel the familiar mottling creeping up her neck onto her cheeks. How she hated that telltale trait.

Before Wash was able to mount the driver's perch, she heard a familiar voice. "Amanda?"

Amanda looked up, startled, to see Claire peering into the cab. "I thought that was you. Have you received bad news?" Her voice broke.

"No, well, yes. I mean . . . Kent's alive. I . . . I hadn't heard from him in so very long that I feared he had been killed. Or had forgotten me. But, oh, Claire, he's been captured. He's in prison here in Texas at Camp Ford."

Claire's hand fluttered to her cheek as she exhaled a long breath. "Thank God he's alive. Is he . . . has he been wounded? How does he fare?"

"As well as can be expected, I suppose. He didn't mention that he'd been wounded again. There are only three beds to five men in his cabin, and there're lice and all kinds of horrible things. I can hardly bear to think of him suffering so."

"At least you know he's alive." Claire looked down and shook her head. "I've not heard from Daniel since he was reported as missing."

Her eyes reddened and she fought to maintain her composure. "I don't know if he's dead or alive. Or out there wounded somewhere and unable to get home. Or perhaps unconscious in some Yankee hospital." She sniffled. "Oh, Amanda, sometimes I think I cannot stand this anymore."

"Claire, get in the buggy with me."

"No, thank you. I was just on my way to Hettie's house for the Ladies' Society meeting when I saw you."

"Oh, I completely forgot about that today." She leaned out of the buggy and grasped Claire's hand. "I need you to get in here for a moment. I have something I need to tell you."

"Very well, just for a moment." Claire climbed in and sat next to Amanda.

Turning to Claire, Amanda took both of her hands. "Claire, Daniel's well."

Claire's hand flew to her mouth. "You've heard from him?"

Amanda smiled. "You could say that."

"Is he well? Where is he? Why was he reported as missing?"

"He is well. He was reported as missing because he was wounded, and they didn't know who he was for a while."

"Did you get a letter from him? Let me read it. Please, Amanda, let me read it." Claire glanced around the buggy. "What's that—paint?"

"I need to get home."

"Why won't you let me read the letter? And why did you buy paint?"

"There is no letter from Daniel. And our fence needs painting."

"So does everybody's in town, but no one has enough help to be painting these days. Amanda, if there's no letter from Daniel, how did you know . . . ? Is . . . oh, could it possibly be? Has Daniel come home? Is he here?"

Amanda stared at the anticipation and dread in her friend's eyes, and she could not bear to deceive her. She wove her handkerchief back and forth between her fingers and felt beads of perspiration on her upper lip. She dabbed it with the hankie. "He's home, Claire. He walked all the way from Georgia, but he's home. He's alive."

"He's home? He's here in Indianola? Oh, thank you, Lord. Our prayers have been answered." She clasped her hands in front of her, and smiled at Amanda through a veil of tears. "When? When did he get home?"

"Just last evening."

Claire hugged Amanda. "I'll get my driver and follow you out to Bellevue." Claire started to disembark from the buggy.

"Wait a minute, Claire. Sit back down. There's something you need to know first."

Claire resumed her seat, her eyes searching Amanda's. "What is it? Is something wrong?"

Amanda nodded her head. "No, but—"

"But what? What are you keeping from me?"

"Claire, he was wounded. He lost an arm."

"Oh, oh, no." Claire covered her mouth with her fist.

"He is completely healed from it, physically anyway, but he's not ready to see you yet. I think he's afraid you won't want him with only one arm."

"Won't want him? How ridiculous. I *love* him, Amanda. I don't want to live without him. It doesn't matter to me if he has only one arm, I'm just glad he's alive. I want to marry him." She fell into Amanda's arms. "Oh, Amanda, I must go to him. I must see him."

Amanda patted her friend on the back as she cried. "I don't know if he will see you right now, Claire."

"How can he do this to me?" She pulled away from Amanda's

embrace. "I'm going out to Bellevue. He's going to see me whether he wants to or not. I will not allow him to do this to us." Her dark eyes flashed with anger and determination.

"I promised Daniel I would not tell you that he was home. He's going to be very angry with me." She hesitated. "He's changed, Claire. There's still the same smile and eyes, and teasing nature, but with a hard edge. He seems bitter. I suppose that's to be expected after having been at war for over three years, and all the evil and death he's seen firsthand."

"I don't care. I know he must be changed, but I want to share his burden." Her voice tightened with emotion. "Please, Amanda. Don't keep me away from him. He needs me."

"I agree. Let me prepare him. I'll tell him exactly what happened—that you saw me and guessed, and that you are coming out later this afternoon. I'll tell him you wouldn't take no for an answer." Amanda smiled. "And that's the truth. Better still, bring your mother and come out for supper, after he's had a chance to finish work for the day and clean up. He won't turn both you and your mother away." Amanda squeezed Claire's hand as her friend exited the buggy. "Don't worry. We'll get through this."

Daniel was going to be furious. But in spite of her apprehension at confronting him, Amanda was excited. For the time being her angst over Kent's situation was overshadowed by the elation of her brother's homecoming and the reunion of the two lovers. She just had to convince Daniel that this was for the best.

Wash drove directly to the barn. Hiram walked up with firewood in his arms.

Amanda exited the buggy and tugged on the paint can. "Where's Daniel, Hiram?"

"Mista Daniel?" Hiram grinned a toothy smile at her. "He

working on the fence. He say as soon as you get back to bring that paint to him." The young boy balanced the wood in the crook of one arm and pointed. Amanda saw her brother kneeling in front of the gate.

"Ah, I didn't see him when we came around."

"I'll get that, Miss Amanda." Wash tied the horse to the hitching rail. "Then I'll come back and take care of the horse."

"Go ahead and take the buggy into the barn and get some brushes while you're in there, please. Take it all to Daniel. I'll go change, and then I'll start painting."

"Yes'm." Wash turned to put up the horse, grumbling. "Jes don't seem fittin' for you to be paintin' and workin' in the fields. Jes don't seem fittin.' "

"Oh, my soul, Wash. You're as bad as your mother. These are not 'fittin' times. They are 'unfittin' times, and we all have to do what needs to be done. Now go on."

"Yes'm." He walked away, shaking his head, as Amanda went into the house.

She changed quickly and braided her long hair, twisted it into a knot at the back. Plopping on a wide-brimmed sun hat, she headed out the front door. Wash had already delivered the whitewash and brushes, and Daniel was opening the can.

He stood and wiped his forehead with his sleeve as she rushed up.

"What took you so long? It's nearly time for dinner."

"I got a letter from Kent."

"And . . . ?"

"He's been captured and is in a prisoner of war camp in Tyler."

"Camp Ford? I hear the conditions are bad there since the Red River Campaign. He'll be lucky to get out alive." Daniel knelt and began stirring the whitewash. He shielded his eyes and squinted in the sun at his sister. "Forget him, Mandy. Don't open yourself up for more heartache."

"Is that what you're doing as far as Claire is concerned? Thinking that you are protecting you both from heartache?"

Daniel stood, his mouth downturned. "That's none of your concern. I'll handle my own personal affairs."

"No, it *is* my concern. You're my younger brother, whom I have helped to raise. I promised Mama I would look after you, and I intend to continue to do that, although you are now a grown man and quite capable." She smiled up at him and touched his arm. "But, Daniel, you are wrong on this point. Claire loves you, loves you deeply—has loved you since we all were children. She loves your character and your integrity. She loves your sense of humor. She loves everything about you. Whether you have two arms, one arm, or no arms, she still loves you and wants to marry you. You mustn't shut her out."

Daniel's eyes clouded over. "I cannot ask her to saddle herself to a cripple for the rest of her life."

"You don't have to ask her. She's already made her choice. Before you left, she made her decision to wait for you and to be faithful to you, knowing what the future might hold. Don't make her decisions for her."

"How can I support her, a family?"

Amanda shrugged her shoulders. "By working. We'll all work together and do whatever we have to do to survive."

Daniel blew his nose on a bandana he pulled from his pocket. "I'll think about it. Right now we've work to do." He handed her a paintbrush. "I hate our place looking so run-down."

"I do too." She dipped the brush into the whitewash.

They worked a few moments in silence.

"You'd best do your thinking quickly."

He frowned at her. "What do you mean?"

Amanda didn't look up at him. "I mean that you need to get your thinking done before supper tonight."

"Before . . . before supper? What does that matter?" He grabbed her arm and turned her toward him. "Amanda, what have you done?"

She looked down at his hand gripping her arm and tried to pull away from him, but he kept her in a viselike grasp. "Daniel, you're hurting me."

He let her go and shook his head. "I'm sorry. I'm sorry, Mandy. You see? I'm not fit for a lady's company yet. I need some time."

"I can see that you're going to need some time to adjust to being a civilian again. That's to be expected. But don't shut out the ones who love you while you are making that adjustment."

Daniel threw his paintbrush down on the ground and walked toward the front door.

"Daniel!"

"Leave me be." He went into the house and closed the front door.

Hiram came out to help Amanda, apparently sent by Daniel, and they painted until Elsie rang the bell for dinner. The family exchanged small talk in the outdoor kitchen. Elsie clucked over Daniel, and the young Belle sisters bantered back and forth.

But Daniel avoided Amanda's eyes. He grabbed his hat and left the meal quickly. "I want to check the back property to see what we have left in the way of crops. Wash, what about our cattle?"

"Mostly gone. The Union army slaughtered most of 'em for their men. We have to go into town and get a permit for some of our own beef."

Daniel swore and shoved his plate back.

Amanda glared at him. The little sisters' conversation ceased all at once as they also stared.

He swung his legs over the bench and stood. "I'm taking Wash with me. Amanda, you and Hiram get as far as you can on the fence before it gets dark. Please forgive my language." He strode down the steps toward the barn.

Amanda called after him. "Supper at seven o'clock, Daniel. Be on time and be dressed."

He ignored her.

"Daniel! Did you hear me?"

He flicked his hand. "I heard you."

"Elsie, we'll eat in the dining room tonight. We're entertaining guests—Claire and her mother are coming for supper."

CHAPTER TWENTY-ONE

> *The soldier lad I love the best*
> *Shall have my heart and hand.*
>
> CARRIE BELLE SINCLAIR,
> "THE HOMESPUN DRESS"

The candles flickered brightly from the silver candelabra Elsie had retrieved from hiding and placed on the dark polished table. Amanda swept into the dining room, having changed into a dinner dress that she wore only on special occasions—and those special occasions had occurred very rarely during the war.

Dressed in her formal maid's uniform, Elsie came through the swinging door with a platter of onions, tomatoes, and oysters on the shell.

"Elsie, you are a genius. I don't know how you always manage to come up with something." Amanda took the platter and set it on the table. "What's for supper?"

"All's I gots fixin's for is shrimp and crayfish for gumbo again. We still has okra from the garden and rice. That'll jes have to do."

"It'll be fine. Daniel loves it."

The old servant chuckled. "I made a chess pie. I scraped up enough flour for Masta Daniel's homecoming."

"You know how he loves your chess pie."

"Yes'm, but Masta Daniel don't sound too happy 'bout our dinner guests."

"He'll be fine once they get here."

"I hopes so. I sho hopes so." She bustled through the swinging door into the kitchen.

Amanda went to the bottom of the staircase. "Emmaline! You all come on down. Our guests will be here momentarily."

The door knocker sounded softly. Kitty, also dressed in a black dress and white apron, answered the door. "Good evening, Mistress Claire, Mrs. Beecham."

Claire handed her light wrap and gloves to Kitty and went straight to Amanda as her mother removed her gloves as well.

Amanda embraced her friend. "You look beautiful tonight, Claire."

"It's Daniel's favorite dress."

"You're trembling."

"I'm excited. I'm nervous. Is Daniel . . . ?"

Amanda turned to Claire's mother. "Good evening, Mrs. Beecham. I'm so delighted you could come on such short notice." She cupped Claire's mother's elbow in her hand and ushered the two women into the parlor. "Daniel will be down in a moment. Let's wait for him in the parlor."

Amanda showed Claire and her mother to the larger sofa, and she sat in a wingback chair across from them.

"Something smells wonderful." Mrs. Beecham took out her fan and flitted it nervously in front of her face.

"Yes, Elsie made gumbo."

"I thought I smelled something sweet—like pie or cake."

"She managed one of her chess pies."

"Hmm." Mrs. Beecham nodded.

Claire remained silent, wadding her handkerchief in her fist.

The ticking of the clock marked the passing of minute after minute. Footsteps sounded on the stairs, and the three younger Belle sisters burst into the room.

"Girls. Mind your manners."

All three sisters curtsied, and then sat on a small sofa.

"Go on into the kitchen, girls. You may eat in there this evening."

Mary and Catherine jumped up and ran through the dining room. Emmaline lingered behind. "May I eat with the adults tonight?"

Amanda smiled at her. "Not tonight, sweet pea."

"But . . . but I'm almost an adult."

"I know, but I need you to take charge of Mary and Catherine this evening."

"Ma-a-a-ndy." Her voice moved up and down in a sliding whine.

"Now *that* is not grown up."

"Yes, ma'am." The girl disappeared into the dining room, and the swinging door banged as she went into the kitchen.

Seven o'clock came and went, and Daniel did not appear.

Claire stood. "Perhaps this was not such a good idea. Maybe I should give him more time."

"No, wait here. I'll go check on him."

Amanda went up the stairs to his room. She rapped on his closed door.

"I'm not coming down."

She tried the door knob. It was not locked. Cracking open the door, she saw her brother sitting on the edge of the bed, half dressed with a shoe in his good hand. He looked up as she eased into the room and set the shoe down.

"I've learned how to compensate and get my military boots off and on, but these dress shoes . . . I can't tie them." He looked at her with eyes that reflected his pain. "Mandy, I can't even put on my own shoes. How can I expect to support a family?" He dropped the shoe on the floor and leaned over with his one elbow on his knee. "Tell Claire to go home. This is not going to work."

"Oh, yes, it will work. I cannot believe you are giving up this easily. Either put on your military boots . . ." She looked at the worn and muddy boots standing in the corner. They were not fit to wear for dinner. "Wait here. Papa had some dress shoes with buckles. I'll get those."

Amanda went out the door and ran to Father's room, which she now occupied. She threw open the doors of the wardrobe and fished out a pair of black shoes with buckles. Dusting them off with her sleeve, she took them to Daniel and set them on the floor in front of him. "Now, see if you can manage those."

He shook his head. "No. I told you I'm not joining you for dinner. Tell Claire to go home."

"I'm not leaving, Daniel." Claire stood in the open doorway.

"Claire." Daniel stood, his suspenders hanging loose from his pants. "I'm not . . . not presentable." He pulled the suspenders around his shoulders, the empty shirt sleeve swinging. He looked at his childhood sweetheart. "The truth is I'll never be presentable ever again."

Claire walked toward him. "Who says? You look wonderful to me, Daniel." A sob stopped her as she covered her mouth with her hand.

He turned his back on her. "Please go, Claire. I . . . I can't. I can't work like a normal man. I don't know how I would support our family." He turned and faced her. "What kind of father could I be to our children?"

She reached up and stroked his beard with the tips of her slender fingers. "I'll tell you what kind of father you would be. You would be the kindest, gentlest, most devoted father of any man I know. We will support our family, and we'll do it together."

Daniel hung his head. "You do not want to spend the rest of your life with half a man."

"Who's half a man?" She looked around the room. "I don't see half a man, do you, Amanda?"

Amanda smiled and shook her head.

Claire took Daniel's face in her hands. "You are the only man I've ever loved, ever wanted. We'll do this together, Daniel. Don't turn me away."

Daniel embraced Claire with his good arm and drew her to him. She turned her face toward him, and he covered her cheeks with kisses.

Claire took his hand in hers. "Here, sit down, Daniel."

He sat down on the bed, and Claire knelt in front of him. She picked up the shoe and put it on his foot, and they buckled it together. Tears flowed down Daniel's face as his shoulders heaved.

Amanda backed out of the room. She went downstairs and entered the parlor, where Claire's mother stood at the window.

"Where's Claire?"

"Upstairs with Daniel."

"Oh, oh, my. That's not proper. Not acceptable at all." She started for the staircase.

"Come now, Mrs. Beecham. Let's give them some privacy. It might not have been acceptable before the war, but you would agree that times have certainly changed, wouldn't you?"

"Well, yes, but . . ."

"They need just a few minutes for Daniel to get dressed."

Mrs. Beecham gasped and her hand fluttered to her face.

Amanda shook her head and ushered the widow into the dining room. "I mean, he's dressed, he was simply having trouble with his shoes. They'll be down shortly."

Daniel and Claire came into the dining room arm in arm after a few minutes, smiling at each other. They seemed unable to take their eyes off of one another. Claire's dark ringlets framed her face. The pink dress she had chosen for that evening accentuated her blushing cheeks. She fairly glowed.

Daniel sat at one end of the table in Father's former place, with Amanda at the other end. Claire and her mother sat on the sides facing one another. Daniel ate heartily, but Claire barely dabbled at her food. She touched Daniel's arm from time to time and patted him. Daniel gazed into her eyes and kissed her fingers over and over.

He pushed his chair back after dinner and stood. Looking at Claire, he smiled. "We have an announcement to make."

Amanda and Mrs. Beecham waited.

"Claire and I are to be married."

Squeals and giggles burst through the swinging door at the precise moment that the Belle sisters burst through. Mary jumped up and down and threw herself into Daniel's arms. Catherine started chanting in a singsongy voice, "Daniel's getting mar-ried, Daniel's getting mar-ried."

Daniel threw back his head and laughed and set Mary down. "Yes, your brother's getting married." He pulled Claire up from her chair and embraced her. "And it's going to be soon. We feel we've waited long enough."

"How soon?" Claire's mother rose from her seat. "We need to make plans."

"No, Mother. No plans. We are simply going to be married here at Bellevue with family and a few friends."

"When?"

"Next week." She looked up at Daniel. "And I don't know if I can wait even that long."

Amanda stood and walked to the couple. "Well, it will take us that long to get the house ready. So please allow us that much time at least."

Daniel nodded. "I do agree with that. Today's Friday. We're thinking about a week from tomorrow."

A wave of emotion swept over Amanda amidst the well wishing and congratulations. She yearned to feel the arms of her beloved around her once more. And she was jealous of her brother and her friend. Not that she would deem it any other way. But she wanted her sweetheart home too. She longed to see Kent's love for her reflected in his eyes. She wanted a hurried-up wedding. But with Kent in prison, she feared that was far in the future . . . if he survived at all.

Kent covered his head with a filthy, flimsy blanket and tried to scoot from the cold raindrops that pelted the porous roof of the shebang. It was his turn on the floor, and he was miserable. The packed dirt turned slowly throughout the night into a slimy, muddy mess. Kent groaned and stood up. He limped to the fireplace and hunkered down in front of it. Stirring the embers, he coaxed a small flame, then put a few small branches on the fire that he had gathered the day before.

Smoke billowed into the room. "C'mon, don't smoke, burn." He bent toward the smoldering flame and blew. Finally a twig caught, then another, and he had a decent blaze going. He held his hands over the meager fire. "Better than nothing, I suppose."

"Is it morning already?" Lieutenant Warner leaned up on his elbow and squinted at the fire.

"Just barely."

The young lieutenant rolled over and was snoring again in minutes. Kent smiled. It seemed Roscoe could sleep no matter what the conditions. He was grateful for the friendship of this strong young man. He shuddered at visions of Roscoe's punishment after the escape attempt— standing on a barrel barefoot in the Texas sun for over eight hours. But they got no information out of him. He and Roscoe took delight in the fact that Lieutenant Selvidge's escape attempt had proven successful.

Kent hunched his shoulders under his blanket and wrapped his arms around his knees. Lightning flashed, and a loud clap of thunder followed immediately.

Roscoe suddenly sat up and put his hand into the mud forming around his bedroll. He swore as he leapt to his feet. "Dad-blast it. I'm soaking wet. Why didn't you awaken me, Littlefield?"

"I was about to. This driving rain just started."

The lieutenant huddled in front of the fireplace with Kent. "The fire feels good."

Kent stared at the flame and poked the wood with a stick. He looked at the lieutenant. "I think it's time."

"Time for what?"

"Time to attempt another escape."

"Now? Today?"

"No, no. But I think it would be to our advantage to start making plans. Winter is just around the corner."

"I agree. Are you thinking about the tunnel?"

"No. I'm thinking of hiding in the garbage wagon. But we need horses." Kent tapped his leg and grinned. "I wouldn't get far on foot with this leg."

"Now that could prove daunting."

"Maybe not. I've written to Amanda, and if she catches the clues in my letter . . . perhaps . . ."

Roscoe scratched his head. "This Southern belle sweetheart of yours may prove to be valuable after all. Who all are you thinking of including?"

"You and me. That's all. If I could release everybody I would do so, but the more men who know, the more likely we'll be found out. Besides that, I've developed a contact."

"A spy? Here in the stockade?"

"Not a spy, but a guard who is a Union sympathizer. He has relatives in Pennsylvania close to my hometown. I think he will help us."

"Whe-w-w-w." Roscoe stood and stretched. "That's fortuitous." He sat in a rickety wooden chair in front of an equally rickety table. "I'll get the 'coffee' going. This is the third go-round for these grounds."

"And fortunate we are to have any grounds whatsoever—thanks to the 'good mother.' "

The lieutenant nodded and went to the door of the shebang with the metal coffeepot. He held the container for the rain to fill, then dumped the leftover grounds into it. He settled it into the fire. The pleasant aroma filled the shebang as the coffee started to heat up.

"Even those old grounds smell good, don't they?"

"Are you always so positive, Major Littlefield?"

"I try to be."

"How do you manage that here in prison?"

Kent poured a tin cup with the weak brew and handed it to the lieutenant, then poured one for himself. "It's simple. I believe God is in control of our destinies, and we've but to trust him and praise him in spite of the circumstances to see his best worked out for us."

"Even with all you've seen of death and the heinous treatment of our fellow man in this war?"

Kent warmed his hands around the cup. "I must admit my faith has wavered—many times. But where else do we go for Truth? His is the only steadfast standard."

"You're a better man than I."

"No. But perhaps more experienced."

The two sipped their brew in silence, and Kent thought of escape. He prayed Amanda would be clever enough to read between the lines of his last letter. His life could depend upon it.

CHAPTER TWENTY-TWO

> *Oh, now I'm going to find her,*
> *For my heart is full of woe,*
> *And we'll sing the song together,*
> *That we sang so long ago.*
> *We'll play the banjo gaily,*
> *And we'll sing the songs of yore,*
> *And the Yellow Rose of Texas*
> *Shall be mine forevermore*
>
> "The Yellow Rose of Texas"

Tomorrow was Daniel and Claire's wedding day. They had finished painting and repairing the fence; Wash got the shutters nailed down; Kitty and the girls weeded the flower beds and trimmed the hedges. Elsie had worked all week preparing her kitchen miracles for the festive occasion. And Daniel was even whistling as he worked. Life seemed somewhat normal once again.

When the household had settled down after supper, Amanda retreated to the privacy of her own room and read Kent's last letter for the third time.

August 13, 1864

My beloved Amanda,

    I am sitting under the stars in the most rickety chair you can imagine in front of my shebang wondering if you are looking at the same stars on your veranda at Bellevue. How I miss the pleasantries of the gentle life as it was with you at Bellevue before the war: long walks at twilight, church dinner on the grounds, Elsie's good cooking, and the beautiful sterling that graced the table in your dining room. Oh, I long to be out of this prison—to be able to ride up to your gate, walk to the door, and invite you to ride with me on the beach, but more than that, for us to be married. I know that's not possible at the moment, but please tell me that you are willing to come here to see me, if only for the briefest of moments. I'm not certain as to the distance, but I think you could make it in about ten days. And I know this sounds absurd, but I know you will recall how I loved sterling. Would it be possible to bring some, just to remind me of you? I don't know if the guards will allow you to get past them with it, but do try. It would afford me a small sense of freedom.

Amanda drummed her fingers on the table. She stood and poured water from the ewer into the washbasin and splashed the cool liquid on her face. Unbraiding her hair, she stepped out of her dress and pulled on her nightdress, then sat back down at the table.

Sterling. Why the sudden interest in sterling? He'd never mentioned it before, much less commented about his affinity for it.

I am so sorry that Daniel has been reported as missing. Please be encouraged. There's always a chance that he's wounded in a hospital somewhere, or he may be on his way home. Don't give up on him.

There's not much to report here, except that more and more prisoners continue to flood into the camp. Our somewhat "benevolent" commandant has been replaced by a much stricter one, Colonel J.P. Borders. He has ordered that anyone attempting escape be shot immediately by whoever discovers them.————————

————————————————

——————————————————————The colonel sports an unusually large handlebar mustache and hooded eyes that miss nothing.

Amanda feared what had been obliterated in the censoring. What atrocities was Kent having to endure?

I keep hoping that any day we will hear that the war is over. When it is over, I will head straight for your arms, my dearest. And I hope that you will agree to be married soon after I return. I long for us to begin our lives together.

When I look around at these miserable surroundings, it seems I have been sentenced to someplace akin to Dante's Inferno. Sometimes I fear I will never get home. But I am trusting God to bring us through this affliction. Please believe that with me. Is the Scripture true when it says that if two or more are agreed on touching any one thing, that it will be accomplished? (I cannot remember the exact wording.) Would you agree with me that we will get through this and one day be husband and wife? I desperately need you to believe with me.

Your sweet face hovers in all my waking and sleeping hours. Please come. Please come. I must see you. And don't forget the sterling.

Devotedly yours,
Kent Littlefield

Amanda lay down on her bed—or rather Daniel's old bed that they had transferred into Father's room for her. Daniel and Claire were taking Father's larger bed, but Daniel preferred to stay in his room. His bedroom had the best view of the ocean, although all the bedrooms upstairs looked out over the water. She was excited at the prospect of having her friend, now to be her sister-in-law, in the house.

Amanda would make her father's room her own. It would be a nice one for her and Kent when they married. Her mother's touches remained here and there—her vanity, a sitting area—and it had a seldom-used fireplace and two large windows overlooking the bay.

Clutching Kent's letter to her chest, she closed her eyes and drifted off to sleep. Feathery dreams and visions danced through her head of weddings and bridal gowns and music and . . . Sterling. Kent's horse, Sterling, rearing on his hind legs, then galloping off into the night. She sat up with a start, her heart banging against her chest. It wasn't sterling *silver* Kent was writing about; he was writing in code about a horse. He wanted her to bring him horses to help him escape.

She turned the wick up on the lantern and reread the letter. *And don't forget sterling.*

She smiled. How clever he was. How she loved him. Her love grew for him every day.

She would do it. She would go to him, as quickly as possible. How she would manage it, she did not know, but her mind was made up. She blew out the lantern and spent a sleepless night with Sterling galloping through her head as she formulated plans to rescue her Union sweetheart.

❧

The two bridesmaids, Amanda and Rebecca, couldn't stop their tears during the wedding ceremony. Sniffles could be heard throughout the crowd. In spite of initially planning for a small wedding, it seemed the whole town came to participate in the gay festivities in the midst of a beleaguered, weary season. As Rebecca's father had officiated at Father's funeral, he officiated at Claire and Daniel's wedding, and if one looked closely, one could see tears in his eyes as well.

Emmaline straightened the wreath of flowers in Mary's hair as she hugged her littlest sister close to her. She had plaited the Texas laurel leaves and blossoms into matching headpieces for all three of the younger girls.

Amanda loved Claire's simple wedding dress of white satin. Her friend had sewn the gown while Daniel was gone, believing with all her heart that he would return to her. Her long Limerick guipure lace veil with floral motifs framed her face. Her countenance radiated with love for Daniel as she gazed steadily into his eyes and smiled. Amanda didn't know how she could have been any more beautiful.

And Daniel wore one of his father's black suits with a black string tie. He was so thin that the suit hung around his shoulders, but it was not too awfully noticeable. He still was a handsome man.

As the elder pronounced the couple man and wife, the whole congregation broke out in spontaneous applause. "You may kiss your bride, Daniel."

Daniel pulled Claire to him with his good arm and kissed her gently. She threw her arms around him and deepened the kiss. When they finally parted, Daniel was blushing and grinning. He seemed the old Daniel.

Mr. Davis pulled out a large handkerchief and blew his nose—and the congregation laughed. "Now let the festivities begin."

Daniel and Claire cut the simple wedding cake, but how Elsie had been able to find the ingredients to bake a pound cake, Amanda didn't know. The woman was a master when it came to figuring out ways to feed people.

Daniel quieted everyone as he raised his glass of wine to toast his bride. "This is the happiest day of my life. I honestly did not believe I would live through the cruelty and violence of . . ." His voice broke. He looked down. "Please forgive me." He cleared his throat. "My bride, Claire Beecham . . . Belle, now . . ."—chuckles sounded throughout the crowd—". . . is the loveliest, most beautiful, most loyal sweetheart that anyone could hope or dream of. She is a strong woman, as well. I consider myself the most fortunate and blessed man on earth to be her husband." He held his crystal goblet up. "To Claire, and to our life together."

"Hear, hear." Glasses clinked as the well-wishers joined in.

"Now, we want you all to stay and enjoy Elsie's lavish spread— stay as long as you like. But you'll understand, given the state of our times and our circumstances, that we would prefer the foregoing of any tomfoolery tonight. No shivaree, please. No capturing the bride away. Enjoy the evening, but when it comes time to go home, please just go home."

Ripples of laughter floated through the friends and onlookers. A tall, curly-headed young man called out, "C'mon, now, Daniel. You've done your share of shivaree nonsense!"

"You're right, my friend. And I've done the last of my shivaree-ing too." He pointed at the man. "I pledge to you that when you get married, I'll do everything in my power to discourage the same."

"You got it. Okay, you heard what the man said. No nonsense." He stepped up beside Daniel and put his arm around his shoulders. "These two have suffered enough. Let 'em be."

Murmurs of consent were heard all around. The ladies rushed forward to congratulate Claire and embrace her, and the men gathered around Daniel to clap him on the back and guffaw as men did.

As dusk began to fall, the guests left one by one, till only the family remained in the yard. Claire began picking up dishes from the table.

Elsie thrust herself in front of her. "Oh, no, you don't, Miss Claire. This is yo' wedding night, and you not gonna work cleaning up on yo' wedding night. It's bad enough that ladies hafta work like field hands these days, but I puts my foot down about workin' today. No, ma'am. You and Mista Daniel go on up to yo' room and enjoy each other's company."

Claire blushed and snuggled up to her new husband standing by.

"You'd best do as she says, dearest. If the truth be known, she's the real boss of Bellevue."

"Pshaw, you go on, Mista Daniel. Kitty done put goodies in yo' room for you. Go on, now. Shoo."

Amanda embraced the two of them. "I agree. We'll take care of all of this. Go on and start your lives together. I love you both dearly."

"We love you as well, Mandy." Daniel started toward the house with Claire. "Oh, by the way, Amanda. Thank you."

"Thank you for what?"

"Thank you for not listening to me, and for encouraging Claire to come for supper last week."

Amanda smiled. "You're welcome. I . . ." She wanted to tell Daniel about Kent's letter, but decided to wait until morning.

"Yes?"

"Never mind. I've something I need to discuss with you, but it can wait until morning. Good night, you two."

"Good night."

Later on that evening, after putting things away, Amanda and the girls climbed the stairs.

Mary darted for Daniel's room. "I'm going to tell Daniel good night."

Emmaline and Amanda caught hold of her at the same time. "Oh, no, you don't. We're going to bed."

"But I always tell Daniel good night."

"Not tonight you don't. He's with Claire, and they . . . well, they need to be alone. In fact, when that door is closed"—Amanda pointed down the hallway—"you knock and wait to be invited in from now on."

Catherine stood on the landing watching the tug-of-war. "It's different when you're married, isn't it? Even though he's still our brother?"

"Yes, Catherine, that's right. It's different."

She giggled as she took the floral wreath from her blond hair. "I thought so."

Emmaline smiled at Amanda, and she took her younger sisters to their room. "Good night, Mandy."

"Good night, Emmaline."

Amanda stood in the hallway until Emmaline closed their door. Claire's soft laughter filtered through their door and down the hall. Amanda smiled and took a deep breath. "I'm so grateful, Father, for your goodness to Daniel and Claire. For your mercy and compassion. My heart is full to overflowing." She opened the door to her room. "Now, help me know what to do about Kent."

⁂

"Absolutely not!" Daniel stood and pounded his fist on the breakfast table.

Claire blinked her eyes at each report. "Dear, calm down."

"You will not go to see Kent Littlefield in prison in Tyler. You will not pursue this supposed love for him. I will not have a Blue Belly Yankee in this house." He resumed his seat.

Mary and Catherine started to sniffle.

"And don't start crying, girls."

"But you're yelling at us. You're angry."

"I'm not yelling at you, and I'm not angry."

Claire began to tear up as well.

Daniel threw his napkin on the table. "Well, I guess this is what is going to be like in a house full of women. Are you going to cry too, Mandy?"

"No, but that's what we are—women. And now that you are the man of the house, you'd better learn how to deal with women." She rose to her feet as tears sprang to her eyes. "Maybe I am going to cry, but I'm not asking your permission, Daniel. I was asking for your help. And if you will not help me, I'll go by myself." She put her hand to her neck as she felt the embarrassing mottling begin.

"Don't be ridiculous, Mandy. It's too dangerous. You'll encounter all kinds of thieving trash, soldiers, animals. It's out of the question. This discussion is over."

"No, it's not over. I'm telling you that I am going. You can either help me or not, but I am going."

Daniel began to yell again and clenched his fist. "I say you are not."

Mary burst into sobs, covering her ears. "Stop it. Stop it. If this is how it's going to be, I wish you'd never come home." She ran from the room and up the stairs.

"Me too." Catherine followed her.

Claire pushed back from the table. "I'll take care of them, Amanda.

You and Daniel finish your . . . your discussion. Come, Emmaline, let's see if we can calm them down."

"Thank you, Claire. I think we are finished."

Daniel leaned forward. "Let me make myself clear. If you leave Bellevue to go after your Blue-Bellied lover, you will not be allowed to come back home . . . at least with him."

Amanda stared at him. "You don't mean that."

"I do. With all that I can muster, I do mean that." He took a deep breath. "You don't know what the Yankees have done to our country. They are plundering the South, burning the crops, destroying everything in sight. They are ravaging the land. There will be nothing left of our country but charred hills and cities and ruined women and families."

"That's not Kent."

"Oh, Kent's not only participated in it . . . he's an officer. He's commanding it. I'll admit that I liked the man. He seemed decent enough, and if he weren't a Union officer, I would approve of him for you. But the fact is that he *is* a Union officer, our enemy."

Amanda looked down at her fork as she slid it back and forth on the table. "Let me ask you this. When this war is over, are we going to continue to fight the war in our hearts, hate each other, brothers and fathers and sons? Will there never be reconciliation? Forgiveness? Healing?"

"It will take a long time for some of us to forget and forgive what we've seen, what we've been through."

"But we must if the land is to heal."

Daniel shook his head. "I'm sorry. I simply cannot sanction this. You'll not go."

Amanda stood. "I am going, one way or another." She walked out of the dining room, not knowing how she was going to accomplish the feat, but determined to do so. She stopped in the parlor, not sure whether to go upstairs and start packing or go outside and start working.

Wash met her in the hallway. "I'll take you, Miss Amanda. When do you want to leave?"

CHAPTER TWENTY-THREE

In "Southern prisons" pining, meager, tattered, pale and gaunt,
Growing weaker, weaker daily from pinching cold and want—
Are husbands, sons and brothers who hopeless captives lie,
And ye who yet can save us—Will you leave us here to die?

WILLIAM COMFORT,
"A CRY FROM PRISON"

Major Littlefield."

Kent took two envelopes from the corporal handing out the mail. Both bore familiar handwriting from women he loved: his mother and Amanda. Stuffing both letters into his jacket, he limped back to his shebang before reading them. Leaves had begun to carpet the ground with shades of gold, brown, and orange, and occasionally red. The fall colors in East Texas were nothing compared to the brilliant shades he was accustomed to in Pennsylvania, but the changing scenery still offered a beauty of its own. The pine trees maintained their stately evergreen status like soldiers on guard duty.

He entered the shebang and sat in the chair beside the fireplace. Tearing open the letter from Amanda first, he read:

My dearest Kent,

I bear wonderful news. Daniel has come home to us. Unfortunately he lost an arm in battle, and he is changed by the trauma of this war, but he is home in the warmth and love of his family. He and Claire married just a week after his return. Life seems almost normal again. Almost . . .

I must admit that pangs of jealousy pricked my heart as my good friend and my precious brother were reunited. All my hopes and dreams for them have been realized, and I would want nothing less, but my soul longs for the same for us, my dear heart. I long for you to come home and for us to be married.

I fear, however, that Daniel is going to prove to be an obstacle to our coming together. He is so bitter, Kent, at what he has endured and experienced. He trusts no one from the North, and has forbidden me to come to you. But in spite of his objections, I am coming. Wash is bringing me. Faithful Wash. We must pray for God to change Daniel's heart.

I'll bring blankets for the winter, socks, mufflers, and anything else I think you might need. Do not write me back as I am leaving straightaway. Expect me soon. Oh, and I am bringing you the special item you requested. I did remember how much you loved sterling, and I think you will be pleased with what I shall bring.

My undying love,

Amanda

She decoded my message. She's bringing at least one horse. Kent jumped up and hopped around in glee, slapping his knee. *That's my girl.* He looked at the postmark on the letter—nearly three weeks ago. She could be showing up any day.

He opened the second letter, from his mother.

My Only Son,

I can hardly bear to write this letter to you. You can tell from my shaking hand and stains on the ink and paper how difficult it is to tell you this. We received word just days ago that our much-loved father and husband is gone. He was wounded in the Atlanta campaign and developed pneumonia in the hospital. They could not save him.

How can this be happening to our family, our country? Those whom we once considered loved ones and brothers are taking our lives. The land we once tread upon in safety and gratefulness to our God is now treacherous and bloody from the wounds of our soldiers.

Oh, could God be so gracious as to bring you back to us? We pray constantly for you. We need you home so desperately. We will manage somehow until you come to us, but the days will be long and arduous until that time.

We long for your return.

Your adoring mother and sisters

Kent's elation turned to pain in that instant. He resumed his seat and clenched his mother's letter in his fist. He ground his teeth, but could not contain his tears. Burying his head in his hands, he wept—wept for his mother and sisters left alone; wept for the vacant hole left in his heart from losing his father; wept for his country. He had heard it said that a man doesn't really become a man until his father is gone, and he felt that truth closing in on him. He now felt a crushing responsibility for his family. The need to escape was more urgent than ever

"How much farther, Wash?" Amanda pulled on her gloves as she exited the inn in Nacogdoches.

"The groomsman in the stable told me we'd reach Tyler in a couple more days."

The two horses pulled at their harnesses, not used to being hitched together. Amanda patted the neck of a shiny black gelding they had managed to keep even during the Yankee occupation. "Just a little bit farther and you can get loose from this assignment."

He looked at her, and his shoulders shimmied as if trying to shake off the harness.

Wash loaded her trunk onto the back as she got into the carriage. The palm trees and salt cedar of the coast had given way to pine trees and oak trees and heavy underbrush. It seemed every mile they were either climbing up a hill or racing down one. Lakes and streams dotted the countryside. What a varied state the Republic of Texas was— coastal beaches, piney woods, the rugged hills near Austin.

Austin—once again her Uncle John had proven to be an ally. Amanda looked in her bag and touched the telegraph wherein he had agreed to request the commandant at Camp Ford to allow her to see Kent. He did not respond to her pleas for prisoner exchange, and she knew he would be angry when he got word of Kent's escape, but she must do what she could.

Daniel had refused to see them off. He ignored their preparations and disappeared into the field the morning they left. Claire and the girls waved them good-bye. As Claire embraced her she whispered, "He will come around. Follow your heart."

Amanda sincerely hoped Claire was right—for she didn't intend to come home until she was Mrs. Kent Littlefield.

The sun stood straight overhead as Wash pulled the carriage up to the gate of the stockade of Camp Ford prison two days later. Two guards stepped forward and halted them. Wash climbed down and opened the carriage door for Amanda.

She took a deep breath and held her head up high. Putting on her brightest smile, she offered her hand to one of the guards, who didn't seem to know what to do.

He simply nodded and tipped his hat, still holding his gun. "Ma'am. May we assist you?"

"Why, sir, I'm not rightly sure what the procedure is here."

"Corporal, ma'am."

"Oh, my soul! I'm not very good at all this military rank protocol."

The Rebel guard seemed to relax. "How may we help you, ma'am? It's good to see a pretty Southern lady."

Wash held the reins to the team and stood close by.

"Yes, well, I have a message here from my Uncle John—Uncle John 'Rip' Ford, that is." She smiled again at the guards and held it up for them to see. "I'd like to see the commandant, please."

"Yes, ma'am." The guard snapped to attention and motioned to his colleague to open the gate. "Just follow Corporal McReynolds there after you get past the gate. He'll show you where to find Colonel Allen."

"Thank you so kindly, Corporal. You've been most helpful."

Amanda reentered the carriage, her knees shaking so hard she feared the guard could hear them. She brushed the perspiration off her upper lip and clasped her hands in her lap. She'd worn a dress with a high collar to hide the mottling on her neck that betrayed her nervousness.

Wash waited as they pushed the eight-foot log gate open and let the carriage pass.

Amanda was not prepared for what she saw. In every direction, men were sitting or lying down on the ground, leaning against trees—skin-and-bones men who looked like broken marionettes with barely enough strength to glance their way; men with overgrown beards and long hair in tattered uniform; barefooted men in the cool autumn weather. Log huts sat helter-skelter dotting the interior of the camp, some with mud roofs, others with roofs made of thatch. Some shelters were merely mud lean-tos. Many men sat outside their huts in a chair or cross-legged in the mud, staring into space.

They pulled in front of a rustic cabin that obviously served as the commandant's headquarters, with the Confederate flag waving in the slight breeze—a flag like the many Amanda had sewed to send to their Confederate forces. She waited for Wash to open the carriage door for her. She wanted whoever might be watching to know that a lady had arrived. A captain stood at the door of the cabin and took her hand as she offered it.

"Captain James Granger at your service, ma'am. How may we help you?"

Amanda gave a slight curtsy as she went through the narrow door, leaving Wash on the small porch. "Thank you, Captain. I would like to see the commandant, please. I believe that is . . ." She pulled out the envelope. ". . . Colonel Borders?"

"That's correct. And what matter of business might you have with Colonel Borders?"

She handed the telegraph message to the captain. "Colonel Ford happens to be my uncle, and I have . . . shall we say . . . assisted the Confederate cause in the past with certain information that came my way. But I am here today on a purely social call. Major Kent Littlefield, whom I understand is incarcerated here, was a guest in our home several times before the war. I would like to see him. I've blankets and socks—purely a humanitarian mission, I assure you."

"I see. Right this way."

Captain Granger escorted Amanda through a door into the back room where Colonel Borders sat at a small desk. The captain whispered a few words to the commandant, then handed him the telegraph.

Colonel Borders, who, unlike most soldiers, was completely clean-shaven, stood and greeted Amanda. "Sit down, my dear." Resuming his seat, he looked at her. "So Colonel Ford is your uncle?"

"Yes, sir. My favorite uncle, I might add."

"Good man." He read through the message quickly. "When did you last see him?"

"A few months ago, in Austin." Amanda returned the colonel's stare.

"And you live where?"

"On the coast, in Indianola."

"I see. You didn't make this trip yourself, did you? It's not safe these days."

"No, I have my . . . my boy with me."

"You came all this way just to bring blankets to Major Littlefield."

Lord, forgive me. "Oh, my soul, no. We have relatives in Tyler, and my family sent us up here to check on them. A new baby and all. Plus our poor, dear aunt is ill and . . . you know, with the war and all . . ."

Colonel Borders held up his hand and smiled. "I see. Very well. I'll send for Major Littlefield. Do I detect that there might be a stronger incentive than simply benevolent concern?"

Amanda looked down. Should she be truthful? She decided to risk it. "My, you are discerning, Colonel Borders. Yes, Major Littlefield and I did enjoy each other's company somewhat before the war. Who knows what might happen when this is over? And I do hate to hear of him needing blankets and such. You understand, don't you?"

He stroked his chin and stood. "Of course. Captain Granger will fetch him for you. You may use my office." He put on his hat and bowed. "I have rounds to make. Very nice to have made your acquaintance."

"The pleasure is mutual. Oh, may I have Uncle John's note back, please? One never knows if I might need it on the return trip."

"Of course. I'll have Major Littlefield brought around immediately." He handed her the missive and left.

Amanda collapsed in a chair and took a deep breath.

⁂

Finally the door creaked open, and Kent stepped into the room. A guard came in behind him and positioned himself at the door.

Amanda gasped and stood. She didn't know if she should rush into his arms or to wait for permission to speak.

He smiled and limped toward her with his arm extended. "What a sight for sore eyes you are, my dear."

She went into his arms and embraced him, fighting the tears that filled her eyes. She could feel his thin shoulders through his jacket. "Let me look at you." His face had grown gaunt, but the dimple was still there when he smiled, and his blue eyes had not lost their sparkle.

"I'm not much to look at, I fear. Let me look at *you*. Now that's a banquet for starved eyes." He caressed her cheek. "You are more beautiful than ever." Turning to the guard, Kent said, "Could you give us some privacy? I'm not going anywhere."

The guard frowned. "I don't know, sir. I'm supposed to keep my eye on you."

"Where am I going to go? I simply would like some privacy with my sweetheart. Surely you understand, don't you?"

"Well . . . I suppose it won't be of any harm. But I'll be right outside this door. No shenanigans."

Kent turned back to Amanda. "You have my word, Private." He smiled at her and began to kiss her as the soldier closed the door. He kissed her cheeks and moved to her lips, pulling her closer to his chest. His cane fell to the floor with a thud, and the soldier threw open the door.

Kent hardly looked up from covering Amanda's face with his kisses. "Just my cane."

"Humphf." The guard backed out and closed the door.

"Oh, my beloved, this is a little bit of heaven in the midst of hell on earth. To feel you in my arms. To kiss your sweet lips." He nuzzled her hair. "To smell the fragrant lavender once again in your hair." He pulled back. "I know I don't smell good at all. I apologize. We don't have the amenities and niceties here that one needs to be a gentleman in every aspect."

"Kent, the little bit I saw coming in—what an awful place this is, and what you must have suffered. I brought blankets, socks, and mufflers. And coffee. I was able to get coffee for you. I also brought soap and towels. Will they let you have these things?"

"I think so." He cocked his head and looked at her. "Did you bring any 'sterling'?"

Amanda smiled and walked to the window, motioning for him to follow her. She pointed outside to Wash and the carriage. "Will black sterling do?"

Kent squeezed her until she thought her ribs would crack. "Good girl. I knew I could count on you."

"What do we do now? Do you have a plan?"

"One of the guards is a Union sympathizer, and I have befriended him. He has relatives in my hometown, and those relatives happen to be my best friend's parents, the Peifers. Every day a Negro man drives a cart into the prison to gather trash. This particular guard usually walks through the compound with the trash cart. He has agreed to help me and my fellow officer, Lieutenant Warner, hide underneath the refuse and ride out."

"Can you trust him?"

"I think so. Guess what his name is?"

Amanda shrugged her shoulders. "I have no idea."

"Sergeant Zeke Miller. Ezekiel." Kent chucked. "I thought that was more than coincidence."

"Go on."

"They take the garbage to dump in a pond about two miles north of here on the outskirts of Tyler. Meet me there with the horses tomorrow afternoon around two o'clock."

"How long before they discover you're gone? Will they come after you?"

"The nemesis of most of the escapes has been the dogs. They send the hounds out after them, and the poor fellows cannot get very far through these thick woods with those dogs chasing them. But if we ride out and then mount horses, we might have a chance. And with the stench of the garbage, well . . . perhaps it will cover our tracks." He scratched his beard and grinned at her. "I certainly won't smell good after that ride. Do you think you could find a change of clothes for us?"

"I already thought of that. I brought some of father's shirts and trousers. And it won't matter how you smell as long as you are free, and we can be together."

Kent took her hands and looked into her eyes. "Sweet Amanda, there is still a war going on. I will have to return to my unit. And . . ."

He hesitated and brought her hands to his lips and kissed them. "I received word a few days ago that my father has been killed . . . in the Atlanta campaign."

"Oh, Kent. I am so sorry to hear that." She embraced him again. "I can truly empathize with you."

"Yes, of course you can. Forgive me, I've not even asked how your family is faring since the death of your father."

"It was very difficult, but now that Daniel's home, things will be better."

"I'm so relieved that he is back at Bellevue. You need him there." He paused. "Has he changed his mind about us?"

"Not yet. But don't fret over that. He will come around. I am sure of it." Amanda searched his eyes. "I cannot go home . . ." She looked toward the door and lowered her voice. "After you escape."

"Only until the war is over."

Her heart plummeted, and she bit her lip to keep from crying. "I cannot. Daniel will not allow me to return. He . . . he . . . said not to come back if I came here to you." A sob interrupted her. "You must let me go with you."

Kent took her by the shoulders. "I love you more than life itself, but I cannot desert my men. The war is surely close to being over. Daniel will not refuse to let you return home. That was anger speaking."

The door opened and the guard came in with his rifle. "Time's up. Back to your barracks."

Kent nodded. He kissed Amanda's hand once more. "Thank you for coming."

She turned to the guard. "May I give him the blankets and things I brought for him?"

"I'll take them. They'll have to be inspected."

She nodded and her eyes glistened with unshed tears. "I'll have my boy get them for you."

Kent started toward the door as the guard ushered him out with the rifle. "This will soon be over, and we can be together as we've planned."

Amanda followed them out and watched as Kent limped through the miserable maze of humanity gathered around the she-bangs and in the muddy road. She turned to Wash. "You may give Major Littlefield's package to the private here."

The soldier leaned his rifle against the wall and took the bundle from Wash.

Amanda pointed to it. "You'll find no problem with the package—only blankets and socks and a few other necessities to help him get through the winter."

"We'll see that he gets it." He gestured toward the horses. "Nice team of horses you have there."

Wash spoke up. "The black gelding is new. We thought this trip would be a good time to break him in."

The guard stared at the Negro and picked up his rifle. "I was speaking to the lady."

Amanda stepped between the two and offered her hand. "Thank you for your hospitality in these trying circumstances." She looked at the young private and saw reflected in his eyes merely a boy, weary with the war himself. Her heart went out to him, and she smiled. "I hope for all your sakes that this horrible war is nearly over."

CHAPTER TWENTY-FOUR

LATE OCTOBER 1864

How we talked of liberty by day, and dreamed of it by night!
How some of our gallant fellows resolved that they would strike for
it; or, at least, endeavor to strike some path that might lead to it!
A.J.H. DUGANNE,
"TWENTY MONTHS IN THE DEPARTMENT OF THE GULF,"
WRITTEN FROM CAMP FORD, TYLER, TEXAS

The dump cart rattled over the ruts and potholes inside the prison, picking up rotting meat, discarded bloody bandages, and human refuse from the shebangs. An unseen cloud of stench surrounded the cart, but the prisoners paid no heed to the disgusting cargo as it passed them by.

Kent and Roscoe stood at the side of their shebang waiting for the cart to pull between their shelter and the one next to it. Lieutenant Warner peered around the corner and swore. "Zeke's not the guard today."

Kent whispered. "Who is?"

"Sullivan."

Kent groaned at the news that one of the meanest, most thorough guards stood at the front of the cart. "We have to go anyway."

"Are you crazy, sir? We won't even get out of the compound."

"We've got to try. Amanda's waiting for us with horses. If we don't go now . . ."

Another guard approached. It was Zeke. "Have you eaten yet, Sullivan?"

"Naw, not yet."

"Go ahead, I just finished. I'll take the cart out."

"Don't mind if I do. Thanks, Zeke."

Kent watched the stocky figure of Private Sullivan amble toward the mess hall. Sergeant Miller walked to the back of the cart, lighting a cigar. Keeping his head down, he mumbled as he lit it. "C'mon. Get in now."

Kent crawled in first; then Roscoe scooted in beside him. Kent gagged and covered his mouth with his fist. Maggots covered the wooden planks of the floor.

Zeke threw burlap bags over them. "Here, this might help some. Godspeed. I'll walk out with the cart."

The cart moved away from their shebang to the next one.

"My cane. I left my cane."

"Shh. Too late, sir. We're headed for the gate."

The two officers held their breath as the wagon lumbered toward fresh air and freedom.

"Whoa. Whoa, there."

The driver halted the team of mules. "Yessuh?"

A low voice rumbled. "Need to check the load."

"It's clear. I've already checked it out." Zeke walked to the back of the wagon.

The low voice again. "Let me just poke around a bit."

Kent held his breath as he heard the soldier's bayonet slicing into the swill. The blade poked into the refuse, releasing the disgusting odors. He came closer and closer and sliced into the cuff of Kent's jacket, cutting into his hand. He bit his tongue to prevent crying out in pain.

Zeke spoke up again. "You're gonna mess up your rifle, soldier, with that garbage. Besides that, you're tearing the bags and spilling all that mess into the wagon."

The slicing noise ceased, and the low voice burst out in expletives. "Go on, old man. Get that out of here."

They proceeded ahead, and the wooden gate scraped shut.

<hr />

"Miss Amanda, here they come."

Amanda stuck her head through the window in the carriage. She opened the door and stepped out into the warmth of the afternoon sun.

An old Negro man sat atop the driver's bench of a broken down buckboard.

Wash waved to them as they pulled alongside the bank of the pond and jumped down. As soon as the cart stopped, Kent and Lieutenant Warner emerged from underneath burlap bags separating them from the rubbish, both men coughing and sputtering.

"Whew! Didn't know if I could stand that for another mile."

Kent grinned at Amanda and held up his hand for her to stay away from him. "Told you we wouldn't smell too good." He turned his lapel inside out, and grinned as he sniffed the perfume button. "I guess I used up all the lavender." Motioning to Lieutenant Warner, he said, "May I present Miss Amanda Belle?"

Roscoe nodded and tipped his cap. "The pleasure is all mine, I assure you."

"Amanda, this is my colleague, Lieutenant Roscoe Warner."

Amanda curtsied. "Here's your change of clothes . . . and soap." She pointed to a line of trees beyond the pond. "There's a small creek over there. Water's cold, but you can freshen up some. I brought underthings and jackets. Winter's not far behind."

"I brought the blanket, too, and stuck the package of coffee you just brought to me in my pocket." Kent examined his hand that had bled onto his jacket.

"Is that serious?"

"No, just a close call. I'll wash it out good."

"Hurry. We'll wait with your horse."

The Negro man went to work unloading the trash and throwing it into the pond as Kent and Roscoe ran to the creek to wash up, Kent limping behind Roscoe.

"Yowee! Whoo!" The two men hollered in glee and shock as they stepped into the cold water. They bathed quickly and returned to the carriage. Kent had rolled up the sleeves of Ezekiel Belle's shirt and had tucked the too-long pants into his boots. He carried his uniform wrapped in his shirt, as did Roscoe. "We need to keep these . . . in case we get stopped. We'll wash them as soon as we can."

Kent went to the driver and shook his hand. "Much obliged. I pray God's protection on you."

The old man took off his hat and scratched his kinky gray head. "You don't need to thank me, sir. I thanks you fo what y'all has done for us." He replaced his dilapidated straw hat. "Now I needs to get out of here, and so do you."

"Yes. Go about your routine as usual. I hope they don't suspect you. It won't go well with you if they do."

"Don't you worry none 'bout that, sir. I'll be jes fine." The man pulled himself into the wagon and chucked the reins on the team of mules and left.

Amanda stared at Kent. "I've never seen you in civilian clothes. Even when you were wounded and we nursed you, all you had was your uniform. You look so different."

He embraced her. "I hope it wasn't simply the uniform you fell in love with."

"Well, I must admit that you are so very handsome in uniform, but that's not what I fell in love with."

He smiled and stepped back from her. "We must go."

"I hid a bridle in my trunk, along with one saddle. You're going to have to ride double."

Wash was already saddling the black gelding.

"No problem. We can do that."

"And there are a few provisions in the saddlebags. Where will you go?"

"New Orleans. I have a hunch my unit is still there. Plus if they come after us, they'll suspect we headed north. Fortunately, they won't know we're missing until roll call tomorrow morning, and we'll be long gone by then. Did you by any chance think to bring weapons?"

"We have a rifle and a pistol in the carriage. And I brought you a knife."

"You need to keep one of them. I'll take the rifle." He took Amanda's hand and kissed it. "As much as my heart longs to remain with you, I must take my leave."

Her eyes filled with tears. "No, please take me with you, Kent. I cannot return to Bellevue." She clung to him. "You can't make me go back. Please, Kent. I want to be with you wherever you are."

Roscoe cleared his throat and gathered the horse and waited.

She started to cry. "What if I never see you again? What if we never get married? What if . . . ?"

"Amanda, we can spend this time apart worrying about what could happen, or we can trust God to bring us through." He brushed her tears away with his fingertips. "Go home and wait for me. Daniel will allow you to return if I'm not with you."

"Please don't send me away. I-I-I . . ." Her voice broke.

"Washington and Lieutenant Warner, come here, please. Come in close. I want you to witness something."

The two men moved into a circle with Kent and Amanda.

Kent took both of her hands. "Look at me, and listen to me carefully. We shall have to wait for our wedding in the future, but we can touch tomorrow now." His eyes bored into hers, refusing to let her go. "I marry you, Amanda Irene Belle. For now and for eternity, in my heart, I marry you. I commit myself to you. I will come for you as soon as I possibly can. Please trust me. I will return for you. Will you agree to wait for me?"

Amanda's knees grew weak as she listened to their makeshift marriage ceremony in the woods, the Texas sky as their wedding bower, a slave and a recently escaped prisoner as their witnesses. Tears coursed down her cheeks. She answered softly, "I will wait for you. And I marry you in my heart, my love."

Kent kissed her tenderly once more. He grinned. "It's official. We have witnesses."

He swung up on the gelding as it backed up a few steps and yanked at the bridle. "Whoa, boy, easy now. You're gonna like me, I promise. What's his name?"

"We've always just called him Black. But I think that Black Sterling would be most appropriate, don't you?" Amanda reached up to take Kent's hand.

Kent kissed it once more. "I love you, Amanda Irene Belle . . . Littlefield."

"And I love you, too, Major Kent Littlefield. I do love you so."

Kent turned to Wash. "Take care of her, Wash."

Wash smiled. "Yessuh. Been doing that most of my life."

Kent pulled Roscoe up behind him, and the two soldiers rode off into the woods until they disappeared from sight. Amanda sniffled and turned to Wash. "Let's go home. Let's go home and pray for the war to end."

Kent urged his new steed on, and the two officers rode as hard as they dared for several hours. The change of terrain from wooded hills into muddy marshland that first night told Kent they were close to Louisiana. The moon rose and cast eerie luminescent shadows through the pine trees. Cryptic curtains of Spanish moss hung from cypress trees that spread their wide trunks in the swampy water.

Kent swiveled in the saddle. "How're you faring back there?"

"Wouldn't mind my own horse, but I'm doing all right." Roscoe stretched his long legs out and rubbed his back. " 'Course, I'll probably be sore for a few days. Strange country. Unnerves me." He squirmed behind Kent.

The horse pulled on the bridle and pranced to the side.

"Be still. You're agitating the horse. It's hard enough for him to be carrying a double load."

The shot of a pistol echoed through the trees. Then another, followed by an agonizing scream.

Kent pulled the horse up and listened. They could hear men laughing and jeering. Another pistol shot, another scream, more laughter.

"We'd better check this out." Kent turned off the road and walked Black Sterling slowly through the trees in the direction of the voices. "Get off, Lieutenant Warner. Take the knife and stay out of sight until I need you."

"Yes, sir. I'm right behind you."

Kent urged the horse forward until they came to a clearing. Nothing he had experienced in the past four years prepared him for what he saw. Two Confederate soldiers sat on one side of a campfire holding a Union soldier on the other side at bay with their pistols, and—could it be so? They were taking turns shooting at him. The poor fellow was in agony, his right hand had been blown away and his right leg shredded.

Kent removed his kepi, drew his rifle, and called to the men, employing a Southern drawl. "Gentlemen, I think y'all have had enough fun for today."

The two Confederates whirled around to confront him, but only one had a pistol. The other was unarmed. The older man with the pistol pointed it at Kent and looked him over from head to toe. "Now who might you be to be giving us orders?"

"Major Kent Littlefield. Out of unifohm, to be shuh. Ran into a little trouble. You men go on now. I'll take this man as my prisoner."

The men guffawed. "Not much of this Billy Yank left to take." They turned back toward the unfortunate man.

Kent pointed his rifle at them. "I said that I will take care of this."

"Hey, how do we know you're even an officer anyway?"

"I can assure you I'm an officer. Drop your weapon. Lieutenant Warner?"

The older man with the pistol pointed it at Kent, as Lieutenant Warner emerged from the brush wielding the knife. "I don't think I'd do that if I were you."

Kent dismounted. "Slowly now. Put your pistol down and take off your boots."

Reluctantly the two complied.

"Tie them up, Lieutenant Warner. We'll help ourselves to that pistol and one of their horses. I'm thinking these two are probably deserters."

Kent walked to the battered soldier. The man was still breathing, but barely. He opened his eyes and spoke in a raspy croak. "Pl-pl-ease." The soldier would soon bleed to death. Kent knew what had to be done, but he could not bear to think about it.

He went back to Roscoe who had just finished tying up their prisoners. The lieutenant looked at Kent. "We cannot leave him like that." He nodded in the direction of the Union soldier.

"I know." He looked at the two Rebs. "We are going to take one of your horses. We'll let the other loose in the woods with your boots. Perhaps you'd best find your way back to your unit—after you find your boots and your horse. We should take you in and have you tried for war crimes and desertion, but we simply haven't the time nor the resources to do so."

The older man spit at Kent and swore. "I don't believe you're no officer. Why're you outta uniform?"

Kent replaced his kepi.

"Blue Belly!"

"Come with me, Lieutenant Warner."

They went to the victim of the Rebs' torture. Kent felt his pulse. "He's gone—blessedly." Kent picked up the entrenching tool leaning against a tree. "Take this, Lieutenant, and go bury this unfortunate fellow. I'll take care of setting the horse loose with their boots and keep an eye on these two. Bring that spade back. It'll come in handy."

Roscoe came back after performing his grisly task, wiping his forehead on his sleeve.

Kent handed his colleague the reins of the remaining horse and mounted. "Let's get out of here." He pointed at the men. "You'd better pray to God that I never see you two again."

❧

Entering Indianola Amanda looked out the carriage window at the Union troops encamped around town. Except for their constant presence, one would almost think the war was over. As difficult as it had been, their community seemed to have escaped the devastation that was sweeping through the Confederate states at the hands of the Union army, according to newspaper reports and what Daniel told them.

She couldn't imagine Kent being party to that kind of brutality—burning plantations, ravaging the provisions of the local citizenry, raping women, slave and free. He was not that kind of man. But what did he do when ordered to destroy a town or village? The tears that had fallen steadily on the return trip home began to gather again. And she wasn't naïve enough to think that Daniel had not been caught up in the horrible cruelties either. War seemed to strip men of their finer character and replace it with barbarism. Or was the barbarism there all the time, just waiting to be uncovered?

There is none righteous, no, not one.

She remembered Father quoting the Scripture from the pulpit, and she had wondered at the time what it meant. Now she knew. *Without God we are all barbaric, all cruel, all heathen, all sinful. We are not good people who simply make mistakes. We are undone with no hope without the atoning blood of Jesus. I was raised in a home and church that proclaimed the truth of the gospel. Why has it taken me so long to understand it?*

Wash pulled the carriage around to the side door. Amanda stepped out and looked at the repaired windows. The house almost looked as if it were standing straighter and prouder as Daniel took care of the neglected chores one by one.

Zachary bounded out of the door and flung himself into Wash's arms. "Daddy, Daddy!" He wrapped his chubby arms around his father's neck and wouldn't let go.

"Whoa, son. You're chokin' me." He pried the boy's arms loose and kissed him on his cheek. "Help me with Miss Amanda's trunk." He set Zachary down and let him think he was helping his father lift the heavy luggage.

"Would you take it to my room, please?"

"I dunno. Zach, do you think we can manage to get this heavy thing upstairs?"

Zachary vigorously bobbed his head up and down.

"Here we go then." The two headed through the hall to the staircase, laughing and grunting under the weight of the chest.

Amanda walked through the back parlor into the kitchen where Elsie and Kitty were busy preparing for the evening meal.

Kitty looked up and put down the knife she was using to cut up a chicken. "Miss Amanda. You're home. Thank goodness, you is home!"

Elsie wiped her hands on her apron and bustled toward her. "I sho am glad to see you, Miss Amanda. I didn't know if you's coming back or not. Welcome home."

"Am I welcome home, Elsie? Will Daniel welcome me home?"

"Aw, pshaw, Miss Amanda. You know he will. He jes trying to protect his family."

"Where is everyone?"

"Miss Claire and the girls gone into town to the store and to see Miss Rebekah. Miss Claire, she hardly move from Masta Daniel's sight, but she finally agreed to take the girls into town today."

"Where is Daniel?"

"He and Hiram looking at the hogs to see what we can slaughter what with the cooler weather on us now."

Wash entered the kitchen carrying Zachary. "I'll take care of the horses and get changed. I can get in a good half day's work before sundown."

"Can I go with you, Daddy?"

"You bet you can. You can help with the horses."

"I'll go, too. I want to see Daniel."

Elsie stammered, her speech hesitant. "Miss Amanda . . . Masta Kent? Is he . . . did you see him?"

"Mister Kent is back with his unit. That's all I'm at liberty to say." She patted the servant's arm and smiled, blinking back tears. "He's well, and we hope that someday . . ." Her voice broke, and she cleared her throat. "It's all in God's hands now."

"It always is, honey. We chooses whether we're gonna fight it or get in the flow." She chuckled. "And the flow is much easier on the nerves. Yessuh. The flow is much easier." She turned back to her work.

Amanda followed Wash and Zach out the kitchen door. She walked toward the barn, but didn't see Daniel and Hiram. She turned the corner of the barn and saw them at the hog pen.

Daniel stood with one foot on the fence, while Hiram prodded different hogs for him to look at. Amanda sidled up to Daniel. "We're fortunate to have any left."

Daniel started and wheeled around. "You're home." He looked toward the barn and then the house. "Alone?"

"Alone."

He encircled her with his good arm. "I knew you'd come to your senses. You are a wise woman."

Amanda shook her head. "I'm alone—now. But you need to know that as soon as the war is over, Kent will come for me, and we plan to marry."

Daniel stepped back. His eyes flashed with a fire that frightened Amanda. It communicated pure hatred. "Never. Not with my blessing."

"Not now, Daniel. Let's don't fight. I am too weary."

"Is he still in prison?"

"No."

"So you managed to break him out?"

She reached up and caressed her brother's cheek. "I love you too much to argue. Can we simply enjoy the fact that our family is together?"

He took her hand and kissed it. "I will not change my mind. And if I don't miss my bet, I'll wager that Major Kent Littlefield will not come for you after the war. We'll never see him again."

"You may be right, but that remains to be seen, doesn't it?"

"You look as if you've been crying for days."

"It looks like I've been crying for days because that's exactly what I have been doing. I laid all my dignity aside and begged Kent to take me with him, but he refused." She sniffled.

"That was a good decision, Mandy."

"It was humiliating, but I know he was right. The hardest thing I've ever done was to watch him ride away."

"Ride away. Yes, I noticed that Black was missing. One of our best horses, Amanda. What were you thinking?"

"Don't be mad at me, Daniel. I had to help him escape. The conditions in that prison were horrible. Even you would have been shocked."

He pointed his finger at her and growled. "And Wash helped you, didn't he?"

"Don't be mad at Wash either." She caught hold of his arm. "He did it because I asked him to."

"That boy would follow you into hell." He brushed her aside and strode toward the barn.

CHAPTER TWENTY-FIVE

A soldier has fallen; but long shall remain
The star-spangled flag which he died to sustain;
For, sooner than let our loved country be lost,
A nation of freemen will die at their post!

J. W. HOLMAN,
"HE DIED AT HIS POST"

A lacy curtain of light snow danced in the air between Kent and the house. He was grateful for leave to go see his family before reporting to his new duty station on General Grant's staff in Washington, DC. Candles perched atop a Christmas tree winked at him through the windowpanes. He pulled around to the familiar stable and dismounted, handing Black Sterling over to the family groomsman.

"Good to see you back home, sir. You have a new horse."

"Yes, it's wonderful to be back. I'm afraid Sterling Prancer went down under me in battle. This is Black Sterling."

"Black Sterling, sir?"

Kent chuckled. "Long story."

"Sir, I am very sorry about General Littlefield." The servant shook his head. "Your mother didn't take the news well. She's not been in good health since. And she was so worried about you."

"Yes, I know."

Kent used to enjoy the beautiful scenery created by the wintery powder, but the brutality of the bitter cold of winter in wartime had changed his perspective. He stomped his boots on the back porch and opened the door into the warm kitchen.

Mathilda swung around with a wooden spoon in her hand. "Mister Kent, oh, my goodness. We've been waitin' and waitin' for you to get here. I've been cookin' this leg o' mutton stew for days, thinkin' you gonna be here any day. Welcome home." She waved the spoon over her head in her excitement.

"Where's Mother?"

"In the front parlor with your sisters, lightin' the candles on the Christmas tree."

"Thank you, Mathilda. You get that stew ready. I'm starving."

"Yes, sir. I'm doing just that."

Kent walked down the hallway to the parlor. Someone was playing "Silent Night" on the piano. Young voices were singing the familiar carol, not quite in tempo and not quite on key, but it sounded heavenly to him. He slowed and waited beside the door, listening. On the last chorus he stepped into the room, singing, "Sleep in heavenly peace. Sleep in heavenly peace."

Luvenia Littlefield rose from her chair and rushed to Kent. "Oh, my son. You're home at last." She embraced him as Fannie stopped playing. The three children—Jacob and Elizabeth's twin girls, Naomi and Hannah—clapped their hands, mimicking the glee of the adults.

His mother clung to him and began to cry tears of grief that they had been unable to share before now. Kent cried with her as the room grew quiet. He cradled the tiny figure of his mother in his arms.

"I'm so sorry, Mother. I'm so sorry I wasn't here. But I'm here now." He continued to embrace her, then reached out for his sisters and nieces and nephews. "Full house tonight, eh, Fannie, Elizabeth? How fare your husbands?"

Fannie spoke up. "Samuel and Robert are both with General Sherman. It's a full house every night these days."

"I see. Were they with Father when he was wounded?"

"Samuel was."

"What happened?"

"Why don't we talk about that later? It's Christmas Eve, and Mathilda will have supper ready soon."

Kent chuckled at Fannie's usual manner of taking charge.

"How were you able to obtain leave? You didn't give us much information in your letter."

His mother stood back and looked at him, at his cane. "I think there's something else you have neglected to tell us."

"What, my promotion? Yes, I'm now Colonel Littlefield." He executed an exaggerated bow. "And I have been reassigned to General Grant's staff as an *aide-de-camp*."

"Oh, that's wonderful, son. I'm so glad to hear that. That means you won't be in the heat of battle, correct?"

"Um, somewhat correct."

"But that's not what I'm talking about. I think you conveniently forgot to inform us that you were wounded."

He tapped his foot with his cane. "This? It's getting better every day. I'm still walking with a cane, but I'm not in pain."

"When did it happen?"

"As Fannie said, we'll have plenty of time to talk later. Let's enjoy the evening and each other. Let's sing and eat one of Mathilda's wonderful meals and forget the war that's destroying our country." He pulled his mother to him. "That's what Father would want us to do. He would want us to love each other and be happy. Would he not?"

Luvenia sniffled and nodded. "Yes, he would. I just miss him so. I keep thinking he will ride up at any moment and burst into the house with his usual flourish."

"We shall all be together again one day."

"I know, son, but I want him here with me now. Life is so empty without him by my side. We were married a long time." Her chin quivered. "Sometimes I don't even know what to do to get through the day." She reached for Fannie's hand. "If it weren't for Fannie and Elizabeth being here, I'd be lost in this big house by myself. I'm looking forward to the day when you come back home and get married, son."

Elizabeth chuckled and flicked her wrist at Kent. "He has to find someone who would agree to marry him first, eh, little brother?"

Kent looked down and shifted his weight on his cane. "In point of fact . . . well, actually, I *have* found someone who wants to marry me—wants to marry me very much."

Fannie frowned at him. "Would this be your Southern belle from Texas?"

"It would be."

The room grew quiet, except for the children's bantering with each other around the Christmas tree.

Mathilda's voice floated in from the kitchen as she reprised "Silent Night."

Luvenia wadded her handkerchief in her fist. "You cannot be serious, son."

"I'm very serious. We are deeply in love with one another. And, Mother, you will love her, too, if you'll give her a chance and get to know her."

His mother walked to the fireplace, then whirled about to face her children and grandchildren. She straightened herself up to all of her small stature and spoke in a firm, steady tone. "How can you entertain such an idea even for a moment? We are at war with the South, for goodness' sake, and your father was killed in . . . that . . . war." Her voice rose almost to a shout.

"But, Mother, when the war's over—"

She held up her hand. "When the war's over, our lives will be changed forever. The country will remain divided for years to come. If it ever mends, it will be after we're all dead and gone. There's been far too much killing and bloodshed."

Fannie moved to Luvenia's side. "Mother's right. It's going to be difficult enough to adjust when this thing ends, if it ever does." She shook her head. "But to invite the enemy into our family and ask us to accept her as a daughter and a sister—that's too much, Kent. Surely you understand. Don't ask that of us."

"Where's our Christian charity? Amanda is not the enemy. There's something you don't know about that I need to tell you." Kent hesitated, not knowing exactly how to broach the subject. "I really had not intended to tell you right away."

"Well? We are waiting." Fannie's dark hair glinted red in the firelight.

"I was in a prisoner of war camp for several weeks."

Luvenia gave a small cry. "Oh, my dear. Where? How did you get out?"

"In Tyler, Texas. I was captured in a campaign up through Louisiana in an attempt to put a Union flag on Texas soil, but it did not go well for the Union troops."

"Thank God you are all right, son."

"Yes, thank God and Amanda Belle."

"Amanda?" Fannie said.

"She used her wiles and influence with her uncle, Colonel John S. Ford, to break us out. If it were not for her, I would still be in that vermin-infested prison. I don't know that I would even be alive." He turned to his mother. "Amanda didn't kill Father, and she saved my life—for a second time, actually."

"No, she didn't kill your father, but her countrymen did." Luvenia turned her back and stared into the crackling flames, then faced Kent once more. "Please don't get the wrong impression. I am grateful that she saved your life, but you will never bring a Southern woman into this house, much less marry one. I will simply not allow it." She turned and left the room, and Fannie followed.

Only Elizabeth and Kent remained. "Is this how you feel as well, Elizabeth?"

Elizabeth, closest to him in age, took his hand and pressed it to her cheek. "You are the highly favored son in this family. You know that. Mother is speaking out of her fear of losing you. I agree it will be difficult, perhaps impossible, but maybe in time. But let's not ruin Christmas debating the war. Can we just enjoy you while you're home?"

"I agree." He hugged her and kissed the top of her head. "You look more like Mother every day."

"That's what everyone says."

"Go get Mother and Fannie, and let's have supper. It's Christmas—a time to celebrate life."

Kent leaned his cane against the hearth and unbuttoned his jacket.

Mathilda brought a tray of glasses filled with blackberry wine. "Where did everyone go? We're about ready to eat."

"They will be right back. And I'll have some of that wine, thank you."

Fannie, Elizabeth, and Luvenia came through the large wooden archway leading from the hallway into the parlor. Luvenia replaced her handkerchief in her sleeve and offered her arm to Kent. "We shall not speak of this again. It is settled."

Kent patted her hand and escorted her into the dining room, where Mathilda had outdone herself with more food than he had seen since dining with the Belles at Bellevue before the war. So much on the table reminded him of Amanda—the smoked oysters, the ham, the turnips and potatoes, and most of all the pies. He thought about their first meeting. "Have you all ever heard of—?" He stopped himself. *Better not bring up Southern cooking.*

"Have we ever heard of what?" Fannie held her wine glass in midair.

"Oh, I was just going to say, have you ever heard of such a spread as Mathilda can produce even in the midst of war?"

They all laughed and clinked their wine glasses in a Christmas toast.

Kent wondered what Amanda was doing this Christmas Eve. Were the Belles enjoying a sumptuous supper? Was his beloved well?

Next Christmas I pray we will be together, my sweet Amanda. Amanda Littlefield. It sounds natural. Soon, my dear, soon.

⚜

Kent knocked on the front door of the Peifer house early the next morning. He heard rustling in the hallway of the modest home, and Jewel Peifer opened the door.

The plump matron opened her arms and pulled him into her embrace, throwing him off balance. "Kent Littlefield. How good to see you."

He recovered his equilibrium and steadied himself with his cane.

"Come in this house. We are letting cold air in. She ushered him in and closed the door. My, my, don't you look fine? And what is this?" She pointed to his cane. Tucking her nut-brown hair under her Moravian head covering, she continued to chatter without giving Kent time to respond as they moved to the parlor. "I'll get James. He's out back getting water from the well."

"Thank you."

"Sit. Sit. I'm just getting something out of the oven."

"Um. Do I smell cinnamon? Reminds me of when we were boys."

Mrs. Peifer laughed. "Have you had breakfast?"

"Just coffee. You know I'd save room for some of your wonderful rolls."

She turned back toward the kitchen, but Kent stopped her.

"Mistress Peifer? You know James and I had an argument before I left for the war. I wanted to see him before I leave this time and . . . well, I didn't like the fact that we left on such bad terms . . . not knowing . . . You understand what I am making a feeble attempt to say?"

"Of course, my boy. You all were mere boys when you left Bethlehem to march off to war, and you've returned as men. James will be glad to see you." She headed for the back door, picking up a broom on her way.

Kent sat in a straight-back chair and looked around the familiar room. The windows sparkled, even in the winter, looking as if they'd just been washed. The house smelled of soap and cinnamon, fragrances that blended in a surprisingly pleasant odor—one that brought memories of childhood flooding into Kent's head. Memories of two small boys playing tag through the house while James's mother did her baking; memories of spying on James's sisters as they gossiped with their friends while embroidering; memories of James's father's stern reading of Scripture in the evenings before supper. Sparsely decorated, the room still offered a warm welcome to all who entered.

The back door slammed shut, and James bounded through the kitchen to the door of the parlor and paused. He broke into a wide grin, his brown eyes animated as he hastened toward his friend.

Kent rose and stuck out his hand.

James brushed his hand aside and enclosed his friend in a bear hug. "Oh, dear friend. I am beholden to our heavenly Father for bringing you home safely." He stepped back and eyed the cane. "Looks like you ran into some trouble along the way, but you are home."

"Just on leave. Have you been dismissed from the volunteers?"

"Yes. You have to go back?"

"Yes, I've been assigned to General Grant's staff in Virginia."

James took off his cap and jacket, smoothing his brown hair—the same color as his mother's—with his hand. "Why are you in uniform if you're on leave?"

"I have some official business to take care of before I go back to the house."

James motioned to Kent to sit down again and sat opposite his friend. "How long is this going to continue—this killing, this division?"

"It's my opinion that the Confederates cannot hold out much longer. Although we've lost some important battles, we simply have more resources and supplies and men than they do. It would be suicide for them to continue beyond this year."

"It has been a nightmare of confusion for both sides, hasn't it?"

Kent nodded and shifted in his chair. "We live in exhausting and dispiriting days. Right seems wrong, and wrong seems right. Leaders with fearless courage and moral clarity are desperately needed. I know President Lincoln is not a popular president, but I do believe he is God's appointed man to lead our nation in this hour."

They sat silent for a moment, then both men spoke at once.

"I . . ."

"I . . ."

"Go ahead, James."

"No, you first, Kent."

"Very well." He looked down at his cap in his hands. "I regret heartily how we parted." He leaned toward James. "Life is too fragile for friendship such as ours to be divided—divided even as our country is divided. Slavery is indeed a serious issue, but I want very much for us to be able to disagree . . . agreeably."

James shook his head and held up his hand. "I'm not sure we even disagree anymore. Don't get me wrong—I believe in our cause more than ever. No human being should own another person. I wish the issue could have been settled without this terrible war, but it was not to be. I've seen that not all of our side were good-willed, and not all Johnny Rebs were evil." The corners of his mouth lifted slightly. "I suppose I've grown up."

"We all have."

"Kent, I am so sorry about your father. Is there anything that we can do?"

"Actually, there is. If you would check on Mother from time to time, see if there are any chores that she needs done. We have Felix and Mathilda, of course, but with no men in the house, it's difficult for them."

"I've already been doing that. And Mother takes food over now and then."

"Thank you. I suppose I'd best be going." Kent stood. "But there is one more thing that you could do for me."

"Name it."

"There's a girl from Texas whose hand I have requested in marriage."

James grinned.

"But as you can imagine, there are complications. Her family objects, and my family objects. When you go by the house, if you could just try to soften the situation. Tell Mother and Fannie your experiences. Elizabeth is not as adamant. Amanda's a wonderful woman. In fact, she has saved my life twice—once when I sustained the leg wound, and then she . . ." He hesitated and smiled. "She broke me out of prison."

"Prison? Wait a minute, I think you'd better sit back down and catch me up. Tell me about this. Where? How?"

Mistress Peifer came into the parlor with a tray of hot sweet rolls and coffee, the spicy fragrance of cinnamon surrounding her.

Kent slapped his knee. "I believe I could be persuaded to stay a bit longer. I know not whether the memory of the deprivation of fine food and coffee in the field will ever leave me. I relish both now."

The two old friends laughed and indulged in the buttery sweet rolls. After an hour of good conversation and good food, Kent rose to take his leave.

"Must you leave so soon? It's only midmorning."

"I need to take care of this other matter. I'll see you again before I leave." He grabbed James's arm. "You are important to me, dear friend."

"And you to me."

"Good-bye, my friend, for now. I pray I shall return someday. I anticipate the days to come will prove to be fearsome."

The pair embraced, and Kent left. As he rode away, he turned to see James on the porch, his hands in his pockets against the cold.

Kent traveled to the edge of town and turned southwest toward Emmaus. The snow had stopped during the night, and it was a brilliant, sparkly winter day. No wind. Just sun and snow. He found the small farmhouse after about half an hour, tucked into the side of a hill, a neat fence lining each side of the road to the house. An older man and two adolescents were hitching horses to a sleigh. Kent could hear them talking and laughing as he rode up. The chatter stopped as they spotted the Union officer.

Kent pulled up to the hitching rail and dismounted. The older man motioned to the younger men to stay with the sleigh as he walked toward Kent. The wind had picked up, sending flurries of snow into the air. It tugged at Kent's hat, and he slapped his hand on top of the crown. He stuck out his hand to Mr. Yost. "Colonel Kent Littlefield, sir. You are Mr. Yost?"

"Yes, sir. I am." He looked at Kent, a bewildered expression in his eyes. "We received word two years ago of young Henry's being killed at Shiloh. Is there . . . is there a problem?"

"No, sir. Please accept my sincere condolences concerning the death of your son."

The two young men held the team of horses and stared at Kent. A woman came around the side of the house wrapping a muffler around her neck, accompanied by a girl about ten. Mr. Yost held out his hand for his wife, and she came to his side.

Kent tipped his hat. "Ma'am."

"Your sympathies are accepted, Colonel Littlefield."

"I was with your son when he died."

Mrs. Yost inhaled a quick breath as tears sprang to her eyes. "You were with him? He didn't have to . . . to die alone?" A sob broke off her sentence.

"No, ma'am, he didn't. In fact, I held his head in my lap as he passed. He was a good, brave soldier."

She held her muffler to her mouth and buried her head in her husband's shoulder.

"He wanted you to know that he was thinking of you in the end." Kent reached into his pocket and pulled out the locket. "And he wanted me to return this to Amy."

Mrs. Yost reached out and took the necklace.

"Would you tell her that he wanted nothing more than to come home to her and have a son?"

"Why don't you tell her yourself?" Mr. Yost pointed behind Kent.

Kent turned to face a young girl with blond hair, the same color as Amanda's, and about her same size. She carried a child who looked to be about a year and a half. She handed the baby to Mrs. Yost as she took the locket and held it to her lips, with her head bowed. Kent could barely discern her words.

"Thank you, Colonel. I asked God for some sort of sign that he was thinking of me." She looked up at Kent with cinnamon-brown eyes brimming with tears. "Thank you."

"My pleasure, ma'am." He turned to the older Mrs. Yost and the child. "Is this . . . ?"

Amy nodded. "This is our son, Henry the third. We call him Hank." She smiled. "Henry never knew about him. Shiloh was his first battle, and I didn't even know that I was carrying a child when I wrote to him. It all came about so swiftly—his enlisting, getting married, his leaving, then . . . Shiloh." She sniffled. "I just wish he had known about Hank."

Kent patted the boy on his back. "I'm sure he knows, ma'am." He said his good-byes quickly and left, more eager than ever to go back to Texas to get Amanda.

CHAPTER TWENTY-SIX

APRIL 9, 1865

> *Glory to God in the highest!*
> *Peace on earth, goodwill to men!*
> *Thank God, Lee has surrendered, and the war will soon end.*
>
> COLONEL ELISHA RHODES

K ent hurriedly buttoned his coat after being roused in the early dawn by an adjutant and rushed toward the farmhouse where General Grant had spent the night. Staff members scurried from their quarters through the mist and dew. The general had summoned his staff, and it sounded urgent. It was Palm Sunday, and the cool, pleasant morning air soothed the countryside. Wildflowers had begun to appear on the meadow, signaling that all was not death and destruction. The abundant Creator of life still reigned.

Grant had followed the Army of the Potomac to the rear of General Robert E. Lee, hoping to cut the Confederate troops off as they moved west of Richmond. After sending a message to General Lee requesting an interview between the lines, General Grant retired, complaining of a sick headache.

Kent entered the farmhouse to find the general almost finished dressing. Kent saluted.

The general returned a half salute as he pulled on his boots. "Good morning, Colonel Littlefield. We received a reply during the night from General Lee." He stood, and Kent helped the general with his soldier's blouse.

"How's the headache this morning, sir?"

"Not much better, I'm afraid. The mustard plasters and hot foot bath felt soothing at the moment, but did little to eradicate the pain."

"I'm sorry, sir."

General Grant donned his hat and picked up his gloves. "No matter. I want to get to the head of the column. General Lee is proposing an interview between the lines this morning at Appomattox Court House at ten o'clock. He's not yet ready to surrender, but I believe he is close." The general looked at Kent, his mild blue eyes clouded with the pressing responsibility of his office and sharpened by the headache. "We're not more than two or three miles from the court house, but to go direct, we would have to go through Lee's army. We'll need to move south in order to find a road coming from another direction."

"Yes, sir."

Kent and his fellow officers mounted quickly, and the entourage rode south to find an alternate route. There was very little conversation. Shortly before noon they halted in a field for rest and a bite to eat. Kent sat down with the general's chief cipher.

"What do you think, Captain Beckwith? Are we knocking at the door that will lead to the end of this?"

The captain took a swig of water from his canteen and wiped his long handlebar moustache with the back of his hand. "I hope so, Colonel. I hope to God we are close."

Horses galloping at full speed came up behind them. Kent stood and turned to face the riders, an officer with an escort, who was waving his hat above his head and shouting. The riders jumped off their horses, saluted, and handed General Grant an envelope. The air was charged with tension. Kent held his breath as the general opened the envelope and handed it to General Rawlins to read aloud:

> I received your note of this morning on the picket line whither I had come to meet you and ascertain definitely what terms were embraced in your proposal of yesterday with reference to the surrender of this army. I now request an interview in accordance with the offer contained in your letter of yesterday for that purpose.
>
> General Robert E. Lee

No one spoke. No one looked his fellow colleague in the face. Kent stared at his boots, muddy and worn. He poked the ground with his cane.

One of the men jumped on a log and proposed three cheers, but only a few feeble hurrahs resounded before all the men broke down in tears. It was over. The war was finally over. Kent should be elated, but he felt nothing. He felt empty.

General Grant's face was devoid of emotion. His jaw was set in a firm line as he rose and signaled to his men to mount. He said nothing except, "My headache is gone." He dictated a response to Captain Beckwith to inform General Lee that he had received the message and was proceeding to the front to meet with him.

The staff rode in silence toward the front where General Sheridan was located with his troops. The soldiers were lined up in battle formation facing the Confederate army close by. An atmosphere of excitement seemed to be running through the lines. Kent dismounted with the other officers.

A lieutenant with a tan, leathery complexion approached with campstools for the men.

"Thank you, Lieutenant."

"Yes, sir, you are welcome."

Kent remained standing as he surveyed the men. "Lots of excitement this morning."

"Yes, sir. Ever since Lee dispatched the white flag, the camp's been abuzz with speculations."

"What are the men saying?"

"The men, and even Generals Sheridan and Meade, are concerned that the surrender is not in good faith—that it is a deception perpetrated to offer an escape for the Army of Northern Virginia. The men feel they can whip the Rebs in five minutes, if General Grant would let them go in. They think it's a ruse."

Kent leaned on his cane. "I doubt that. General Lee is a man of impeccable character. I believe we are witnessing the conclusion of one of the most hideous periods of our country's history. And it will not end with glorious battle, but with the sad snivel of defeat."

The lieutenant nodded. "I believe your musings are correct, Colonel."

Kent looked at the young lieutenant as he walked away, and thought it wasn't that long ago he had been a lieutenant, eager to serve his country. Only four years later, he felt very old.

General Grant ordered his staff to mount once more and follow an aide who had been sent to escort them to Appomattox Court House. As they approached the building, Kent sighted the head of General Lee's column occupying a hill, a little valley separating the Confederate army from General Sheridan's troops on the crest of another hill to the south. An apple orchard occupied a portion of the sloping landscape.

"Look at that, Beckwith."

The captain answered between the unlighted cigar stuck in his teeth. "I've already seen them. I hope this is no trap."

The officers dismounted and followed General Grant up the steps to the front parlor of the house. General Lee had arrived first and awaited them. Kent smiled at the contrast of the appearances of the two men. Though he was the defeated party, General Lee was the picture of dignity, with his head of gray hair, closely-cropped beard, crisp new gray uniform, and engraved sword by his side.

Kent supposed the swiftness of the negotiations had caught General Grant off guard. He wore only a rough traveling suit, the straps of his uniform with the lieutenant-general insignia the only indication of his rank. His boots and trousers were splattered with mud from the journey.

Kent and the other staff gathered in the rear of the parlor. The two generals shook hands and began a casual conversation of prior meetings. Kent shifted his weight and wished they would get to the primary purpose.

Finally General Lee broached the subject. They soon reached an agreement on terms. Kent was glad to hear that General Grant would allow all the Confederate men who claimed to own their own horses to keep them, as well as their side arms and personal possessions. And each man would be allowed to return to his home undisturbed by the Union authorities.

"Are your men hungry?" General Grant's usual direct manner held no condemnation.

"They have been living many days on forage, parched corn mainly."

"How many?"

"I no longer know the number . . . probably about 25,000. I'm sure they are all hungry."

"Send your own commissary and quartermaster to the Appomattox Station, and you may have out of the trains there all the provisions you need."

"Thank you, General Grant. This will have the best possible effect on my men and will do much toward conciliating our people."

The two commanders signed the agreement that had been inscribed by one of Grant's staff and the shook hands again.

General Lee left the parlor and stood at the head of the steps for a moment, slapping his hands together as if he didn't know what to do next. He descended the steps and got on his horse, Traveller.

Kent heard bickering behind him and turned to see staff officers bargaining for the parlor furniture as keepsakes. He limped into the middle of the foray. "Have you no respect for what just occurred here?"

The men laughed at him and continued bartering. Kent turned away in disgust and returned to the porch as General Robert E. Lee rode away.

The Union soldiers outside began to cheer and federal artillery started to fire salutes, until General Grant halted it. "The war is over. The Confederates are our countrymen again."

Lee's men lined the road. The general's reins hung loose and his head was bent down. As he approached his men, they began to cheer. He took off his hat as he passed by them. What began as cheers for many of the men ended in a whimper. They reached out and touched Traveller as he passed by. Some of the gaunt, grimy solders knelt on the ground and buried their heads in their hands and wept. Officers sat astride their horses and sobbed aloud, unashamed.

Kent wept with them.

❧

The lilac bushes surrounding the Littlefield house, laden with fragrant purple clouds of color, greeted Kent as he approached his home for the second time in just four months. Tulips and hyacinths dotted the front yard, nodding their heads in the gentle breeze as if to say "welcome home."

He tied Black Sterling to the hitching post and went in through the front gate. He smiled to himself and pounded on the door, then stood to the side as he heard muffled voices and the shuffling of feet.

Felix opened the door and peered out.

The old servant nodded. "Welcome home, sir, yes sir." He grinned, showing missing teeth on both sides of his mouth. He stepped back and ushered Kent inside the hallway.

"Who is it, Felix?" Fannie called from the front parlor.

Kent stepped into the room. "It's Kent, Fannie. I'm home. Where's Mother?"

Fannie embraced her brother quickly and pointed to the back parlor.

Kent removed his gloves and hat and tossed them onto the sofa. No longer needing his cane, but still limping slightly, he stole quietly to the archway of the back room.

His mother stood in front of a round, ornately carved oak table, arranging lilacs and forsythia in a large porcelain urn. Sunlight streamed through the shutters of the bay window, gleaming on the highly polished table and wood floors.

"Those flowers are not half as lovely as the one arranging them."

Luvenia whirled around and gasped. She dropped a branch of lilacs on the table and ran to her son. "At last, at last! You're home for good, my son. Oh, at last." She embraced him and stroked his cheeks.

Kent picked her up and twirled her around, and she threw her head back and laughed. "Put me down. I'm too old for this."

He set her down and gave her another hug. "Never."

She clasped his arms and looked at him. "Your leg? You don't have a cane any longer?"

"No, ma'am. Ever since the war ended, it has improved more each day." He patted it. "I still limp a bit, but I'm believing for that to eventually go away as well."

"That's wonderful. I'm sure it will."

Elizabeth came down the stairs and joined the family reunion. "Welcome home, Kent. It's so good to have you back."

"What about your husbands? Have they returned?"

"Both of them. Samuel is back at the steel mill in his old manager's position, and Robert is working there as well."

"That's good news. I'm glad that there is a man . . . men . . . in the house."

"And there is one more man in the house now that you are back."

Mathilda bustled into the room, throwing her hands up and exclaiming. "Lawse, Mister Kent. Welcome home. I hadn't planned anythin' special fo supper. I'll have to see what I can come up with."

Kent laughed. "Anything you fix will be special after having eaten food in the field for four years, believe me."

Luvenia picked up the lilac branch she dropped and stuck it into the vase. "You're still in uniform." She avoided his eyes.

"Yes."

"Do you intend to stay in uniform?"

Kent walked to the table and traced along the carving on the edge. "You know I chose the military as a career when I graduated from West Point. That hasn't changed."

"I thought perhaps the war might have changed your mind." She turned her back to him and brushed a tear away.

"I have given the matter much thought. My country needs me

more than ever now. General Grant has asked me to remain on his staff, and I have accepted."

His mother looked down, still facing away from him. "I see."

Kent gently took her by her shoulders and turned her around. "The war's over. We will be rebuilding the country. It's an honorable profession."

"I know, son. But I selfishly want you home—with us—since your father is gone."

"I'll be able to come home often. For right now I'm to be stationed in Washington. It was Father's desire for me to have a military career."

"That's true, but when he was killed, things changed."

She looked up at Kent, and his convictions began to waver as he peered into his mother's face.

"Don't you think your father would want you to reconsider and assume the role of head of the Littlefield household now? Won't you at least think about it?"

He kissed his mother's hand. "Let me mull it over a bit more. I've not signed my reenlistment papers yet. I promise you I'll think about it."

"Thank you, son."

Kent rang for Felix. "Would you take my things upstairs, please? I'd like to change before dinner."

Felix slung Kent's backpack over his shoulder and started up the stairs. Kent gave his mother and sisters a final hug and followed behind the servant.

"Anything else, sir?" Felix set the backpack on a chair beside Kent's old dresser.

"No, not right now. Would you mind coming back a little later and cleaning up my boots for me? I'll leave them outside the door."

"Yes, sir. That would be my pleasure. Yes, sir." Felix backed out the door.

Kent flung his hat and gloves on top of his backpack. Sitting on the edge of his bed, he pulled off his boots and set them outside his door. Little flecks of dried mud littered the floor where he had walked. He wondered if he had tracked mud all through the house. Probably. Something he had not concerned himself with for months. He wondered in how many other ways he had become uncouth.

He opened his wardrobe and took out a pair of pants and a shirt and changed into civilian clothing. He hung his uniform in the wardrobe. Strange. He felt like he was a guest in a hotel, rather than being in the house in which he grew up.

His leave was for a month; however, he didn't intend to stay in Bethlehem but a few days. His thoughts were on traveling to Texas to get Amanda. That would meet with much resistance from his family. They did not want him to leave at all, much less travel halfway across the country to claim a Southern woman for his bride.

God, I need wisdom on how to proceed with my life. What is it that you desire for me to do? Should I stay here with my family and work in the steel factory, or pursue my military career as I've always planned? Do I go to Texas and get Amanda when both families oppose the union?

He had not written to Amanda yet. She would be wondering about him—if he were safe, where he was stationed now, if he was coming for her. It was not his intention to be insensitive to her by not writing, he simply wanted to see his family first and discern whether their attitudes had changed since the conclusion of the war. Obviously they had not.

If he followed his heart, he would stay in the military, go after Amanda, marry her, and bequeath the role of head of the Littlefield household to Fannie's husband, Samuel. He clasped his hands in front of him and leaned over with his elbows on his knees.

Heavenly Father, I'm asking you for very clear direction. Please show me what to do.

He lay down on his bed and folded his arms behind his head. After sleeping on a cot for these many months, his bed felt incredibly cozy. He closed his eyes, and all he could see was Amanda's face—her honey-colored hair and hazel eyes. She pleaded with him in the shadows of the pine trees in East Texas, her tears dampening his cheek as he held her in his arms. She grew smaller and smaller as he rode away. The scene shifted—shells along the beach crunched beneath their feet, and the ocean waves swooshed in steady rhythm onto the sand. She held an envelope in her hand, and with the other she reached toward him, but could not touch him. He opened his eyes. He was in his own bedroom in Pennsylvania.

Kent reached for his watch in the pocket of his pants. It had only been a few moments, but he had his answer.

He walked to the small writing table by the shuttered window. Opening the drawer he pulled out stationery and pen. An ink bottle sat atop the desk. Holding it up to the light, he shook it. A small amount of the dark liquid splashed around in the jar.

My dearest Amanda,

    As I am certain you are aware by now, this terrible war is over. I thank God every day that the carnage has ended, and our country can start the long road to unification and restoration. I pray you and your family are well and that the fair community of Indianola is beginning to recover.

    I have been asked to remain on General Grant's staff. We are in Washington, DC for now, but the general is planning to travel across the country for the president to make an assessment of conditions. We will return to the capital as our headquarters.

At the moment I am with my family in Pennsylvania, but I am coming for you soon. The image of your beautiful face is indelibly impressed upon my memory—every time I close my eyes you are there. I feel I can reach out and almost touch your soft cheeks. I remember our few short days together with much fondness, and trust that the coming days and years will only expand and deepen the love that we have for each other.

I am praying that you still have the same affections for me. Amanda, I hope to prove to be a husband worthy of you. I desire to make you happy. Can you be content as a military wife? I feel this is my calling—to serve my country.

You have no need to answer this brief correspondence. There are a few items of business here at home that I need to take care of, then I will start the journey back to your arms, and we can be married, never to be parted again.

I am as I ever was, devotedly yours,
Colonel Kent Littlefield

CHAPTER TWENTY-SEVEN

Where the Rio Grande is flowing,
And the starry skies are bright,
She walks along the river
In the quiet summer night.
She thinks, if I remember,
When we parted long ago,
I promised to come back again,
And not to leave her so.

"THE YELLOW ROSE OF TEXAS"

Amanda opened the window at the end of the landing where she was watering plants and looked down as Wash pulled the wagon around to the back door and tied the horses to the railing.

Elsie opened the door and stuck her bandana-swathed head out. "Did they have flour? I wants to make biscuits. We's all tired of cornbread."

"Yes, Mama. We got flour." Wash helped Claire and Emmaline down from the buckboard. "Since the blockade lifted, the stores gettin' supplies again in good order."

"Sugar and coffee too, Elsie." Emmaline went up the steps, gripping a bag in her hands.

"Whatcha got there, sweet pea?"

Emmaline smiled and reaching into the parcel, pulled out a rainbow of color. "Hair ribbons. They had ribbons again."

Elsie chuckled and held the door open for Claire and Wash. "I guess the war truly is over if we be buyin' hair ribbons again."

Amanda moved down the stairs with a watering can in her hands and into the kitchen.

Claire set the sack of coffee on the kitchen table, the smoky aroma filtering through the room. "Doesn't that smell heavenly?"

Amanda leaned over the bag of coffee, inhaling. "Oh-h-h-h, it certainly does. Elsie, let's make a pot of coffee right now."

"Yes'm. I do that right away."

Claire removed the haversack from her shoulder and pointed to it. She motioned for Amanda to follow her into the hall. Claire stopped and untied her hat, hanging it on a hook on the hall tree. Her dark eyes gleamed as she removed an envelope from her pouch.

"It's from Kent."

"Oh, my soul, Claire. Oh, my." Amanda's pulse began to throb in her temples. She clutched the ornate banister Elsie had polished that morning and looked at Claire. "What if he says he's changed his mind? What if he's not coming? What if he *is* coming? What shall we do about Daniel?"

"Open it, Mandy. Open it."

Amanda sat on the bottom step and held the letter in her lap. "I'm afraid to." She chewed on her lip.

"Your cheeks are blotching."

"I can imagine." She fanned herself with the letter.

"That's not a fan. It's a letter from the man you love. Open it now before I die of curiosity."

"Very well." She broke the seal and read quickly, then looked at Claire and smiled. "He's coming for me. Soon." She looked at the letter again. "He will be here . . . next week. Next week, Claire."

Her sister-in-law clapped her hands and sat beside Amanda on the step, adjusting her skirt over her swollen belly. "I knew he would come for you. I was sure of it."

"We need to decide what to do about Daniel. He's not going to be happy about this."

"Let me handle Daniel."

"No, this is not between you and Daniel; it's between Daniel and me. I'll talk to him." Amanda stuffed the letter back in the envelope. She smiled. "Kent has been promoted to colonel. He's going to stay in the military."

"That means you'll be leaving, doesn't it?"

Tears gathered in Amanda's eyes as she nodded her head. "But what about the girls? I promised Mother—"

"We'll take care of them. You know that."

Amanda wiped her eyes with the corner of her apron. "It's going to be difficult to leave them . . . after all these years." She fingered the cameo ring.

"You have fulfilled your promise. You have taken fine care of them. I do not think your mother intended for you to sacrifice your chance for marriage and family to stay with the girls until they marry and leave. Then where would you be?" She placed her hand on Amanda's arm. "If Daniel and I were not here, it might be different, but they have a home here at Bellevue. They have family to care for them. No, your soul needn't be troubled about this."

Amanda embraced Claire. "Thank you. You're the best friend and sister-in-law anyone could ever hope to have." She stood and helped Claire rise. "I'll miss the big event."

Claire smiled and patted her tummy. "Not too much longer, I don't think. Maybe a month at the most."

"He *could* come early before his Aunt Mandy leaves, you know."

"He?"

"Oh, it's a boy. I'm sure of it."

"I hope so, for Daniel's sake. But I want girls too. They are so much fun."

"Hmm, sometimes." Amanda laughed. "My mind is already swirling with plans. The wedding . . . where shall we marry? Elsie and Kitty need to help me get my clothes cleaned and ready to pack." She started up the stairs. "Should I talk to Daniel first?"

"Are you going to marry Kent with or without Daniel's permission?"

"Yes, I am."

"Then start getting ready. Tonight will be time enough to speak to your brother."

Amanda picked up her skirt and ran up the stairs.

"Oh, Amanda."

She stopped and turned at the head of the stairs. "Yes?"

"Don't forget to pray—pray for the Lord to soften Daniel's heart."

"I've already been doing that. I've come to a place of rest and peace with the Lord. I know he will see us through." She went into her room and closed the door. She could not keep the smile from her face. Kent was coming for her just as he said he would.

She laid the letter on the washstand and walked to a large trunk in the corner of the room. She unlatched the lock and pushed the heavy lid open. The familiar fragrance of lavender filtered up from the fabric as she dug down through the dresses and laid them on her bed one by one until she reached the bottom.

A thin cedar shelf separated Amanda's clothing from the treasure beneath. She removed the protective piece of wood and then lifted the heavy garment wrapped in a sheet out of the trunk. She laid it on the bed and unwrapped the contents carefully. Memories of her mother flooded her very being as she lifted the voluminous wedding gown.

Amanda held the dress against her body and swayed in front of the mirror. Would it fit her? Perhaps Elsie could help tailor it, if it didn't. The soft yellow fabric, looped on each side with dusky rose bows puffing the skirt into flounces, suited her coloring. She retrieved a hanger and hung the dress on the open wardrobe door. As she started to close the trunk, something caught her eye—a veil. She didn't know there was a veil. Gently she burrowed her hands underneath and raised it from where it had been stored long ago. Her mother had never showed her the veil.

She unfolded the yards of lace, and gloves fell out. Laying the gloves aside on the bed, she held the veil up to her head. It reached all the way to the floor. She could picture a wreath of fresh flowers around her head with the veil trailing from them. The filmy fabric swirled around her as she spun in front of the mirror. She laughed at herself and removed it, placing it over the shoulders of the dress.

Lastly she found shoes in the corner of the chest. She set them on the floor and eyed them. Definitely too small. She untied her boots, and as she attempted to wriggle her toes into the shoes, she felt something. She held up the shoe, reached into the toe, and tugged on a piece of paper. She yanked on it, and it tore. "Oh, my soul, no."

She opened the piece of the one-page note that she held in her hand.

My dear Amanda,

    I hope that you have found this note because it is the happy occasion of your impending wedding. Oh, how my mother's heart wishes I could be with you. I am leaving this note, fearing that I will not recover from the horrible sickness from which I currently suffer.

Oh, my. She knew she was dying. Amanda wiped a tear from her cheek with the back of her finger.

    I know the young man you have chosen must be of the highest character and integrity. I pray the two of you find . . .

The rest of the note remained in the shoe. Amanda felt around the lining and pried it out, crumbling the edges, but she could still read the faint script as she pieced it together on her lap.

    . . . as loving a union as your father and I have had. I am so proud of you. When you find the love of your life, please continue to take care of your siblings,

Amanda's breath caught. Her mother's last wish—how could she not honor it? She read on, her hand beginning to tremble.

    . . . unless your fiancé by necessity of his vocation must settle elsewhere. In that case, leave the responsibility of raising them to Daniel and his wife, whom I believe will be Claire. A woman must go where her husband bids her. Do not shoulder that burden any longer, my child.

Only when you have children will you understand how great
is a mother's love. You are my firstborn, and I love you dearly.

Love extravagantly and be loved extravagantly,

Your Mother

Amanda looked at the yellowed paper in her lap, then at the
cameo ring on her finger. A weight that had entwined itself around
her shoulders for years suddenly released. Hot tears burned her eyes
as she began to cry. "Thank you, Mother, thank you." She rocked
back and forth on the edge of her bed and released the emotional
burden she had carried as a premature parent.

*Oh, Mother, can I truly let this go now? Is it what you really wished? I
can marry my beloved and go where he bids me go without the nagging guilt
that I'm abandoning my primary responsibility? What a gift. Thank you,
my sweet mother.*

Someone rapped on the bedroom door softly.

"Yes? Who is it?"

"It's Emmie."

Amanda looked at the wedding dress hanging on the wardrobe, and the thought danced across her mind to decline to invite
Emmaline into the room. However, she reconsidered and opened the
door.

"Mandy, Catherine's supposed to help with the chickens and
she . . . oh-h-h. How beautiful." She moved to the wedding dress and
stroked the fabric. "Was this Mother's?"

"Yes, it was. Isn't it lovely?"

Emmaline, now maturing into a young lady, took the veil and
cocooned herself in the swaths of lace. "Are you going to wear this
one day?"

Amanda nodded her head. "I hope to." She took the veil from

Emmaline and put it back over the dress. She looked at her little sister, whose eyes were the same hazel with blue rims and whose hair was exactly the same color as hers. "It's more than hope, Emmaline."

Emmaline caught her breath, and her eyes widened. "You're getting married? When? To Major Littlefield?"

Amanda smiled. "Yes. He's supposed to come for me sometime next week. And it's now Colonel Littlefield."

"You're really getting married!" Emmaline embraced her sister.

"Emmaline, I need you to keep this between us . . . the two older sisters. Can you do that?"

"Why?"

"Because Daniel doesn't know yet, and I need to talk to him before, well, before we make a public announcement." She gathered Emmaline in her arms. "He's not going to be happy about this, but pray with me that he will accept it."

"Just you and me know?"

"And Claire."

"Won't she tell Daniel?"

"No, not until I do. I plan to discuss it with him tonight." She touched Emmaline's lips softly with her finger. "Can I count on you?"

Emmaline looked down, and her long lashes lay on her cheeks. She spoke without looking at Amanda. "Does this mean you will be leaving us?"

Amanda embraced the child again and said nothing, but the two sisters cried together in each other's arms.

⁂

"Amanda, you are unusually quiet tonight." Daniel waited for Kitty to take his plate from the table. "Is there any of Elsie's pound cake left?"

"Yessuh. And we're getting strawberries already. Picked some today. Miss Mary helped me. Would you likes some berries on that cake?"

"Absolutely, and put a little cream on top." He patted his stomach. "I can't seem to get enough to eat since I've been home." He chuckled. "Seems both of us are dealing with expanding waistlines." He reached over to a blushing Claire and caressed her hand.

Mary handed her plate to Kitty. "Could I have some strawberries too, please?"

"No cake?"

Mary shook her head.

"I'll have cake and strawberries." Catherine tossed a blond curl behind her shoulder. "I love the strawberries, but I'll never set foot in the fields again." She shuddered. "I don't ever want to see another snake again in my whole life."

"You can't spend the rest of your life indoors just because you came across a snake one day." Daniel smiled at his little sister.

"Well, I don't have to go back in the field anymore, do I?"

Amanda stood. "We don't have to worry about that now. Daniel, could I speak to you in the library after you finish your dessert, please?"

"This sounds ominous. But of course. Are you not having any dessert?"

"I don't think so. Not right now."

Emmaline put her napkin on the table. "May I be excused, also?"

"No dessert for you either?" Daniel lifted his eyebrows as Kitty set down the plate of cake topped with the red berries and cream. "Look what you're missing."

"I'm sure it's wonderful, but I'm full. I'd like to go to my room."

"Very well."

Amanda started for the hallway behind Emmaline. "Kitty, would you bring us coffee in the library, please?"

"Yes'm. Right away."

Daniel picked up his dessert. "Let's get this over with, whatever it is." His fork fell off the plate and clanked onto the floor. He turned to set his dessert on the table to pick it up, but Claire and Amanda bent down to retrieve it for him. He grimaced. "I'm certainly capable of picking a fork up off of the floor."

Amanda placed the fork back on the table. "I'll have Kitty get you another."

"No, this is fine." He motioned with his head and picked his plate up once more. "Lead the way."

Daniel followed Amanda into the library and sat opposite her in matching upholstered chairs. The musty odor of leather bindings on the books reminded her of the night she and Kent spent holding each other on the settee. Everything in the room was the same, except one of the servants had returned the dueling pistols to the mantel above the fireplace. Amanda lit a lantern in the darkening room.

Daniel balanced his dessert on his lap, finishing it quickly. He wiped his mouth with the back of his sleeve and set the plate on the desk.

"Daniel, where's your napkin?"

He laughed and pointed into the dining room. "Always the big sister. Forgive my bad manners. I must be more diligent to relearn my good Southern courtesies after having lived like a barbarian on the battlefield."

"Is that what it was like? Did you feel like a barbarian?"

"Somewhat. One has to put aside all sensibilities in order to carry out the . . . killing that must be done." He cleared his throat. "But that's not what you want to speak to me about, is it?"

"No, no, it's not." She folded her hands in her lap, then looked directly into her brother's dark eyes. "I received a letter from Kent today."

Daniel stood. "I thought you understood my position on this. I will entertain no further discussions involving Major Littlefield in this house."

"Sit down. You are going to hear me out. And it's Colonel Littlefield now."

Surprisingly, Daniel returned to his seat. He glared at his sister. "He must be some kind of warrior to have advanced to colonel at his young age."

"I don't know about that. But I do know he is a man of high character and integrity and that he loves me and wants to marry me."

"I'll not give my permission.'

"He's coming for me next week. We are to be married."

"With or without my permission? You are determined to defy your family?"

Amanda nodded slowly, watching Daniel's face drain of color. He stood again and clenched his fist. "Don't do this, Mandy. It will tear the family apart."

"It won't if you would but let go of your bitterness and anger. The war's over. Kent is not your enemy—he never was."

Daniel jabbed his finger toward her face as he spit out his words. "You didn't see what I saw. You didn't see the Blue Bellies pillaging the countryside, burning homes, stealing hogs and cattle and chickens until there was nothing for the people to eat. And what they did to the women is unspeakable. There's not a town in the whole of the South that was not touched in some way by the destruction. You didn't see the Yanks ripping boots and jackets from dead bodies. You didn't see a young Rebel soldier no more than fifteen begging for his life, and a dirty, despicable Yankee soldier blow his head off. That, my dear sister, is what the army of your intended did to our beloved South. It is ruined. It will never recover."

Tears stood in Amanda's eyes, ready to spill onto her cheeks. Her chin quivered. "No, you're right. I didn't see all of that. And I'm sorry that you had to . . . had to witness the carnage that you did. I don't understand how human beings can treat each other with such cruelty, especially men of our own blood and heritage." She wiped the tears from her cheeks with her hand. "But are you telling me that the Confederates were entirely innocent of their share of useless slaughter? I think not." She pointed toward the dining room. "And Claire still loves you, despite what you may have gone through or done in the war. She loves you because of the good man that you are beneath the hard crust you have built around yourself. She can see through to who you truly are. Isn't it time to forgive and move on—move on toward unifying the country instead of harboring hatred and bitterness that will only widen the division between the North and the South? Isn't it time . . . ?" She covered her mouth with her hand as a sob halted her.

Daniel shook his head and suddenly all the weariness of the war years seemed to rest on his shoulders. "I cannot. I simply cannot."

"Cannot? Or will not?"

"I will never agree to or bless a union between my sister and a Union officer. Forget him, Mandy. Forget *Colonel* Kent Littlefield."

Chapter Twenty-Eight

Oh, now I'm going to find her,
For my heart is full of woe,
And we'll sing the song together
That we sang so long ago.
We'll play the banjo gaily,
And we'll sing the songs of yore,
And the Yellow Rose of Texas
Shall be mine forever more.

"The Yellow Rose of Texas"

Amanda went into her room, closed the door, and leaned against it. The wedding dress seemed to float above her in the flickering light of her lantern, shadows dancing in and out of the folds of the fabric. She set the lantern on the night-stand and sat on the bed, staring at the gossamer gown. The lid of the trunk still stood open in the corner of the room. Her mother's note to her lay on the table, pieced together where she left it earlier in the day.

She picked up her mother's dainty wedding slippers and set them on the table. Folding the note together, she put it back into the toe of the shoe and set them in the corner of the bottom of the trunk. She took the veil from around the shoulders of the dress, folded it neatly, tucked the gloves in the center of the folds, and laid it across the floor of the chest. Then she removed the wedding dress from the hanger, folded it, and wrapped the protective sheet around it before placing the precious treasure in the trunk. She inserted the cedar shelf into the grooves lining the walls of the trunk and closed the lid. It appeared that she would not be needing the wedding dress at Bellevue, but she would take it with her for wherever and whenever she and Kent would marry. She would marry Kent Littlefield and she would wear her mother's wedding dress.

If Daniel persisted in refusing to give his approval and blessing, she would depart without it. She could hardly stand to think about leaving her family after the separation they had already endured, but she could not let Kent walk out of her life after God had so obviously brought them together.

Heavenly Father, you made a way for our family to survive the war. You brought Daniel home to us, and you saved Kent out of prison. Can you rescue us again, Lord? Would you change Daniel's mind? Would you show him he's wrong to keep Kent and me apart? And I suppose I should pray that you show me if I'm wrong.

She paused in her prayer and looked around the room at the clothes she had taken out of drawers, the jewelry on her vanity ready to pack, her hats and bonnets hanging on the bed poster. Sticking her jewelry in a velvet pouch, she looked at her hand with her mother's cameo ring on the ring finger of her left hand. She removed it, put it in the pouch, tied the cords of the small bag, and packed it in the trunk.

Kent finished packing his saddlebags and went down the stairs for breakfast. He could hear his sisters and their husbands as they chatted across the table.

"Quit fidgeting, Jacob, and eat your hotcakes."

"More butter?"

"Pass the molasses, please."

His mother's soft laughter fell on his ears like the ring of a crystal bell. He set his gear down at the front door and went into the dining room. "Good morning, everyone."

Luvenia rose and greeted her son with a quick kiss and motioned toward his father's vacant place at the head of the table where she had insisted he sit all week.

"Good morning, Mother. Samuel, Robert." He shook hands with his brothers-in-law as he walked to his place and sat down.

"Would you say grace for us this morning, son?"

"Yes, of course," Kent reached out and waited for everyone to join hands around the table. "Heavenly Father, how grateful we are to be together once again as a family." He heard his mother sniffle. "Thou hast been good to us with abundance far more than we deserve. We thank thee for thy mercy and thy protection. Please bless this food and our time together. In the blessed name of our Lord and Savior, Jesus Christ, Amen."

Kent put his napkin in his lap. "I'd hoped I could catch everyone together this morning."

Samuel responded as he helped himself to a piece of ham. "You're lucky. Robert and I are usually gone by six thirty or seven."

Fannie reached over and caressed his shoulder. "I worry about him. He works entirely too many hours. I hardly ever see him."

Samuel was average height with thinning brown hair and soft blue eyes . . . nobody one would notice in a crowd. But Kent thought he'd never known a better man, other than his father. Fannie had made a good match.

Elizabeth's Robert laughed. "Yes, to go in at seven o'clock instead of six is quite a reprieve." He smoothed his blond beard and put his napkin on the table. He leaned toward Naomi and wiped molasses off her mouth with the napkin.

Kent liked Robert as well. He'd grown up on a farm in upstate Pennsylvania and met Elizabeth when his parents brought their vegetables to market one weekend. He fell in love with Elizabeth at first sight and had married her before the war started.

The child turned her head and pushed his hand away. "Don't, Daddy." The four-year-old twins had just recently begun eating in the dining room with the adults.

Jacob, six years old now, made a face at his cousin and mimicked her.

Fannie frowned at her son. "Are you finished?"

He nodded and pushed his plate aside.

Mathilda came into the dining room with a fresh pot of coffee and poured a cup for Kent.

"Thank you." As the servant turned to leave, he halted her. "Would you wait just a moment, please?" He looked to his sisters. "If the children are finished . . . could Mathilda take them into the kitchen? I'd like to speak to the rest of you."

Fannie rose and took Jacob by the hand, shooing him toward Mathilda. "Of course."

"Come along, you children. Let's go outside. It's such a beautiful day." She picked Naomi up in her ample arms and grabbing Hannah's hand, helped her out of her chair. "C'mon, Jacob. You too."

The boy jumped out of his chair and ran to the servant's side.

"Would you ask Felix to ready my horse, please, Mathilda?"

The room grew silent.

"Yes, sir, I'll tell him." Mumbling affectionately to the children, she exited the dining room.

Kent looked around the table at his family. All faces turned toward him.

Samuel leaned back in his chair and pulled his watch out of his vest pocket.

"This won't take long." Kent cleared his throat. "After much prayer and consideration, I've reached a decision, and I hope that you will support me in this. It is my belief and conviction that God's will for my life is to serve my country. I plan to reenlist upon my return to Washington."

Luvenia gave a slight nod. "I cannot say that I am surprised, my dear. Of course, I had hoped otherwise." She looked down and sighed. "At least the war is over." She traced the lace designs on the tablecloth with her finger. "But that's not the primary reason for this meeting, is it, son?"

"No, it's not. I have also decided to go to Texas for Amanda and marry her. It would mean a great deal to me if I could leave here with the approval of my family. I know that to gain her brother's consent is going to prove to be a major hurdle. We may not attain it. But if I could have your support . . ." He looked around the table. "I know this is difficult . . . if you just knew her . . ." He stood. "You need to know, however, that I *am* going after her. I plan to leave later this morning."

Luvenia stood as well at the opposite end of the table. "Sit down, please, Kent."

They both resumed their seats. Luvenia stacked her plate on top of Fannie's and folded her hands in front of her. "We have already met together about this." She nodded toward her two daughters and sons-in-law. ". . . The five of us. We had hoped that you would come back home as a civilian, and that you would give up the idea of marrying this Southern woman. However, you are a grown man—and a wonderful man. You have to know how proud we are of you. So we have decided . . ." She paused and looked at her daughters. "We have decided to trust your judgment. Although Amanda is from the South, if you love her that much and feel she would be a good wife for you, then we—with reservations, you understand—will offer our approval."

A grin spread over Kent's face. He leaned forward toward his mother. "You will? You really will?" He stood and went to her as she rose to meet him. He embraced her and kissed her cheek. "Thank you, Mother. You will love Amanda. I'm certain of it."

Fannie and Samuel, together with Elizabeth and Robert, gathered around, amid handshakes, hugs and kisses—and tears.

"What changed your minds, if I may ask?"

Elizabeth pointed at Robert and Samuel. "Our husbands agreed, together with James Peifer's encouragement, that if they as Union soldiers were willing to accept a Southern woman as your wife—and they could—then the women should be willing as well. We decided the healing has to start somewhere, and we want it to start in small measure here—in our home."

"You won't be sorry." Kent hugged his sister.

Luvenia pointed her finger at Kent. "One thing I ask of you."

He took his mother's hand and kissed it. "I'll do anything I can."

"Bring your bride home to meet us before you go back to Washington."

Kent pursed his lips. "We shall try, but if we run out of time before I have to report back, we will come soon."

"And one more thing." She pulled her wedding ring off her finger. "I want you to give this to Amanda as my wedding gift to her."

A loud rap resounded upon the front door of the Belle home. Daniel paused as he moved through the hall from the dining room to the library. He grabbed his hat from the hall tree and opened the door.

A tall young man, with a shirt on whose too-short sleeves left his wrists dangling, stood with an envelope in his hand. "Telegraph for . . ." He glanced at the address. ". . . Miss Amanda Belle."

"I'm her brother. I'll give it to her."

The young man tipped his hat and loped down the porch steps.

Daniel held the envelope against his chest with his stump and tore it open with his hand. He pulled the message out and let the envelope flutter to the floor.

Amanda stepped into the hallway from the kitchen. "I believe I heard the gentleman say the telegraph was for me."

Daniel handed the message to Amanda, put on his hat, and went out the front door without a word.

She picked up the envelope and sat on the hall tree to read the telegraph.

In Houston. Expect me tomorrow or the next day. First day of the rest of our lives. Devotedly, Kent

Truly, he was coming for her as he said he would. Had Daniel read the message? She did not know. Perhaps he caught a glimpse of it. The communication was so short he could have read it in that instant that he tore the envelope open.

She would need to be ready to depart when he came. If Daniel continued in his stand against welcoming Kent into the family, they would have to leave quickly. Picking up her skirt, Amanda ran through the kitchen and outside to the barn. She found Wash repairing the door on the chicken coop.

Their new rooster strutted his stuff close by with several hens and their chicks pecking at the ground. Their gentle clucking, punctuated by the rooster's occasional crow, filled the pen.

Zachary held a small hammer and followed behind his father, rapping on the wood, mimicking Wash's rhythm.

Amanda patted the child on his head. "You are a good helper for your papa, aren't you?"

"Uh-huh."

"Zachary. What did you say?" Wash stopped his hammering and knelt in front of his son.

The little boy's eyes widened. "Yes'm." He looked up at Amanda with his hauntingly beautiful green eyes he had inherited from Harriet.

"What do you say, son?"

"Sorry."

Amanda chuckled and pulled him against her skirt in a loose hug. "No harm done."

Wash stood and shoved his hammer into his belt. "Yes'm, Miss Amanda? Did you need me for somethin'?"

Amanda had not bothered to put on a bonnet, and the wind blowing in from the bay pulled curls from her bun and sent them swirling into her face.

"I just received a telegraph from Kent. He's in Houston and will be here tomorrow or the next day for me." She paused and sighed. "My heart's desire would be to marry here at Bellevue, but Daniel will not agree to our marriage at all—he feels I am being a traitor to the South by marrying a Union officer."

"Does Masta Daniel know 'bout our trip to Austin? What you did for the Confederate army?"

"I don't think it would make any difference to him. And the memory of that trip is so very painful for me. I don't know if we did the right thing, and then we lost Harriet."

Wash took off his hat and wiped his forehead. "No need in dredgin' all that up, Miss Amanda. It's time to move forward."

"That's what I want to talk to you about. Wash, I want you and Zachary to go with us. Harriet's dream was for your son to be educated in the North. We could get him in school and see to it that he has the best education possible. He's smart. He deserves that chance." She looked at the little boy diligently hammering holes in the wood. She patted his shoulder again. "And besides that . . ." Her voice trailed off, and she squinted into the sun at her life-long friend. ". . . Besides that, I cannot stand to leave you behind. We've been together a long time, the two of us. Through deaths and births, war and poverty. I want you to come with us, not as a slave, but by our side as our companion."

Wash replaced his hat and turned away from Amanda. He shifted his weight and leaned across the fence. "What 'bout Masta Daniel? Don't he need me here? And I'd be taking Zachary away from his grandma and family."

"Yes, Daniel will miss your help sorely, but he will have Hiram, and the new hired help. He's going to have to let much of the land go anyway. There's no way to keep it running without the slaves. Your being here won't change that." She walked to the fence and put her hand on his arm. "Will you think about it?"

He looked up at her. "I'll pray about it."

Daniel slipped down the stairs in the early morning stillness of the house and paused, holding his breath as one of the steps creaked beneath him. He waited, but no sound came from the other bedrooms. His lantern cast a circle of light at his feet. He figured he had about half an hour before Elsie would begin preparations for breakfast and the rest of the household began stirring. He pushed the door open to the library and eased in quickly, shutting the door behind him. He set the lantern on the desk.

He walked to the window and opened the shutters to let the gray of dawn begin to seep in. The sky was cloudy. He opened the window. It looked and smelled like rain. Fitting. He needed to hurry. Turning on his heels toward the fireplace, he stared at the case containing the dueling pistols. He reached up with his good arm and removed the case from its mounting.

He will come today. I'm sure of it. Being as close as Houston, he will not want to waste another day to come after his . . . his beloved.

He heard the door scrape against the floor. Whirling around with the dueling case in his hand, he saw Claire standing at the entrance.

"I heard you get up. I was worried that perhaps you were ill."

He set the case on the desk. "I'm fine. Go back to bed."

She looked at the case, then back to Daniel. "I'm having trouble sleeping. The baby is kicking so much that he keeps me awake." She walked to her husband and cuddled up against him.

He gave her a cursory hug and kiss on the forehead. "Go back to bed, Claire."

She kept her arms around him and her head buried in his chest.

He sighed and gathered her in his arm and stump. "I wish I had both arms with which to embrace you."

"You do just fine, my darling." She patted her abdomen and smiled. Reaching up, she stroked his cheek and searched his eyes in the early-morning dimness. "Daniel, you cannot do this. If you do, you will lose your sister forever."

"If I don't, I lose her . . . to a Yankee."

Claire pulled him down on the settee with her and took his hand. It was trembling. He pulled it out of hers and stood up.

Claire looked up at him, tears brimming in her eyes. "You don't want to do this. I know you don't."

"I have to. It's a matter of honor."

"Honor? Or pride? Misplaced, stubborn pride. And for what? We've no place for pride in these times. All of our energy must go to rebuilding our homes and our families, not destroying them. The war's over. There are no longer Blue Bellies and Johnny Rebs. Can you not find it in your heart to forgive and move on?"

"I can try to move on. I can work around Bellevue and try to rebuild it. I can ride out over the property and survey the fields that we don't have enough help to plant, but I can put that aside as long as we have enough to eat from the garden. I can look at the livestock we are replenishing little by little and be thankful that they are reproducing. I can walk through the house and be grateful that it wasn't burned to the ground, that we still have a house to live in. But when I look at *this* . . ." He held up his stump. "I am reminded every minute of every day that a Yankee blew my arm off . . . and for what? Because we simply wanted to live our lives as we chose. How can I forget that?"

"We are grateful you came home at all. Many families lost their loved ones, including mine. My father didn't come home." She sniffled and brushed her tears away. "Your father preached a sermon on forgiveness shortly after we received word that Father had been killed. Something he said guided me through my own struggle with forgiveness. He said, how can we gaze upon our Savior, Jesus Christ, hanging on the cross, saying 'Father, forgive them,' and refuse to offer that same forgiveness to our fellow man? God doesn't require us to forget, Daniel, but he does ask us to forgive."

"It's too much. I cannot do it. And I certainly don't intend to have a Blue Belly for a brother-in-law."

CHAPTER TWENTY-NINE

MAY 1865

The gentleman does not needlessly and unnecessarily remind an offender of a wrong he may have committed against him. He can not only forgive; he can forget; and he strives for that nobleness of self and mildness of character which imparts sufficient strength to let the past be put in the past.

ROBERT E. LEE

Daniel strode around the corner of the house to the barn, dueling case under his arm, to saddle Cannonade. He got his saddlebags from the tack room and set them on a bale of hay along with the case.

The horse nickered as Daniel approached with his bridle. "Want to go for a ride this morning, boy?" He rubbed the horse's forehead and gave him a handful of feed.

Wash and Hiram came into the barn with milk pails. Hiram picked up his milking stool and started with the morning ritual, the ping of the milk against the metal pail signaling the beginning of the chores for the day.

Wash stopped beside Cannonade. "Mornin', Masta Daniel. You're up early. Goin' into town?" He eyed the saddlebags and case on the hay bale. "Can I help you with that?"

"No." Daniel stuck the case in the saddlebag. "Go on with the milking. I have an errand to run. I may be gone most of the day."

"Yessuh." Wash got his stool, clanging his bucket against it as he turned. "Any orders for the day while you gone?"

"Did you get the repairs on the chicken coop done yesterday?"

"Yessuh."

"Onions and lettuce are already coming on in the garden. Have Kitty keep up with that weeding. Show the new hired hand around the property. Have his wife help Kitty."

"Yessuh."

Daniel finished bridling Cannonade and placed the saddle blanket on the gelding.

"I'd be happy to help you with that, Masta Daniel."

"I'm perfectly capable of doing this myself," Daniel snapped. "Go about your chores." He swung the saddle up with his good arm and cinched the girth using both his stump and his arm. Then he slung the saddlebags on the back.

Wash smiled. "Yessuh, I can see that." The servant walked to the cows and started milking alongside Hiram.

Daniel mounted and rode out of the barn.

⚜

"Wake up, Amanda. Wake up."

Someone was shaking her shoulder. She opened her eyes. The room was still dark. Amanda sat up. "Did I oversleep?"

Claire went to the windows and opened the shutters. It was just the beginning of daylight. "No."

"What is it? The girls? What's wrong?" Amanda swung her legs over the side of the bed and reached for her robe.

"The girls are still asleep. It's Daniel."

Amanda tied her robe. "What's wrong with him? Is he ill?"

"No. Oh, he will be so angry with me, but I have to let you know. He . . . I heard him get up a bit ago, and when he didn't come back, I went looking for him. I found him in the library getting the dueling pistols. Mandy, he's going after Kent."

"No! He mustn't. Why'd you let him go?" Amanda put on her slippers, ran to the door and down the stairs, with Claire following after her.

"I couldn't stop him. He's . . ."

The two women ran to the back door in time to see Daniel riding out.

"Daniel!" Amanda ran down the back steps after him as the dust from Cannonade's hooves swirled around her. "Daniel, come back."

Wash and Hiram stood in the entrance of the barn.

"Wash!" Amanda darted to the servant. "He's going to kill Kent. You must stop him." She turned back to the house. "I'll get dressed and go with you."

Wash caught her by her arm. "No'm. I'll go, but I'll go by myself."

"But—"

"Wash is right, Mandy." Claire came up behind Amanda. "Let him go by himself. This is not for a lady to deal with."

The clouds hovered over them like a curtain, and it began to sprinkle.

"Go on to the house, Miss Amanda. I'll take care of this." Wash looked at Claire. "I don't think he'll do no harm to Colonel Kent when it comes down to it. He's got an awful lot of bitterness that he still needs to deal with. But he's been brought up right. He'll do what's right in the end." He shooed the two women toward the house like they were chickens. "Go on now. You're gonna get all wet."

The rain had started in earnest, pelting them with large, cool raindrops.

Claire ran for the house.

Amanda looked at Wash, with her wet hair stringing into her face. She brushed it back with her hand. "Don't let anything happen to either one of them, Wash."

"No, ma'am. I'll try."

"Take a rifle with you."

She thought at first that he was going to refuse to arm himself, but he nodded.

"I better get saddled up so I can catch Masta Daniel."

"What will you say to him?"

The two moved into the barn, and Amanda watched as Wash saddled a small buckskin mare.

"I'll tell him he needs a second if he's intending on challenging Colonel Kent to a duel."

Amanda gasped and shook her head. "No, Wash."

"Aw, I'm not really intendin' to do any such thing, Miss Amanda. I'll just tell Masta Daniel that's what I'm doin'. In the meantime, I'll do my best to talk him out of it."

Wash tied the mare to the railing of the stall, got the rifle they kept in the barn and some ammunition. "I'd better get a canteen of water and some biscuits from the kitchen. I don't think Masta Daniel took any food with him, tho I don't think we be gone that long. My guess is that Colonel Kent wants to get here right soon, and if he was in Houston yesterday . . ."

The two ran through the rain to the kitchen, where Elsie was making coffee. "Miss Claire come in here looking like a drownded rat, now here come you two. You getting my kitchen flo' all muddy."

Wash stepped backward on the small porch and wiped his feet. "Sorry, Mama. You got any leftover biscuits I can take?"

"Take? Where you goin' in this rain?"

Wash wrinkled up his forehead and looked at Amanda. "Miss Amanda sending me after Masta Daniel to help him with an errand he going on."

"This storm look like it settlin' in."

"We'll be back before too long. Any biscuits?" He poured water into a canteen from a pitcher on the table.

"No, but I has some Johnny cakes."

"That will do."

Elsie wrapped several in a cloth and handed them to him. "What's goin' on here, son? What's so all-fired important that you has to go off riding in dis rain?"

Amanda pulled a towel from a drawer in the cabinet and dried her face. "I'll explain it to you later, Elsie. Go on, Wash, and hurry. I'll be praying."

"Me too, Miss Amanda." Wash stuck his bundle under his shirt and dashed back to the barn.

Sam barked and ran behind Wash.

"Come back, Sam. You can't go." The dog circled and came back, hunkering under the protection of the small porch as the rain started.

Amanda watched as Wash rode out with a poncho thrown over his shoulders and his hat down low. She left the kitchen with Elsie still wondering what was going on, and went upstairs to finish her packing.

❦

Wash rode at an easy canter until he sighted Daniel ahead. "Masta Daniel! Masta Daniel!"

Daniel whirled Cannonade around so quickly that the horse reared. "Wash? What are you doing? I don't need anyone along with me."

"Well, I saw that you had the dueling pistol case and figured that if you's thinkin' about a duel you'd need a second."

"Humph. If I'd wanted a second, I'd have asked you when I left."

"And I brought water and Johnny cakes, in case we have a bit of a wait . . . for Colonel Kent."

"Oh, I see. My wife sent you after me."

"And Miss Amanda."

Daniel ducked his head, and the rain dripped off his hat onto his poncho. "Humph."

"Where you plan to wait for him?"

"Not planning on waiting for him. I figure he'll come through Lavaca and start down the road to Indianola. Plan on meeting him on the road."

"Nice day for a duel."

Daniel whipped his head around and glared at his longtime slave.

Wash held his hand up. "Not meanin' no disrespect, Masta Daniel. Just meant that a duel's a nasty thing, and this is a nasty day."

"You don't approve, do you?"

"Not for me to approve or disapprove. I just come along to see if I can help in any way."

They rode in silence for several minutes. "What did Amanda say?"

"What you expect she say?"

"I expect that she wanted you to stop me."

"Yessuh."

"But you're not going to try to do that?"

"No, suh. If you're bent on killin' Miss Amanda's intended, I don't suppose I can stop you."

Daniel halted Cannonade. "Why don't you turn around and go back home, Wash?"

"No, suh."

They had nearly reached Lavaca when Daniel pulled over to a small grove of cedar trees. "I don't want to go any farther. Let's wait here."

The two hunkered down beneath the low-lying branches of the salt cedars as the rain continued. "This is miserable, Masta Daniel. Are you sure he comin' today?"

"Today or tomorrow."

"You mean we're gonna sit here in the rain maybe all day, all night, and maybe all day tomorrow?"

"You don't have to stay with me."

"I'm stayin'."

The rain slowed to a depressing drizzle. Thunder rumbled in the distance from time to time. An hour passed.

Wash shielded his eyes from the water dripping from his hat and looked down the road. A lone horseman on a black horse riding at a fast clip—not a gallop but moving smartly along. "There he is."

Daniel mounted and laid his rifle across his saddle, waiting for Kent to approach.

Wash remained with his horse in the trees.

Kent reined Black Sterling in and raised his hand in greeting. "Daniel, I'm glad to see you are well."

Daniel raised his stump. "Not whole, but reasonably well."

"I'm sorry, my friend."

"You are not my friend."

"We were friends at one time."

"That was a long time ago. You are in civilian clothes. Are you still in the military?"

"Yes, but I'm on leave." Kent dismounted, limped toward Daniel, and extended his hand. "I've come for Amanda. I love her so very much and want to make her my wife. I greatly desire your blessing."

"Never." Daniel motioned toward the horse with rifle in hand. "Nice horse. In fact, I believe he belongs to us, does he not?"

"He does. I've brought him back and intend on leaving him with you." Kent looked at Daniel's rifle. "Do you intend on shooting me? If you do, you might as well go ahead and get it over with. I'm no match for a Terry's Texas Ranger."

Daniel holstered his rifle and swung off his horse. He pulled the dueling pistols out of his saddlebag. "Colonel Littlefield, I've come out to meet you to ask you as a gentleman, although I have my doubts that any Yankee officer is a gentleman, to turn around and go back without seeing my sister. There is too wide a chasm dividing the Northern way of life and the Southern culture for a marriage to work between you."

"We fought a war to unify the country. That chasm will become less and less as time goes on. A marriage between two people who love each other from opposite sides could begin the healing process. Do you not agree?"

"I will not allow my sister's marriage to be an experimental field for the healing of our nation. If you refuse to abandon this ridiculous notion, I shall challenge you to a duel—here and now."

"Hmm. This appears to be pretty irregular procedure, is it not? No planning, no seconds."

"Wash."

The servant stepped from behind the cedar grove with his rifle in his hands.

"I see. Well, you have a second, but I do not. However, that is immaterial." Kent stepped back with his hands up. "I will not accept your challenge to a duel. The barbarism has to end. I'll not participate in any further unnecessary carnage."

The rain *pitter-patted* on their ponchos and almost came to a stop.

It seemed to Wash as if the weeping of heaven was about to cease, and as soon as these two men made peace, that it would.

Kent put his hands down. "What I will do is ask you to forgive us. I won't ask forgiveness for what I feel was a just cause. The slavery issue had to be dealt with. But as an officer in the Union army, I ask you to forgive us for all the heartache and ruin that resulted from the march through the South." He stepped toward Daniel. "I ask you to forgive us for the mistreatment that your prisoners of war received."

Daniel stared at Kent. "You were in prison at Camp Ford."

"Yes." Kent's voice was barely above a whisper.

"Were you treated well?"

Kent didn't answer him. "And I ask you to forgive us for . . . for crippling you, for taking your arm." He shook his head. "So much useless suffering."

"I see you walk with a limp now."

"Yes, but thanks to Amanda and Dr. Greer we were able to save the leg." Kent shifted his weight and extended his hand again. "Can we forgive each other and let the bitterness and anger go? Please?"

❧

Cannonade nickered as Daniel turned toward him with the dueling pistol case in his hand. Daniel looked back at Kent, and then over at Wash. Leaning against his saddle, he buried his face in his hand and took several deep breaths. Every horrific battle scene, every buddy that he had held as his life blood oozed out of his body, every charge and retreat that turned the fields and meadows of the South into slaughter houses, every scream as a limb was amputated flashed and echoed through his mind. How could he simply forgive all that had been done in the name of freedom and country?

He couldn't. He returned the case to the saddlebag, then turned his back on Kent and Wash and walked toward the trees. He just could not bring himself to erase the gruesome scenes from his mind. They invaded his thinking and gripped his heart like a vise. Every time he heard a gunshot he started to tremble. Every time he was startled by a horse or a bird flying from its nest, his heart started to pound. How could he overcome his involuntary reactions, much less accept one of the enemy into his family? He turned and peered from under the brim of his hat at Kent.

This man had suffered as much as he, perhaps more. He had been in a prison camp. Kent was willing to forgive. Why couldn't he?

A picture in his father's Bible of the crucifixion flashed through his mind. "Father, forgive them, for they know not what they do" read the caption beneath it.

We didn't know what we were doing either. We didn't know the devastation it would bring. We dashed out like foolish boys to an adventure and came home broken men . . . all of us. Yankees and Johnny Rebs.

His heart wrenched within him as he recalled Claire's admonition. How could he claim to be a Christian and look at Jesus forgiving mankind from the cross and refuse to forgive his brother? He had no choice.

Daniel looked down at the rain pooling around his boots. Thunder grumbled in the distance. *Father, I know I need to do this. I don't feel forgiving, but I know I need to offer forgiveness for the sake of our family. Help me.* Minutes passed.

Then he turned and started toward Kent. As he walked, he gained the strength to do what he had to do. Holding out his good hand, he said, "You're a better man than I, Kent Littlefield—a man that I would be proud to call my brother-in-law."

Kent pulled the younger man into an embrace and slapped his back over and over. "Thank you, my friend. Thank you." He looked toward the sky. "The rain has finally stopped. May we please go get Amanda?"

Amanda dragged the trunk into the hall, leaving it for Hiram to carry downstairs. She took one more look around the room now devoid of her belongings.

Claire stood in the doorway. "You have on a traveling dress. Are you expecting to leave immediately when Kent arrives?"

Amanda picked up her purse and gloves. "I don't know what to expect. What if Daniel has hurt Kent, or even . . . ?" She shook her head. "Or what if Daniel is harmed in the fray? For these two men to make it through the war and then be wounded or killed in a ridiculous duel is beyond comprehension. I cannot stand to even entertain those thoughts. Whether Kent comes for me in spite of Daniel's objections or whether Daniel has made him turn back, I'm leaving."

"But what if Daniel finally agrees to give you his blessing?"

Amanda stared at Claire. "Do you think that he might?"

"I think once Daniel sees that his objections are simply bitterness and anger, he will quickly give his approval."

"I pray that happens before anyone gets hurt."

"I do too."

"I'm going to wait on the porch for them, for whoever comes back. Will you sit with me?"

"Of course."

The two friends walked down the stairs, out the front door, onto the porch. They pulled two rocking chairs together, facing the road, and began their vigil. Sam sat at the top of the steps looking toward the road as if he knew what was at stake.

Elsie bustled out with a pitcher of milk and pieces of chess pie. "Thought you two might like somethin' to eat."

Water dripped from the eaves of the house, but the sun had

begun to poke through the clouds. The pair sipped their milk, but the pie sat untouched. Claire spread a napkin over the slices.

Amanda couldn't keep her eyes off the road. Finally she stood. "I'm going after them. I can't bear to wait here any longer."

"Don't be ridiculous. There's nothing you can do but wait and pray." Claire stood with her hand to her back and stretched.

"I truly am trusting God to bring Kent safely to me, but it's so hard to wait here doing nothing." Amanda walked to the railing and stared down the road. Her breath caught in her throat. "Is that . . . ? Do I see . . . ? Someone's coming down the road. Claire, someone's coming." She stepped out onto the front steps.

"You're going to get all muddy, Amanda."

"I don't care." She stood on the bottom step and shielded her eyes with her hand. "There are two . . . no, Claire, it's all three of them! Claire! It's three men!" Amanda picked up her skirt and ran toward the gate as three horsemen pulled up to the fence through the haze. Sam ran in front of her, his tail wagging, barking incessantly.

The handsome young man from the North jumped off his horse, ran toward his Southern sweetheart, and gathered her in his arms.

Relief flooded through her. He was safe. "You came. You really came."

Kent laughed and tilted her chin toward him with his hand. "I told you I would. I knew God would bring us back together."

Daniel dismounted and handed the horses over to Wash, then walked to Claire. He shoved his hat back on his forehead and shook his head sheepishly. "I don't know what I was thinking. Continuing to fight this war is of no value to any of us."

Amanda turned to her brother and caught hold of his arm. "Thank you, Daniel."

Kent nodded. "Yes, thank you, sir. I am forever in your debt."

He took hold of Amanda's hands. "Oh, my dearest, at last—at last we can be together. I am hopelessly in love with you. Will you marry me?" The dimple in his cheek deepened as he grinned. "Officially this time?"

She removed his hat and smoothed down his curls, wet from the rain. "What about your family?"

Kent reached into his pocket and pulled out a black velvet pouch. He opened the container and shook it into his hand. A small gold filigree wedding band fell into his palm. He looked at her, excitement dancing in his eyes. "Mother sent this with her blessing and her prayer that in some small measure the healing might begin with us."

Amanda held out her trembling hand as he placed the treasure on her ring finger.

Claire snuggled up against her husband. "Looks like we're going to have another wedding."

The two couples moved up the steps to the porch, the men shaking the moisture from their ponchos. Taking Kent's rain gear, Amanda pointed to the table. "Elsie made chess pie."

Chuckling, Kent embraced her around the shoulders. "What more could a man ask—the love of his life by his side and a piece of Elsie's chess pie?"

Amanda thought Kent's eyes had never looked bluer.

ACKNOWLEDGMENTS

No book is ever written in complete isolation. Editors and proofreaders and critique groups are all major players who invest time, energy, and expertise in each and every book. But this one seemed to require more than the usual number of supporting cast, and I am indebted to them.

First of all, renewed thanks to my agent, Mary Beth Chappell, Zachary, Schuster, Harmsworth Literary and Entertainment Agency, who continues to believe in my writing and is always willing and very able to stand in the gap for me. Thanks to the fiction team at Thomas Nelson and my editors, Natalie Hanemann, Jamie Chavez, and LB Norton, who make my stories read better than I can write them. To Katie Bond and Eric Mullett for their work on the publicity and marketing end. To Eric Wilson for editing help on the synopsis. To Jennifer Wilford, my virtual research assistant, who seems to be able to dredge up any tiny bit of information, no matter how remote. My critique group, Linda LaRoque, Lynn Dean, and Lynnette Sowell, who read far more pages than normal just to help me meet deadline.

Friends who are truly interested are an added bonus. Many thanks to Gary and Susan Heffner, who went with us on a trip to Jefferson, TX, to observe the community's commemoration of the send-off of the Confederate soldiers, the battle reenactment, and the fascinating tours of the Civil War homes in Jefferson, not to mention our visit to Camp Ford in Tyler, TX, where Kent was imprisoned in the novel. To our friends Joe and Gayle Bailey who accompanied us on our trip to the coast to visit the actual site of Indianola. The highlight of that trip was being able to actually go through the home that served as the prototype for Bellevue. My grateful thanks to the owners of that beautiful house. The gals at the Calhoun Country Museum were most helpful, especially George Anne Cormier, the director of the museum who read through the manuscript to check for any errors I might have made in local terrain, flora, or history. That meant volumes.

My neighbor, Kathy Hinton, who works in the Texas Collection at Baylor University in Waco, TX, who loaned me her personal books about the Civil War, *Texas Tears and Texas Sunshine, Voices of Frontier Women*, Jo Ella Powell Exley, and *The Slave Narratives of Texas*, Ron Tyler and Lawrence R. Murphy. Much of the story of the residents of Indianola during the occupation of the Federal troops was sparked by the memoirs in those two books. I buried myself in books and films of the Civil War, from *Gone with the Wind* to *Gods and Generals*, but found particularly helpful a copy of *The Civil War, An Illustrated History*, based on the documentary film by Geoffrey C. Ward, Ric Burns, and Ken Burns.

One of my most favorite things to do is to speak to book clubs. One club in particular has been such an encouragement and has invited me to discuss every one of my books with them—the Ladies Only Book Club in Dallas. So to Jami, Annette, Michelle, and Chanda, and the two virtual members who have read along with them, Barb and Courtnee, and my daughter, Amanda, who goes with me when we meet—a million thanks!

And my thanks always to CLASS. Without the encouragement, networking, and support of that organization, I doubt that any of my books would be published today.

Thank you, Jesus, that you are the Author and Finisher of my faith.

READING GROUP GUIDE

-1. Amanda's love and loyalty to her Southern family were tested by her love for her Union officer sweetheart. She was torn between the two. In your opinion, which one—her family or her sweetheart—should have commanded her first priority? Do you think she handled the dichotomy well? Why or why not?

2. Prior to the war, Amanda's faith was in word only. She was riding on the coattails of her father's faith, but it wasn't enough. She had gone to church all her life, but she didn't really believe that God was to be trusted because He allowed the trauma and atrocities of war. Then she came to the end of herself and realized that God is faithful and she could trust Him. Have you had a similar journey? Share it with the group.

3. What were your feelings when Amanda decided to take information of the Red River invasion to her Confederate colonel uncle? Did you think she was being disloyal to Kent?

4. Who was your favorite character? Why?

5. What was your favorite scene? Why?

6. Whether your empathies were with the North or the South prior to reading *His Steadfast Love*, did your perspective change at all? In what way?

7. Did you learn anything new about the Civil War? What was it?

8. Did Daniel have a "right" to be bitter? Why or why not?

9. What would you imagine is going to be the most difficult obstacle for Kent and Amanda to overcome in building their lives together?

One family fights against King Louis XIV
for the freedom to live a life of faith.

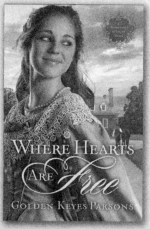

The Darkness to Light
Historical Romance Series

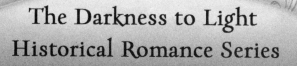